A Wi Time Solves Nine Parts 1, 2, and 3: 1906, 1916, 1923

Rosie Reed

A Witch in Time Solves Nine Parts 1, 2, and 3: 1906, 1916, and 1923 by Rosie Reed

Chapter One

Listen… can you hear the upbeat jazz music spilling from the Fat Pussycat Club? It makes you want to dance, doesn't it? Go on, tap your toes – it's jolly good fun!

Now, picture the scene: it's a warm spring evening, and a pair of buckled high heels are striding confidently down a city thoroughfare. Allow your mind's eye to scan upwards and you'll find a gorgeous pair of stocking-clad legs. And higher still is the knee-length hem of my tasselled gown. But scan no higher, cheeky!

Now you can see the back of me, walking away – curves in all the right places. Let me turn around so I can greet you with a grin!

Well, hello! Lady Joanforth Eldritch at your service. The location: London. The year: 1926. And just like me, this city is alive with dazzling, roaring magic!

It's official: this fun and frivolous decade is my favourite so far. And I've seen several *centuries*, for I am a witch, and over four hundred years old. I've lived through some terribly turbulent times – with some unbelievably oppressive underwear.

Up with freedom, down with the corset!

But you can't stop progress. So on with the story…

As I neared the entrance of the boozy nightclub, I saw Lord Vincent Vilnius loitering outside, smoking gaspers with his friends. Oh drat! This was *not* good news. Lord Vilnius was certainly pleasing on the eye

– dashing as ever in his leather aviator jacket and fedora hat. But he was trouble with a capital T. And I was public enemy number one. His cool expression didn't flicker as he noticed me click-clacking his way.

His voice was deep and measured. "Well, well, what do we have here? Joanforth Eldritch, what the devil have you done to your hair?"

I patted my blonde, waved crop. "Delighted you noticed, Vinnie. And don't be so dreadfully old-fashioned. I'll wear my hair – and my hemlines – as short as I choose."

He blew out a languid smoke ring, making me wait. "You wouldn't if *we* were still engaged."

"Bully for me we're not then. Do excuse me, I came here to dance – not talk hairstyles."

I stifled my fear of that brooding villain and sauntered inside the Fat Pussycat Club. The swinging music and smoky atmosphere swept me up, dissolving my tension. How I loved jazz, with all its sax and violins!

Ah yes. This was what life was all about – music, dancing, and fun! I air-kissed my friends, then shimmied over to squeeze in at the bar – ordering a vodka martini and knocking it back. *Down the hatch and bottoms up. I drink to your health. Another? Yup!*

This was going to be a night to remember! The rousing horns, clanging piano, and driving drumbeat whooshed through me, making my body sway. *I* wasn't a wallflower who waited for a man to invite me to dance. But first another drink!

"Make it a large one, Freddy," I purred.

The scrummy chap behind the bar threw me a flirty grin as he handed me another vodka martini. "Your ladyship…"

Down the hatch and – oh good heavens!

My hand froze, glass to lips. Lord Vilnius was now leaning against the wall opposite, staring coolly at me across the dancefloor.

His stance said: You'd better watch out, Joanforth Eldritch.

I gulped my drink so vigorously that I almost swallowed my olive. *Gaghh*! Trying to act cool, I eased that oily orb back into my glass with a plop. I couldn't look away from Lord Vilnius though. I needed to at least *seem* unaffected by his unflinching stare – even if my heart was pounding in my chest harder than the big bass drum.

Lord Vilnius and I were both Beings of Magic, childhood friends from powerful families. Everyone had assumed we'd marry and rule the magical land of Marvelton together. But he'd returned from the Great War… dark. Oh, he was *impressive* – handsome, charming, and seven-foot-tall. He was magically talented and destined for greatness. But the war had changed him. It'd changed us all – stolen our faith and hope. But Lord Vilnius more than most. *He'd* seen the war as an opportunity for personal advancement. And then he'd hooked up with this new tutor…

A male voice by my side spoke loudly above the jazz. "You've been staring at that man for over a minute, your ladyship."

I didn't know this fellow, but he was young and good-looking, and a welcome distraction from Lord Vilnius. I sensed straight away he wasn't a fellow Being of Magic, meaning he wouldn't see Lord Vilnius as he really was. The human mind tended to block out magic as an exercise in sanity-saving. As long as Lord Vilnius didn't start throwing fireballs around, we should be okay. Perhaps if I flirted with this chap, Lord Vilnius might go away.

"And *you* are?" I asked.

He bowed. "Captain Sebastian Loveday at your service, your ladyship."

"*Love*day? Gosh, now there's a name that holds a promise."

He smiled knowingly. "And you're Lady Joanforth Eldritch."

"Have we met?"

"No, your ladyship." He leaned conspiratorially towards me. "I asked the barman."

"How terribly clever of you."

"Here on your own?"

"Not anymore, Captain Loveday. I'll have a Champagne cocktail. Then we can dance."

The captain ordered our drinks. He wasn't that young, now I came to look at him – not that I was one to judge. He looked perhaps forty. His thick brown hair and round boyish face made him appear youthful. But he was given away by the lines around his eyes and flecks of grey in his swept-over fringe. He certainly kept up with the fashion – his suit was modern, and he was wearing spats. Good dancing shoes!

"Cheers," I said, clinking his glass.

He drained his drink, then spoke with grim melancholy. "Here's to better times."

"Surely these are better times, Captain?"

"I suppose so." He pensively twiddled the cocktail stick in his empty glass.

Oh bother. Why did I always attract the dark, brooding type? Men with problems were drawn to me like flies to jam at a picnic. It was a jolly *unfortunate* curse, because I wasn't even a sympathetic listener. I just wanted to have fun and dance the night away.

But my curiosity got the better of me. "Come on then, let's hear it."

He smiled thinly. "You're jolly kind to be interested."

"Oh I'm not interested. So... shall we dance?"

I headed off, but he drew me back by the upper-arm. "Know any priests?"

I gestured to myself. "Do you think that's likely?"

"They're not allowed to tell the police what you confess, are they?"

Police? Uh-oh. "What don't you want the *police* to know?"

"It's a weight on my conscience. My soul is stained."

"Your soul is stained?" Oh golly...

"Your ladyship, I need to tell someone – if I don't, I'll burst."

The band launched into *The Charleston*. "Look, would you mind awfully if you refrained from bursting until after this dance? Then you can tell me all about it, yes?"

I downed my drink, grabbed Captain Loveday's unresisting hand, and joined the throng of joyously jerking bodies. *Everyone* loved the Charleston – the tune, the dance, the carefree attitude. The crowd moved as one, each of us abandoning our 'small sense of self' to the marvellous music.

Despite apparently needing a priest, Captain Sebastian Loveday was a good mover. He wrapped one arm around my waist and we held hands at shoulder height, swinging our hips and jigging vigorously. I broke away, kicking up my heels, then thrusting my hands down to my knees and knocking them together.

"What jolly good fun!" he shouted above the music.

"Isn't it!" I waved my hands in the air, grinning with glee. Then, laughing, I turned on the spot in a circle, sharing smiles with my fellow dancers who were high on the jazz, like me.

As I turned back to the captain, my happy mood bombed like a bi-plane. Suddenly, his face was stricken with terror. His wide eyes were bulging. His hand clutched at his chest… oh I *say*, he was dying!

The captain opened his mouth to speak, but *blood* rather than words spurted out. He slumped into me – his deadweight dragging me down. I grappled, shoving him upright, but I pushed him too hard, and he toppled backwards like a felled tree.

Screaming women leapt out the way. The music screeched to a halt. Captain Loveday crashed to the sticky floor. In the stunned silence, I could hear the sound of *no one* breathing.

I knelt to hold his hand. "Captain Loveday? Can you hear me? Can you speak?"

"Lady Joa… I know who…"

"Who *what*!"

His grimacing face relaxed. He exhaled heavily. His fingers unfolded from my hand.

"Captain Loveday?"

I stared at his lifeless face, willing this not to be true. But his body was as still as a statue. His staring eyes… dead.

The air around me felt thick and dreamlike. How… what…*why*…?

A man's voice shouted. "Watch out!"

I jerked out the way as a pool of blood collided with my dress. My gaze followed the stream of sticky liquid. It was oozing from the dead captain's back.

"Someone stabbed him…" I whispered.

Through giddy eyes, I glanced around for the culprit, but saw no one with a knife.

Poor Captain Sebastian Loveday. Whatever it was he'd wanted to confess, it was too late now.

Chapter Two

"Stand back, I'm a doctor!"

A young man pushed through the stunned crowd, then crouched to check the captain's pulse. "He's *dead…*"

Well, this chap was sure to go far in the medical profession…

"Bartender," the doctor shouted. "Telephone the police!"

A wave of panic surged through the club. No one wanted the police here. We weren't doing anything illegal, but… who'd honestly want to get caught up in a murder case? Certainly not me.

My friends drifted over to see if I was okay. They – *we* – all looked ridiculous now, dressed in our sparkly gowns and feathered headbands. In mere moments, this gay venue had become a tomb of severity. The Fat Pussycat Club felt as dead as the corpse sprawled on the floor.

But why had this happened? Who'd done this?

I glanced around, wondering where Lord Vilnius had got to. Would *he* do this?

"Lady Joanforth?" The barman pushed a brandy into my hands.

"Oh… thank you, Freddy. What a dreadful business."

We both glanced up at the sound of men shouting wildly in the street, followed by the frantic tooting of brass whistles.

I rolled my eyes. "They always like to burst in like *The Charge of the Light Brigade*, don't they?"

Four uniformed coppers stormed into the still-stunned nightclub, looking efficient and powerful in their smart blue tunics and tall, domed policeman's hats. One of the officers shouted that no one was to leave, whilst another turned on the lights – and the stark brightness made me feel even more overdressed. Then, like chorus girls at an opera, the uniformed officers stood to one side, as the main event arrived – a middle-aged, plain-clothed, pockmarked detective inspector.

A younger plain-clothed copper entered with him, and they quickly took control of the situation, locating the nightclub owner and all his staff. The uniformed officers started taking witness statements, but my heart sank as the barman pointed straight at me, muttering something to the detective inspector – oh *thanks* Freddy.

The detective inspector clumped over, eyeballing me. "Barman says *you* were seen dancing with the deceased."

Good manners might cost nothing, but this chap *certainly* wasn't giving them away.

I stood tall. "I don't recall dancing being a crime, Inspector."

"Don't get cocky with me, madam. How long have you known the captain?"

I glanced at my elegant wristwatch. "About forty-five minutes. But he was only *alive* for ten."

"You met him for the first time this evening then?"

"I can see why they made you a detective, Inspector."

"And yet, *madam*, you were seen dancing and laughing together."

"Does one need to be formally betrothed to dance and laugh in 1926?"

"You're a suspect. Don't leave London." He called over his shoulder. "Detective Constable, witness statement here, *now*."

"A *suspect!*" I spluttered to the retreating inspector. "But I had my back to Captain Loveday when he was stabbed… *in* the back – I was in front of him… Well, *really*…suspect, indeed!" I glanced at the detective constable. "Is your boss always so rude to – oh…"

This chap was much easier on the eye than his gruff superior. He was dressed in a brown pinstripe suit, a long police coat, and fedora hat. But his stubbly chin and cocky grin betrayed his formal clothing. His tie was wonky too.

I took an immediate liking to this young man – and not just because he was ruggedly handsome. But I sensed, like me, he refused to know his place. He went through life with a twinkle in his eye – as if he'd heard the joke of reality, but wasn't put off by the terrible punchline.

As he looked at me, I noticed he had one blue eye and one brown eye. What an intriguing young man.

He spoke with a gravelly cockney accent. "Name, madam?"

I automatically went into flirt mode. "Why don't you tell me yours, and we can go from there?"

He grinned coolly into my eyes. "Detective Constable Anderson, madam."

"Do you have a first name, DC Anderson?"

"What's *your* name, madam?"

"Joanforth."

"Joan*forth*?"

Gosh, my name sounded delicious on his lips…

He wrote it down on his notepad. "And is that Miss or Mrs?"

"It's *Lady* Joanforth Eldritch."

The grumpy inspector was still in earshot. He spoke with scorn. "Lady Joanforth Eldritch? I've heard about *you*. All true, I suppose?"

"Oh, I never listen to gossip, Inspector, especially not about myself. You *know* what Oscar Wilde said."

DC Anderson wrapped his long fingers around my sequined clutch. "I'll need to search your handbag, madam."

"I don't think Oscar Wilde ever said *that*."

"Your handbag, madam."

I opened it wide for him. "See, no concealed daggers – although I do think my lipstick is to-die-for. Don't you?"

I pressed my lips together and winked.

DC Anderson cleared his throat and referred to his notepad. "So *are* you a Miss or a Mrs?"

"Why are you so keen to know if I'm married?"

"I need to put your marital status in my report. And – begging your pardon, madam – but also your age."

"My marital status is Free and Single. And as for my age, honestly, Constable, if I told you, you wouldn't believe me."

"I'll just put 'Single' and 'Undisclosed'. What's your address?"

I told him where I lived, line by line.

14

He stuffed his notebook into his pocket. "Um… due to a lack of lady policemen, I'm afraid *I'm* going to have to… search you, your ladyship."

I threw a hand to my hip. "Oh what a pity, *you* have to search me? Please tell me it ain't so!"

He stepped closer. "Just a quick pat down. If you could hold your arms out to the side…"

He bent so we were eye-level, then gently ran his hands down the sides of my torso.

I twitched.

"Did that tickle?"

"Yes…"

"I'll try to be gentle…"

"Please don't…"

He stifled his grin, running his hands down to my hips.

"We should ask them to play a tune for us, Constable. I feel like we ought to be dancing."

He paused at my outer-thigh and fingered the object tucked in my garter. "What's this?"

I hitched up my skirt, revealing my stocking-clad thigh.

DC Anderson glanced away. He was a cocky young thing, but clearly unused to such bold behaviour from the 'fairer sex'.

I slid the thin wooden baton from my garter. It was about a foot long, made of ebony, and decorated with ornate swirls. It crackled with centuries of ancient magic. "Here, Constable. As you can see, it's not a dagger."

He took it from my hands, gazing at it in confusion. I didn't let many people touch it, but I liked this young man.

"What is it?" he asked, with genuine interest.

"My magic wand."

He smirked. "Of course. Well, I can see it's just a harmless piece of wood."

"If you say so, Constable. But it certainly *wasn't* used to murder Captain Loveday. Do you need to continue searching me? Please say yes."

He grinned, enjoying the flirtation. "No, your ladyship."

"What a pity."

"I've got all these other witnesses to talk to. But you've been most helpful."

I stepped closer, gazing at him with my big brown eyes. "Thank you, Constable. I'll never forget our brief – yet thrilling – time together. I hope to meet you again. Perhaps I'll break the law intentionally, just to get your attention."

He laughed. "I'll have to keep my eye on you."

"Oh goody, the blue eye or the brown eye?"

"Goodnight, Lady Joanforth."

"Goodnight, Detective Constable Anderson."

Chapter Three

Despite outward appearances, I was actually rather shaken by the murder of Captain Loveday. I'd seen plenty of dead men during the war, but for my dance partner to be brutally stabbed right in front of me… well… that was jolly disturbing. It wouldn't do to blub though. What I needed was a cup of tea, with perhaps a dash of brandy for luck.

As it was May, the sun was rising as I walked home. But, because this was England, it was obscured by grey clouds. Apparently even the weather wanted to mourn the murder.

Oh drat! After all that flirting, I'd totally forgotten to tell the constable about Captain Loveday's desire to confess something to a priest – but not to the police. If *only* I'd let the captain talk… Ah well, I'd go and see the lovely DC Anderson tomorrow and fill him in...

I shook myself out of my downcast mood and focused on the positives. I lived in a delightful little London street called Cherry Garden Avenue – which was flanked with tall Georgian townhouses, and cherry trees all in a row. Their pink, fluffy blossoms beguiled me this and every springtime – a glorious explosion before a summer of lush, green leaves.

I loved living here. Naturally, our butler would've turned in hours ago, so I tip-toed down the stone steps for the servants' entrance in the basement. I fumbled for the key under the doormat… but discovered mere empty space. Right…

Our butler was a loyal hard worker, but he didn't hide his views about my habit of staying out all night – and this key removal was obviously *his* doing. I could image his stern expression as I confronted him about it. "I discovered the key under the mat, your ladyship, and deemed it a security risk, so I removed the offending item…"

Pompous arse. Ah well, there was more than one way to sneak into your own property. My magic was weak this far from Marvelton, but I summoned up all my powers and cast the Lock-picking spell.

Like opening a solid rock, magic now will pick this lock.

Yes! The sturdy lock opened with a satisfying clunk. How I loved magic!

I crept into the corridor of the servants' hall, feeling like a thief in the twilight. How thrilling!

Whoops, I almost tripped over a silver-headed cane propped against the wall. Was this an obstacle course left for me by the butler? Perhaps not… this cane belonged to Lord Vilnius – and even the butler wouldn't dare cross him. I cast my mind back to the nightclub. Lord Vilnius hadn't had his cane with him, had he? So how did it get here? I sighed. He'd probably dropped in to visit my uncle earlier, and left his cane on purpose, giving him an excuse to return – and see *me* at the same time.

Trepidation tingled in my chest. Why had he been staring at me across the dancefloor like that? It was as if he'd been taking one long last look at me…

I pushed away my worry and grabbed a saucepan to make the tea. The cook wouldn't mind, as long as I cleared up after myself. Despite having a rather grumpy butler, our servants were wonderful. They endured a great deal, what with my Uncle Frog and his wild inventions.

The servants didn't know this, but my Uncle Frog was a wizard, and it was his mission to invent a time machine so he could collect all the magical jewels that the Council of Magical Beings had scattered throughout time, after the last Major Mage War.

The magical jewels had been scattered to prevent the Beings of Evil from ever rising again – well, that was the intention. But there were rumours flying that the current evil Empower planned to travel in time and collect the jewels for his own use. No one knew how the Empower planned to do this. Had *he* invented time travel? Uncle Frog was determined to get to the jewels before the Empower did, and then cast a protection spell around them, to keep them safe forever.

"Just make sure you keep the Empower away from your time machine," I'd said to my uncle. "Otherwise *you* might inadvertently give *him* the power to collect them up."

But Uncle Frog was a pioneer and a dreamer, and he wouldn't be told. It was a family trait…

I sat at the long servants' table, poured my tea, then checked my Amulet of Seeing for messages. The Amulet was a magical bracelet that I wore around my wrist, in order to communicate with other Beings of Magic. It projected their image into the air in front of me, like a flickering sepia film – a great way to keep in touch.

I only had one message this evening – from my mother, a witch who lived in a quaint little village called Maiden-Upon-Avon. I really ought to call her back because we hadn't spoken for a week or so. But then I'd have to tell her about the murder, and right now, I needed to get my thoughts in order.

And besides, it was only five in the morning.

Wait a minute, *the murder!* I quickly grabbed a mirror from the servants' dressing room and cast a spell to make it temporarily magical. Then I cast another spell.

This spell gave me the ability to look back at my memories, as if my eyes were a film camera. But the great thing was, I could also look around the *edges* of my vision – at the people and objects in my peripheral field that I hadn't noticed when I'd actually been there.

I focused on the events of tonight. From my detached place, I saw not only the things I'd actually looked at – Lord Vilnius, the dancefloor, Captain Loveday – but also *around* my vision, which included faces in the crowd.

I watched the entire scene from when I'd arrived at the club to when I'd left – including the moment Captain Loveday had slumped into me and died. But alas, I was unable to see anyone acting suspiciously amongst the throng. There was no knife-wielder lurking in the background. What a pity I'd turned around as Captain Loveday had been stabbed. If I hadn't had my back to him, I'd be able to see the murderer in my mirror now!

I finished off my tea, deciding I'd better turn in. But a scratching sound at the backdoor made my breath catch with dread. What if the murderer had seen me dancing with Captain Loveday and thought I'd witnessed something? With my heart pounding hard, I grabbed a poker from the aga and crept to the door, pressing myself against the wall. Then I yanked the door open, ready to strike! *Rahh!*

"Oh, it's you…"

Two big, puppy eyes gazed up at me from the doormat. A fluffy tail wagged with affection. Then Wispu, the stray dog who hung around our kitchen, trotted inside. She was so cute and woolly – like a cross between a sheepdog and a poodle. How I adored her.

Wispu was carrying the latest edition of *Society* in her mouth, so I took it from her, and we both sat at the kitchen table.

"I'm in it again, am I?" I asked.

She barked, sitting up in the chair opposite me. I was sure she could understand me. It was probably all the magic leaking from Uncle Frog's study.

"Right, let's have a look then." I flicked through the pages. "Ah, here we are. *Despite being in her fourth decade, Lady Joanforth has brains as well as beauty. After her bust-up with Lord Vincent Vilnius a few years ago, she's wealthy, fun-loving, and still eligible – but beware! She won't be tamed easily. Good luck to any bachelor who dares take her on!*"

"How about *that*, Wispu? They think I'm in my forties."

Wispu winked her eye. I was about to read more, but a renewed scuffing at the backdoor made me pause. Once again, with trepidation jangling, I grabbed the poker and crept to investigate.

Oh drat! I hadn't closed the backdoor properly after letting Wispu in. Although I couldn't see him, it was obvious from his shadow that the man outside was strong, muscular, and over six-foot tall. And there was nothing but an ajar door between us… Gulp!

Perhaps Lord Vilnius had returned for his cane? But I wasn't detecting any magical vibes from this shadowy lurker. Fear oozed through my chest. Should I quickly try to slam the door shut?

No, Lady Joanforth Eldritch did *not* run from danger. Instead, a *plan*! I'd rip the door open, zap him with a spell of debilitati—

Too late! The door burst open. On autopilot, I cast the Strength spell and raised my poker-wielding arm to attack. But he blocked me, pushing me backwards. I yelped and grabbed his wrist, pulling him down. We landed together with a thud on the floor – him sprawled on top of me, knees around my hips. I moved to kick him in the groin and–

Wait! His eyes – one blue, one brown. "*You…*"

His voice was as deep as an ocean. "Your ladyship…"

I lay there, panting. "Well, I *was* hoping to see you again, Constable…"

"I do beg your pardon, Lady Joanforth. I er… I wasn't sure if any of the servants would be up yet."

"Then why were you lurking at my backdoor?"

"It was unlocked. I saw movement. I thought someone had broken in."

"Ah yes. That was me."

He frowned. "You broke into your own home?"

"My butler has rather old-fashioned views. Shall we perhaps get up off the floor?"

He offered his hand to help me up, grabbing his fallen hat on the way.

I brushed myself down. "Would you like some cocoa, Constable?"

"I wanted to ask you a few questions actually."

"More questions?"

"Well, the truth is… if you recall… I didn't actually ask you any questions pertinent to the murder earlier. I only got as far as your – *ahem* – particulars… The inspector'll go spare if he finds out I didn't get all the details."

Pride prickled through me. I'd managed to distract this lovely young man with my particulars! "Well, you can ask me now. Over cocoa."

I heated the cocoa while DC Anderson made a fuss of Wispu. They made an instant connection, which warmed my heart. Wispu was a lovely soul, and her tail wagged contentedly as the handsome policeman ruffled her woolly brown ears.

"Here we are," I said, placing the cocoa down on the table.

"Thank you, your ladyship." DC Anderson sat opposite me – next to Wispu – and took out his notebook. "All the other witnesses have confirmed that you were dancing, drinking, and laughing with Captain Loveday just before he was stabbed."

I shrugged. "I don't deny that. As I said to your grumpy inspector, I'd never seen Captain Loveday before tonight. We were merely doing the

Charleston. Not a motive for murder, is it? He was a pretty good mover – I liked him. But there is something I need to tell you, which slipped my mind earlier."

"Oh yeah?"

"Well, the captain was in a melancholy mood when we met. He said he needed to confess something to a priest – but he didn't want the police to know. He said his soul was stained."

DC Anderson leaned forward. "And what did he confess?"

"Unfortunately the Charleston came on and we danced. And then… well, he…"

"Died."

"Yes."

"Pity he didn't spill the beans, eh?"

"I know. Perhaps you'll discover something when you start checking his background?"

"Perhaps." DC Anderson wrapped his hands around his mug of cocoa. "Did you see anyone acting suspiciously?"

I was about to answer, but I noticed a blue swallow inked onto his hand between his thumb and forefinger. From this one tattoo, I suddenly knew a lot about this young man. Almost hypnotically, I ran my fingers over the inch-long bird. This resulted in me pushing up his cuff to reveal another tattoo – a rope twisting around his wrist. "You were in the navy, DC Anderson? A deckhand?"

He held me in his inquisitive gaze. "You know your tattoos, Lady Joanforth."

"I've known some sailors, Constable."

He looked surprised. "With *tattoos*? Not officers, I mean?"

I smirked. "I won't bore you with my encounters with seamen. I'm just surprised *you've* had time to be in the navy – as well as presumably going to war, *and* making detective constable in your... thirty years?"

"Twenty-eight. But I joined the navy when I was fourteen. I've crammed a lot in."

"You joined the navy at fourteen?"

He tried to stifle his grin. "I stowed away. After we'd reached the middle of the Mediterranean, the skipper either had to throw me overboard or let me stay. Luckily for me, they needed a deckhand on their two-year journey to India and back."

"What an adventure." I gazed at him. "But what were you running away from so young? You broke the law?"

He stared into his cocoa. "It was a *crime* to force me into the workhouse at the age of ten, your ladyship."

"Ah. So you escaped the workhouse, then… let me guess… you fell in with a gang of crooks? And it was them you were fleeing?"

He frowned. "Are you a… mind-reader, or something?"

Call it witchy perception. "So how did you end up a copper?"

"I'm here to be ask *you* questions, your ladyship."

"Oh come on, you must finish the story. You went off to war, then joined the police in 1918?"

"Yeah. I'd never officially joined the navy, so when war broke out, I left a life on the ocean waves and enlisted in the army instead. Just before it all ended, somehow I was promoted to sergeant." His carefree expression clouded. "Probably because they were running out of better men by then. But anyway, my military rank gave me the clout to become a copper." He raised a playful eyebrow. "Obviously I didn't tell them about the workhouse and stowing away… Now, your ladyship, back to my investigation…"

I was tempted to ask him if he'd like to investigate my sheets, but he'd probably arrest me for indecency…

He must've noticed my salacious grin, because he said, "What is it?"

"I was just wondering if you'd like to stay for breakfast?"

He chuckled. "From *that* look I get the feeling *I'm* on the menu."

"Oh no, Constable – not breakfast. You're an exquisite meal to be savoured."

He swallowed hard, making his Adam's apple bob. "I should probably get back to the station."

"I thought you wanted to question me?"

"I'm slightly worried about the answers I might get…"

The magnetic tension between us made me want to reach over and grab him. But we were interrupted by a loud bang from upstairs followed by frantic shouting.

DC Anderson grabbed his hat and, with Wispu following, we ran to investigate.

Chapter Four

The bang had come from Uncle Frog's study. Nothing unusual there – his magical inventions often exploded. But whoever was in there with him was angrily yelling, and it sounded like they might turn violent.

I needed to help my uncle. However, I was reluctant for DC Anderson to see Uncle Frog or his magical workshop. Ordinarily, it would've been fine as long as no magic was happening at the moment, but the trouble was, ten years ago, my uncle had been turned into a frogman – and not of the diving variety! He'd been kissed by an evil princess and he was now stuck with the head of a frog and the body of a man – just like a footman in *Alice in Wonderland*. The servants had become accustomed to his amphibian features, but DC Anderson was a bright spark and might start asking awkward questions.

I grabbed the constable's arm. "You can't go in there!"

There was another crash and the sound of Uncle Frog crying out in pain.

DC Anderson shook me away and rattled the locked door. "Open up, it's the police!"

"Help!" Uncle Frog shouted, as another crash erupted from inside.

DC Anderson shoulder-slammed the door, forcing it open. Gosh he was hunky!

Inside the invention-crammed study, I ignored the wooden shelves laden with clocks of varying sizes, the steam-powered gizmos, and the giant lightbulbs flashing on and off. There, in the centre of the Persian rug, *Lord Vilnius's* hands were wrapped around my frog-headed uncle's throat. That dastardly villain must've been here the whole time!

"Get your hands off my uncle, Vincent!" I shouted.

Keeping ahold of the struggling Uncle Frog, Lord Vilnius eyed me up. "Joanforth, you should've married me when you had the chance."

I hitched up my skirt and whipped out my wand. "I *said*, let him go!"

"Don't cast any magic, Joanie!" Uncle Frog croaked. "The time machine's unstable. It could blow any moment!"

Oh no, he was right! Behind the tableau of Uncle Frog and Lord Vilnius, the ceiling-to-floor circular steel machine whirred and crackled – discharging electrical sparks like a giant frenzied blow torch.

Uncle Frog spoke pleadingly to Lord Vilnius. "Vincent. Don't do this, please! Let me switch it off…" My uncle raised his hand, revealing a flashing five-inch cube. The time controls!

DC Anderson brandished his heavy wooden police baton and spoke in a growl. "I don't know what's going on here, but *you*, sir, are under arrest. Unhand Her Ladyship's uncle and put your hands on your head."

The atmosphere in the room plunged to freezing as Lord Vilnius laughed sinisterly. Far too obediently, he let go of Uncle Frog and turned to face the constable. "*I'm* under arrest, am I?"

I held out my wand. "Don't you hurt him, Vinnie! Uncle, what's going on?"

Uncle Frog gestured to the machine. "Vincent asked me to show him how it worked. I thought he was just curious… But he attacked me – said he planned to travel in time to steal the nine magical jewels!"

Lord Vilnius threw me a wicked smile. "If I can get all the magical gems, I'll be lord of all Marvelton – I can even overthrow my tutor, the Empower! Come with me, Joanforth! We can rule together!"

"Never!"

"As you wish!"

"Sir, I said put your hands on your head – you're under arrest!"

Ignoring the constable, Lord Vilnius grabbed the time control cube from Uncle Frog and pushed him to the floor. "Ow!"

I rushed to stop him – grabbing his arm. "Please, Vinnie!"

"Get away from me, witch!" He shook me away, took a frenzied run up, then threw himself into the middle of the sparkling steel circle – before vanishing into inky darkness.

Goodness gracious! Had it worked? Had he time-travelled?

"Where'd he go?" DC Anderson shouted. "What's happening?"

There was no time for discussion, because suddenly the room started to shake like an earthquake. *Oh no!*

"It's a tremor in space/time!" Uncle Frog shouted. "The backwash from magical time travel. Hold on to something!"

Lacking anything solid to hold, I grabbed the constable – which was jolly nice. His *biceps* were pretty darn solid! Hanging onto him, I bounced up and down, as the books and ornaments on Frog's shelves juddered. The antique writing desk jumped across the rug and the multitude of clocks chimed in unison. But worst of all, squealing like a runaway train, the giant, circular time machine spun fast, discharging devilish sparks of hot, white light – which sprayed all over the room.

"I'm going after him!" Frog shouted, raising his hand up against the sparks.

"No, Uncle – you don't even know if it works yet!"

"I can't let Lord Vilnius loose in time – imagine the damage he'll cause. Not to mention the magical jewels! If he finds them, we're all done for! I can't let him – owff!"

Uncle Frog was thrown to the floor as a statuette from the bookshelf crashed on his head. He tried to scramble to his feet, but he was dazed and flopped down. "Joanforth, he mustn't get away with this!"

I sighed. "Looks like I'm going after him then."

"Will someone tell me what the *hell* is happening!" DC Anderson shouted. "Pardon my language, your ladyship. But where did that reprobate disappear to?"

"No time to explain. Must go and do brave daring feats. Existence at risk!"

I darted towards the whirring steel circle, preparing to jump to goodness-knew where. But DC Anderson grabbed my arm, pulling me towards him. "I can't let you do that. Tell me what's happening, or I'll arrest you!"

"Let go of me!"

"Your ladyship, please?"

I lurched towards the time portal, trying to shake off this meddlesome policeman. "Let go, I said!"

I pushed him away as I leapt – but he grabbed me again, and we fell into the time machine together. DC Anderson let out a frantic roar of confusion.

Then we were sucked into the swirling inky void…

-

Chapter Five

We landed with an inglorious thud in a cobbled alleyway. DC Anderson continued crying out for a moment, then suddenly fell silent, patting the ground gingerly.

I scrambled to my feet. "We've stopped. It's all right."

But had we travelled in time? It was impossible to tell in this alley.

The constable shoved his hat on his head. "What… what happened?"

"You shouldn't have grabbed me like that, you stupid boy."

I checked all my bits were present and correct. Yes, I was all in one piece, but something felt… off. My magic seemed weak – as if I only had enough oomph for one spell, perhaps two at a push.

I grasped DC Anderson's upper-arm. Golly, such muscles! "Let's try and find Lord Vilnius and get the time controls back. You can arrest him if you like, in fact, it would be jolly helpful. Not that he's likely to come quietly. But nevertheless, we need to stop him from stealing the magical jewels." I bunched my fist. "I'll knock his block off if he does anything fiendish."

DC Anderson frowned. "Magical jewels? Lady Joanforth, what are you talking about?"

"Um…" I glanced up as a horse and cart trotted past the end of the alleyway. Well, *that* didn't prove anything – people rode horses in 1926. "Wait there a sec, Constable."

I sidled along the wall and peeked around the corner. We were still in Cherry Garden Avenue. But, oh my goodness! Dressed in their long gowns and big hats, a one-hundred-strong Women's Social and Political Union march was heading this way. Suffragettes, gosh! I hadn't seen them since before the war. I'd been an active member, of course. That's why I'd given Wispu that name, because of the Women's Social and Political Union. They'd transformed my life – all our lives.

My eyes welled with tears as I remembered how much Emily Davison had given to the cause. Arrests, hunger strikes … and the ultimate sacrifice in 1913 when she'd walked in front of the king's horse, bringing our plight directly to His Majesty. By giving her life she'd given me the right to vote.

I smiled at the banner the Suffragettes were proudly carrying: WSPU – 1906.

1906? So we *had* time-travelled. And Emily Davison was still alive. Perhaps she was even part of this march! If I saw her, would I warn her?

DC Anderson halted behind me. "Lady Joanforth?"

I positioned myself so he couldn't see around the corner. "Er, Detective Constable Ander… er… do you have a first name?"

"Charles… Charlie."

"Charlie. Right…" How to explain? "Tell me, Charlie, can you feel a golden dappled glow of innocence in the air?"

"Um… no?"

34

"Right. Well, do you remember the Edwardian era? You know, the time of country house parties? Messing about on the river? The age of innocence?"

"I was a child in poverty then, your ladyship. You'll be unsurprised at the complete lack of invites to country house parties I had."

"Yes, of course. Well, let me explain. Don't be cross, but – as you probably noticed – my uncle's been inventing a special machine... without the correct papers and licences."

"He's created an illegal machine?"

"Yes. But that's not the worst of it."

"Right?"

"You see, this machine he's invented, he's discovered a way to move people and things from one, er, *place* to another."

"Oh really?"

"Yes. But *that's* not the worst of it. You see, when I say 'place', I mean 'time'."

"Your uncle has invented an illegal time machine?"

"Yes! But that's not the worst of it."

"*That's* not the worst of it?"

"No. You see, the... um... *thing* that powers my uncle's illegal time machine is... without wanting to beat around the bush *or* put too fine a point on it... it is in fact operated by... magic."

Charlie's face was utterly deadpan. "He's created an illegal magical time machine?"

"That's right. But..."

"*That's* not the worst of it?"

"You're a very bright young man, Charlie. You see, the thing is, I must tell you, I'm a Being of Magic – a witch – and when we leapt into Uncle Frog's time machine, we were sucked back to 1906. And we're sort of stuck here unless we can find my former-fiancé, who – as it turns out – is a megalomanic, hell-bent on ruling the world."

"Ah. And is *that* the worst of it?"

"It doesn't really get much worse than that, does it? Here comes the Suffragette march. Look at the date on their banner – 1906. And see how they're dressed…"

We watched the proud marchers trail past the alleyway, with their heads held high. They looked so old-fashioned, compared to 1926… the women with their high lace collars, puff-sleeved blouses, and ankle-length skirts. Their long hair was poofed up on their head, with a giant hat balanced on top. And the bustle! Such a bizarre undergarment, which made the posterior protrude out from the back of one's gown like a closed peacock tail. It looked elegant, but greatly restricted one's movement. No striding for the Edwardian gentlewoman!

The few men we could see wore typical Edwardian top hats, tails, and boots. Well, the middle and upper classes did. The working classes were dressed in their own 'uniform'. Everyone knew their place in 1906, and their clothing shouted it out loud and clear.

Charlie was speaking. "Lady Joanforth, are you trying to tell me that this is 1906?"

"I'm afraid so."

"The war hasn't started yet." He threw me a cocky grin. "We can stop it!"

"Charlie, you're a very adaptable young man, and I commend you for taking this so calmly. But how could *we* stop the war? And *should* we?"

"But I thought you said you were magical."

Oh bless him, he was adorable! "Let's focus on trying to avert the impending disaster of Lord Vilnius taking over the world, all right? *And* on getting back to 1926."

"How? And what about money?"

I held up my arm, making my bangles jingle. "I have plenty of gold. But we need to blend in. Come on, let's find some suitable clothing…"

I'd learnt over the centuries of a life amongst humans that confidence was a state of mind. And power came to those who looked and spoke as if they already had it. In other words, fake it 'til you make it!

I strode out of the alleyway with my head held high, approaching the crowd of spectators. Some people were cheering; many were booing. But, thanks to my knee-length 1920s dress and cropped hair, *I* was suddenly the focus of attention.

Charlie had realised I was being stared at like a circus sideshow. He whipped off his coat and draped it over my shoulders. "Put this on, your ladyship."

I pulled it around me. "Thank you, darling."

A young middle-class woman was standing nearby. She spoke approvingly. "Did you come dressed in your underwear to protest against the treatment of women?"

"Actually I was mugged in that alleyway over there, and my dress was torn in the tussle."

The woman gasped. "Gosh. And the mugger also cut off your hair and stole your hat?"

"Ye-es…"

"Goodness gracious!" The woman clutched her lacy blouse and inspected Charlie. "And *you*, sir, must've got all dirty defending this lady's honour?"

I noticed that Charlie's trousers were grubby and torn at the back. It must've been when he'd landed in the cobbled alley just now.

The woman was still speaking. "You must find some suitable clothing at once – and alert the police."

Hmm… perhaps this lady could help us?

I thrust out my hand. "I'm Lady Joanforth Eldritch. You are?"

The woman seemed flustered at my aristocratic credentials. She was clearly one of the rising middle classes, and keen to suck up to the gentry. She took my fingers in her gloved hand, practically curtseying. "It's a pleasure to meet you, your ladyship. I'm Mrs Sandhurst – Elizabeth Sandhurst. You must come back to my house – it's only a street away. I'll lend you some clothing and be honoured if you'd take tea with us?"

Before I could reply, Mrs Sandhurst spoke to her maid who was loitering in a long black dress and sensible hat. "Millie, run and tell Mrs Grace that we'll be providing tea to Lady Joanforth Eldritch!"

"Yes, m'm." The maid rushed away.

"You're too kind," I said.

A woman in a long dress cycled past on a clunky bicycle, so we stepped out the way. Mrs Sandhurst smiled at Charlie. "How do you do, er…?"

"This is Mr Anderson," I said.

Charlie tipped his fedora. "How do you do, Mrs Sandhurst."

Mrs Sandhurst raised an inquisitive eyebrow. "You're… related?"

"Er, Mr Anderson is my…"

"Son?" Charlie suggested.

"No!"

"Fancy man?"

"You wish…"

"Cousin?"

"That'll do. This is Mister Charles Anderson. My cousin."

The journey back to Mrs Sandhurst's townhouse was a matter of minutes – in fact, it was just down the road from where I lived in 1926. As we walked, she spoke of her admiration for Christabel Pankhurst and Annie Kenny, who'd purposely got themselves arrested last year as a WSPU publicity stunt in Manchester.

"They heckled that young politician, Winston Churchill," Mrs Sandhurst said. "I doubt he'll amount to much. But they went to prison for their cause, and a crowd of cheering women greeted them when they came out of Strangeways. It was a triumph!"

"And that's what got you interested in the WSPU?" I asked.

She grinned proudly. "Yes!"

I liked Elizabeth Sandhurst. She seemed like a woman who wanted to change the world. A dreamer, like me.

As we approached the house, Charlie headed towards the metal steps for the servants' door. I yanked him towards me,

"What are you doing?" I hissed. "You're supposed to be my cousin. You can't use the tradesmen's entrance."

For someone so cocky, he sounded panicky. "*I* can't use the *front* door, your ladyship!"

"Of course you can. And don't call me 'your ladyship'. Call me 'Cousin Joanie'."

Mrs Sandhurst turned on the doorstep. "Are you quite well, your ladyship?"

I smiled innocently. "Indeed. We were just saying how dreadfully kind you are."

"You're very welcome. Come inside. Greyson and Millie will help you freshen up."

Chapter Six

I was whisked up the carpeted stairs by Millie the maid, and Charlie was taken elsewhere by the butler. Charlie looked reluctant to go, but surely even *he* knew that one couldn't take tea in an Edwardian drawing room wearing torn, grubby trousers.

Millie ushered me into a lavish spare bedroom, then popped back out into the hallway, saying she was fetching me some clothes. I flopped onto the springy double bed and tried to get my bearings. This room was bright and airy, and expensively decorated with a full-length mirror, sturdy dressing table, and ornate fireplace. *I was in 1906!*

I glanced at my Amulet of Seeing, wondering if there was time to connect with Uncle Frog. How long was Millie going to be? If memory served me well, she'd currently be collecting *a lot* of clothing, including… argh, Edwardian undies.

But my underwear issues were trivial in the grand scheme of things. Poor Uncle Frog, I wanted to check he was okay after that bump on the head. But also I needed to know how to track down Lord Vilnius and get Charlie and I out of here!

But at least we'd found ourselves in a nice house with a kind hostess. This townhouse was similar to where I lived in 1926, and Mr and Mrs Sandhurst were clearly doing all right for themselves. Far from aristocracy, I suspected Mr Sandhurst probably owned a factory or was a senior bank clerk. Perhaps I'd meet the man of the house later.

Millie swept back in, so I stood up and... oh drat... there was enough material to cover Trafalgar Square – *including* Nelson's Column – slung over both her arms. "Here we are, your ladyship."

I wilted internally. Here we go then. I knew from experience that this was like being wrapped up for that children's game, pass the parcel. Did I really have time for this? But, alas, I needed to blend in.

Millie plonked the clothing down on the bed. Oh no... the dreaded bustle and corset!

"I've picked out a nice tea-dress for you, your ladyship." She frowned at me. "Are you quite well, madam?"

"Yes..." *No!* I was about to be ambushed by undies! "Um... Mrs Sandhurst doesn't mind me wearing one of her dresses?"

Millie spoke with a gentle cockney accent. "No, madam. She's very generous. Sometimes she even lets me dress up in her clothes. Just for pretend, of course."

"She sounds like a fair mistress."

"She's wonderful."

I picked up the corset and sighed wearily. No matter what Charlie was enduring right now, it was nothing compared to this...

Millie took the corset from me. "I'll help you undress, madam. If you'd like to turn around."

I turned slowly, as if she was holding a gun to my head.

She unbuttoned the back of my dress. "Did someone really come up and cut your hair in the street, my lady?"

I caught her gaze in the mirror and realised I wanted to tell her the truth. Well, some of the truth. "Actually, I did my hair like this myself. Well, I paid a hairdresser to do it."

Millie gasped. "You *wanted* your hair to look like that?" She blushed. "Oh please excuse my impertinence, your ladyship. I do beg your pardon for speaking out of turn!"

"It's all right, Millie. I'm sure it's a truly shocking hairdo." In fact, it was pretty shocking even in 1926, when most women still wore their hair long – but tied it back to give the illusion of a crop.

Millie handed me a cotton slip to pull over my head, then brandished a pair of knee-length drawers. Oh cripes, here came the layers of undergarments… I stepped into the drawers, and Millie tucked my slip into the waistband then fastened the drawers at the back. Next came the petticoats. Millie had brought in three, but I insisted one would do. All this extra padding was such a faff – but it created the illusion of the Edwardian woman's S-shaped figure. I did admit all this underwear made one look elegant and feminine, but I'd always enjoyed *breathing* over style.

Millie brandished the stiff corset. "Goodness, madam, I've never seen a lady so scared of undergarments. Come now, turn around."

Millie wrapped the stiff corset under my bust. I fastened the hooks at the front. Then, taking delight in her work, Millie tugged hard at the laces at the back.

"Oof!" I grunted.

Suddenly my waist was half the size. I felt like I was being constricted by one of those giant anacondas from South America. How quickly I'd become accustomed to the modern 1920s clothing, which was loose-fitting, simple, and didn't require extra help.

Then came more faff – the bustle at the back then another petticoat… and finally the dress. It was a beautiful, silk, high-necked gown, which covered everything – including my ankles. I was taller than Mrs Sandhurst, so I was surprised she didn't trip over this thing when walking. I gazed into the full-length mirror and ran a finger under the lacy collar, feeling restrained.

The war had been dreadful, but I'd been delighted when it had well and truly killed off the Edwardian gentlewoman.

Millie inspected me. "Now what shall we do with your hair? The mistress has this fashionable wig. Shall I affix it, your ladyship?"

"Thank you, Millie."

"Sit here at the dressing table, your ladyship." She spoke dreamily as she fastened the fluffy, brown pompadour wig to my short hair – giving me the quintessential Edwardian hairstyle of puffy on top and rolled under at the nape. "The dress suits you, madam. I did read in the newspaper that Queen Alexandra wore one similar to the Royal Command Performance at the London Coliseum."

"You enjoy reading the newspaper?" I asked.

"I do, madam. Mr Greyson, the butler, isn't in favour. He says it's the duty of a husband or male employer to tell women about current affairs. We women are shockable and hysterical, that's what he says."

I winked at her. "Well, they certainly wouldn't want you expanding your mind and getting above your station, would they? Imagine if you started expressing your opinions!"

Millie gazed at me in the reflection. "I wouldn't do nothing to risk my position here, my lady. And I do love my mistress. I do worry about her."

"Why?"

"She's been experiencing some… accidents."

"Accidents? What sort of accidents?"

"I don't like to accuse people, your ladyship. But some of them seem a little, well, fishy."

"Fishy?"

"Yes, madam."

"Can you tell me what's happened? Perhaps I can help?"

Millie smoothed down the puffy wig on my head. "Well, firstly, there was the threatening note. And then there was a pistol that was fired at her…"

"A pistol? And a threatening note? They don't sound like accidents, Millie."

She started to reply, but she was interrupted by a knock on the door. She gathered up my discarded clothing. "I've said too much."

"Come in," I called to the knocker.

Mrs Sandhurst swept in. "Your ladyship… oh, that's much better – you look wonderful. What a clever girl you are, Millie."

"Thank you, m'm."

Millie curtsied, then left. I was eager to ask Mrs Sandhurst about these attempts on her life, but I didn't want to get Millie in trouble. Gossiping servants were frowned upon in 1906, especially if they dared to speak freely with their 'betters'.

"Tea will be served in the library," Mrs Sandhurst said. "And we've got a couple of other guests joining us. Please, do come…"

Chapter Seven

Feeling like my ribs were being squeezed in a vice, I glided down the stairs, and found Charlie adjusting his cravat in the ornate hallway mirror. He'd been trussed up, just like I had. But he looked devilishly handsome in his suit, waistcoat, and silk cravat.

"You look beautiful," he said… He swallowed his laughter. "I see the hair's grown back. Changed colour too."

"I feel like I'm about to snap in half. How did you get along with the butler?"

"He didn't get very far when he tried to take my clothes off me!"

I chuckled. "It's normal for a gentleman to be dressed by his valet or a butler, Charlie."

"I'm not a gentleman. Anyway, he only managed to get my overcoat off me. He soon backed away when he found a wooden cosh in one pocket and a knuckleduster in the other."

"Golly, you don't take any chances, do you?"

"It's tough being a copper, Lady Joanforth." Charlie rolled his eyes. "Anyway, the butler confiscated them as if I was a naughty schoolboy, saying we don't have weapons in this household. Snooty so-and-so." Charlie lowered his voice. "Luckily he didn't notice my boot knife."

He pulled up the bottom of his trousers, and I glimpsed a knife nestled in a sheath clipped to the side of his boot.

"Goodness. Don't tell me you've got a pistol stuffed down your trousers too, darling."

I was just joking, but his expression darkened. "I'll never pick up a gun again, so long as I live."

"Because of the war. I understand."

"I don't mean to be impertinent, your ladyship, but you most certainly do not understand. No one does, not unless they were there."

I opened my mouth to explain that actually I *did*, but Mrs Sandhurst headed over with a man in tow. He had bushy sideburns, a rather plain face, and he wrung his hands nervously as he approached.

"Lady Joanforth, may I present my husband, Mr Alfred Sandhurst."

I extended my hand. "How do you do. And this is my cousin, Mr Charles Anderson."

Mr Alfred Sandhurst squeezed my fingers gently. "A pleasure to welcome you and your cousin, your ladyship."

Mrs Sandhurst ushered us into the library. It was a beautiful room for entertaining – an open, decorative space, containing bookshelves crammed with Jules Verne and Charles Dickens novels. There were several overstuffed armchairs near the shelves, inviting one to sit and read. To the side stood a long table for serving the tea, which currently held a silver tea service and china teacups. The large windows overlooking the garden let in plenty of light and, judging from the mahogany bureau at the far end, Mr Sandhurst also used this room as an office.

There were two leather sofas in the middle of the large rug, facing each other. Each sofa currently contained a man – one of whom had his back to us.

The man facing us was an older gentleman, and he was waffling loudly about the general election that had taken place in February. He wasn't a fan of the new Liberal government – and was happy to let the world know.

Before I could discover who the other man was, the butler entered, carrying Charlie's heavy wooden baton and knuckleduster as if they might explode. Like any archetypal butler, Greyson was slightly overweight, light of foot, and snootier than even the aristocracy. He spoke quietly to Mr Sandhurst, who returned Charlie's weapons. "My apologies, Mr Anderson, Greyson was just concerned. We've had a few... accidents here recently."

"Accidents, my eye," said the older man on the sofa, clambering to his feet.

As the other man turned around, I almost fell off my dainty heeled slippers.

Charlie gasped sharply, also unable to believe his eyes.

"Captain Sebastian Loveday!" Charlie whispered to me.

The captain was twenty years younger, and he was wearing Edwardian clothing, but he was definitely the man I'd seen stabbed in 1926.

My mind churred with a million thoughts. Should I warn him about his fate? Would telling him change not just his future but *the* future in unimaginably bad ways? It *could* certainly result in me getting locked up in an asylum if I started talking about magical time travel!

Charlie and I were introduced to the two men. The captain frowned as we shook hands. "If I may say so, you're staring at me rather curiously, your ladyship. Have we met?"

"Um… How… how do you know the Sandhursts?"

"Beth – Mrs Sandhurst – and I were childhood friends." He winked at her. "But she threw me over for Alfred whilst I was off fighting the Boers!"

"Oh Sebastian," Mrs Sandhurst said. "Don't say it like that. Alfred simply swept me off my feet…"

Mr and Mrs Sandhurst exchanged a look of love. Of the two men, Captain Loveday was more attractive, so there must be something else appealing about Alfred Sandhurst that had made Beth marry him. Perhaps she just preferred a more stable type of man – one that didn't go around getting himself stabbed in twenty years from now!

But I sensed dejection coming from Captain Loveday. Perhaps it was my overactive romantic soul, but I'd swear that the captain was in love with Mrs Sandhurst. Was that what he'd wanted to confess back in 1926? That he was in love with a married woman?

Or perhaps they were lovers…

The older gentleman turned out to be a stuffy old soldier called Major Payne. His moustache made him look like a walrus, and I knew his opinions would be as baked-in as the craggy lines etched on his face.

I found myself sitting next to the major and Mr Sandhurst, opposite Charlie, Captain Loveday, and Mrs Sandhurst. The butler served the tea, then made himself scarce.

"This is jolly nice," Mr Sandhurst said. "How lovely to have company."

The small talk continued in the same strained, dull manner.

I watched as Mrs Sandhurst absent-mindedly fiddled with a silver brooch pinned to her high lace collar. The brooch was several inches across and shaped like a rose – and I suddenly realised it was emitting magical vibes! I tried to remember everything Uncle Frog had told me about the magical jewels that were scattered throughout time. I knew they were made of various precious metals and gems. Was one of them silver? I'd have to ask him when I eventually made contact.

But if this *was* one of the magical jewels, did *that* mean Lord Vilnius was nearby? He'd made his mission jolly clear. I needed to be on my guard in case he turned up.

"That's a pretty brooch, Mrs Sandhurst," I said.

"Oh thank you, your ladyship. It comes from a silver mine in South Africa. Family heirloom."

She exchanged a glance with Captain Loveday. What did that mean? *Were* they lovers? Had he given it to her? What was he doing here anyway?

Those certainly weren't questions one could blurt out over tea. I needed to be subtle. "And, Mr Sandhurst, what line of business are you in?"

This was also a rather personal question for tea – especially from a lady. But I was aristocracy, which meant I could get away with a lot. Class mattered in England – it always had, and I suspected even in a hundred years from now, it still would.

Mr Sandhurst sipped his tea. "I'm an industrialist, your ladyship. I own a cotton mill in Essex and also have shares in a coalmine in South Wales."

"How terribly fascinating…" Excuse me while I watch this paint dry…

"Let's get down to my reason for being here," Major Payne said. "These accidents you've been encountering, Beth?"

Mrs Sandhurst glanced at her husband. "You asked the major here to talk about that? We don't want a scandal, Alfred."

The major waved this away. "Nonsense, nonsense… No point in Alfred having the chief constable as an old family friend if I can't help you here and there."

"You're the chief constable of the Met Police?" I asked.

He grunted. "Certainly am, your ladyship. Now, Beth, tell me what's happened. You've apparently received a threatening note?"

Mrs Sandhurst rummaged in the long sleeve of her blouse and pulled out a crumpled sheet of paper, which she handed to the Major.

I read it out loud. "*Watch your head. You'll soon be dead.*"

Charlie plopped a sugar cube into his tea. "How charming. A poet."

"Tell them about the gun attack, Beth," Mr Sandhurst said.

She wrung a lacy handkerchief in her hands. "It was when I was in here the day before yesterday. I had my back to the door, and I heard the click of a gun being… what do you call it?"

"Cocked," Charlie said, stirring his tea with a silver teaspoon.

She blushed. "Yes. Thank heavens I ducked to the floor as the shot was fired. You can see where the bullet landed in the bookshelf over there."

We all craned to look. There was indeed a bullet hole in the far bookshelf.

"Then what happened?" I asked. "Did they fire again?"

"I screamed and Alfred came running. But the gunman had vanished."

Mr Sandhurst nodded. "I heard the shot of course, *and* my wife's scream. But the front door was wide open with no sign of the assailant."

"Did the butler let anyone in?" Charlie asked.

Mrs Sandhurst shook her head. "Greyson says no. The gunman must've broken in."

"Any witnesses see anyone running away?" Charlie asked.

The major grumbled. "Excuse me, young man, I'll ask the questions around here! Now, Beth… did any witnesses see anyone running away?"

Charlie rolled his eyes, exasperated with this old walrus. I stifled my smile.

"No," Mrs Sandhurst said. "None of the servants saw anything."

"And what else, m'dear?" the major asked. "Alfred said there was a potted plant?"

Mrs Sandhurst sighed wearily. "Yesterday, a heavy terracotta plant pot in the garden fell off a high wall and almost hit me. But… I'm sure that was just bad luck."

"Doesn't sound like it," the major said. "Sounds like the fellow came back to finish you off."

"But you saw no one?" I asked.

She shook her head. "I was alone in the garden. I'd asked Millie to run in and get my parasol, because it was rather warm in the sunshine. The wall is part of an ornate stone archway. As I'd strolled through the archway to look at the roses growing against it, *that's* when the pot fell. Luckily, I moved in time. The wall leads to the roof, so I suppose they slipped off that way."

"You didn't see anyone on the wall?" Charlie asked – ignoring the major's glare. "Running to the roof?"

"I saw a glimpse – a blur. But no, I couldn't even say if it was a man or a woman."

"Of course it wasn't a woman," the major said. "The fairer sex wouldn't possess either the physical strength or the intelligence for such a plan. And as for firing a gun… Well, if *was* a woman it might explain why they missed you, m'dear!"

I was tempted to turn the major into a mouse. Or worse still, a woman. But I refrained. For now.

Mrs Sandhurst pressed her hanky against her lips and whimpered. Her husband rose and wrapped his arm around her. "Shh, darling. We'll catch the fellow. Won't we, Major?"

The major muttered his agreement and stuffed a shortbread biscuit in his mouth.

I sipped my tea. "Major, Mrs Sandhurst's maid, Millie, wanted to tell me something about these so-called accidents just now. I think perhaps you ought to talk to her?"

"Oh, *please* don't upset Millie," Mrs Sandhurst said anxiously. "Poor girl is too sweet and innocent to be drawn into this."

"Yes, I agree," Major Payne said. "No need to upset the domestics. Once we start talking to *them*, rumours spread like wildfire. Before we know it, they'll all swear they've seen Genghis Khan riding around on his horse!"

"I think you should ask her what she knows," Charlie said. "It sounds like it might be important."

"Don't tell me how to do my job, boy."

"I'm not a boy."

"I know what maids are like – they swoon and get hysterical at the drop of a hat. It's just this Suffragette nonsense stirring her up. Women voting, indeed? Whatever next, women Members of Parliament!"

"Why not?" Captain Loveday asked.

Major Payne grunted. "Women shouldn't be worrying about politics. They should be worrying about *us*. And besides, imagine the scenes in the House of Commons – the women's big hats would obscure the views for all the chaps!"

"I suppose they could take them off?" Mrs Sandhurst said. "The *men* don't wear hats inside the chamber."

"Women going about hatless?" Alfred asked in shock. "Beth, have you gone mad?"

Major Payne started to agree, but he coughed and wheezed, going red in the face and banging the sofa angrily. "See, this is just the sort of suggestion we're up against! Go about hatless, I ask you. Here is conclusive proof that women are frail, illogical, and hysterical."

I glared at the half-dinosaur/half-walrus next to me. "Queen Victoria was a splendid *female* monarch, was she not, Major?"

"I won't hear a word against their majesties," he grumbled.

"Quite."

I looked away from Major Payne and saw Charlie covertly slipping a teaspoon up his sleeve. A thieving copper – now I'd seen it all!

Before anyone else could air their views on votes for women, the butler swept in, carrying a silver platter, which he lowered for Mr Sandhurst. "A telegram has arrived for Mrs Sandhurst, sir."

"Thank you, Greyson."

Mrs Sandhurst smiled at me. "I keep asking Alfred if we can get one of those new-fangled telephone devices, but he says they're dangerous."

Mr Sandhurst read his wife's telegram, then passed it to her.

"Oh," she said. "The next WSPU march will be outside the Houses of Parliament next week. Alfred, you don't mind me joining them, do you, darling?"

He glanced at the major, who snorted.

"Of course not, my love. But you must let me come with you. I don't like these attempts on your life, and I worry the killer might succeed next time."

Mrs Sandhurst agreed. Tea was declared over, and everyone dispersed, so Charlie and I went over to inspect the bullet hole in the bookshelf.

"I could run a ballistics test on this," he said, pensively.

"What's that?" I asked.

"It's a new form of firearms forensics – like, fingerprinting for guns. It was only invented last year… well, it *will be* invented in 1925."

"But if anyone *sees* you carrying out this ballistic thingy, *you'll* be credited with inventing it!"

He grinned at this prospect. "I'd better not then, eh, your ladyship?"

"Precisely. And… don't be cross, but… Charlie… I think you'd better put back the teaspoon."

He smirked and shook his arm, easing the stashed silverware back into his hand. "Sorry, force of habit. You should know– before I joined the police – I was a thief."

"I rather worked that out for myself, darling."

"But I *did* manage to swipe something useful just now." He pulled Mrs Sandhurst's threatening note from his pocket.

I took it from him. It was difficult to focus because he stepped behind me and read over my shoulder. "*Watch your head. You'll soon be dead.* It's not exactly Shakespeare, but it gets the message done."

"I wonder if the police have checked the handwriting?" Charlie said. "Or dusted the paper for fingerprints. That's what I'd do. But this is 1906. And the major is an idiot."

"I don't disagree with you. But if *I* were to send a threatening note, I wouldn't use my usual writing hand, would you?"

"True. And I suppose it's covered in all sorts of fingerprints now, if she's been passing it around."

I turned and popped the note into Charlie's jacket pocket, relishing being so close to him. "Let's go out to the garden. We need somewhere secluded."

He raised a flirty eyebrow. "All right."

"To contact my uncle! And we'll see what happens from there…"

Chapter Eight

But first thing's first, I needed a hat…

I found Millie cleaning in Mrs Sandhurst's sitting room, next door to the library.

She lowered her feather duster and spoke nervously. "Your ladyship, the mistress will be back down momentarily – she said she wishes to write some letters. Did you want to see her?"

"It's all right, Millie, no need to disturb Mrs Sandhurst. Mr Anderson and I are going for a stroll in the back garden. Would you be so kind as to lend me one of your mistress's hats? I wouldn't want to give any men like the major heart failure."

"Of course, madam."

"Wait, Millie… what were you going to tell me earlier when–"

"Oh, I do beg your pardon…" Alfred Sandhurst walked in and started riffling through his wife's letters on her writing desk. Drat, I couldn't speak freely with him here. Not after the major had warned me off speaking to the 'hysterical' servants.

"Never mind," I said to Millie kindly.

Millie returned with a large hat to match my dress, fixing it with a hat pin. Then Charlie and I made our way down the high-ceilinged hallway and out the back French windows.

The garden had been designed and cultivated in the typical Edwardian 'back to nature' style. The flagstone pathway down the middle was flanked by flower beds overflowing with peonies, lavender bushes, and roses. It smelt glorious!

Two lofty stone arches divided the garden into three separate spaces – perfect for a tryst. Or for conducting some surreptitious magic…

Charlie and I innocently promenaded towards the end of the garden, enjoying the sunshine and birdsong. It was impossible to relax in all this underwear, but at least I was in the company of a handsome young sailor. Soldier. Police officer. Gosh, so many uniforms, so little time!

"Were you a professional thief?" I teased as we strolled. "Or just for fun?"

"No, your ladyship, I needed to eat."

"Oh… sorry, Charlie."

"It's all right. But the truth is, I wasn't just running away from the workhouse when I stowed away. As you rightly guessed, I'd fallen in with a gang of crooks, and I was being chased by a couple of coppers for nicking some toff's purse."

"Goodness, your life sounds like a Mr Dickens novel! So you ran to the docks – purse in hand – and hid on a ship moored there?"

"Exactly that, your ladyship. I never expected it to become unmoored, but next thing I knew, I was sailing to Italy as a deckhand."

"And from there, India?"

"Yep. Via Egypt and Arabia… those were great days. Everything was simple. Then I came back and there was a bloody great war on."

"Well, at least the toff probably forgot about her stolen purse." We strolled under the furthest archway and I dragged Charlie behind the rose-clad wall. "Come on, let's hide here…"

"Whatever you say, your ladyship. Er… what are you doing?"

I unbuttoned my fiddly cuffs to reveal my Amulet of Seeing. "I hope this works here in 1906…"

My only other plan was to go and find Uncle Frog or even *myself* in this time. But I'd prefer not to involve anyone else. Even if it *was* me.

Thankfully, the flickering image of Uncle Frog whooshed up from my wrist.

Charlie gasped. "Your uncle! Is he here?"

"No, he's in 1926. This is magic. Oh look, there's Wispu. Hello, Uncle; hello Wispu!"

Wispu barked. How I adored that woolly dog. They were sitting in Uncle Frog's workshop, with the time machine in the background. It looked… dead.

"My dearest Joanie," Uncle Frog said. "I'm relieved you're safe. Where are you? *When* are you?"

"1906, Uncle! Charlie and I have been enjoying the hospitality of the Sandhursts."

"Charlie?" he asked.

"DC Anderson here."

"Oh… Have you seen Lord Vilnius?"

"No, but we need to find him, don't we. To get the time controls."

"Yes. But I've been consulting the runes. If you can find *one* of the magical jewels, it should provide enough of a magic surge to initiate time travel – to get you back here. It might just work. *If* you can find one of the jewels."

"Actually, Uncle, I think Fate has intervened. Mrs Sandhurst's silver brooch is fairly buzzing with magical vibes."

"Silver brooch? It's not in the shape of a rose by any chance?"

"It is!"

"Well, that's it! Bless, Fate. If you can, by chance, convince Mrs Sandhurst to part with the brooch, it might get you back here."

"I can't ask her to give it to me. She's clearly very attached to it."

Charlie grinned. "I might be able to help with that."

I smiled. "You'll need to get very close to her to swipe it."

"I'll see what I can do."

Uncle Frog rolled his eyes. "Just sort it out, Joanforth. And watch out for Lord Vilnius." Uncle Frog waved a red magical crystal in the air in front of him. "Oh dear…"

"What?"

"I'm detecting an abundance of negative vibes around your projected image – coming from *you*. Has something terrible happened?"

"Yes! I've been forced to wear a corset. Look…" I held up my arms and showed him my pinched waist.

"Something more serious than your undergarments, Joanforth!"

"What about the death threats?" Charlie asked. "The 'accidents' that Mrs Sandhurst has encountered?"

"That could be it," Uncle Frog said.

"Well, what about it?"

"It's blocking your magic. And I'm worried that the negativity surrounding you might prevent the magic from catching when it's time to leave – even *with* the silver rose."

"How do we cleanse the negative vibes?" I asked.

Uncle Frog stared at the crystal. "I think… yes… Make sure she doesn't die… *and* make sure justice is done – catch the person who's threatening her. That should unblock the negativity."

"Then we'd better get to it. I'm not spending the next twenty years squeezed into a corset. It was bad enough the first time around."

"We'd have to go through the war again," Charlie said glumly.

I squeezed his arm. "It's all right, Charlie. We'll get back."

"We need to. I've got a murder to solve in 1926."

"Yes. Speaking of which, Uncle, can you believe it, Captain Loveday's here! We've met him."

Uncle Frog frowned. "Captain Loveday? Oh… you mean that chap who was murdered last night? Yes, a rather grumpy police inspector turned up looking for you earlier. He said that *you* were dancing with a Captain Sebastian Loveday at the Fat Pussycat Club – just before he was stabbed to death."

"All true, alas. And that grumpy inspector is Charlie's boss."

"Oh… well, perhaps you can gather a clue or two whilst you're there, young man. Might cheer him up a bit, eh?"

Charlie muttered, "Unlikely…"

Uncle Frog spoke pensively. "But how interesting that you've met the murder victim back there in the past. Fate has well and truly been tinkering, hasn't she?"

"She does like to tinker," I said, keeping my voice jolly – in case she was listening.

"Well, as it happens," Uncle Frog said. "I've discovered some information about Sebastian Loveday myself. As soon as the inspector said *you* might be involved, Joanie, I asked him some questions of my own."

"I'm not involved, Uncle. But what have you discovered?"

"Apparently, here in 1926, Captain Loveday has recently returned from South Africa. But interestingly, he left England in August 1906 – shortly after when you are now."

Charlie scratched his stubble. "Mrs Sandhurst said that the captain had been out fighting in the Boer War. He must've returned from Africa after that – and now he's about to leave again for the next twenty years."

"Could *he* be behind the attempts on Mrs Sandhurst's life?" I asked pensively.

"It could explain why he's suddenly about to leave the country and not return for twenty years." Charlie said.

"Yes, but why would anyone kill *him* in 1926?" Uncle Frog asked.

"That's what we need to find out. And keep Mrs Sandhurst safe. Uncle Frog, can you gather some background information on the people we were at tea with? Cast the Invisibility spell and get the files from the police station or public records library?"

"You think one of *them* might be behind the murder attempts?" Charlie asked.

I shrugged. "No idea, but they're a good place to start. Don't you think so, Detective Constable?"

He threw me a flirty grin. "Indeed, your ladyship."

Uncle Frog grabbed a pen from his desk and dipped it in the inkwell. "What are their names?"

"There was a Mr Alfred Sandhurst and a Major Payne. Also, see if you can get any more info on the captain."

"Will do. And what about the servants?"

"So far we've met Millie – a maid. And Greyson, the butler."

"I can speak to the cook and any other servants," Charlie said. "Perhaps one of *them* wants their mistress out the way."

"Good plan," Uncle Frog said. "But try not to change anything. Don't step on any butterflies. They might be your grandmother."

"My grandmother was a butterfly?" I asked playfully. "How marvellous!"

"You know what I mean. Don't make any changes that might affect the future."

"Other than keeping Mrs Sandhurst alive and ensuring justice is done?" I said flatly.

"It's the only way to purge the negative vibes," Uncle Frog said. "Now, I'd better get on. Come on, Wispu, you can help me. Stay in touch, Joanforth. And 'best of British' to you both!"

Uncle Frog's projected image disappeared.

Charlie gazed at me in awe. "That was incredible."

"Why thank you, Charlie – not the first time I've heard *that* from the lips of a handsome young man."

He started to chuckle, but a shrill scream from the other end of the garden made us both jump. Oh golly, what now?

Chapter Nine

Fate had a nasty habit of giving with one hand and taking with the other.

As Charlie and I dashed to the other end of the garden, I saw Mrs Sandhurst sprawled in the middle of the garden path, completely still. Deathly still…

Charlie and I stood over her. I rubbed my ankle. "Ow, these shoes were *not* made for running..."

Charlie crouched and pressed his fingers to her wrist. "She's dead, your ladyship. Murdered, I'd say – judging from that frightened scream."

I knelt and eased Mrs Sandhurst's hair from her face. "But… but this isn't Mrs Sandhurst!"

"It's Millie…" Charlie whispered. "Why's she wearing Mrs Sandhurst's topcoat?"

"No idea. But whoever killed her obviously mistook her for her mistress."

Charlie gazed into my eyes. "Someone familiar with Mrs Sandhurst's *coats* then?"

We looked up at the sound of approaching footsteps. Mr and Mrs Sandhurst were rushing over from the direction of the backdoor.

Mrs Sandhurst spoke frantically. "What happened? We heard a scream, and… oh my goodness, Millie!"

Alfred Sandhurst drew his wife into his arms. "Beth, stay back. What happened to her? Did you see?"

Charlie and I stood up. "No, sir," Charlie said. "It looks like the killer came up behind her and thwacked her over the head with a blunt instrument – a club, or something."

"Neither of you saw anyone?" Mr Sandhurst asked. "You were out here, weren't you?"

"We were at the other end of the garden," I said. "Looking at the… er… flowers behind the far wall. Where were you two? Did *you* see anyone?"

"I was in the library," Alfred said. "When I heard the scream, I ran to the backdoor, bumping into Beth in the hallway."

"And where were you, Mrs Sandhurst?" I asked.

"Writing letters in my sitting room. Like Alfred, I came running when I heard the scream."

"Why was Millie wearing your coat, Mrs Sandhurst?" Charlie asked.

"She… I don't know. She sometimes wears my clothes indoors and I don't mind. I know how hard she works. Worked. Oh goodness, is this really happening?"

"Any idea who might've done this?" Charlie asked. "Thinking that Millie was you?"

"I don't know. Perhaps… perhaps... I'm not sure." Mrs Sandhurst clutched her silver brooch for comfort. "I didn't know she planned to borrow my coat… That should be me... oh good heavens…"

"Where was she going?" Charlie asked.

"She was taking this basket of unwanted clothing to the church. Donations for the needy."

I gazed at the upturned wicker basket of old clothes, which Millie must've been carrying.

I frowned. "Hold on, what was Millie doing in the back garden if she was heading for the church? There's no access to the street from here, is there?"

Mrs Sandhurst rubbed her brow. "I… I asked Millie to gather some pretty flowers for the church ladies. They decorate the tables, you see. We do what we can to help… Don't we, Alfred?"

"We do, my darling. But come now, let's get you inside. Greyson can get Major Payne back here."

Mr Sandhurst practically carried his trembling wife back into the house. Charlie grabbed a blanket from the pile that had spewed from the wicker basket and covered Millie.

I gazed at the motionless shape under the blanket for a respectful moment – feeling sadness mingle with my anger. If only Charlie and I had been nearer, perhaps that lovely young woman would still be alive…

"We'd better leave the crime scene as it is for the major," Charlie said. "I don't respect the man's values, but he's the chief constable of the Met, so he must know a thing or two about murder."

"Yes, I expect he does."

I wandered over to the first stone archway, hiding my distress from Charlie. He was a policeman and probably used to this sort of thing, but for me it was utterly heart-wrenching.

Right… *when in doubt, do something about…*

I absentmindedly picked up a piece of smashed terracotta pot from in front of the wall. "Look, Charlie, this mess must be what's left after the attempt on Mrs Sandhurst yesterday. She said someone had pushed a plant pot off the wall and almost hit her."

Charlie inspected the pieces of smashed terracotta scattered on the ground. "It must've been very heavy to create all this mess. Mrs Sandhurst was lucky she moved out the way in time."

An idea struck me. "What if the killer tried the same method *this* time, and ended up killing *Millie* with a plant pot – thinking she was Mrs Sandhurst? There are *a lot* of smashed pieces here. Surely enough for two pots?"

"But… that doesn't make sense, your ladyship. Look, Millie's at least three yards away from this wall."

"Perhaps she didn't die instantly? She staggered along the path then fell?"

Charlie crouched down and respectfully checked Millie's injuries. "Forgive me, your ladyship, but this huge dent in her head would've killed her immediately."

"So she can't have staggered along? All right… it *wasn't* the plant pot that killed her. But I wonder…"

"Your ladyship, what are you doing!"

Charlie tried to pull me back as I hitched up my heavy dress and clambered on top of a large planter that was pushed against the wall. "I want to take in the entire scene…"

"You can't climb up there!"

"Want to bet?"

I won the bet… Being careful not to trip on my petticoats, I hoisted myself to the top of the wall and crouched on the archway, scanning the entire garden. Other than the lifeless Millie and upturned basket, I

70

couldn't see anything out of place. What a shame the pathway was made of flagstones. A gravel path might've held a convenient footprint left by the killer.

I was about to clamber down again, when my eye caught a blue scrap of material snagged on the corner of the wall. "Look, Charlie – this must've come from the killer's clothing when they were waiting for Mrs Sandhurst yesterday – when they tried to push the pot on top of her!"

Charlie offered his hand to help me down, but instead I handed him the two-inch scrap and jumped down on my own. Ow… my ankle didn't appreciate *that*. I must find some flat shoes.

"So we're looking for a man with clothing of this colour?" Charlie said. "We need to ask him what he was doing up there."

Oh, but I suddenly realised something! I tugged Millie's blanket back an inch and… yes! "Except, *this* blue scrap is an exact match for the coat Millie's wearing, look!"

Charlie sounded baffled. "What was *she* doing up there?"

"Surely *she* wasn't behind the attacks on Mrs Sandhurst?"

"I think it's highly unlikely Millie would've climbed that wall, your ladyship. If I hadn't seen you do it, I would've sworn it wasn't possible for a woman to climb like that."

"Well, you've learnt more than a few things today, haven't you? Can you see a murder weapon anywhere? You think it was some sort of blunt object?"

"Yes, like a club."

"Or a police baton, like yours?"

"You don't think *I* did it?"

"Of course not – you were with me behind the wall at the other end of the garden. I just mean, perhaps… another copper?"

"Oh… Well, let's wait to see what the experts think before we start making accusations."

"All right. But Mrs Sandhurst is still at risk. Uncle Frog said if we can protect her and ensure justice is done – *and* get the silver brooch – we might be able to travel home."

"Don't we also need the time controls from Lord Vilnius?" Charlie asked.

"One step at a time." I gazed at the lush garden, which was a haven of peace and innocence again. "Right, I suggest first we have a little chat with anyone who was nearby at the time of this latest attempt on Mrs Sandhurst. Everyone who was at tea with us for example… where did *they* disperse to?"

"All right. But, your ladyship, I'm the detective around here. *I* should be in charge of this."

"Is that right? Well, Charlie, I'm the 'your ladyship' around here, and this is 1906. You know as well as I do how important class is in this country, so I'm in charge."

He tried to suppress his smirk. "No one's above the law, your ladyship."

"Quite right. So I suggest you stop breaking it. Come along."

Chapter Ten

Back inside the house, Charlie volunteered to go and speak to the servants – to find out if this household consisted of more than just the butler, cook, and now-late maid. I decided to speak to Mrs Sandhurst, wherever she'd got to. She'd had a dreadful shock and I wanted to check if she was well. But also, I needed to learn more about these threats and so-called accidents.

Her husband informed me that she was lying down, so I made my way up to her bedroom. It was a lovely, bright room, with a four-poster bed and a separate dressing room. But Mrs Sandhurst wasn't there – in fact, there was no one on this floor at all.

At the end of this light and lavish hallway, my witchy senses compelled me to pass through the green baize door – the dividing line between master and servant. I climbed the creaky narrow staircase to the sparse attic. What did I expect to find up here? Perhaps I might discover some vital information on that butler. He was so snooty and stuck-up. Did *he* have a reason to want Mrs Sandhurst dead?

I crept past several closed doors in the drab corridor but halted suddenly at the sound of a crash. *Uh-oh!*

As I burst into a poky bedroom, I was relieved to find Mrs Sandhurst crouched in front of the open wardrobe, picking up a pair of boots she'd dropped.

She was alive and well. Thank goodness.

"Your ladyship." She shoved the boots back into the wardrobe. "I know Alfred wanted me to rest, but I simply can't. Not until I find out what happened to poor Millie. Why would anyone do this to her?"

I joined her by the open wardrobe. "Mrs Sandhurst, surely you must know this was another attempt on *your* life? Millie was wearing your coat…"

Mrs Sandhurst seemed frail and defeated. She sank onto the small bed, which boinged beneath her. "Poor Millie… Your ladyship, do you know *how*… what happened?"

"It seems she was hit with a heavy object, such as a club."

As Mrs Sandhurst replied, I gazed into the wardrobe and noticed how few personal belongings servants really had. Millie owned a couple of day dresses, but mostly her clothing consisted of her uniform – two pressed blouses, two long black skirts, two white aprons. Several white caps. No wonder she wanted to dress up in her mistress's finer clothing.

I sat on the bed with Mrs Sandhurst and picked up Millie's nightdress from the pillow, rubbing my fingers forlornly over the soft cotton. It would never be worn again by that lovely young woman. My fingertips brushed the collar and I realised she'd sewn some letters into the material. MJ. "What was Millie's surname?"

"Um… Jones, I think. Yes. Mildred Jones."

"She embroidered her initials into her clothing?"

"She previously worked in a bigger house, your ladyship. They all sew their initials in their uniforms, otherwise things get mixed up in the laundry. I wouldn't expect a lady like your ladyship to be aware of what goes on below stairs, of course." Mrs Sandhurst swallowed her emotion. "I just don't know what her parents will think. We feel our servants are in our care somehow. And there's still someone out there who… who…"

I placed my hand supportively on her back. "We'll keep you safe."

"Thank you, your ladyship." She rubbed her brow. "What a dreadful day. And… I know it's not a time to speak of this, but Millie was taking that basket of old clothes to the church for the poor. The vicar's always so grateful for our donations – there are so many needy souls in this city." She bit back her tears. "I'd hate to think of some wretched urchin being cold, because… because…"

"Don't you worry about that now, Mrs Sandhurst. Mr Anderson and I will take the donations. Is it the local parish church?"

"Yes." She gazed at me through teary eyes. "You're ever-so kind, Lady Joanforth. And now, I think I will lie down."

I helped her back down the stairs to her bedroom, where she flopped onto the soft double bed. After I'd covered her with a snuggly woollen blanket, I went to fetch Charlie. We had a murderer to find!

Chapter Eleven

As I descended the main staircase, my heart leapt at the sight of Charlie loitering in the hallway. He was standing in front of a mahogany table, which held a collection of Mrs Sandhurst's antique bronze figurines. I watched as he inspected each one briefly then put it back down. Hmm… was he up to his old pilfering tricks?

I halted stealthily behind him. "Should I frisk you before we leave?"

In the hallway mirror, I saw his face break into a grin. "You can frisk me, your ladyship – certainly."

"Well, *you* frisked *me*. It's only fair."

He turned slowly and held out his arms, gazing into my eyes. "Go on then."

Gosh, I was tempted...

But I glanced coolly at my fingernails. "Get any information from the butler?"

Charlie fell serious. "Not really. Apparently the entire household consists of himself, the cook, and the now late-Millie."

"Millie cleaned the entire house by herself?"

"Greyson said a couple of women come in twice a week."

"Ah. And did you ask him who might want to harm Mrs Sandhurst?"

"I did. But he told me he was very busy and refused to talk. He also instructed the cook not to answer my questions – right in front of me."

"Suspicious?"

"Just the usual obstructive butler."

"What a pity. However, we now have a mission from Mrs Sandhurst."

"Oh yeah?"

"We're to take the basket of clothing to the church for the needy. Come on, the walk will do us good."

"All right. Let me just put this back…"

I rolled my eyes and walked off. It was probably best not to know…

Now that Mrs Sandhurst's knick-knacks were once again safe from Charlie's thieving hands, we stepped out into the garden to collect the basket. But I was dismayed to discover that the peaceful haven was now a hive of police action. Major Payne was standing near the first stone archway, shouting orders at his constables. The only motionless thing out here now was Millie's rigid body, which remained covered under the blanket. Poor, sweet girl.

I put on my haughtiest voice. "Major Payne, Mrs Sandhurst has asked me to take this basket of clothes to the church. *That's* where Millie was off to before… this happened."

The major glanced at the now-upright basket. He waved his hand dismissively. "Yes, yes, you have my permission. My sergeant has rummaged through the clothes and found no weapon concealed within."

I hoisted the basket to my hip. "Any idea about the murder weapon, Major?"

He shrugged. "Looks to be a cosh or a club, dear lady."

Charlie spoke pensively. "How about one of the bronze figurines on the table by the front door?"

The major eyeballed Charlie. "I say, boy, I saw *you* with a cosh that looked similar to a police baton. Where'd you get it?"

"My... *uncle* is a police officer. And he gave it to me to protect myself – and certainly *not* to murder innocent young women."

"Nevertheless, I want to look at it. Hand it over."

Charlie handed his baton to the major. "See, no blood marks? Not fresh ones, anyway."

Major Payne passed it to the nearby constable. "We're confiscating it for the time being. Once we're satisfied that it wasn't used to commit this dreadful crime, you can have it back. You're free to leave. For now."

Duly dismissed, we headed out.

The local church was only a few minutes away on foot. It was an imposing medieval gothic building, famous for surviving the Great Fire of London back in the seventeenth century. It was stone and sturdy, with huge stained-glass windows – making its purpose clear to all who walked past.

Charlie and I dropped off the basket of clothes, explaining to the vicar that they were courtesy of Mrs Sandhurst. The vicar was sad to hear about Millie, saying what a nice girl she was. I was more determined than ever to solve her murder. But where to start?

We strolled a little further along the road, taking in the sights and sounds of 1906. Even though it looked terribly old-fashioned to my 1926 eyes, things *had* changed since King Edward VII had taken over from his glorious mother, Her Majesty Queen

Victoria. The fashion was *slightly* less stuffy than the Victorian era, despite the corset, and there was a little class mobility now that the middle classes were buying factories and businesses.

This street was busy with all sorts of different people, but it was easy to distinguish between the classes, with the very wealthy wearing only the best and brightest materials, and the workers wearing drab, darker clothing. Everyone, but everyone, was wearing a hat.

Edwardian London was noisy and smelly, with horses, factories, and people loudly mixing together in close quarters. But even with its noise and smog, this was an age of innocence – which was about to be shattered in the most dreadful way.

I halted outside a familiar landmark. "Oh look, Charlie, it's the building where we first met. This will become The Fat Pussycat!"

"Looks like it's currently an officers' club."

Out here in the street was as near as *I'd* ever be permitted to such a place. But I gasped as I spotted someone we knew, sitting at a table, drinking brandy, and smoking a cigar.

"It's Captain Loveday. Let's go in and ask him where he went to after tea."

"We can't go in there, your ladyship," Charlie said. "It's a place for gentlemen to drink, socialise, and unwind. I'm neither an officer nor a gentleman, and you're…"

"Disadvantaged by having a womb. yes… Charlie, did you put back that silver teaspoon like I asked?"

"Um… I forgot in all the excitement."

"Never mind. Go back to the church and make a donation of one silver spoon. Then ask the vicar for some britches for me and a gentleman's jacket for you. There's bound to be something in the clothing donations for the poor."

Charlie groaned. "It'll never work, your ladyship. Captain Loveday's met us both – and only an hour ago."

"That's true. Get some spectacles too. And a hat."

"This isn't a penny dreadful, Lady Joanforth – or Sherlock Holmes."

"It's quite dimly lit in there. I think it might work."

"Shall I grow a beard and moustache in the next five minutes too?"

"Just go."

If only I had more magic in me. I was almost a senior witch and would've ordinarily cast the Creator spell to conjure up whatever I needed. But, exactly as Uncle Frog had said, the magic was weak around here, and I needed to save it for our trip home.

Charlie came back dressed in a top hat and tails, wearing a monocle, and carrying a cane. He certainly looked the part! He handed me a pair of britches and a red officer's jacket. I sidled behind a convenient oak tree, and pulled the britches up over my dress, making it look like I had a big, fat stomach.

I pulled on the jacket. "How do I look?"

"Like a woman dressed up for vaudeville."

I removed the pompadour wig. "At least I've got short hair. Any better?"

"Nope. Still feminine." He stared at the pavement. "Too pretty for a man…"

Bless him… I scrutinised Charlie. The 1920s men's style was to have short hair and be clean-shaven, whereas the Edwardians grew bushy beards, lamb-chop sideburns, and long moustaches. He'd been joking just now about growing a beard, but maybe… I glanced around the busy street for inspiration.

Ah ha! "Look, Charlie, the backdoor to that music hall's open. Let's sneak in and raid their wig box."

He groaned. "A music hall? You can't be serious."

"Oh don't be like that. I'm not asking you to actually *watch* any of the dreadful acts."

"That's not really what I meant…"

I grabbed his hand and we hurried across the cobbled street. Then we crept through the backdoor and found a tiny dressing room, which was stuffed to bursting with rails of costumes. Every shelf was crammed with hats, theatre props, and pots of greasepaint.

I rummaged through a cardboard box of wigs. "Look, here's a bushy moustache for me. And this beard would be perfect for you!"

I hooked the curly beard over Charlie's ears, relishing being so close to him.

"You look like Moses!" I raised an eyebrow. "Don't even think about giving me any commandments."

He grinned. "I wouldn't dare."

I lost myself in his blue and brown eyes, looking from one to the other.

"We should hurry," I said slowly. "We'll lose the captain."

"Yeah…"

I pulled myself together and sat down in front of the mirror, which had lightbulbs around the frame – several of which weren't working. On the dressing table, I found some wig glue, and set about affixing my moustache.

Charlie wandered to the other side of the small room. "Oh, there's a bowl of fruit here. Do you want anything?"

"It's probably wax, darling."

He unpeeled a banana. "No, it's real."

I pressed the moustache onto my upper-lip. Charlie stepped over and handed me a peeled banana, which I gratefully polished off. "Mmm, thank you…"

He chuckled. "Don't get any on your moustache, your ladyship!"

I was about to reply, but a man walked in, catching us in the act. "Hey, what are you two doing in my dressing roooo—wah!"

I burst into laughter as the poor chap slipped on a banana peel.

Charlie helped him stand. "Sorry, guv, I must've dropped that. Are you all right?"

The man was in his late-teens, pale-faced, and rather moody. "I don't know what *you're* laughing at."

I stifled my smile. "Sorry, but it *was* rather amusing."

"What's so funny about someone slipping on a banana peel?" He pointed accusingly. "And what are *you* doing wearing my comical moustache, lady?"

"May we borrow it just for a moment? We're trying to solve a murder. Here, I'll leave my pompadour wig as collateral. How about it?"

"Well… I suppose so."

Charlie shook the man's hand. "Thanks, mate. What's your name?"

"Chaplin. Charles Chaplin."

Oh my word, it was Charlie Chaplin! "Thank you, Mr Chaplin. Tell me, do you like it here working in music hall? I hear those silent movie things are paying rather well."

He grumbled. "If I got the right offer I'd *consider* working in the flicks. I could earn a bit of money, then when the film fad is over, I could come back to vaudeville,"

"Or you could stay in films, if you liked it?"

"Nah, I can't see a future in it."

"I'm sure you'll know what's best. Come along, Charlie, let's go before we lose Captain Loveday."

We left Mr Chaplin inspecting the banana peel. "Hmm… *Charlie*? And slipping on a banana peel? I suppose it *is* quite funny..."

Chapter Twelve

Back at the officers' club, we hid out of sight, and waited for the doorman to pop to the cloakroom, then we snuck into the opulent marble and stone foyer.

I adjusted my stance to what *I* thought was manly, and was about to stride into the main space, but Charlie grabbed my hand. "Your ladyship, wait."

"What is it?"

"It's falling off…" He smoothed down my moustache. "… that's better."

His touch and proximity set off fireworks in my chest. But I refused to get side-tracked. "Let's go."

It was rather dark and seedy in the Reading Room, which would definitely help with our disguises. Unsurprisingly, not much reading was happening, but plenty of drinking, smoking, and guffawing. It was old-fashioned, even for 1906, with its heavy wall panelling, mahogany furniture, and men in tails topping up glasses for the gentlemen. The air was thick with cigar smoke, and raucous chatter was interspersed with boisterous jeers, as the men let their hair down away from their wives. Most of the gentlemen were dressed in red military jackets and sported bushy facial hair. The fashion would inevitably change in the future, but I knew these sorts of elitist clubs would go on forever.

We sidled up to the table near the window, where Captain Loveday was sitting alone.

"Captain Sebastian Loveday?" I said in my deepest voice.

"Er, yes?"

I saluted. "Sir, Corporeal Squiffy, sir – remember me?" I slapped my thigh and added a manly, "Phwoar!"

We sat uninvited. Charlie spoke with a bad upper-class accent – aspirating his vowels but then dropping his h's in all the wrong places. "Forgive the h-intrusion, sir, but we was in South Africa, together. 'Appy days, they was. H-apart from the scorching 'eat, blood, and squalor. You *do* remember us, don'tcha, sir?"

Captain Loveday squinted at Charlie. Then he told a lie. "*Remember*? How could I forget you two?"

Charlie fished some stray beard out of his mouth. "What time did you h-arrive 'ere today, sir?"

"Er, why?"

I slapped my thigh. "*Phwoar…* Sir, we've been here a couple of hours, sir, drinking and talking about cricket, and drinking and smoking cigars, and drinking… and… I'm just surprised we didn't see you before, sir. *Phwoar.*"

"Oh, I arrived a couple of hours ago myself."

That was another lie, because he'd still been having tea with us then. But was his confusion being caused by the three empty brandy glasses in front of him? Or was he trying to give himself an alibi?

"Funny bumping into you here, sir… *phwoar…* All these miles from where we met. Did you ever marry that young woman you often spoke of? The one you were bally-well smitten with, eh? Beth, wasn't it? Phwoar."

His face darkened. "No, I didn't marry Beth."

"Why-h-ever not, sah?" Charlie asked. "Some h-other chap beat you to it, eh?"

Captain Loveday sighed wearily. "Yes, but I'm probably better off without her really."

"You still love 'er?" Charlie asked.

"Oh yes, I do still love her."

We exchanged a glance. Did this mean they *were* lovers?

"But?" Charlie asked.

"Her family... well, her father... he can be tight with the old purse strings, as her new husband is finding out."

"How so? Phwoar."

He leaned forward to speak quietly. "Well, naturally when they married, Mr Sandhurst acquired the rights to Beth's fortune, but her father isn't a man to let go of the purse strings just like that. He gives Alfred a monthly allowance, taken from his wife's inheritance. Well, it's Alfred's inheritance now, of course."

"So Alfred's business h-investments must all go through the father-in-law for h-approval? Is there no h-way Alfred could get his 'ands on the lump sum?"

Captain Loveday swigged his brandy. "I suppose if she were to die, Beth's fortune would *have* to be transferred to her husband. He ought to have it all now really, but as I say, Beth's father can be... difficult."

"You've known Beth's family since childhood, phwoar? Yet, this arrangement wouldn't have worried *you*? Marrying the daughter of – phwoar – someone so tight?"

"I have my own money. Did pretty well out of a silver mine I started up in South Africa. Probably should've stayed there rather than coming back for Beth. Yes, Alfred Sandhurst is a lucky man, but also... unlucky too."

Charlie pretended to be pensive. "Alfred Sandhurst? Squiffy, old chap, why does that name ring a bell?"

"Hmm… Oh *I* know, phwoar, it's because of that murder we heard about. Mrs Sandhurst's maid was killed earlier today. Awful shame, phwoar… Wonder if it's the same Sandhursts?"

Captain Loveday sat to attention. "Mrs Sandhurst's *maid* is dead!"

"Yes," I said. "Someone bonked her on the head – knocked her dead instantly. Poor gel."

Captain Loveday gazed at me as if more was required.

"Er… *phwoar.*"

Charlie leaned forward. "H-apparently the maid was dressed in 'er mistress's coat."

"It was an accident?" Captain Loveday whispered. "She was killed by mistake…?"

"Tragic," I said. "Looks like someone intended to bump off Mrs Sandhurst, but accidentally killed the maid instead."

"He'll 'ang for it nonetheless," Charlie said. "And quite h-right too."

The captain had gone very pale.

I thought back to my conversation with Captain Loveday in 1926. "Er, phwoar, sir… Anything you'd like to confess? How's your soul today? A little stained? Phwoar?"

He stood up suddenly. "Excuse me…"

Captain Loveday's face took on a green hue as he rushed to the cloakroom for his coat and hat. Charlie and I watched agape, as the captain hurried out the club, momentarily disappeared, then dashed past the window at full pelt.

Was it something we said?

I absent-mindedly smoothed down my moustache. "What did you make of that?"

Charlie helped himself to the discarded brandy, then spoke in his normal deep cockney tones. "Utterly ridiculous. I've never heard a man say 'phwoar' before in all me life."

"Oh I have, lots of times. Always saying it, phwoar, phwoar, phwoar. But what about the Cap? He seemed surprised to hear about Millie dying. Was *that* what he wanted to confess to me just before he died? The murder of Millie?"

"Because he *intended* to kill Mrs Sandhurst?"

"Precisely. Phwoar."

Charlie swigged the brandy. "And the question is, is he still planning to kill Mrs Sandhurst? Did he want to confess a *double* murder when you two spoke?"

I stood up. "Come on, Charlie, we'd better follow him."

Charlie puffed languidly on the captain's abandoned cigar, resting his feet on the chair opposite. "Can't we stay a bit longer? You do look delightful in that fabulous moustache."

"No, come on. What if he's going back to the Sandhursts to get the job done properly?"

We ditched our disguises and returned our borrowed facial hair to Mr Chaplin – who was vigorously practising slipping on a banana peel. Then we strode out into the bustling street, taking in the ambience of Edwardian England.

I smoothed down my pompadour wig and adjusted my bustle. "Gosh, I'd forgotten how far we'd come by 1926. Look at all these people – such fabulous wealth mixed with desolate poverty. I don't say it's all right, but perhaps those Zeppelin raids over London were just what the slums needed. At least the government was forced to build slightly better housing for the poor. Charlie?"

Charlie was gazing forlornly at an imposing Victorian grey-stone building, which was surrounded by a sturdy iron fence. His usual cockiness had plunged into a deep sadness.

"You know this place?"

"I grew up there, your ladyship. Orphanage."

The building was greyer, colder, and damper than the English Channel. "How did you end up *there*?"

"I'm the youngest of ten brothers and sisters. Our parents died when I was six, so we had nowhere else to go."

"And then the workhouse?"

"At ten. My dad was always generously giving me things – a good hiding, a thick ear… a shedload of gambling debts… Those needed paying off after he snuffed it."

I rested my hand on his arm. "I am sorry it was like that for you."

He threw me a grin. "It's made me the man I am today."

I chuckled kindly. "A kleptomaniac stowaway?"

He laughed too. "Something like that, your ladyship."

I linked my arm through his as we strolled. "Looks like we've lost Captain Loveday. Listen, you'd better call me 'Joanie', okay? We don't want to draw attention to ourselves."

"If you say so, Lady Joanie."

We shared a smile.

The clip-clop of hooves rang in my ears as a couple of horse-drawn carriages sped past, mixing with the hustle and bustle of the busy street. But then a BANG up ahead caught my attention.

"Oh look, Charlie, it's an old Rolls-Royce."

"Or rather, a *new* Rolls-Royce for 1906."

This car was so flimsy compared to my Rolls-Royce back in 1926. This early prototype was noisy and smelly, and the engine was straining under the weight of the open-topped vehicle. It looked like it might fall to bits any second.

"It's astounding the progress they made in such a short time, isn't it? Rolls-Royce transformed the motorcar from an unreliable toy to the beautiful beast I drive *myself* around in!"

The car banged again. Black smoke billowed from the engine.

I spoke to the man bent over the open bonnet. "Need a hand, mister?"

His face was covered in soot and, as he lifted his driving goggles, it left a white patch around his eyes. "I'm sure no one can make this car work but me, madam."

"Budge over and hand me your tool bag. I have a knack for taming naughty motors."

I flexed my fingers, bent over the smoking engine, and did what always worked on my car – I thwacked it hard with a hefty spanner.

"Madam!" the driver yelped, snatching the spanner from me. "This is a delicate instrume— oh…"

I tried not to sound too smug. "It's okay, you can thank me later."

The driver opened the back door for us. "No, no, I can thank you now. Allow me to drive you home. Providing you don't live more than two miles away…"

We climbed in the back, where the seats were rather hard. I spoke above the juddering engine. "You might think about adding cushions."

"Splendid idea."

He drove us along the road so slowly that we were overtaken not only by horses, but by pedestrians. I was tempted to wave regally at the people staring.

I raised my voice to shout at Charlie. "It seems we'd better talk to Alfred Sandhurst about his father-in-law's tight purse strings. A motive if I ever heard one."

"Yes. And I'm just realising something, your ladysh... Lady Joanie. I didn't notice it before, because I was so distracted by the murder. But I think the library window overlooks the garden."

I let this fact bed-in. "You think perhaps Alfred Sandhurst climbed out the library window, bonked Millie on the head, then quickly climbed back in again? Then when we all heard the scream, he ran out of the library *door* and into the hallway – where he bumped into Mrs Sandhurst. And they ran together out the backdoor and into the garden?"

"It's certainly a possibility. If he was alone in the library after tea."

"I believe he was. Mrs Sandhurst said *she'd* gone to write some letters in her sitting room. But, Charlie, there's one thing wrong with that…"

"Go on?"

"If Alfred hit Millie with a blunt object – killing her clean dead – and *then* he leapt in the window... Well, how on earth did Millie scream *after* she'd died?"

"Ah… Well, Millie must've screamed when she saw Mr Sandhurst attacking her. Then he quickly climbed back in the library window after he'd done the deed."

I thought about this. "I don't know. There's something…"

Charlie spoke firmly. "Let's check how far the library window is from where we found Millie."

"Yes. And then we'll talk to Mr Sandhurst…"

The driver parked outside the Sandhurst residence and let us out of the car.

"That was fun," I said. "Thank you, sir."

He gestured proudly to his car. "I doubt this toy will ever become a popular form of transport – I can only dream."

"Don't give up on your dreams," I said. "You never know."

"Thank you. May I know your names?"

"I'm Lady Joanforth Eldritch. And this is my... this is Charles Anderson."

"And you are?" Charlie asked.

"Henry Royce. Myself and my partner Charles Rolls have recently gone into business together. Perhaps you'll buy one of our prototypes, your ladyship?"

"Yes, I have a feeling I might. We wish you the very best of British, Mr Royce. And please, never give up."

Chapter Thirteen

Charlie and I stood on the doorstep at the Sandhurst residence, gazing at the solid front door. The solid front door gazed right back at us. Hmm…

"I don't think we ought to announce ourselves," I said. "Not if we want to sneak into the back garden and have a proper look at the crime scene."

"Agreed. But…" Charlie gave the door a tentative push. "Locked – as expected."

I raised my hands. "That's not a problem for a witch like me, darling. I don't have much magic in me at the moment, but if you'd like to move out the… oh…"

While I'd been nattering, Charlie had been busy with a lockpick. Stifling a smirk, he pushed open the front door. "After you, Lady Joanie."

Checking there was no one around, we crept down the wide hallway and past the closed doors of the library and the sitting room. This was fun! Back in the dark ages I'd been educated at a strict witch academy, where I was always sneaking out of my dorm in search of freedom. Now, because of that, I was skilled at creeping along corridors, shinning down drainpipes, and blending into the background. And how lovely to be doing it with a handsome young chap who seemed to be enjoying our adventure as much as I was!

Stifling giggles of rebellious joy, Charlie and I rushed out of the French windows and into the sunny garden, where we halted abruptly. Major Payne was around the corner, barking orders at his men.

We caught our breath for a moment, composed ourselves, then strolled casually over to investigate that pesky library window.

"Search those bushes next. We need to find that weapon!" Major Payne barely paused for breath as he noticed us. "What are you two doing out here again? This is a murder scene!"

Charlie squared up to the major. "I'd like my baton back please, sir."

While Major Payne was distracted by reluctantly giving Charlie back his property, I inspected the side of the house and realised that the library window did indeed look over the garden – as did the sitting room window. It was a nice sunny day, so both large sash windows were currently open. I tried to cast my mind back to earlier. Had the library window been open all along?

Alfred Sandhurst could've easily climbed out the library window, killed the woman he *thought* was his wife, then quickly climbed back in again. And then he'd rushed out of the library door, bumped into his wife in the hallway… but, hmm… seeing Beth alive would've been a shock, wouldn't it? If he'd thought he'd just killed her! Perhaps he'd managed to turn his shock into *pretend* shock.

I pictured the scene in my mind – Alfred seeing her alive in the hallway. "Good heavens, Beth, *you're…* I heard a scream. From the garden!"

"I did too!"

And then they'd run outside together, and found Charlie and I. But how lucky for Alfred that he *had* bumped into Beth in the hallway, because now he had an alibi…

Major Payne's gruff voice broke into my thoughts. "And now you'll both need to leave."

I ignored his demands. "Major, you've known Mr Sandhurst's family a long time, haven't you? Do *you* think he and Mrs Sandhurst are a good match?"

The Major couldn't resist the opportunity to have a grumble. "Oh goodness me no, I never liked the woman. We all know he married her for the money. But she's not what I'd call a proper wife, always waffling on about women's rights and votes and such forth. If they're so keen on acting like men, they should be rounded up and shot by firing squad. Live like a man, die like a man – that's what I say."

Charlie and I exchanged a glance. Was *this* a motive for murder? Or just the ramblings of an old military man who'd probably had too much intense South African sunshine?

I spoke carefully. "So you don't think very highly of Mrs Sandhurst's politics?"

"Good heavens, no." Major Payne huffed disapprovingly. "Especially after she made that dreadful spectacle of herself last week at dinner."

"What happened?" I asked.

"Not my place to say."

Charlie folded his arms across his chest. "Where were *you* at the time of the murder, Major?"

The Major's walrus moustache twitched as he spluttered. "What are you suggesting!"

"Well, you were *here* at tea," Charlie said. "So where did you go afterwards?"

"Not that it's any of your business, but *I* went back to the police station straight after tea. When I arrived there, I heard about this dreadful business, so I turned around and came back. Now, if you'll excuse me, I've got a murder weapon to find."

Chapter Fourteen

Charlie and I made our way back into the house. "We'd better check on Mrs Sandhurst," I said. "Just in case… well, you know."

"Yeah, I know."

Alas, in the hallway, we were rumbled by the butler. "What are you two doing here! Er… I mean, your ladyship, I don't recall admitting your good self and your most gentlemanly cousin across the threshold of this welcoming abode, but if you–"

"Yes all right, Greyson, that's enough of that. We'd like to speak to Mrs Sandhurst please."

"Certainly. If her ladyship would be so kind as to follow me?"

Greyson led us into the library, where Mr Sandhurst was writing a letter at his desk. Greyson ducked out, closing the library door behind him. So much for us going to check on Beth…

Mr Sandhurst stood to greet us. "Your ladyship, Mr Anderson, do come in and sit down. Tea, please Greyson… oh, he's gone. I'll ring the bell – he'll catch my drift."

I hustled my bustle out the way as I sat. "We'd like to check on Mrs Sandhurst. She was very shaken."

"Mrs Sandhurst is lying down. Our cook has sent for her niece to attend to my wife until we can find a new maid."

"Oh I see." I spoke sympathetically to Mr Sandhurst. "The major was just telling us about the spectacle Mrs Sandhurst made of herself at dinner the other night?"

He looked embarrassed. "Gosh… I do love my wife, but yes… her behaviour was unacceptable."

"Why do you think she did it?" Charlie asked, pretending to know all the details.

"She'd had too much wine." Mr Sandhurst shook his head. "I know she's passionate about the issue of women's suffrage and I do support her, but she shouldn't be arguing like that at the dinner table with my business associates. One or two of them have already broken ties with me. My father-in-law is furious."

"She argued with your business associates?" I asked.

He groaned. "She became extremely voluble. Beth is eloquent and always puts forth her case well, but she must understand that men expect a wife to make polite conversation over dinner – not to confront them about votes for women! Major Payne was there too. It was… humiliating. And it might give other wives bad ideas. What will their husbands think of me then?"

"You argued with her about this afterwards?" I asked.

"I insisted she hold her tongue in future. She's so… angry. So unladylike. And now someone's trying to do her in. Poor Beth – I am jolly fond of her. She would've made a good politician – if she were a man."

Greyson swept in with the tea tray. I gazed at him, wondering if *he* was capable of murder. What would be his motive? Perhaps I'd try to get him alone later. I might have more luck than Charlie.

We waited silently as Greyson poured the tea, distributed the cups and saucers, then swept out again.

I focused my attention back to Alfred. "Mr Sandhurst, where were you at the time of the murder?"

He paused with his teacup to his lips. "I was… er… as I told you, I was here in the library. I heard the scream from the garden, then Beth and I ran out and found you there with… Millie. I just hope whoever did this doesn't come back and try to finish off my darling Beth. All these dreadful threats and accidents... But I can't think why anyone would want to hurt her."

Charlie laid down his teacup with a rattle. "I'd like another look at that bullet hole."

Mr Sandhurst and I watched as Charlie stood in front of the bookshelf and frowned at the small impact crater. He pressed one finger against it, then stretched his other arm out across the room. "Hmm… interesting…"

"What is it, Charlie?"

"Well, judging by the angle of entry, the bullet came from in front of… the desk."

"*Your* desk, Mr Sandhurst?" I asked.

"Well… yes, it's my desk… but…"

"Mr Sandhurst," Charlie said flatly. "Is there a firearm in this house?"

Alfred's guilty glance skirted over the top drawer of his desk. "Of course not," he spluttered. "And what business is it of yours anyway?"

I pointed. "Charlie, the drawer."

He tried it. "It's locked."

"I can unlock it," I said, rolling up my sleeves.

"No need." Charlie dipped his hand into his pocket and pulled out his lockpick. The drawer was open in seconds. He lifted out a pistol. "Yours, sir?"

Mr Sandhurst sighed. "It's my father-in-law's. He insisted we keep it here after Beth received the threatening note."

"Where is your father-in-law now?" Charlie asked.

"In France on business."

"How very convenient for him. So he left you a gun?"

"He doesn't trust that I can protect my wife. But I *can* – and I don't need a gun to do that!"

Charlie opened the gun's bullet chamber and measured a bullet against the hole in the wood. "Looks like a match to me. Who knows about this gun?"

"Just myself and Beth. The key is always kept in my dressing room."

"None of the servants know about it?"

"Surely you're not suggesting one of the servants tried to shoot my wife?"

"No, sir. But I *am* suggesting that *one* of the two people who knew about the gun might've."

"I assure you, I did not fire that gun! I've never even held it. My father-in-law showed us how to use it, but I've never touched it. I'm not lying!"

Charlie laid the gun on the desk. "The police can test it for fingerprints."

Alfred looked terrified. "Police?"

"Mr Sandhurst, a murder has been committed. After they've finished searching the crime scene, I'd imagine they'll want a little look around."

Chapter Fifteen

I desperately wanted to check on Mrs Sandhurst, but her husband insisted that we leave *immediately*. It didn't help that Greyson 'accidentally' revealed that he hadn't let Charlie and I into the house. Mr Sandhurst accused us of breaking in (quite justifiably) then threatened to set the major on us!

Hmm… were any of those men in it together?

Duly turfed-out, Charlie and I decided to take some fresh air and think about how we might match up the scattered pieces of this jigsaw.

Hyde Park was beautiful at this time of year. We strolled together along a wide thoroughfare, which was flanked by lofty horse chestnut trees. I felt as peaceful and vibrant as they looked. The green grass seemed to go on forever, broken up only by the large flower beds crammed with orange marigolds. The long winding River Serpentine was full of ducklings, cygnets, and several Edwardian gentlemen who were messing about on the water in punts, filling the air with raucous laughter.

"It's nice to feel the sun on my face," Charlie said. "I don't come to this park often enough."

"Why not?"

"I'm usually too busy working to spend time larking about like those toffs."

"Work's important, Charlie. But one must take time to *live*. Otherwise, what's the point of it all?"

"A discussion for another time perhaps, Lady Joanie?"

"All right. Let's talk about this ghastly business. After everything we've discovered, *who* would be the greatest threat to Mrs Sandhurst? Her husband? The butler? The captain?"

"I'd love to pin it on Major Payne," Charlie said. "He's so high and mighty."

"It *was* strange how he didn't want to interview Millie about Mrs Sandhurst's so-called accidents at tea. Do you remember? I asked him to, but he refused."

"Do you think he might've killed Millie because *he* was trying to bump off Mrs Sandhurst and Millie found out somehow?"

"Which would mean it *wasn't* mistaken identity after all."

"Yeah. But we still don't really have a motive for why the major might want to get rid of Mrs Sandhurst in the first place."

We walked silently for a moment.

"What about Alfred Sandhurst?" Charlie said. "The humiliated husband?"

"Is he fed up with his opinionated wife showing him up at dinner?"

"Or is he upset that all his money comes via her father?"

"Alfred Sandhurst was alone in the library when Millie was killed. He could've easily jumped in and out of that window in the shake of a lamb's tail."

Charlie scratched his stubble. "He *said* no one else knows about the gun apart from him and his wife. But *I* wonder if someone else found out about it. Greyson could've easily swiped the desk drawer key."

"Perhaps. But one thing's for sure, the killer must be someone close to Beth. Someone who can sneak around the house and try to shoot her or push a terracotta pot on her head. It's got to be someone who can blend in."

"How about friend-of-the-family Captain Sebastian Loveday? Our victim back in 1926?"

"Yes, why did *he* have to die? Uncle Frog said that the captain is due to head back to South Africa in August of this year. Was he fleeing a murder – the accidental murder of Millie?"

"Then," Charlie said, "when he thought the coast was clear, he returned to England in 1926."

"And ended up dead."

"He does seem to be acting suspiciously," Charlie said. "He lied to us, saying he'd been at the club at the time of the murder, when we know he was still at the Sandhursts."

"But that memory lapse might be due to the three large brandies…"

Charlie sounded puzzled. "But who killed him in 1926? One of our suspects from here in 1906?"

"And why?"

We walked in silence again, letting the information bed down.

I linked my arm through Charlie's. "This sunshine is glorious."

He smiled kindly at me. "Are you well, Lady Joanie?"

"Perfectly. But I wanted to tell you, Charlie. I do understand… about the war."

He sighed. "I'm sure you did your bit."

"I certainly did."

"Yeah, let me guess, you ran a hospital for wounded officers in a big posh house? Well, begging your pardon, but that doesn't mean you know what it was really like at the Front… in the trenches."

"You're right, Charlie – I did run a hospital. I opened up our stately home, Locksleigh Manor in Maiden-Upon-Avon – converted it into a hospital. I couldn't believe the dreadful injuries – physical and mental."

"Forgive me, Lady Joanie, but a few wounded officers was nothing compared to the full horrors in Belgium."

"I know that. That's why, in 1915, I travelled to Belgium to work as an auxiliary nurse. I ran a field hospital for wounded soldiers of all ranks."

He halted. "Did you?"

"Yes. I have exemplary leadership skills, what can I say!"

He smiled. "I've no doubt."

The memories I'd tried to forget flooded back. "We commissioned an old chateau about a mile from the Front, and turned it into a well-oiled machine… patching up the wounded simply so they could be sent back to the horrors again. I saw for myself the trenches… the mud, the blood. Granted, I was never ordered to go over the top – to slowly march to my almost-certain death. But I do understand, Charlie. I was there."

"In 1915?"

"And 1916, 17, and 18."

He inspected me with his different-coloured eyes. "You're a remarkable woman, Lady Joanforth."

"Darling, you ain't seen nothing yet!"

He flashed me a grin. "I'm hoping to see more."

"Cheeky!"

We strolled in silence again for a moment, listening to the sweet birdsong in the trees.

"So," Charlie said. "This Lord Vilnius… is he your betrothed?"

"I was engaged to him before the war. But…" I shook my head.

"You broke it off? Why?"

"He loves power too much."

"Power?"

"Look, I haven't told anyone else this, but… I discovered that Vincent was selling arms to the Germans in 1916… and continued to do so for the next few years. He did well out of the war,"

"He was a spy?"

"Just a mercenary."

"Then he should be hanged as a traitor."

"You'll have to catch him first. His family in Marvelton are powerful. And he's fallen in with a bad lot."

Charlie gasped. "Did *he* murder Captain Loveday in 1926?"

"Possibly. But I don't know how they'd know each other."

"You should stay away from him, Lady Joanie."

"Yes I know. But he does look rather dashing in black leathers."

Charlie chuckled. "And besides, we need to get the time controls from him so we can go home, don't we?"

"We certainly do. But first… let's see if we can solve this murder."

"And try to prevent another one."

"Yes, we *must* check on Mrs Sandhurst. Come on, let's go back and insist we see her."

Chapter Sixteen

Once again Charlie and I found ourselves on the doorstep of the Sandhurst residence.

"Right, Charlie," I said. "You pick the lock, then we'll sneak upstairs and find Mrs Sandhurst – hopefully still alive."

"Right you are, Lady Joanie." He rolled up his sleeves…

But before Charlie could get to work, the door was yanked open, and an angry Captain Loveday shoved past and stormed off down the driveway.

"Woh-ahh!"

Charlie caught me in his arms – how delightful! I scrabbled to my feet, enjoying a quick grope as he helped me to stand. What muscles!

"All right, Lady Joanie?"

"Wonderful, darling – gosh, those are big, aren't they? What? Hmm? Oh yes…" I straightened my hat. "I'm fine. Seemingly better than Captain Loveday anyway."

Charlie glanced down the street. "I wonder what that was all about?"

"Perhaps he's discovered that *someone* finished off his brandy earlier. Come on, let's find Mrs Sandhurst."

As we stepped into the hallway, the very woman came dashing out of her sitting room, crying and grasping her throat. "Lady Joanforth, did you see who it was? Who attacked me!"

Oh my goodness, the poor woman had scratches on her cheek and throttle marks on her neck! So… it *had* been the captain all along… I wrapped my arm around her. "My dear, what happened?"

She started to babble an explanation but Mr Sandhurst and Major Payne stepped into the hallway from the garden.

Alfred ran to comfort his wife. "Good lord, Beth, what now?"

"I was in the sitting room, arranging flowers… and… and…"

She pointed weakly at the sitting room door, so Charlie and I led the way. In 1906, the sitting room was the domain of the Edwardian gentlewoman, with its armchair for embroidering, upright piano, and a few wholesome books. But as we stepped in, the usual serenity was gone. A table had been tipped over, and a smashed vase was strewn with some flowers on the rug. It didn't take my witchy perceptions to detect a recent struggle.

"Well Beth?" Major Payne asked. "What was it this time?"

"It was dreadful," she whimpered. "I can't… I can't…."

"It must've been Captain Loveday," I said. "Mr Anderson and I saw him storming off just now. Fairly pushed *me* over!"

Major Payne poured Mrs Sandhurst a brandy from the decanter on the sideboard. "Stop these tears now, Beth. Sit down and tell us what the devil happened."

With her husband supporting her, Mrs Sandhurst flopped into an armchair and sipped her brandy.

"I didn't see who it was," she said in a feeble voice. "He grabbed me from behind and tried to choke me. He was shouting that he was going to kill me."

"Was it the captain's voice?" I asked.

She shook her head. "I don't know. Perhaps he was disguising his voice?"

"Mrs Sandhurst," I said. "Excuse my indelicacy, but what's your relationship with Captain Loveday?"

She looked offended. "Whatever do you mean!"

"I mean…"

What did I mean? Was I asking if they were lovers? He was a handsome man, and she clearly had issues with her husband after that outburst at dinner.

"He's just an old family friend," Mrs Sandhurst said firmly. "We've known each other since we were children. We're practically brother and sister."

Alfred Sandhurst took it upon himself to explain. "When Captain Loveday returned from South Africa four years ago, he needed somewhere to stay. The Boer War had taken its toll on the poor man. So my wife's father's household gladly took him in and helped him recover. I met him shortly after that, when I became engaged to Beth. He seemed like a decent enough chap… But I suppose you never really know a person…"

Charlie perched on the arm of Beth's chair. "You have scratches on your face, Mrs Sandhurst." He gently grasped her chin in his fingers. "They look painful…"

She sniffled. "They are."

"And I see you have blood under your nails." He lifted Beth's wrist and inspected her fingers. "You scratched your attacker, and he scratched you?"

"I… don't know… It must've happened in the struggle."

Major Payne grunted. "So we're looking for someone with scratch marks somewhere about their person… I'll go and speak to the captain. He has some questions to answer."

"I'd arrest him if I were you, sir," Charlie said.

The Major treated Charlie to a glare. "I'll ask him a few questions and make up my own mind!"

Charlie muttered 'pompous arse' under his breath, and I was inclined to agree. But was the major simply inept and stubborn, or was *he* in this with Captain Loveday? Where *exactly* had he and Alfred Sandhurst appeared from just now? The garden? Beth had been attacked from behind again, and the sitting room window was open… which led directly to the garden…

Like an English summer picnic, this mystery was becoming cloudier by the minute.

But at least Mrs Sandhurst was still alive, and I hoped to keep her that way. But… oh drat! Fate was being unkind again. I realised with dismay that the silver rose brooch was no longer pinned to her lacy collar. *Blast*! Had Captain Loveday taken it in the struggle? Was *that* what this whole thing was about? Or… my heart sunk… had Lord Vilnius been here?

And if so, where was he now?

Chapter Seventeen

Major Payne went off to find Captain Loveday, and Alfred took his wife upstairs for a lie down. I almost didn't want her to be alone with him, because I felt he was our main suspect, but I could hardly forbid a husband from being alone with his own wife, especially not here in 1906.

Charlie and I had nowhere else to go, so we sat in the library and rang for some tea.

The butler brought it up.

"Thank you, Greyson," I said. "By the way, how long was Captain Loveday here just now? When did you let him in?"

Greyson frowned. "I did *not* let the captain in, your ladyship. Not since he arrived for tea this morning. But it seems to be a day for people barging in unannounced. Do enjoy your tea, my lady."

Charlie and I shared a smirk, feeling like a couple of naughty schoolchildren who'd been admonished by the headmaster.

Charlie poured the tea and we sat opposite each other on the sofas, surrounded by the lovely bookshelves. The sun was streaming through the open window, overlooking the beautiful garden. It was blissful.

I stirred my tea. "If we don't figure this out, Mrs Sandhurst might soon be joining Millie in the morgue. And if Mrs Sandhurst *is* killed, then the negative vibes surrounding us won't dissipate and we won't be able to jump home. We need to crack this, Charlie! Tell me, is this how you usually go about solving these things?"

He dropped a sugar cube into his tea. "Actually, Lady Joanie, this is my first murder case."

"What!"

"Well, the one in 1926 is… was… I only became a detective last week. An opening became available, so they put me forward."

"What happened to your predecessor?"

"Have you ever heard the expression 'dead man's boots'?"

"Right, so you're a bit inexperienced… but you've been a copper a few years, you've sailed around the world, been to war… I'm almost a senior witch, I'm highly educated, and just generally brilliant. We must be able to solve this between us."

Charlie sighed. "How can it not be Captain Loveday? Otherwise, what was he doing here without Greyson knowing?"

"Yes, you're right. It's probably him. Or her husband. Or them both."

"But…" Charlie wrapped his hands around his teacup. "I wonder why all the murder attempts have used *different* methods. Usually, killers just stick to their one same method."

"Really? I thought this was your first murder case?"

"It is. But I've read a lot of Sherlock Holmes."

"I *see*. What a pity there were no conspicuous footprints or some exotic cigar ash lying around, or you would've cracked it straight away." A realisation struck me. "Don't you think it's strange that none of the murder attempts have been successful though? Apart from young Millie's, which was a case of mistaken identity. You've got to wonder if their heart's really in it. I mean, do they want her dead, or not?"

My Amulet of Seeing bleeped, so I pressed the button for Uncle Frog's image to project upwards from my wrist. "Hi, Uncle. Hi Wispu!"

Wispu barked. Her lovely woolly face cheered my spirits as always.

"Any news?" I asked.

Uncle Frog sounded excited. "Yes Joanforth. I've researched the suspects and discovered something very interesting."

"Oh yes?"

"I've discovered that the late Captain Sebastian Loveday was riddled with cancer on the day he died. He was about to die in the next few months."

"But… why would anyone kill a *dying* man?"

Charlie sat up tall. "He must've known something that his killer didn't want him to confess!"

"Confess, yes!" I gasped. "He wanted to tell a priest something that was weighing heavy on his soul. Blast, if only I'd let him tell me."

Uncle Frog waved this away. "Joanforth, calm down and listen – there's more. Captain Loveday has been formally identified here in 1926 by his fingerprints and dental records. And listen to this – his real name is actually James Lawless!"

"What? He wasn't really in the Boer War?"

"Oh yes, he was. James Lawless fought in the same battalion as the *real* Captain Loveday."

I dreaded the answer to my next question. "So what happened to the real Captain Loveday?"

Charlie winced. "James Lawless presumably stole Captain Loveday's identity. After the real Captain Loveday somehow… died…"

"So it would seem," Uncle Frog said.

"That's why he's been acting suspiciously," I said. "When we approached him in the officers' club, he looked all panicky. He must've thought we'd blown his cover. Uncle, why did James Lawless steal Captain Loveday's identity? Was he wealthy?"

"Very wealthy. No family, but he'd bought a silver mine out in South Africa."

My thoughts whirred into place. "It must've been all too tempting for James Lawless… When his colleague Captain Loveday was killed in a battle… or by some other method… it would've been easy for James Lawless to steal his personal papers – his identity and his name. And then take the silver mine for his own."

"Are we to assume that James Lawless *killed* the real Captain Loveday?" Charlie asked bluntly.

Uncle Frog shrugged. "The police here aren't saying that. At least, not yet. But… well… what do you two think?"

I spoke slowly. "Mrs Sandhurst must know the truth. She and *our* Captain Loveday have known each other all their lives. She *knows* he's an imposter."

"About Mrs Sandhurst," Uncle Frog said. "I've discovered that her pre-married name was… Miss Elizabeth Lawless. They're cousins."

"She's covering for him," I said quietly. "And so must be her father. He must know the truth – it's *his* nephew after all."

"But why would this imposter want to *kill* his cousin?" Uncle Frog asked. "And why did *he* have to die in 1926?"

Charlie chewed his lip. "Because… because someone in 1926 was about to reveal the truth about this little scam. Perhaps Mrs Sandhurst and her father are blackmailing the captain in order to protect his true identity. Hush money, you know? And… he… I don't know." He rubbed his eyes. "Or perhaps it's something else. Someone acting alone."

A thought went *clang* inside my head. "*Someone acting alone?*"

Uncle Frog's voice sounded remote to my ears. "Joanie, what are you thinking? Have you worked something out?"

I fished in my pocket and pulled out the scrap of material from Mrs Sandhurst's coat that I'd found on the garden wall. When I'd found it, I'd wondered what Millie had been doing up that wall, because she'd been the last person to wear the coat. But what if someone else had been wearing it?

I frowned. "What happened to *Millie's* coat?"

"Millie's coat?" Charlie asked. "What do you mean?"

"Millie was wearing Mrs Sandhurst's topcoat… just before she died."

"Yeah. And so someone killed her thinking she was her mistress…"

"Yes. But when I looked in Millie's wardrobe earlier… Oh Charlie, we need to go back to the church and search Mrs Sandhurst's clothing for the needy. I think I know what happened!"

Chapter Eighteen

My brain buzzed like a bee in a biscuit box as Charlie and I rushed down the aisle of the cavernous church. My fingertips itched. Why was this aisle so long!

Oh *drat…* the vicar stepped out from a row of pews halfway down. Luckily for him, the gentle smile on his face prevented me from rugby tackling him out the way.

"Welcome and bless you. How may I help?"

"We just wanted to… er… pray," I said anxiously.

"How lovely…"

The vicar left us to it, so Charlie led me to the room where he knew the clothing donations were kept. I grabbed Mrs Sandhurst's basket and frantically pulled out her old dresses, skirts, and blouses. And then… there it was. A straight, black coat made of cheap, sensible material. The needy would undoubtedly be grateful for such a garment, especially as there was nothing wrong with it – an important fact which meant its owner would never have parted with it. *Make do and mend* was the motto of the servant classes.

I eagerly inspected the collar. And yes! The initials MJ were stitched into the material. "This wasn't hanging up in her wardrobe, Charlie. Because it was already in the basket."

"Millie put her coat in the basket when she put on her mistress's coat?"

"I don't think so. I think the *killer* removed Millie's coat and *hid* it in the basket."

Charlie was confused. "Are you saying the killer *wanted* Millie to look like Mrs Sandhurst?"

"Think about it, detective constable. There's only *one* person who'd ever remove Millie's coat. Yes… *that's* it – it's got to be."

"You'd better tell me everything, Lady Joanie."

I did. He listened attentively, asking questions. But he believed me.

"We must tell the Major," Charlie said. "Make *him* believe it."

"Yes. Then perhaps we can try to get out of here." But how? Without the magic from the silver rose… without the time controls from Lord Vilnius… we were as good as stranded.

As we walked towards the church entrance, my voice echoed off the stone walls. "It's a shame we couldn't get the silver rose – it means we'll have to… what?"

Charlie smirked. "Do you mean *this* silver rose?"

I gasped. "Charlie, did you pilfer that off Mrs Sandhurst?"

"I can't lie to you, Lady Joanie. It was when I was comforting her in the sitting room after her most recent attack. You said it was important." He half-bowed. "Your wish is my command."

"But I didn't see you take it. You must be extremely swift of hand."

"I do have rather nimble fingers… or so I've been told."

I almost blushed. "I'm sure that's true. And this street gang you were in before you went off to be a sailor clearly taught you a trick or two."

He halted. "I'm not bent, Lady Joanie. I just… sometimes I bend the rules for the greater good."

"I like the sound of that. Come on, let's find Major Payne."

With our feet clicking merrily on the stone church floor, Charlie and I strode towards the door. I grinned, feeling triumphant. What an adventure! But we'd successfully solved the mystery, and soon – thanks to Charlie's thieving talents – we'd be back in 1926!

But… oh *no*… Worry tingled up my spine. My instincts screamed *danger*! And yes… *there* it was. Outside the open church door, I saw shadows dancing on the pavement in the street. The shadows *might've* been mistaken for a trick of the light – the setting sun flowing through the branches of a nearby tree. But my witchy senses knew better. Evil was lurking.

I thrust out my hand, making Charlie halt.

His voice echoed off the high ceiling. "What?"

I whispered my reply. "He's *here*. Out there."

"Who?"

Oh yes… he always did have a sense of drama. I froze as the shadows solidified, blackening with apocalyptic doom. And then, in the church doorway, seething like a vengeful Adonis, Lord Vilnius stepped into view. "Hello, Joanforth. I heard a rumour that *you* have the silver rose."

Charlie was brave – or merely ignorant. "Ah, Lord Vilnius, so glad you found us. We've been hoping to bump into you."

Lord Vilnius didn't take his accusing eyes off me. "And who, may I ask, is this fool?"

"I'm a police officer, and you're *still* under arrest, sir!"

I held out my trembling hands. "Vinnie, please, just give us back the time controls. We'll take them to Uncle Frog and say no more about it…"

He stepped closer to me. "I need the silver rose. Give it to me now."

"You know I can't do–"

"Silence!" Moving like lightning, he grabbed my wrist, yanked me back against himself, and held me tight. A pistol went click by my temple. "How nice to hold you in my arms again, Joanie."

"Let her go!" Charlie commanded. "Unhand her now!"

"Shut it, *mortal*!"

Trying not to *breathe* lest he shoot me, I went inside myself, desperately trying to cast a spell, but Vincent's powers were strong.

"Stop trying to cast magic against me, Joanforth. It won't work."

I made eye contact with Charlie. I wanted to tell him not to get involved, but of course he already was. And he needed to get back to 1926… If Lord Vilnius activated the time controls and took *me* off, Charlie would be stranded here. I wasn't having *that* on my conscience for all eternity.

Slowly shifting my weight, I sensed a solid, five-inch cube pressing into my back. The time controls were hanging from Lord V's belt! If I could reach around and press the button, I might be able to quickly break free and send *him* off in time… then use the magic from the silver rose to get Charlie and I home.

Lord Vilnius's voice was deep in my ear. "I do love human weapons. It's a shame we can't cross them over the Standing Stones portal – imagine the power I'd have in Marvelton with a gun. But no matter, when I get all the magical jewels, I'll be even more powerful than any mage who's ever lived!"

Charlie stalled for time. "Lord Vilnius, how could you hold a gun to the woman you claim to love?"

"I do love her."

"You don't. You can't."

"You don't know anything about me, mortal."

"Yes I do. *Now* I do. I know everything about you."

My powers of empathy told me that Charlie's words had struck deep – to a hidden place that probably even Lord Vilnius had forgotten existed. But alas, this flicker of love, or guilt, or kindness was quickly snuffed out by a tidal wave of fury. Lord Vilnius gripped me hard, pressing the cold steel painfully to my temple. "Listen you stupid boy, if I push the activator button on the time controls now, I'll take *her* with me, leaving you here. Now hand over that silver rose."

"Don't, Charlie!" I shouted. "If he gets the jewels, it'll spell disaster for us all."

Charlie held out the brooch. "I can't let him kill you, Lady Joanie."

Charlie stepped forward, offering up the prize. But… Lord Vilnius's hands were *both* occupied – one with the gun, one holding me.

"Put it in my coat pocket," he growled.

"Certainly, your lordship…" Charlie halted almost nose-to-nose with him, squashing me between both men, which would've been delightful had I not been shaking with fear.

"I *said*, put it in my pocket! Do it now!"

Charlie held the rose over Lord Vilnius's pocket, flourishing it theatrically.

"As you wish…" Charlie stared Lord Vilnius firmly in the eye. Then he grinned.

He had a plan! Maintaining cocky eye contact, Charlie flicked his wrist and sent the brooch clattering to the floor. Lord Vilnius growled in anger, but *I* sprang into action – leaping like a cat and shoving him hard in the chest.

"Oof!" He was so surprised, he stumbled backwards.

Charlie leapt, punched him in the face, then grabbed his wrist, squeezing hard.

To my amazement, Lord Vilnius dropped the gun. Why wasn't he casting magic? Too shocked? *Or* did he want to prove he could beat this 'mere mortal' with mere brute strength? Whatever it was, Charlie didn't flinch – but he *did* fight dirty. He kneed Lord Vilnius in the groin, then punched him again. Of course, Lord Vilnius fought back, and–

Now his swirling magic surged – mixing with his raging anger. Something brutal was brewing and *I*

126

couldn't allow that! I threw myself on top of the fighting men, grappled with the time controls, and shouted, "Charlie, move!"

Charlie rolled to one side as I pressed the flashing button. Then I leapt out the way…

With a screeching squeal, reality imploded. Time froze… but then it lurched to a slur. The edges of the church smudged into darkness, as Lord Vilnius's expression rushed with shock. His words came out a heavy drawl, striking my brain with raw terror. "I'll get you, Joanforth Eldritch – I'll take you apart atom by atom!"

Strewn on the stone floor, Charlie and I watched – captivated by the metallic blue lightning writhing all over Lord V's body like streams of electric eels. He roared in agony, convulsing and shaking, and I almost wanted to run and help but… it was too late. He paused like a tableau… then vanished…

Charlie and I stared at the empty space. It crackled and fizzed with discharging magic.

"Where'd he go?" Charlie whispered.

"Home perhaps?"

I pulled myself back to reality and scrambled to my feet, grabbing the silver rose and shoving it up my long sleeve for safe keeping.

Charlie hauled himself to standing. "I can't believe what I just saw."

"Well… you'd better believe it. Because it happened."

He stepped closer. "Are you well, Lady Joanie? Did he hurt you?"

Oh, the agony of being scrutinised by those blue and brown eyes! "Yes, I'm well. You were very brave."

"Oh… not really." We shared a smile of relief. Charlie grinned, then laughed. "This is a day I won't forget in a hurry."

"No… Right, I'd better warn Frog that he might expect Lord Vilnius." I pressed the button on my Amulet of Seeing. My hand trembled with the aftermath of danger.

Uncle Frog's image whooshed into view. "Joanforth, what's happening?"

"Uncle, we've got the silver rose, but we've just sent Lord Vilnius… *somewhere*. He's still got the time controls!"

"All right, don't panic. You should have enough magic in the rose for your jump home. Have you removed the negative vibes?"

"We just need to go to the police station now," I said. "But we know what happened."

"Right-o. Contact me again when you need the Coming Home spell. Oh and, Joanforth…"

"Yes, Uncle Frog?"

"Jolly well done, that woman."

Chapter Nineteen

I was tempted to send a telegram to the police station ahead of our arrival:

For the attention for Major Payne (STOP) Sit down and grip onto something firm (STOP) A woman has solved your murder case (STOP) Now she hopes your bigotry against women will… STOP!

I could hardly wait to see the look on his walrus face. I was going to enjoy this!

Although Major Payne was based at The Met's Scotland Yard, Charlie was certain he would've taken Captain Loveday to our local police station for questioning, so we strolled there via the busy Edwardian streets. The traditional blue lamp shone proudly outside, with the word POLICE boldly inscribed.

On the steps of the redbrick building, Charlie offered his arm. "Shall we, my lady?"

"Honoured, kind sir… *oh wait!*" I glanced around and eyed up a public convenience on the other side of the road. "I just need to pop down there."

"Um, right… of course."

I sped off. He followed.

"Not for *that*," I said. "I need a mirror."

"You look lovely, Lady Joanie."

I absent-mindedly patted my hair. "Look, just stand at the top of these steps and keep watch."

"What are you going to do?"

"Magic. I've got just enough for one spell."

"Magic!" He beamed. "I'm coming with you. I want to see you do this magic spell."

"*You* need to keep watch."

"Oh come on, Lady Joanie, you can't leave me out of this."

"Oh all right. Come along then."

One useful thing that the Victorians *had* done for women was to build public lavatories for the ladies as well as the gentlemen. This meant it was now possible for women to travel longer distances, without needing to worry about being – *ahem* – inconvenienced. But because the Victorians had some funny ideas about basic body functions, most lavatories were hidden out of sight, underground. Charlie and I jogged down the wrought-iron steps and into the large musty, tiled room, which echoed with the sound of dripping water from the cubicles.

An ornate mirror spanned the length of the ceramic washbasins. "This is what I need."

Charlie folded his arms and watched keenly. "This I've gotta see."

I held out my hands to the mirror. "*Mirror, mirror on the wall…*"

"You can't be serious?"

"Shh, I'm trying to concentrate… *Mirror, mirror on the wall, show me memories so I see all…*"

I blocked out the sound of Charlie's gasps and focused my thoughts solely on so-called Captain Loveday's murder in 1926. On the mirror's shiny surface, clear images of that fateful night played out like a film. But my *magic* film was crisp and realistic – nothing like those flickering, black and white moving pictures we had in the 1920s.

Pouring all my magical might into the spell, I scanned the nightclub crowd for familiar faces. Of course, when I'd cast this spell back in 1926, I hadn't seen anyone I'd known other than Lord Vilnius, but now… yes… *that* was who I'd been expecting to see.

And now I knew the truth for sure.

I allowed the mirror to return to normal. Charlie was staring, stunned.

"Pretty nifty, ain't it?"

"It's… unbelievable. And… in the background… in the crowd… it was…"

"Mrs Elizabeth Sandhurst. Twenty years older and dressed in 1920s clothing, but most definitely her. I *did* cast this spell on the night of the murder – just before you arrived. But it was meaningless, because I hadn't met her – she just looked like another face in the crowd."

Charlie spoke in awe. "But now we know she was there on the night that Captain Loveday – or should I say James Lawless – was murdered."

"Precisely. Come on, let's get to the police station. We need to tell the Major who the killer is."

We headed for the steps, but an older lady bustled in. She pointed at Charlie in horror. "What… what's that!"

"It's a man," I said, dragging Charlie up the stairs. "Nothing to worry about!"

We ran up the steps, laughing like children. I was really going to miss this lovely chap when we got back home. But we certainly couldn't stay *here*…

In the police station foyer, Charlie strode confidently past the desk sergeant. He knew his way around, and was clearly a fellow fan of *fake it 'til you make it*!

He led me to Major Payne's office and burst in without knocking. "S'cuse us, sir…"

The major was sitting behind a huge mahogany desk, in mid-conversation with Mr and Mrs Sandhurst. He clambered to his feet and spluttered. "What is the meaning of this intrusion!"

I waved amiably at the Sandhursts. "Oh look, Charlie, everyone's here. Isn't it nice to have the gang back together?"

Charlie sounded smug. "Not quite everyone, Lady Joanie… I mean, *Cousin* Joanie."

Major Payne eyeballed me. "You'd better have a jolly good reason for bursting in like this."

"Is Captain Loveday in custody?" I asked.

"He certainly is."

"Please have him brought to your office, Major. I'd like to speak to everyone together, including Mr and Mrs Sandhurst."

The Major looked like he might explode. "*You* want to speak to *everyone*?"

"I strongly suggest you do as she says, sir." Charlie gazed at me. "She's not just a pretty face, this one."

I folded my arms defiantly. "No, I'm a stubborn one too, and I'm not leaving until *you* bring the captain here and hear me out."

"I shall *throw* you out!"

"*I* shall chain myself to your desk."

"Blast the Suffragettes. Militant women, indeed!"

I stood tall, raising an eyebrow at the old walrus.

"Very well, your ladyship, we shall hear your ramblings. And then you *will* leave."

He shouted for a constable to fetch the captain, who was led in, in handcuffs. He stood over by the Sandhursts.

Major Payne sunk down in his cushioned desk chair, waving a hand in my direction. "Go on then, get on with it."

Charlie winked encouragingly at me, filling my heart with confidence.

"Captain Loveday…" I said. "Or should I say, James Lawless?"

Mrs Sandhurst gasped. "*What!*"

Captain Loveday paled. "Oh good heavens…"

"Don't act innocent, Mrs Sandhurst," I said. "You already knew *that*. You two are cousins."

"*Cousins*?" Alfred Sandhurst said.

"*Are* you?" Major Payne asked. "Why didn't you mention that before? And who the devil is James Lawless?"

"*This* is James Lawless, Major."

"I… I've no idea what she's talking about!" Captain Loveday stuttered.

I glared at him. "Well, let me refresh your memory. When you were in South Africa during the Boer War, you murdered the real Captain Loveday and stole his identity."

"Why the bloody hell would I do *that*! Um… excuse my language."

"Because the real Captain Loveday was the owner of a lucrative silver mine and *you* wanted it. You presumably got chatting with him in the officers' mess one night, and he told you about his little nest egg. You probably asked him lots of questions, checking he had no family – ensuring you knew where all his personal papers were kept."

The room was so quiet now that I could almost hear the heartbeat of the murderer pounding with worry. They knew that *I* knew...

I continued explaining. "It was jolly easy for you, James Lawless, to kill the real Captain Loveday in the heat of a battle, then steal his papers. Steal his silver mine. When the war ended you returned to England hoping to marry your cousin, Elizabeth Lawless – to take her back to South Africa with your new wealth. But unfortunately, while you were away, Beth had fallen for Alfred."

"This is ludicrous," Mrs Sandhurst whispered.

"No, Mrs Sandhurst, surely you must remember? In a desperate attempt to convince you to come back with him, James told you everything he'd done. He gave you a beautiful silver brooch as a token of his love. As it happened, you were happy with Alfred – you wanted to stay with him. But, happily for you, you were now in a position to blackmail your own cousin. You probably said something like, 'Give me a percentage of your money, or I'll tell the authorities what you've done.' And, Mrs Sandhurst, if you *had* snitched on him, then James would've been court-martialled for murder." I glanced at Charlie. "Does a court-marital still entail 'death by firing squad', Mr Anderson?"

Charlie raised his chin squarely. "Sometimes…"

Oh drat… I shouldn't have said that. He'd undoubtedly known men shot at dawn, for the 'crime' of fleeing the horrors of the trenches.

Luckily, Alfred Sandhurst spoke up. "Beth, is this true? It's not really. Is it?"

"It is," I said. "Her father's even in on it. The contents of the stolen silver mine have been funding *your* allowance, Mr Sandhurst."

Mr Sandhurst gaped at his wife. "I can't… this is…"

I transferred my attention to the major. "After Beth rejected him, James Lawless knew he *had* to agree to her blackmailing or else he'd be arrested for murdering the real Captain Loveday. So he set up an account for Beth, to buy her silence."

My thoughts turned to poor Millie. "Of course, the tension between the cousins was now fraught. Even though James Lawless was still madly in love with Mrs Sandhurst, they probably argued a lot. I expect, Mrs Sandhurst, that your loyal and lovely maid accidentally overheard you two arguing, did she not? It's the only thing that makes sense. The reason she had to die."

Mrs Sandhurst gazed glassily ahead. "Stupid girl was eavesdropping. But she got it wrong. She overheard the words 'murder' and 'blackmail' and assumed *I* was being threatened by… Captain Loveday. She wanted the police involved. Begged me to tell Alfred – *or she would*. I told her to give me a couple of days…"

"Yes," I said. "Millie knew too much and needed to be silenced permanently – otherwise the police might discover *your* little blackmailing scheme. So you set up a series of accidents on yourself, and faked a threatening note. You made us all believe that someone wanted *you* dead. And then you made it look like Millie had been killed in your place. But, in fact, *you* killed her."

"I'm finding this difficult to believe," the Major said. "Beth, is this really true?"

Mrs Sandhurst stared at her hands.

"Major," I said. "When we found Millie, she was wearing Mrs Sandhurst's coat, so we assumed that Millie had been wearing it all along. But actually, Millie was wearing her *own* coat when Mrs Sandhurst sent her to the church. Mrs Sandhurst then waited high up on the wall for Millie to walk under the arch – and dropped a pot to kill her outright."

Charlie took up the story. "Mrs Sandhurst specifically asked Millie to gather flowers from the garden to take to the church. It was a clever way to ensure Millie would definitely walk through the archway."

"Archway…" Major Payne whispered.

I continued with the grizzly explanation. "Mrs Sandhurst then dragged poor Millie's dead body along the path to make it *look* like Millie had been hit over the head by a club or a blunt instrument – and not by the pot at all!"

"Dragged her along?" the major asked.

"It was indeed cunning," Charlie said. "Because not only did she then have the police searching for a murder weapon, but it also cast suspicion on *me*. Mrs Sandhurst clearly saw my baton at tea. Major… sir… you even confiscated it for a closer look."

Alfred Sandhurst frowned. "But… this coat of Beth's? I don't understand…?"

"Once the dead Millie was in place," I said. "Mrs Sandhurst quickly dressed her dead maid in her own coat – hiding Millie's coat in the basket of clothes. They were utterly alone in that part of the garden, so it was easily done. Of course, Mrs Sandhurst *had* originally been wearing the coat herself – and she left *this* scrap of material on the wall when she was up there pushing the pot onto Millie."

The major took the scrap from me. "But… we found no extra bits of smashed pot."

"We all were taken in by that, Major. You see, Mrs Sandhurst cleverly told us at tea that a *previous* attempt had been made on her life by pushing a plant pot off the wall. Of course, *that* so-called attempt had merely been Mrs Sandhurst stealthily smashing the pot herself. But it meant that no one noticed the *new* shards, which came from the pot that actually bonked Millie on the head."

Alfred Sandhurst was flabbergasted. "This is… just…"

The major sat up suddenly. "No, no, no… it can't have been like that. You *all* said you heard the girl scream. How could Beth have dropped the pot from on high, then climbed down from the wall, and done this dressing-up thing *after* the maid screamed? How long did it take you to run from the other end of the garden, your ladyship? Hmm? Mere seconds?"

The major seemed ready to dismiss my entire theory. I spoke calmly. "But it wasn't Millie who screamed."

"What?"

"It was Mrs Sandhurst. Pretending to be Millie."

"Ah, now… wait a minute…"

"Mrs Sandhurst screamed – attracting us to come running – then she quickly climbed back into the sitting room through the open window. *That's* how she came to be in the garden in the first place, after all."

"She *climbed* in and out the window?"

"Yes. She was in there after tea, pretending to write letters. I guess she must've had the coat in there with her and put it on when she climbed out, rather than carrying it. She climbed up the wall, pushed the pot onto Millie, switched the coats, screamed… then climbed back in through the sitting room window. And *then* she bumped into her husband in the hallway – thus securing an alibi."

"What about the pistol attack?" Mr Sandhurst asked. "Surely you admit that someone tried to shoot her?"

Charlie shrugged. "She stood near the desk and fired it herself, sir. Then she made up a *story* that someone had fired at her – and escaped."

"What about the attempt on her life earlier today?" Major Payne asked. "In the sitting room? *You* saw Captain Loveday running out the front door and down the street."

"We'd been arguing," Captain Loveday said. "I was drunk and trying to convince Beth to come back to South Africa with me… I love you, Beth! Please tell me you haven't done this dreadful thing!"

The major interrupted his dramatics. "But… what about Beth's scratches?"

"After today's attack," Charlie explained, "Mrs Sandhurst had blood under her fingernails. She said she'd scratched her *assailant* in the struggle. But if we were able to test such a thing, we'd undoubtedly discover that it was Mrs Sandhurst's *own* skin under her fingernails. She scratched her own face to fake an assault, knowing the captain had just left in a huff."

Mrs Sandhurst stood up and wailed. "I just wanted my own money! That's why I was blackmailing him. Why should my husband have financial control over me? It's not fair!"

Everyone stared at her. Alfred leaned away.

"I agree with you in principle, Mrs Sandhurst," I said. "But times *are* changing. Murdering a sweet innocent girl like Millie can never be justified."

Major Payne broke the stunned silence by arresting Mrs Sandhurst for the murder of Millie and arresting James Lawless for the murder of the real Captain Loveday.

Charlie and I slipped back out into the night-time street.

"So it was Mrs Sandhurst who killed our Captain Loveday in 1926," Charlie said. "He'd returned to England, wanting to tell the truth – to cleanse his soul before he died. He must've informed her of his plan just before he went out that night. But Mrs Sandhurst knew his confession would incriminate *her*. And so she killed him – just like she'd killed her maid twenty years previously. To keep them both quiet."

I halted on the pavement. "But now none of that will happen, I suppose?"

"They'll both hang for murder back here in 1906. Well, Lawless might be shot at dawn. But either way …"

"That sounds like justice to me, Charlie. I'll contact Uncle Frog for the spell. We've got the silver brooch to fuel our journey." I smiled at him. "Let's go home."

We snuck down an alleyway and I beamed up Uncle Frog on my Amulet of Seeing. He congratulated us again, then told me the magic words for the Coming Home spell.

"We'll hopefully see you very soon," I said, pinning the silver rose to my high collar.

"Best of British to you both!" Frog said triumphantly.

I turned to the gorgeous Charlie. "We'll need to be touching – to ensure we travel together."

He took my hand in his. "I can probably live with that, Lady Joanie."

I crossed my fingers for luck and said the spell out loud "*Now we've travelled back in time, and have justice for this crime, we can leave 1906, and our normal timeline can affix.*"

I grinned into Charlie's eyes. *Home*.

As the spell caught, electric blue sparks flashed all around us, sizzling and crackling with magical glory. Next stop, 1926!

"Hold tight, Charlie!"

"If you insist…" He swept his arm around my waist and pulled me close. *Gosh!*

"Here we go-ohhhhhh!"

Edwardian London, with its dappled golden glow of innocence – those carefree days of tea on the lawn and messing about on the river... Suffragettes... the bustle, the corset, the high lace collars, and the huge feathered hats... the entire glorious era vanished. And then *we* did.

Chapter Twenty

"…ohhhhh!"

We landed in a familiar cobbled alleyway with a bump. Luckily, I landed on top of something soft.

"Owf!" Charlie groaned.

"Thank you for breaking my fall, Charlie."

His voice was strained. "No problem, Lady Joanie."

I pushed myself to my hands and knees and gazed down at him. He smiled playfully. Gosh, I could so easily kiss him from here…

But… we were surely about to say goodbye forever. It'd been fun, but we both led vastly different lives here in 1926. *I* couldn't be friends with a policeman. People would talk.

A booming voice inside me said LET THEM TALK. WHO CARES?

Charlie helped me to my feet. "Are we home?"

I crept around the corner of the alleyway and spotted a newspaper billboard with the headline: *His Majesty King George V…*

Yes! I didn't bother to read the rest – so relieved was I that it was *him* back on the throne, and not his father, Edward VIII, who'd died in 1911.

Charlie spotted it too. "King George the Fifth, we are home then!"

"Thank goodness I can get out of this stupid dress – I never want to see another corset for as long as I live!"

We left the alleyway and strolled along the street. But as worry crept through me, I halted. Something felt… odd. It was daytime now, which was okay. We did *have* daytime in 1926. But the season was wrong. The leaves were red and yellow and gold. Autumn, yes obviously. But it wasn't only the wrong time of year… Something else felt wrong… things were too *serious* for the 1920s!

"I don't think this *is* home, Charlie. Not quite. Look…"

The street contained the usual horses, carts, and a few motorcars. *Old* motorcars… And the women were wearing long, straight, shin-length skirts. I knew from all the shins that we'd definitely left 1906. But we absolutely *weren't* in 1926.

We stepped over to the newspaper billboard and read it properly. *His Majesty King George V to Relinquish All German Titles Next Year! Saxe-Coburg to become Windsor!*

I spoke with dread. "They became the House of Windsor in 1917."

"So this is nineteen-*sixteen*?"

"The magic must've been too weak to get us all the way back." I glanced around at the bustling Londoners. "But just look how much things have changed in ten years! I didn't notice it at the time because I was so absorbed in the war, but when you see it like this, from 1906 to 1916 in an instant, it's incredible."

Charlie grinned. "Look who's driving that bus – a woman!"

I stared at the female bus driver. "All the men are at war."

His grin faded. "This is the first year of conscription."

I linked my arm through his. "Cheer up, Charlie, at least the sun's shining."

"Not where *I* currently am. In Belgium. It never shone there."

"Try not to think about it. Look, I'd better contact Uncle Frog and ask what's happened. And perhaps he'll know the whereabouts of that villain Lord Vilnius too."

Charlie bunched his fist. "If he's here, I'll gladly finish what *he* started earlier."

"Not if he beats us to the next magical gem, you won't. But Uncle Frog can give us all the details about *that*. Perhaps we can intercept it again."

Charlie knew the score by now. "Shall we go somewhere secluded and speak to him then?"

"Yes, all right." I glanced at the sky. "Oh, what a pity about that big grey cloud…"

"Er… that's not a cloud, Lady Joanie."

We stared up at the giant airship overhead. *Uh-oh…* Trying to contain their panic but failing, the men, women, and children in the street darted for cover – fleeing into shops, cafés, and halls – screaming with fear.

Charlie shouted about the whirring engines. "It's a Zeppelin – an air-raid!"

I grabbed Charlie's hand. "Let's get out of here then! Quick, Charlie, *run!*"

Will our heroes escape the zeppelin raid? Will they find the next magical gem before Lord V? Will they ever get home again…?

And when will they jolly-well kiss each other!

Turn the page to 1916 and find out…

A Witch in Time 1916

Chapter One

"Quick, Charlie, run!"

Ah, hello darlings – you've just caught me courageously fleeing for my life, so I'm in a bit of a hurry. But here's the story so far…

I'm Lady Joanforth Eldritch, soon-to-be senior witch, lover of fun, and solver of murders. I'm originally from 1926, but I'm currently travelling around the twentieth century with a dishy young police detective called Charlie. In our last adventure we bravely chased 'wannabe evil overlord' Lord Vilnius into my Uncle Frog's magical time vortex… and vanished! We materialised in 1906, where we solved two murders, found the first of nine magical gems – and inspired a famous movie star to slip on a banana peel for larks.

After my Uncle Frog had given me the magic words to travel back to 1926, Charlie and I had disappeared into the foggy streams of time. But… it's always disappointing, isn't it, when after much strenuous effort, you arrive slightly short of your mark? Well, Charlie and I had arrived a *decade* short – and we were now in 1916.

But getting upset would do us no good! I knew well enough after my four-hundred-odd (sometimes *very* odd!) years on this planet that the only way to get over something was to go through it – especially if that thing was time… which brings you up to speed!

And speaking of speed… Holding hands, Charlie and I fled down the hectic London street, running from the giant airship above. As if *that* wasn't bad enough, I was still wearing my Edwardian tea gown, complete with bustle – which was *not* made for running in. I lost my footing on a slippery cobblestone and fell… dragging Charlie to a halt.

Oh, but bustles *do* have their uses – namely, a bit of extra padding as I landed on my gorgeous little bot. "Owf!"

Charlie helped me up. "All right, Lady Joanie?"

I straightened my hat. "I always did plan to go down in history, but not like *that*."

We glanced up to the gloomy sky. The six-hundred-foot, cigar-shaped Zeppelin loomed overhead like an apocalyptic thundercloud. Even to my 1926 eyes, these giant airships seemed futuristic – like something out of an H G Wells novel. But their cargo of bombs was very real. And if the bombs didn't get you, well… those massive hydrogen-filled balloons had a tendency to explode…

"In here," I said, pushing open a shop door.

The shop turned out to be a bakery, with an attached café. It was rather dark and cramped inside, with wooden floorboards, marble-topped tables, and a glass counter towards the back.

There were no customers in here, but a young man in uniform was stoking the roaring fire. He only looked around eighteen, and his second lieutenant's uniform was clean and ironed. He glanced over his shoulder as we stepped inside. His lovely red hair and bright blue eyes starkly contrasted his scowling face. Here was a troubled young man if I ever saw one. But this was 1916. Troubled young men were ten a-penny.

The other two people in here were a young blonde woman and a middle-aged man. They were deep in discussion behind the glass counter, so presumably this was the workforce. Almost in mid-conversation, the man shrugged off his overcoat and hung it up in the kitchen, then continued talking with the young lady.

I felt self-conscious in my expensive Edwardian tea gown. Whilst it was true that *some* upper-class ladies continued to dress this extravagantly in 1916, it was rather outdated by now. These days, ladies wore shin-length flared skirts, coupled with a blouse or jacket – giving the feminine silhouette straight lines, instead of the Edwardian corset-induced S-shaped curves. Fancy frills and bright silks had been tamed in favour of plainer materials. I needed some modern clothes…

I sensed that Charlie also felt over-dressed, because he subtly tugged off his 1906 silk cravat as we stood there waiting. He removed his hat too, but that was just good hat etiquette.

The young waitress stepped out from behind the counter and took Charlie's hat from him. "Welcome madam, sir…"

She was a pretty young thing, with her long blonde hair knotted back in the 1916 style. Her clothes were fashionable, but not expensive – she was wearing a shin-length woollen skirt with a cotton blouse.

The older man smiled gaily as we approached the counter, smoothing down his suit and straightening his tie. He spoke in a thick German accent. "Welcome to *Hengleberg's Bakery*. I am Herr Rolf Hengleberg, proprietor and head baker! Oh, do not worry – I do not bake the heads! But only the tasty foodstuffs. Will you stay for tea? Or have you heard about mine famous products?"

He gestured to the cakes, breads, and biscuits under the glass counter.

"Excuse the bad news," I said. "But there's a Zeppelin raid overhead."

Herr Hengleberg, the young waitress, and the soldier rushed to the large windows and looked upwards.

"The sky's empty now," the young soldier said with relief. "Must've just been passing over."

"They follow the Thames," the young waitress said with a tiny trace of a German accent. "To draw aerial maps. They come mostly at night. Mostly…"

I shivered at the memories of the Zeppelin raids from when I'd lived through the war the first time around. Charlie misinterpreted my shiver. "We'll have some tea please, Mr Hengleberg. Come, Lady Joanie, stand by the fire."

Herr Hengleberg bustled off to make our tea, so Charlie and I stood in front of the sturdy fireplace together. Charlie squeezed my shoulder. "Did you hurt yourself when you fell?"

"I'm all right, Charlie, thank you."

I glanced at the young soldier, who'd sat himself down at a nearby table. It seemed rather surreal for

Charlie to be concerned about my little stumble, when such horrors were happening on the Continent.

And Charlie would be there now – his *1916* self. And so would I, as a nurse.

Best not to think of it. We'd be out of here soon with any luck. I turned back to the roaring flames and let my mind unwind into the crackling oranges, whites, and lilacs. It was soothing, and I started to relax, but then I noticed a shiny white object in the grate, which was about the size and length of my little finger. How odd.... My witchy senses compelled me to pick it up, but of course the flames were far too hot to plunge my hand in, and my magic was too weak to waste on the Second Skin spell.

The young waitress placed our tea things on a marble-topped table. "Here we are."

Charlie pulled out a chair for me, and we both sat.

"Mmm…that's a good cuppa," I said, letting the warmth fill me up.

"How's your magic?" Charlie asked quietly. "Any stronger in this era?"

I closed my eyes and searched inside. "I feel it's been replenished a little, but I still only have enough oomph for one spell – or two small ones. Certainly not enough to get us home."

The waitress sat down with the soldier. She spoke accusingly to Charlie. "Why aren't you in uniform, sir?"

Charlie tensed, dropping the tea strainer with a clatter. Oh dear... But Charlie *was* in uniform in Belgium… just an earlier version of himself.

"Mr Anderson has a special job within the military," I said.

I waited for the soldier and waitress to get back to their own conversation – then I spoke to Charlie. "Let's finish our tea and contact Uncle Frog. He'll tell us why we're not in 1926."

"It *would* be good to go home, Lady Joanie. But I was thinking… surely that villain Lord Vilnius still has the time controls. And he's *still* hoping to collect all the magical gems – which you said would spell disaster for us all. What if *he's* here in 1916 too."

"Yes." A terrible thought struck me. "And what if he pairs up with his 1916 self! Double trouble."

"Can he do that? Can we interact with our 1916 selves?"

"No idea. I'll check with Uncle Frog. But anyway *we're* both in Belgium at the moment, so no chance for us."

"Hopefully we won't be stuck here long."

I gazed into his eyes. "It was rather fun though, wasn't it? Visiting 1906 and solving that murder. *Both* murders. I felt like I was in a mystery novel. Didn't you?"

He shrugged. "It's my job – I'm a detective."

"Don't be coy, Charlie – you've only been a detective for a week. And your training seemingly consisted of reading the entire back-collection of Sherlock Holmes."

He smiled. "I do like those books, it's true."

I stirred my tea. "How about Agatha Christie, have you read any of her books? They're marvellous."

"I've read some of her short stories starring her Belgian detective and his little grey cells. She kept me guessing until the end – very clever." He raised a flirty eyebrow. "I do like a lady of mystery."

I ignored the swooning effect he had on me. "I'll lend you Mrs Christie's first novel when we get home. You'll love her. She's become quite a hero of mine."

"That's kind, your ladyship. Leave the book in the servants' hall and I'll collect it from the backdoor."

I snorted playfully. "I'm not having *you* sniffing round my backdoor. I might never see my silverware again!"

He laughed. "I wouldn't steal from *you*. You might turn me into a toad!"

Our laughter had caught the attention of the soldier. His voice was sullen. "You've been to war, sir?"

Charlie didn't look up. "Aye."

"George is going tomorrow," the waitress said. "Along with all the other young men from the area."

Oh yes, some bright spark at the war office had come up with *that* idea – to enlist all the local lads into the same battalion. It was no doubt good for camaraderie. But it also meant that entire villages lost *all* their young men in the space of one battle. Twenty thousand men had been killed on the first *day* of the Somme in France. Magic was all very well, but it was powerless against human stupidity.

The German man, Herr Hengleberg, sat down with the two youngsters. *Ah-ha!* I detected magical vibes emanating from him. I wasn't sure what sort of Being of Magic he was, but that wasn't important. Perhaps *he'd* know where we might find the next magical jewel. Charlie was right – whilst we were here, we ought to locate it before Lord Vilnius had the chance.

"We are very proud of George here," Herr Hengleberg said, gesturing to the young soldier. "Aren't we, Becky?"

"Yes, Uncle." Becky stood up. "I'll rinse those cups from earlier."

"I'll come with you," George said grimly. "I need to focus on normal things, before I go off to fight for King and Country."

Herr Hengleberg watched them disappear to the kitchen out the back. He sighed wearily. "Such upsetting times."

"Where are you from?" I asked.

His face flashed with worry. "Hamburg, originally, but let me assure you, I have lived here in London for thirty years. And don't worry, I have been curfewed – I cannot leave my flat above the bakery after dark. I need a permit to even leave London. But I'm lucky to not have been interned, like so many of my fellow 'aliens'."

My heart twisted with sympathy. "Actually, I meant, do you know a place called Marvelton?"

He smiled with relief. "Oh yes – I am familiar with that magical land. I am myself from the German equivalent, Wunderstadt. But I thought you were perhaps another of these anti-German types. I have received several spiteful postcards – anonymous, of course. But I am just a humble baker. I want to serve the people of London the breads, the cakes, and... I want to live peacefully."

"Live peacefully?" Charlie's voice was gruff. "But you're *German*…"

"Charlie!" I said. "Herr Hengleberg is just the same as us. Well… he's just the same as me. He's a…" I lowered my voice. "…Being of Magic…"

Charlie was unimpressed. "He's a *German* Being of Magic."

Herr Hengleberg held up his hands. "It's all right, it's all right. These young men are sent off to fight my fellow countryfolk, I quite understand. I'm *sure* there are also English bakers working in Hamburg who are suffering the same treatment. I can feel their presence in my every breath."

I clicked my fingers. "You're psychic!"

He smiled kindly. "Ja. But my powers are weak at the moment, alas."

"I know that feeling."

"Dark times indeed… But, might I know who *you* are?"

"Lady Joanforth Eldritch. Soon-to-be senior witch."

"Ach, I know of you!"

"And this is Mr Charles Anderson."

Charlie nodded curtly. "How do you do, sir…"

Our introductions were cut short as a middle-aged man dashed suddenly into the bakery. I realised it was dark outside now – how quickly the autumn nights drew in.

Herr Hengleberg stood to greet the newcomer. "Neville, we don't usually see you at… But what is the matter?"

This Neville person was suave and well-dressed – and he was well-spoken behind his neat moustache. "Rolf, there's an air raid – Zeppelins overhead. We must take shelter now!"

Herr Hengleberg turned to us. "Come, Lady Joanforth, Mr Anderson. We will all go down to the cellar where we will be safe."

Neville nodded. "At haste…"

"Ach, Becky and George are in the kitchen…"

"*George* is here?" Neville asked in surprise.

"Ja, I will get them. Come, we have no time to lose!"

Chapter Two

Well, I certainly couldn't contact Uncle Frog down in this cellar, surrounded by all these people. Rolf Hengleberg was a fellow Being of Magic, but the others were human, and we always preferred not to involve humans if possible. Really, we ought not to live amongst humans at all – we should stick to the magical lands. But… they were so captivating.

Especially this one…

I caught Charlie staring at me. It was his eyes that enchanted me the most. One was blue, one was brown. And his confident grin… oh and his handsome face, of course. And underneath that yummy wrapping was a… well, there was a streetwise thief-turned-copper. But under *that*… he was lovely.

But alas, I was a witch and he was a human. I was a highborn member of the aristocracy and he was… salt of the earth. I needed to put him from my mind and focus on getting back to 1926, where I would complete my magical studies.

But for now, we were all stuck together… That was the thing about this war. It had shuffled up the rigid and restrictive roles of class, sex, and age – exposing the old rules for the façade they were. And about time too.

The cellar was large enough to accommodate all six of us, despite being rather cold and stark. There was no electricity down here, and the flickering candlelight cast shadows on the hard stone floor.

There were piles of wooden crates stacked up against the whitewashed walls, as well as a spare table and chairs – which turned out to be in need of repair, but would do for somewhere to sit for now.

Perhaps in an attempt to prove how loyal he was to England, Herr Hengleberg had stuck up a large poster of Their Britannic Majesties, King George and Queen Mary, looking regal and reassuring. But – then again – he'd stuck it up in the cellar, which might not go down well with anyone who was keen to kick up a fuss.

There was also an ancient upright piano down here, which was slightly out of tune – as we discovered when Charlie sat down and played *It's a Long Way to Tipperary*. Nevertheless, we were all soon having a jolly old sing-song, belting out *Pack up Your Troubles in Your Old Kit Pack* and *Jerusalem* – William Blake's patriotic poem, which had, this very year, been set to Hubert Parry's rousing music. And of course, we were obliged to sing *God Save the King*, for which we all stood.

The two youngsters, Becky and George, sat on the cold floor throughout our sing-song, while Herr Hengleberg, Neville Baron, and myself occupied the chairs. I was a strong and independent witch, but I'd probably need assistance if I wanted to sit on the floor in *this* dress…

Charlie closed the piano lid and turned to face us. "Surely the air raid must be over by now?"

Neville Baron stood up. "You stay here. I'll check."

"You could get information from the wireless, Neville," Herr Hengleberg said. "Up in my room.

The door to the flat is open. But be careful of the bombs, yes."

"I'll be back presently. Everyone, stay here."

"He's very bossy, isn't he?" I said, as he left.

Charlie smirked. "Lady Joanie's used to being the bossiest person in the room. She's feeling usurped."

"Oh very funny, Charlie." *He'd worked me out quickly, hadn't he!*

Herr Hengleberg shrugged. "The Right Honourable Neville Baron is our local MP. He's always bossy."

Oh dear, it didn't take a genius to detect tension between Rolf and Neville…

"Did you say you were psychic?" Charlie asked, probably to break the tension.

"Yes, young man, I am."

"Read Lady Joanie's fortune…"

"Oh no," I said, waving this away. "It'll be frightfully dull."

"Nonsense," Herr Hengleberg said. "Give me your hand, your ladyship."

I groaned, but obeyed. "Very well."

Rolf Hengleberg grasped my fingers in his. "Ah… this is far from dull, your ladyship. It seems that you're going to meet a handsome stranger and embark on a long adventurous journey together."

I frowned. "I think you've got last week's predictions there. I've already done that."

"Ach! Perhaps it is because *someone* has been tampering with *time*, hm?" He let this accusation hang in the air.

Charlie and I both became very interested in the stone floor…

"Are you a medium?" I asked, changing the subject back to him.

"Ach, nein!" He patted his round stomach and winked mischievously. "I'm a *large*. All that delicious bread and cake! Und now I must say something amusing about how I should stop eating all my… *prophets*!"

Despite the dreadful pun, I laughed out loud. Herr Hengleberg was a jolly old soul and I liked him a lot.

"Don't encourage him," Becky said affectionately. "He'll think he really is psychic… and amusing."

Herr Hengleberg spoke in a stage whisper. "Mine niece doesn't believe in magic… or too much of the humour."

"Niece?" I asked. "But… no German accent?"

"Ach no. Becky has been living here with me since her parents died years ago. She's British, but her parents were both German. She's eighteen – still a baby. She'll remain in my care until she's twenty-one."

I lowered my voice. "She seems rather attached to young George."

"Ja, ja, but we all must do our bit for King and Country. George knows this. He's eighteen now, so old enough to fight."

Hmm… So they were the same age, but George was old enough to fight, yet Becky was too young to care for herself…

Herr Hengleberg nodded. "Ja, your ladyship, I can see what you're thinking there."

"Oh… can you?"

"I'm afraid I can read your mind a little. I am sorry. But it's true, I do rely on Becky, perhaps too much." He laughed. "I don't even know how many sugars I take in my coffee! She is the closest thing I have to a daughter. To any child."

Neville Baron strode back into the cellar like a hero in a silent film. "The air raid is still ongoing. We'd better stay here for a little longer."

We all groaned. But at least we were safe in this stone bunker.

Neville sat at the table. "So George, my boy, all set for tomorrow?"

George didn't hide his fury. "Yes, but no thanks to you, Uncle Neville! I know you voted for conscription. And how very convenient for *you* that all fit men between eighteen and forty-one are being called up, when *you're* forty-five! And not only that, but I bet Herr Hengleberg doesn't know that *you* supported the internment of aliens!"

Herr Hengleberg started to reply, but Neville Baron spoke over him. "Now look here, George, I know you're still upset about your brother, but –"

"Upset? *You* sent him off to war – you and your government! And now… he's dead…"

"We all must do our bit, George," Neville said. "I'm sure Herr Hengleberg knows that, and you must too."

Herr Hengleberg spoke sadly. "Neville, perhaps it's best if you don't come here anymore."

"Don't be ridiculous, Rolf, we've known each other twenty years."

"But still… And yes, George, I did know that your uncle voted for the internment of aliens. But – as he says – we all must make sacrifices when there's a war on."

George huffed and glowered at the floor.

Neville Baron sat up tall. "Look, it seems we're stuck here for the night. Perhaps we'd better get some sleep?"

"Agreed," I said. "Things might seem better in the morning."

"Not if the entire area has been bombed to rubble!" George said moodily.

"Oi!" Charlie said. "Don't be so flippin' rude, or I'll –"

"Charlie, it's all right," I said, yawning. "Let's do as Mr Baron suggested and try to rest."

I very carefully lowered myself to the floor and shuffled up against a wall. Once again, my bustle was my friend, protecting me from the hardness and the coldness of the ground.

Charlie took his coat off and sat beside me. "Put this around you, Lady Joanie."

His coat was full of his own lovely warmth. "You're sweet, Charlie. But you'll get cold. Here, we can both share it, like this…"

I draped the big coat over us, meaning we had to snuggle up close – any excuse! He gazed at me for a moment, then lifted his arm and wrapped it around me. Despite being slouched against a stone wall in a dank cellar, I knew that I was about to have one of the most comfortable sleeps of my entire life. Even if the air *was* cold and musty, my heart felt as warm and fuzzy as my dog Wispu's cute woolly ears.

162

Chapter Three

I awoke with a start. It was completely dark. A terrifying rat-a-tat sound hammered at my brain via my eardrums. What *was* it? Had the Zeppelins returned? *Oh no!*

Oh… no… I relaxed. Someone down here in the cellar was snoring loudly. I couldn't see who the snorer was because – now that the candles had burnt down – it was as black as coal. I shivered in the chilly air, but Charlie's strong arms and warm coat prevented me from being too uncomfortable. How snugly we fitted together!

I drifted back down to the outskirts of sleep, but the sound of raised voices from up in the bakery jolted me awake. Two people were arguing up there, but their voices were muffled and I couldn't make out who they were, or even if they were young, old, male, or female.

I was tempted to cast the Enhancer spell to increase the volume, but I was exhausted and needed to save my magic. The truth was, after all the tense bickering in the cellar earlier, it could've been *any* of them arguing.

The voices slurred away as I drifted back to a sponge-like, snoozy slumber…

Then… several hours later, a warm masculine voice said, "Lady Joanie?"

My eyes fluttered open. The morning light was spilling down even into this dim space. And what a glorious sight to wake up to. I was lying on the floor now, covered with Charlie's coat, and the man himself was smiling down upon me.

"Good morning, your ladyship. I made you some tea…"

I sat up slowly and stretched. Young George was sitting at the other end of the cellar, staring into space. But the others – Neville Baron, Rolf Hengleberg, and Becky were elsewhere.

I sat down at the wobbly table where Charlie had placed the tea things. Then, after the important ritual of pouring, adding milk, sweetening, and stirring, I sipped my tea gratefully. "Where is everyone?"

Charlie sat opposite me. "I don't know where Neville Baron is – he must've left early. But Becky and Mr Hengleberg are up in the bakery, chatting at a table. Their discussion looked serious, so I quickly made them some coffee, then made our tea, and made me-self scarce."

"I hope Herr Hengleberg hasn't received any renewed threats, poor man."

Becky jogged down the cellar steps. "None today, thank you, your ladyship."

"Glad to hear it."

George clambered to his feet. "I should ready myself to leave."

Becky held out her hand for him. "Good luck to you, George. You'll be in my thoughts."

George grasped her hand, nodded curtly, then stomped off up the cellar steps. Poor chap. Little did he know what horrors awaited.

Becky sighed, watching him go.

"Becky?" I said. "Mr Anderson said you were having a serious discussion with your uncle just now. Is all fine with you both?"

Charlie raised an eyebrow. "It's not our business, Lady Joanie,"

"I'm merely checking on the child."

Becky sat with us at the table. "I'm grateful, your ladyship. And my uncle is okay. He has trouble sleeping these days, due to the stress of merely being German in these terrible times."

"It is a dreadful strain on him," I said. "But he seems to take it in his stride."

"Yes," Becky said. "He tries to keep his spirits up. But these days he often needs a sleeping draught to help him sleep. I don't really approve, because I believe one can become addicted to such things. But we're both always up with the lark to open the bakery, so I do understand why he wants to get *some* sleep."

I squeezed her hand. "Don't worry, the war will be over soon. Just a couple more years."

She frowned. "*You* don't also think you're psychic, do you?"

"Just a feeling I have."

Becky stood up. "I'd better get back up there – I've just opened the front door, and Uncle might need me. I only came down to say you're welcome to come upstairs, your ladyship. It's much more comfortable. I'll make you some breakfast."

My ears pricked up. "Breakfast?"

She chuckled. "Yes. How does bacon, eggs, and our own speciality bread sound?"

Charlie shot to his feet. "Sounds like a dream come true. I'm starving."

Up in the bakery, Rolf Hengleberg was sitting at the table by the window, gazing outside.

"Good morning, Herr Hengleberg," I said to his back.

He continued staring outside. Poor chap. He knew how to put on a jolly front, but there was obviously something troubling him today. Those awful threats and anti-German sentiments must be hard to bear. He was deep in thought, so Charlie and I sat at a table near the fire, leaving him to brood.

The fire hadn't yet been lit but… oh…

There was a white glint in the ashes. It looked like a small piece of bone, and I suddenly realised I'd seen *this* in the flames yesterday. I checked that no one but Charlie was watching and bent to pick it up. My witchy senses were telling me it was important. Could it be the next magical jewel? But surely that wouldn't have been thrown on the fire? And this didn't look precious or feel magical. It just looked like a thin fragment of burnt bone, about the size of my little finger. How odd.

I gently blew the ashes off… "Hmm…"

"What is it?" Charlie asked.

I handed it to him. He wrinkled his nose. "Bone? That's creepy."

Becky came over with two overflowing plates of bacon and eggs, so I shoved the strange item up my long Edwardian sleeve.

We polished off our breakfasts gratefully, but we needed to get out of here and find somewhere secluded to contact Uncle Frog. I was worried about

Lord Vilnius – he was bound to be lurking nearby. Hopefully Frog might suggest how to prevent that evil villain from gathering up all the magical jewels – preferably in a way that didn't involve Charlie and I locating the other eight before he did.

"Charlie," I said. "Your silk cravat should be enough to pay for two breakfasts and their hospitality."

He pulled it out of his pocket. "Poor Alfred Sandhurst. I wonder what happened to him in the end."

"I hope he re-married and –"

I was interrupted by the sound of Becky's voice. She was standing over Herr Hengleberg, gently shaking him. "Uncle, wake up! Honestly, I only left him here to… oh good heavens…"

The sleeping Herr Hengleberg keeled heavily forwards. Oh bless him he must be so tired… But… actually, he wasn't asleep. Dreadful realisation smashed into me as I saw his head loll floppily against the stunned Becky's stomach.

Becky screamed in terror, pushing him backwards. "Uncle, *no*!"

The late Herr Hengleberg dropped off his chair, thumping to the floor with a dead-weight *thud*.

He might've been psychic, but he certainly hadn't seen *that* coming.

Chapter Four

Charlie and I rushed over as Becky dropped to her knees, pressing her fingers against her uncle's wrist. "No pulse! Oh, uncle!"

Charlie threw a strong arm across me. "Stay back, Lady Joanie."

"Don't be ridiculous, Charlie. I'm a nurse! I can help."

Becky's voice was full of juddery shock. "It's too late… he's dead…" Her face contorted with dismay. "He's… cold…"

I stared at the dreadful sight on the floor. She was right. Herr Hengleberg was stock-still. And it was pretty clear what had killed him. There was an ice pick sticking out of his throat, with sticky blood congealing on his pale white neck.

"I thought he was asleep!" Becky whimpered.

Charlie took control. "Miss Hengleberg, I'm a police officer. I'll–"

"*Are* you?" Becky asked.

"I am. I'll run to the police station. You two stay here. Neither of you touch *nothing*."

Charlie ran outside, leaving Becky and I alone in the tense, ringing air.

I helped her to stand. "Come along, Becky. Let's sit over here."

Shaking with shock, she sunk into my arms, then she flopped into a chair and stuttered, "It's the anti-German brigade, I know it is. The door was unlocked

– someone came in and… done it. While I was down in the cellar with you."

I sat down too and gazed sadly at the dead man on the floor. Most of the blood was being stemmed by the ice pick in his neck… *That's* why we hadn't realised he was dead when we'd come up from the cellar just now. If there'd been a pool of *blood* on the floor, I obviously wouldn't have said 'good morning' to him. But I wasn't to know. He'd had his back to me. He'd just looked… slumped and pensive.

Still shaking, Becky was wiping her uncle's blood on her apron. She must've got it on her hands when he'd slumped against her. Poor thing.

There wasn't anything I could do now though. Apart from *one* thing… the thing that the English always did in a time of crisis… I got to my feet.

Becky looked panicky. "Don't leave me!"

"It's all right, my dear. I'm going to make you some tea. Stay here. I'll be back presently."

The kitchen was a simple affair, which seemed strange, considering it was the beating heart of this bakery. I stepped into the small stark space, which had a low ceiling and whitewashed walls. A hefty wooden table stood solidly in the middle of the stone floor, and a huge iron oven took up an entire wall. Another wall held shelves of baking equipment as well as large trays for the finished loaves.

I filled up a copper kettle from the porcelain sink, then lit the gas stove with a taper. Despite being a member of the aristocracy, I'd learnt a lot as an auxiliary nurse and knew how to take care of myself. Skills like those came in handy.

As I waited for the kettle to boil, I noticed that a coat hook by the door had a tatty apron hanging from it, as well as a man's overcoat. I guessed those probably belonged to Herr Hengleberg… Hmm…

Channelling my inner-Charlie, I dipped my hand into the gaping pocket of the apron, but it was empty. Nothing helpful there. How about the overcoat? The kettle started to whistle, so I had a quick rummage in both external pockets, then the inner one. All empty. Ah well, better luck next time.

I took the whistling kettle off the flame with a tea towel and found a tannin-stained teapot. There was a stack of cups and saucers on the counter and… oh, that was odd… there was one less cup than saucer. I already knew there were two cups and saucers on Herr Hengleberg's table. Charlie had said he'd taken them some coffee when making my tea. So that made thirteen cups but fourteen saucers all together. Oh well, it probably wasn't important – one cup had probably just been smashed and not replaced.

I assembled the tea things the best I could on a tray. I couldn't find any brandy, but there was half a bottle of schnapps. I took a quick swig to calm my own nerves, then poured some into a teacup for Becky.

I found the poor girl staring at her dead uncle. "Here, love, drink some tea."

"I can't believe this… who would do this?"

"Becky, forgive me, but I think I heard raised voices overnight."

"Between who?"

"I'm not sure. But perhaps between your uncle and someone who was here with us? George? Neville?"

She sighed. "Uncle Rolf and Mr Neville Baron have known each other a long time. And I know they *have* recently argued."

"Oh yes?"

Becky sipped her tea, then pulled a face. "Eurgh…"

"Oh, I slipped in a little schnapps to calm your nerves. You were saying?"

She sipped more tea. "I overheard my uncle and Mr Baron arguing yesterday afternoon when I went outside to spend a penny. The lavatory backs onto the kitchen, you see, and you can hear people talking when you're… occupied."

"What were they arguing about?"

"Neville Baron was saying to Uncle Rolf, *you'll never get away with it*."

"Away with what?"

"I don't know."

"But you worry that perhaps Mr Baron decided to stop your uncle… permanently?"

She gazed at me with her blue eyes. "Mr Baron will be in parliament today. Perhaps you might talk to him?"

"Me? You really ought to tell the police."

She nodded reluctantly. "Yes."

Before we could talk anymore, Charlie arrived with… oh dear, my heart sank. It was Inspector Grumpy from 1926 – the one who'd attended the murder of Captain Sebastian Loveday at the Fat

Pussycat Club. Well… he *would* do in ten years from now.

As always, he scowled as if the world was a jug of rancid milk and he was being forced to sniff it. I got along with him like a house on fire – he made me want to run away screaming…

He was accompanied by two uniformed officers who immediately set about checking the body. "This one's still a bit warm, sir. Must've only been dead under the hour."

Becky's face washed with pain. "Oh poor Uncle…"

Charlie joined us. "Lady Joanie? Are you all right?"

"I'm not pleased to see your boss again."

"I know – I was shocked to see him at the police station. But he's not my boss yet. And he's only a detective sergeant."

Inspector Grumpy pulled out his notepad and pounced on us. "Right then, I need accounts from you lot about exactly what happened here."

"Inspector Gru… sorry, what is your name?"

"Detective Sergeant Parry. And you are?"

"Lady Joanforth Eldritch."

He scoffed. "Lady Joanforth Eldritch. I've heard about you. All true, I suppose?"

"I believe we've been through *this* before, Inspec… Sergeant."

He eyeballed me. "Just tell me what happened… How did you all come to be here this morning?"

"This is Becky," I said. "She lives here with Herr Hengleberg in the flat upstairs. She's his niece."

"And what happened?" Sergeant Parry asked. "See anything suspicious?"

Becky swallowed her tears. "No. I'd just unlocked the door for the day and gone down to the cellar to speak to Lady Joanforth. Then I made the breakf—"

DS Parry held up a hand. "Just a minute. What was Lady Joanforth doing in your cellar?"

"We all spent the night down there," I explained. "Me, Mr Anderson, Becky, Herr Hengleberg, an MP named Neville Baron, and his nephew, George Baron."

DS Parry was on the cusp of exploding. "But *why* did you all spend the night in the cellar? Little party, was it?"

"Because of the air raid," Charlie said.

"What air raid? There was no air raid last night."

"But Neville Baron announced it when he arrived," I said. "And he went off and checked – and confirmed it was still going on."

DS Parry sighed. "A couple of Zeppelins *were* reported at twilight, but they were simply on manoeuvres. No bombs were dropped. Tell me, Mr Anderson, on your journey to the police station just now, did you not notice the complete lack of bombed-out houses and newly-appeared potholes?"

Charlie ignored his future boss's sarcasm. "Neville Baron lied about the air raid."

I frowned. "Why on earth would he do that?"

Sergeant Parry huffed. "Right, you're not to leave London. None of you that was here last night."

"George is supposed to go to war today," Becky said meekly.

"I'll have a word with his recruiting office. He's a possible witness of a murder. A possible *suspect*. He'll be delayed a short while. And *you'll* need to clear out of here, young lady. We'll be wanting access to all areas… upstairs in your flat. Down in the cellar…"

Becky clambered weakly to her feet. "I can stay with a friend. I'll go and pack."

I watched as she made her way to the back of the space, where a wooden staircase led to the first floor. Perhaps I ought to go with her? But then again, maybe she needed a moment alone…

Sergeant Parry turned to the crime scene. "So… the victim was sitting at that table, was he? Hmm… near the unlocked door. Good position for an intruder to be in and out in a jiffy. Ice pick… nasty."

The sergeant picked up one of the coffee cups on the table and sniffed it.

I spoke quietly to Charlie. "Shouldn't he be wearing gloves? Fingerprints and all that?"

Sergeant Parry had good hearing. "You think the killer perhaps stopped for a cup of tea before brutally stabbing the victim with an ice pick, your ladyship?"

Before I was able to reply with a witty quip, young Becky plodded back down the stairs with a tatty suitcase.

"You packed quickly," I said sympathetically.

"I always have a suitcase ready in case of anti-German attacks."

"Shall we go, Lady Joanie?" Charlie said – clearly eager to contact Uncle Frog and get out of here.

"Not whilst I'm still wearing a bustle and corset, Charlie… Becky, strange question but could I borrow some clothes? I'd love to slip into something more comfortable." I held up my be-ringed hand, making my gold bangles jangle. "I'll pay you, of course."

Chapter Five

We stepped out into the cobbled street, and immediately came face-to-face with a stern, moustached military man, informing us that our country needed us.

"That poster was up everywhere," Charlie said wearily. "*Is* up everywhere in 1916. General Kitchener and his accusing pointy finger, demanding we do our patriotic duty and get slaughtered for King and Country."

Other than the propaganda posters on every flat surface, the Maida Vale street we'd grown accustomed to hadn't changed much in ten years. The road was cobbled, the shops were small and independent, and the weather, of course, was overcast. Well, it was October…

But I was free! Free from the constraints of Edwardian undies at last. Becky had kindly given me a woollen shin-length skirt and a cotton blouse with a tailored jacket. My hat was much smaller than the huge Edwardian styles, and my hair… well, it was still short and blonde because of the 1926 style I'd arrived with – but I should be able to get away with it if I kept my hat on.

Becky had been grateful for the gold ring I'd given her in exchange for the clothes – and she'd also gladly thrown in a handful of assorted coins. She'd even given me a small velvet moneybag, which I'd tied around my wrist. It contained farthings, ha'pennies, a few thruppenny bits, and five half crowns.

It wasn't really done for a lady such as myself to be carrying money and paying for things – it was expected that my maid or man would take care of such complex financial transactions. But I'd always relished my independence. Besides, I loved how random our currency was. Pounds, shillings, and pence. One shilling consisted of twelve pennies, and there were twenty shillings in a pound, which meant two hundred and forty pence to the pound. And that wasn't even mentioning the guinea, which was one pound and one shilling! You could say *this* for us English folk – we were jolly good at complicated mental arithmetic. We had to be!

Charlie and I strolled along the busy street. "Have you still got the silver rose, Lady Joanie – the first magical gem?"

"Yes. I've stashed it in my new 1916 undies, along with that strange piece of bone."

He wrinkled his nose. "Why have you kept that?"

"I don't know… it was sort of calling to me. Anyway, most importantly, the silver rose is safe in my under-garments."

He threw me a flirty grin. "I should hope so."

I stifled my smirk. "Let's find a convenient alleyway and beam up Uncle Frog. Hopefully he'll be able to get us home."

"Sounds good. We seem to be attracting murders, don't we?"

"As you said to me yesterday, Charlie, you're a detective. It's what you do."

"Oh, so Fate has decided to cast me back in time so I can solve murders with you?"

"Perhaps."

He went quiet for a moment. "Well, firstly I want to know why Neville Baron lied about the air raid?"

"Can't you guess, darling?"

He halted by a fruit cart. "No. Can you?"

"I assume it's because he wanted Herr Hengleberg and Becky out of the way so he could snoop in their bakery for some reason. Or in their flat above the bakery."

"Hm, perhaps."

"Don't you remember, darling? Neville Baron was surprised to see George when he arrived, so he hadn't expected him or *us* to be there. *He* was the one who came in shouting about the air raid, and *he* checked it was still happening before we all went to sleep."

"And *that's* when he snuck off to snoop in the flat, you think?"

"That's what I suspect, yes. Think about it – Herr Hengleberg even told Neville to check the wireless up in the flat for information – saying the door was open up there. It was the perfect opportunity for Neville to conduct a thorough search, *alone*. Why *else* would he lie about an air raid and keep us all safely down in the cellar for an entire night?"

"So you're saying that either Hengleberg or Becky possessed something of Neville's that he wanted back?"

"I'd assume so. But I couldn't see anything out of the ordinary when I was up in Becky's bedroom changing just now."

Charlie and I set off again. "Perhaps he found what he was looking for?"

"Perhaps..." I grabbed Charlie's arm. "Come on, let's go down this alleyway and speak to Uncle Frog."

The alleyway led to the secluded backyard of a local tavern, so I sat on a beer barrel and beamed up Uncle Frog on my Amulet of Seeing. I was delighted to see my frog-headed uncle. And how wonderful to see the friendly sheepdog/poodle cross Wispu there too.

She barked a hello.

Uncle Frog was in his study. The time machine was whirring gently in the background. "Joanforth, where are you?"

"1916, Uncle. We arrived here yesterday in the middle of an air raid! Zeppelins, remember those? It turned out to be a false alarm, but we took solace in a baker's cellar. And then the baker was murdered!"

"Another murder, Joanie?"

"I know. He was a nice chap called Rolf Hengleberg. Stabbed by an intruder, by all accounts."

"*Or* by the bloke who lied about the air raid," Charlie said. "The Right Honourable Neville Baron."

Uncle Frog rubbed his chin. "Hmm, I wonder if I can get you some information on the original history... Just hold tight a moment..." He adjusted a few dials and levers on a clunky metal machine to the side of him. "This is a new invention I've recently built, based on the work of Ada Lovelace. I call it the Historitron. I just need to add some parameters, and twist this dial here... pour *this* magic potion into the spout, and... Oh... oh *dear*..."

"Uncle Frog, please don't worry about the original history. Charlie and I just want to get back to 1926. Can you concentrate on *that*, please?"

"Do you know what went wrong, sir?" Charlie asked. "How come we ended up in 1916 instead of 1926?"

Uncle Frog stopped fiddling with his Historitron. "I've calculated that there wasn't *quite* enough magic on the silver rose to bring you all the way back to 1926."

"I thought the silver rose was fairly potent with magic?" I said.

"When all the gems are together, they form a potent spell. That's precisely why the Beings of Magic Council scattered them throughout time – to keep them out of the hands of the evil ones."

Charlie folded his arms across his chest. "But now Lord Vilnius wants them. Any idea where he is?"

"Unfortunately, the runes indicate that he's in 1916 with you – so be careful!"

"Can he team up with himself?" I asked. "His 1916 version?"

"Good heavens, no! None of you must meet your alternative selves, otherwise the entire universe will implode like a flan in the overheated oven of space/time!"

"So what do we do?" Charlie asked. "Must we once again solve the murder? Are there… what did you call them… negative vibes, blocking the magic?"

"You're a fast learner, young man." Uncle Frog sounded impressed. "Bright, isn't he, Joanforth."

I tried to act nonchalant. "I suppose so. For a human."

Charlie grinned at me. "Glad I've impressed you, your ladyship."

"Uncle Frog, what's the next gem?" I asked, ignoring Charlie's penetrating gaze. "Perhaps if we try to find that, we might be able to leap out of here without entangling ourselves in the murder this time?"

"It's a lion made of gold," Uncle Frog said.

"And where would this golden lion be?" I asked.

Uncle Frog picked up a collection of small ivory-coloured tiles and threw them to the carpet of his workshop. "Hmm… the runes are placing the golden lion *somewhere* in 1916 London, but I'm not sure of the precise location. I'll try to find out. You'll need to give me a couple of hours, Joanforth – I'll work as quickly as I can."

Wispu barked.

"Yes," Frog said. "Wispu will help too. But, Joanforth, I must tell you the information from the Historitron – Becky Hengleberg and George Baron are due to *die* tomorrow evening!"

Chapter Six

Charlie and I strode along the bustling London street, still reeling from Frog's news about Becky and George. Apparently, in the original history, their blood-stained clothes had been discovered by the banks of the Thames… tomorrow.

"How awful that their bodies were never found," I said. "Their killer must've thrown them in the river… and you know how dirty and polluted the Thames is. Not to mention how *huge*."

"And tidal," Charlie said. "They could've been washed out to sea."

"Dreadful."

"Lady Joanie, I know you *do* want to stay and prevent their deaths. You pretend to be all 'I don't care about anyone'. But I know you care about Becky. You wouldn't want her to be killed. Come on, let's go to the Palace of Westminster and talk to Neville Baron – that's where he'll be, isn't it? That's where all the MPs go."

How could I refuse such an appeal – especially one from such a deliciously handsome fellow? And the trouble was, he was perfectly right. I cared much more than I liked people to think. "Becky did say Neville would be there today, yes."

"Well, come on then. I want to know why he lied about the air raid."

"I've told you my theory on that. It's because he wanted to get everyone out the way so he could have a snoop."

"And I agree. But whatever he was searching for *must* be something to do with Hengleberg's murder. *And* Becky and George's impending deaths."

I stepped off the kerb into the road. "Charlie, what you – wah!"

With my heart in my throat, I jumped into Charlie's arms, watching as a Harrods motor van swerved wildly – after almost running *me* over. Roadhog…

I eased myself out of Charlie's arms. He was grinning. "That could've been disastrous, Lady Joanie. Imagine if Harrods had killed off their most-valued customer!"

I chuckled. "You've rumbled me – I am rather partial to their food hall."

We checked there was nothing else coming and crossed the road carefully.

"I've never tasted their food," Charlie mused. "Harrods, I mean. I've actually only been in there once."

"Have you? To buy a hat?"

"No, your ladyship. I was there as a copper – used the back entrance, of course. But there was this notorious dealer in narcotics who was nabbed in there, and I helped with the arrest."

"What was a notorious dealer in narcotics doing in Harrods?"

"He thought Harrods still kept those gift boxes of cocaine that they sold until 1916. He was caught nicking boxes of chocolates instead! I don't think he could read very well."

I shook my head in disbelief. "Oh yes, I remember those cocaine gift boxes! *Send our boys at the front a little pick-me-up!* Gosh, the drug laws were certainly ripe for reform, weren't they? I had a friend who was into dope. Liked it a little *too* much, alas."

Charlie winced sympathetically. "Sorry to hear that."

"Thank you." A rumbling noise at my side cut into my sad memories. "Oh look, we can take this motorised bus to Westminster."

"Good idea. Hey, I wonder what Mr Royce who we met back in 1906 would've made of all these motorised vehicles!"

Yes, things had changed a lot in only ten years. There *were* still horse-drawn carts in 1916, but many of the poor wretched beasts had been seized by the government and shipped off to war, so the transport companies had quickly adapted. The bus Charlie and I were climbing onto was still very basic compared to what we had in 1926 – looking rather like an oversized van, with small white wheels, and an open upper-deck. But it was warm and dry on the lower deck. I handed the conductress a couple of farthings for our fare and she gave us both a small cardboard ticket.

The bus was half-full of passengers – some working class, some middle class. Charlie and I sat on a hard wooden bench near the front.

I watched London trundle past the window. "What a pity the lady driver and bus conductress will be sacked when the war is over, so the men can take their jobs."

"So the men can take *their* jobs *back*. So they can support their women."

"Oh? And what about the women who'll lose their husbands in the war? What should they do for income?"

Charlie stared at me. "Well… they'll have to remarry, won't they?"

"Sounds like you've got it all worked out."

Bless him. I did like Charlie, but he was jolly old-fashioned. Perhaps it was my duty to enlighten him. For the benefit of his future… wife.

Let's not go down that road…

I cleared my throat. "Charlie, tell me what happened this morning. When you were making my tea. You also made some coffee for Becky and Herr Hengleberg? But you didn't see anyone lurking outside?"

"No, but I was in the kitchen most of the time. Hengleberg and Becky seemed to be having a serious conversation. Their heads were bent together, and she looked a bit worried. So I didn't want to disturb them."

The bus bumped around, so I grabbed the handrail. "Perhaps someone had popped in earlier that morning and threatened him? The anti-German brigade?"

He shrugged. "I didn't see anyone."

"And when you took their coffee over? How did Hengleberg seem?"

"He had his back to me, but he seemed… sad. Not perky and happy like yesterday. Becky took the coffees from me and then..."

"And then?"

"And then Becky said to Hengleberg, 'We can talk about this later, Uncle.' She patted him on the arm.

He shrugged his shoulders. And then I brought down your tea. She came down shortly after that."

Well, that all sounded perfectly innocent. "Come along. This is our stop."

The Palace of Westminster was probably the most iconic building in the whole of London. It was an imposing gothic edifice, with a steep roof and ornate turrets, looming over the Thames on one side, and dominating the local skyline. The three-hundred-foot clock tower, affectionately known as Big Ben, stood tall and proud, and bonged out its famous chimes as regular as... well, clockwork.

"And another thing," Charlie said, as we squeezed through the throng of top-hatted politicians and civil servants. "Becky told us that Neville Baron and Rolf Hengleberg had a falling-out yesterday. *I* want to know what that was about."

I pointed. "There he is, let's ask him."

The Right Hon Neville Baron was easy to spot with his handsome face and confident swagger. We called his name, making him halt.

He seemed short of breath. "Oh, it's you two again. What is it?"

Charlie tipped his hat and spoke firmly. "Sir, why did you lie and say there was an air raid when there wasn't?"

"And did you really think we wouldn't find out?" I asked.

Despite the accusation, his expression didn't flicker. "I don't have to explain myself to you two."

"No, but you might need to explain yourself to the police," Charlie said.

"The police? For lying about an air raid? I hardly think so, now if you'll excuse m –"

I grabbed his arm. "Your friend Rolf Hengleberg was stabbed to death this morning by an intruder, whilst Becky, Charlie, and I were down in the cellar."

"Good heavens, that's… dreadful news." He absent-mindedly scratched his arm. A guilty nervous tick, perhaps?

"Where were *you* this morning?" Charlie asked. "Lurking outside the bakery so you could stab Hengleberg when the coast was clear?"

"Of course not! Now excuse me, I have a vote in the Commons to get to. Good day to you."

"We know you argued with Rolf Hengleberg yesterday," I called out. "What was that about?"

"And what did you take from the bakery or flat last night?" Charlie added.

Neville Baron turned back to face us. He looked worried. "How did you know that I… oh…"

I spoke smugly. "You just told us, Mr Baron."

Neville Baron kept his voice low. "All right, I admit I made up the air raid so I could search Rolf's flat. He had something of mine that I needed back."

"Which was?"

"That's not important… however…" He pulled a rectangular piece of card from his pocket. "I found *this*. In Rolf's overcoat."

As he passed it to me, I noticed he had burn marks on his fingers. I'd seen such marks before – they were from smoking a pipe. Lots of men smoked a pipe, of course. But Neville Baron's hand was trembling, which made me suspicious… hmm...

188

His pale face and dark eye bags *could've* just been caused by the stress of his job. But he was shaking, scratching, and out of breath simply from walking. I'd seen such symptoms before... But for now, I needed to focus on the piece of cardboard he'd just handed me.

"A third-class train ticket from London Euston to Carlisle?" I said, confused.

"That's in Scotland, isn't it?" Charlie asked.

"It's in the far North of England," I said. "On the border. And you found this in Herr Hengleberg's coat pocket, Mr Baron?"

"Do you often rummage through other people's pockets, Mr Baron?" Charlie asked.

"Of course not. But after I'd been unsuccessful in my search last night, I had a quick look in the kitchen before I left this morning – when Becky and Rolf were busy chatting. And it's a good job I did find this train ticket. Rolf's an alien – he's not allowed to leave London. I can't let him break the law – there's a war on you know."

"So you're going to hand this to the police?" I asked.

"No. I'm… I *was* planning to go back to the bakery this morning and have it out with Rolf. Convince him not to go to Carlisle."

"And what was in Carlisle for him?" Charlie asked.

"How should I know? Anyway, he won't be going now, will he?"

"You don't seem very shocked or upset about your friend's death," Charlie said.

"Look, Rolf was alive and talking to Becky when I left. I had an important meeting first thing that I couldn't get out of, so I slipped off. But… of course I'm shocked. Now, if you please…"

Mr Baron tried to take the ticket from my fingers, but I snatched it back. "*I'll* give it to the police."

"As you wish," he said. "Now I really must go. I'm due in the House."

Charlie raised his hat as Neville Baron hurried away.

"Oh drat, we forgot to ask him what he was looking for in Hengleberg's flat."

"No, we did ask him, Lady Joanie. But he refrained from telling us."

"You're right. Come on, let's go back to the bakery and wait for Uncle Frog to get in touch. We can give your grumpy inspector this train ticket."

Charlie and I glanced up at the sound of raised voices. Neville Baron was now shouting at a man who was clearly *not* a fellow politician. He was dressed in a bowler hat and pinstripe suit, and he was holding a notepad and pencil. Ah, the politician's favourite… a journalist.

Neville Baron shouted angrily over his shoulder. "Leave me alone, Volfson, I mean it!"

Volfson? Where had I heard that name before? It rang a bell… oh yes… the Volfsons were a clan from Marvelton. *This* Mr Volfson had inherited the family traits of thick curly hair, a stocky build, and long fingernails. As we approached him, I could practically taste his magical vibes. Perhaps he could give us a little info…

He ignored us, engrossed in his notebook.

190

I cleared my throat. "Ahem!"

"What?" he growled.

"What do you know about The Right Honourable Neville Baron?"

He waved his notepad at me. "Everything."

"Good. I'd like to know his voting record."

"What's it worth?"

Charlie loomed. "You get to keep your teeth intact."

Mr Volfson raised a cool eyebrow. Charlie had no idea what he was messing with. If it came to it, Charlie might not get to keep his *throat* intact.

"What my colleague means is..." I lowered my voice. "… if you don't tell us everything you know about Mr Baron's voting record, I'll tell your editor that his political correspondent is actually a werewolf."

The journalist flashed me his fangs. "You wouldn't dare!"

I stood my ground, gazing firmly into his yellow eyes. "I'm almost a senior witch. I do hope I won't need to show you what I'm capable of."

We stared at each other for a few tense seconds.

The journalist blinked first. *Yes!*

"Very well," Mr Volson said. "Neville Baron's main focus right now is the Regulation of Drugs Act. He's vocally opposed to alcohol, and wants gin banned from the working classes – deeming them too feeble-minded to handle it."

Charlie grumbled. "He certainly wouldn't get *my* vote."

Mr Volson looked Charlie up and down. "Luckily for him, *you* don't get a vote."

The two men launched into a debate over the working man's right to vote – which didn't yet exist in 1916. I blocked them out and thought about what we'd just discovered: Neville Baron was anti-drugs, and yet he was possibly displaying the symptoms of cocaine abuse...

I smiled politely. "Thank you for your help, Mr Volfson."

The journalist tipped his hat as we walked away.

"What are you thinking Lady Joanie?" Charlie asked. "Apart from how hypocritical Neville Baron is."

"I think that whatever he wanted so badly from Rolf Hengleberg's flat was highly incriminating. And I *really* want to know what it was."

Chapter Seven

Charlie and I took the bus back to the bakery, to discover that the late Rolf Hengleberg's body had been removed. Poor, dear soul…

The door was open, so we stepped inside, looking for Inspector Grumpy – or should I say, Detective Sergeant Parry. There were a couple of uniformed coppers dusting for fingerprints. But no sign of the Sergeant.

"Perhaps he's in the kitchen?" I said.

Charlie and I crept successfully past the police officers but, as we walked into the kitchen, I halted in shock – and Charlie crashed into the back of me.

"Oh!" I gasped.

Becky and George sprung guiltily apart from their kiss! Becky smoothed down her blouse. "Your… your ladyship… Mr Anderson… how can I help?"

"You two are sweethearts?" I asked.

"Please don't tell anyone," George said. "My uncle doesn't approve."

"But I thought your uncles were friends?" I said.

Unless one of them had recently stabbed the other in the throat with an ice pick, of course…

"They *were* friends," George said. "Years ago. But… I think it's the German connection. It's dashed unfair, but there we have it. We must keep our love secret. I don't care though. Becky will wait for me to come home, then we'll marry."

Charlie leaned against the counter. "Your deployment's been delayed?"

George was still wearing his uniform. "I presented myself at the recruiting office, as arranged, but this police fella arrived and told me not to go today. Said he was a detective investigating the death of Rolf Hengleberg. Well, obviously I came straight here to see Becky."

The cogs in my brain started to whirr. Could *George* have stabbed Rolf Hengleberg with the ice pick when he'd left this morning? Becky had been downstairs with us, and it would've been the work of a moment to stab Rolf, then push him forward so he was slumped over – seemingly deep in thought.

George's motive was clear. He and Becky wanted to be together. Herr Hengleberg had admitted last night how heavily he relied on his niece. Had George decided to cut her free of him… forever?

But then again, Uncle Frog said that these two youngsters were due to die tomorrow. Worry tingled down my spine. Could *I* save them? "Becky, I thought you were going to stay with a friend? Perhaps you should leave this area? Just in case…"

Becky nodded slowly. "I will. I was about to leave, when George arrived. George will accompany me to my friend's house, and I'll stay with her."

"Make sure you tell the police where you're staying," Charlie said. "They might want to question you further."

She nodded sadly. "I will."

"George," I said. "Becky mentioned earlier that she overheard your two uncles having words yesterday. Do you know anything about that?"

George frowned. "Not really. I can't say I'm on good terms with Uncle Neville after he voted for conscription. My brother… is gone."

"*And* Mr Baron voted for the internment of Germans," Becky said quietly.

"Yes," George said. "He's not exactly a favourite around here. I say, perhaps *that's* what Uncle Neville was arguing with Mr Hengleberg about – the internment of aliens. Perhaps his government is planning even harsher laws?"

"That could be it." Becky bit back her tears. "Uncle Rolf was very low this morning. When Mr Anderson very kindly made us some coffee, my uncle was talking to me about the possibility of leaving London. Returning to Germany. After all these years."

Returning to Germany, via Carlisle, I wondered.

I realised I was still holding the train ticket that Neville Baron had given me – the one he'd taken from Herr Hengleberg's coat this morning.

I started to ask Becky if she knew anything about her uncle's plans to go to Carlisle, but a young female voice called from the main space of the bakery. "Becky? Are you here?"

"Oh, that's Anne – she must've heard about what happened. Do excuse me, Lady Joanie – this is the friend who I will stay with."

George picked up Becky's suitcase and the two of them went off with Anne.

I gazed at the train ticket. "I had hoped to ask her if she knew about her uncle's *definite* plans to leave London."

"Never mind," Charlie said. "We'll hand it to Sergeant Parry when we next see him."

"All right." I smiled at Charlie. "Any thoughts on George? He could've done it whilst we were all still down in the cellar. The murder took place between Becky coming down to the cellar – after you'd just brought me my tea – and us coming up to the bakery for breakfast. George was up here alone with Herr Hengleberg as he was leaving. What if it *wasn't* an intruder *or* Neville lurking, but George?"

"George doesn't really have a motive, does he?"

"What if George wanted to set Becky free from her uncle – who'd come to rely *so* heavily on her that he didn't even know how many sugars he took in his coffee. He said so himself."

Charlie considered this. "My money's still on Neville Baron. He was the one who lied about the air raid. And he could've easily snuck back in and done the deed while we was in the cellar."

"Perhaps…"

We didn't get any further than that, because a uniformed officer stepped into the kitchen. "We're carrying out a thorough search of this crime scene – every nook and cranny."

"I'm sure you're doing a sterling job, constable," I said.

"Yes, I am, missus. And *that* includes me telling you two to clear off *now*."

So, duly ousted, we cleared off.

Chapter Eight

It was rather chilly on this October afternoon, but the sun was shining, and the sky was gloriously blue. We were still waiting to hear back from Uncle Frog with news on how to get home, so Charlie and I decided to take a stroll in Hyde Park.

I adored the lush landscape of this London park in the spring and summer, but the autumn always brought spectacular scenes of its own. As we walked along, I was beguiled by sunbeams as they shone down on the red, gold, and yellow leaves.

The grass was muddy today, so we stuck to the wide walkways – perfect for a meandering stroll. I inhaled deeply – breathing in the stillness all around. The musky autumn aromas floated into my nostrils, filling me up with snuggly warmth.

Chatting casually and taking in the sights, Charlie and I strolled all the way down to the Albert Memorial Statue – which stood proudly opposite the Royal Albert Hall. In the centre of the ornate podium, below a lofty gothic spire, sat the gilded figure of Prince Albert himself. And on each corner of the podium was a large marble sculpture, commemorating the global reach of the Empire. Those Victorians really knew how to do architecture.

I gazed up into the blue sky, letting my soul unravel into nature and nostalgia. Being out here nourished my nervous system after a night cooped up in that cellar. Nothing could go wrong here.

But… oh drat! My witchy instincts sensed a cloudy gloom of foreboding and…

Lord Vilnius stepped out from behind the Albert Memorial Statue.

"Joanforth… fancy meeting you here in 1916. And your… human."

If he'd had a moustache, he'd be twirling it. He certainly knew how to make an entrance. And he always looked so cool, in his fedora hat, leather jacket, and buckled boots. He was grinning like a smug cat – a vampire smile. And like a vampire *and* a cat, he seemed ready to pounce…

Charlie tensed like a steel rod. "*You…*"

"Yes, me."

Without taking his deep brown eyes off me, Lord Vilnius held up a golden object, about the size of a teapot, which he tossed in the air and caught skilfully. "Recognise this, Joanie?"

I frantically tried to think of an escape plan… "It's a golden lion."

"It's *the* golden lion. The next magical gem. And – you'll never believe this – but I've just walked into the British Museum and lifted this baby from under its glass case. Humans are so trusting, aren't they?"

Charlie spoke in a deep growl. "Why are you still here then?"

"Because I want the silver rose. And if you don't give it to me, Joanforth, not only will *you* regret it for the rest of your life, but any children you may have will also regret it. And grandchildren. And great-grandch –"

"Yes, all right, Vincent, we get the picture. But there's just one problem with your plan."

"I don't think so…"

"Oh *yes*…" I grabbed Charlie's hand and hastily cast the Invisibility spell. "I'll never give you the silver rose!"

Charlie and I ran off, leaving Lord Vilnius to his fury, as he tried to figure out which way we'd fled. "Joanforth, where are you! I'll get you for this!"

My magic was weak, but it did the trick – giving us just enough cover to escape. Holding hands, Charlie and I whooshed back to visible in the middle of the grass, scaring a couple of pigeons, who flapped away. But we'd lost that nefarious villain. For now.

We didn't dare stop running yet though.

"Where to?" Charlie shouted.

My mind *and* legs rushed frantically. "No idea! But it won't take him long to find us. Quick, let's head for that crowd of people on the grass over there. We can try to blend in!"

I quickly realised that Charlie and I would never blend in with this crowd, because it was made up of about a hundred British Army officers. All male, of course – so no witches or working-class folk. But my spirits soared as I realised that the officers were all gathered around a light aircraft. A Sopworth Triplane! Gosh, this must be one of the first outings for this plucky English plane!

I pulled Charlie behind a nearby army truck, and we scrabbled into the open back. The metal frame of this vehicle was covered in a tough, green material and it was tall enough inside for us to stand comfortably. A good hiding place for now.

Charlie and I still had our fingers linked together as we stood opposite each other on the metal floor of the truck. My eyes skimmed over his smiling lips. Gosh, he was dishy. He was an enigma – sweet and youthful, yet strong and masculine. Those sparkling blue and brown eyes were captivating – mischievous, but kind.

He was still a little out of breath. "Are you all right, Lady Joanie?"

"Hm? What?"

"It's just… *that* was a close one."

"It is… *was*…"

He smiled tenderly, making my heart skitter.

I felt exhilarated. But *surely* my excitement was merely the aftermath of our confrontation with Lord Vilnius. Detective Constable Charlie Anderson was *not* the reason for this delightful joy within me, was he? Not I, Lady Joanforth Eldritch – always so cool and in control. Nope… I refused to allow it.

I stepped away from Charlie, disconnecting our fingers and staring fiercely through the back flap of the truck. Charlie moved behind me to look over my shoulder, meaning we were almost touching again. *Gah*! Perhaps I should just kiss him and get it over with… But *that* might make things worse...

I focused my attention on a high-ranking Royal Flying Corps officer who was standing next to the plane, giving a demo to the gathered crowd. This Brigadier General was a musty, crusty old soldier who seemed as stiff and stuffy as his over-starched uniform. Yes, let's focus on *him*…

Charlie spoke in a loud whisper. "I remember hearing about this the first time around. It's a

Sopworth Triplane. The British government's defence against the German Fokkers."

"Charlie, there's no need for that language!"

"That's what the German planes are called, Lady Joanie."

"Oh of course. I knew that..."

I gazed at the triplane. It was a small, flimsy yellow aircraft, with three sets of wings all stacked on top of each other. There was a single cockpit and tiny wheels – which looked in danger of detaching at any moment. And yet, this little aircraft might be our ticket out of here…

I let the flap of the truck close. "Charlie, it won't take long for Lord Vilnius to catch up with us. I doubt he'll cast the Locator spell, because *his* magic is weak here too, so he won't want to waste it. But he's cunning and intelligent."

Charlie held his head high. "Then let him come. I can fight him."

"You're very brave. But he wants the silver rose. And he'll do anything to get it."

"Well, *we* need the golden lion, don't we? *And* the time controls? We'll have to confront him sooner or later."

"That's true. But we must evade him until we can come up with a plan." I glanced at my fingernails. "I… er… I bet I could fly that plane."

He looked unconvinced. "*You* can fly a plane?"

"Yes, actually. I've done it once before. For larks. A friend of mine back in 1926 is an aviatress. She let me have a go."

Charlie pulled back the flap. "We'll never get near it."

I glanced inside the truck and espied a pile of British army uniforms. "Hmm... I've an idea... Ready to get back into uniform, Charlie?"

He frowned at the pile of clothing, realised my plan, and groaned.

We stood with our backs to each other and quickly dressed in dark olive tunics and heavy woollen trousers – tucking our trouser legs into our knee-high socks. I laced up my clumpy leather boots and grabbed a peaked 'trench' cap. All the clothing was far too big for me but, as I turned and saw Charlie... well, let's just say he looked good in uniform.

"Sha-aaaaa jddrrr?" I asked. Oh gosh, he looked *so* good in uniform that I'd been rendered a blithering idiot!

He inspected me. "You make a very boyish soldier, your ladyship. But of course, there's just one vital thing you're missing." He chewed his lip pensively. "But then again, *I* haven't got one either."

"Er, what's that?"

"A moustache... up until 1916, well *this* year, all British soldiers had to have a moustache. By law!"

"Oh drat, I should've kept Mr Chaplin's fake moustache in 1906! Oh well, never mind – they'll probably forget about my lack of moustache when they're busy charging me with impersonating a soldier and stealing a military aircraft. Come along..."

He chuckled. "All right, let's get this over with."

I saluted theatrically, then slipped out of the truck and strode towards the triplane. Charlie marched along beside me.

The Brigadier General stuttered to a halt as he saw us.

"Oh don't worry about us, sir," I called over in a deep voice. "We're just here to show off the plane. Aren't we... Private Anderson?"

Charlie instinctively lowered his voice too. "Er... yes..."

I raised my arms and spoke quietly to Charlie. "Put your hands up like this. Pretend you're a glamorous magician's assistant – I think they might fall for it."

"A glamorous magician's assistant is basically what I *am*, isn't it?"

"Nonsense, darling. I'm a witch, not a magician."

Charlie held up his arms with a flourish and twirled his wrists, smiling like a loon.

I glamorously stroked the aircraft. "I say, Brigadier General, why don't you explain to the chaps how it works?"

The Brigadier General spoke through his moustache. "Er, well... first you must hand-start the aircraft's engines by swinging the propeller."

Charlie glamorously spun the propeller. "Like this, sir?"

"That's right."

I hoisted myself up into the cockpit, struck a sensual pose for a moment, then pulled on a pair of flying goggles. "And then what?" I called.

"It's quite simple," the Brigadier General said. "You need to start the ignition by flicking the control switch."

I gazed at the control panel in front of me. All the buttons and levers were clearly labelled, so I flicked the control switch. The propeller whirred.

I shouted above the roar of the engine. "And then I assume you use *these* levers for taking off and steering?"

"Jolly good guess, that… um… man…"

I got myself comfy. "And tell me, Brigadier, would one of the wings support the weight of a man?"

"Haven't ever tried it, old… boy…?"

"Ah. No time like that present then. Come on, Private Anderson, climb aboard."

Charlie twirled his arms and spoke through a gritted smile. "You're not serious, Lady Joanie!"

"Can *you* fly a plane, Charlie?"

He sighed wearily. "No."

"Come on, climb up."

Charlie waved to his audience like a magician's assistant who was about to be sawn in half – before tentatively hauling himself up to perch on the middle wing. He gripped the metal struts that held the three wings together, posing with his legs crossed like a glamour girl. The wood creaked under his strapping six-foot muscular weight. But we could do this. And if all else failed, I could use my magic to cast the Levitation spell and save us.

If indeed I had enough magic for such a powerful spell...

The plane controls were rather similar to my beautiful Rolls-Royce back in 1926. The brakes were on the floor by my feet but, instead of a steering wheel, I had a rudder like on a boat. *Unlike* my lovely Rolls-Royce, the triplane was crude and rickety. No wonder the pilots I'd known had called their planes 'crates'. The Sopworth Triplane felt as flimsy as a cardboard box.

I eased the throttle slowly to the side and we started to move. Hooray! But I quickly realised that the plane's centre of gravity was unbalanced, meaning the tail swung wildly from side-to-side as we gained speed along the grassy runway. And… oh dear… I'd just discovered another snag – the cockpit was so low that I could hardly see out the front. And what I *could* see was obscured by the whirring propeller.

I shouted at Charlie as we bounced across the grass of Hyde Park. "Hold tight and think of England!"

I glanced at him. He was still grinning like a glamorous assistant and waving one-handed to his public.

I eased the take-off lever backwards – making the flimsy aircraft rattle and the engine whine… But, *yes*! We left the grass with a wobbling judder and… we were flying!

I shouted to the gathered troops below. "Bring it back soon, I promise!"

Now… where should we fly to? Ah yes… I knew just the location.

Chapter Nine

There was only one place to go… the quaint little village of Maiden-Upon-Avon.

Now that we were sky-high, I actually felt quite comfortable, and flying conditions were perfect. It was a bright blue autumn day, and we weren't flying too high – no higher than a hot air balloon. The strong wind was blowing my hair around – after having blown my army cap off ages ago. But it was a fun adventure.

I glanced at Charlie, who was sitting on the wing, gripping the metal struts. The engine was far too noisy for us to talk, but I didn't need words to understand the expression on his face. It was a mixture of awe and disbelief.

I decided to follow the main highway all the way to Somerset. One thing the Romans *had* done for us was to build a lovely straight road between London and Bath. And how wonderful Mother England looked from up here – a patchwork of green fields and leafy forests, with villages and towns dotted around the landscape. There were churches with tall spires, farmsteads with hedgerows, and gushing rivers that flowed into meandering streams.

I shouted above the engine. "Look, Charlie, it's Stonehenge!"

He smiled as we flew over that mystical monument of giant stones, which had been arranged in a perfect circle by ancient Britons to celebrate the summer solstice. How lucky we were to have such wonderful sights in our glorious, green and pleasant land.

And then, at last, I spotted Locksleigh Manor far below. Locksleigh's top field was a short distance from the manor house, so I eased the take-off lever forwards and we began our bumpy descent back to earth. We clattered along the grass, until I skilfully brought the plane to a halt.

I pushed up my goggles to my forehead and grinned at Charlie. "Well, I think we've lost Lord Vilnius."

Charlie hopped off the wing and stumbled, regaining his land-legs. "Good work, Lady Joanie. And now there's only one thing I need…"

"Cup of tea?"

"I thought you'd never ask… Who owns this house?"

As we strolled across the field, I explained that Locksleigh Manor had been in the Eldritch family for years, and it currently belonged to the Earl of Maiden, my Uncle Frog.

"Earl of Maiden?"

"Yes. Our neighbours, the Earl and Countess of Pornphan, reside in Maiden Manor on the other side of the village. We live harmoniously, but I must admit that back in 1926 we aristocrats are struggling to maintain our big houses. The war impacted us all in one way or another."

"It does seem unfair, begging your pardon, your ladyship. That your family should own all this *and* your London home."

"And we have a property in magical Marvelton. And… I do agree with you, Charlie. We can't stop progress."

Locksleigh Manor was beautiful though, and I would be sad to see it sold. It was nestled at the end of the Maiden-Upon-Avon High Street, and it was like magic for the eyes, with its picturesque, wisteria-clad Tudor part, tacked onto the grand Victorian wing. The surrounding land consisted of ancient woods, green fields, and wildflower meadows, as well as a few secret gardens where one could stroll, sit, and read – or simply enjoy the tranquillity.

But for now, I saw our loyal housekeeper, Mrs Evans, striding across the lawn towards us, probably wondering why a triplane had just landed in the top field.

I waved at her "Coo-ee, Mrs Evans. It's me, Lady Joanforth."

Mrs Evans did not wave back. She'd previously worked for the royal household at Buckingham Palace during the reign of Queen Victoria, and she still embodied those strict Victorian values. She always wore a long black dress with a stiff high collar, and her iron-grey hair was always tied back in a severe bun. If I hadn't been such a brave witch, I might've been a little intimidated. But she was a wonderful housekeeper, and we trusted her to take care of Locksleigh while we were in London or Marvelton.

As Mrs Evans joined us, my attention was seized by the little puppy she was clutching in her arms. Wispu wriggled as she saw me, excited by our reunion. Oh *yes*! I'd forgotten that I'd brought Wispu here as a puppy to protect her during the war. My heart surged with love. How I'd missed her since Charlie and I had been stranded in time!

I gently took young Wispu from Mrs Evans, hugging her woolly lamblike body against myself. She yapped with joy. "Hello, darling... oh you're so sweet!"

Mrs Evans needed answers. "Your ladyship, we weren't expecting you back so soon."

"Oh... er... I took an aeroplane for a test flight – all very hush-hush. For the Royal Flying Corps. So... I thought I'd pop in."

"But, my lady, we only got your telegram yesterday. From Belgium!"

"Yes. That's the beauty of flight, you see."

"I see." She looked me up and down. "And I suppose that's why you're dressed as a soldier?"

"Precisely. Now, Mrs Evans, if you'd be so kind to arrange some tea? This is my guest, Mr... um... Private... no, not private, you wouldn't approve of that. This is Captain Anderson."

Charlie snorted at the very thought. "Captain, indeed!"

Mrs Evans nodded tightly, then started to walk away, but she turned back. "Oh, your ladyship... there's a young woman here. Her car broke down in the village this morning, and I said she was welcome to stay until it's repaired. I trust that is acceptable?"

"Of course, Mrs Evans – the more the merrier. Where is this young lady?"

"I believe she's busying herself in the hospital part of the house, your ladyship. I'm given to understand

210

that she's an auxiliary nurse, like your ladyship. She wanted to be useful while she's here."

"I like her already."

Mrs Evans smiled curtly, then turned and scooted off.

I kissed Wispu on the head, making her little tail wag excitedly in my arms.

"This is Wispu?" Charlie ruffled her ears. "I thought she was a stray."

"Oh she isn't *my* dog. But I wanted her to be safe during the war, so I brought her here. But she's a very independent lady, aren't you, darling, yes you are!"

Charlie raised an eyebrow. "They do say dogs are like their owners. Not that you *are* Wispu's owner, of course."

"Precisely. Now let's have some tea. And we'll find out who this mysterious young visitor is."

After a refreshing cuppa and a slice of our cook's mouth-watering Victoria sponge, I led Charlie to a large, high-ceilinged room. Previously a library, the bright and airy space was currently crammed with camp beds containing convalescing officers. There were a couple of nurses in attendance, but I couldn't see our visitor.

Then at the end of the space, I noticed a young woman dressed in a cotton blouse and long skirt, standing behind a high wooden table. She was mixing medicine from an assortment of glass bottles – fully absorbed in her task. Her long hair was wisping out of her 1916 knotted bun, and she'd stuck a pencil behind her ear. What an intriguing young woman…

I halted in front of the table. "How do you do, I'm Lady Joanforth Eldritch."

She looked up and blinked, as if coming back to earth. "Oh… how do you do, your ladyship. It's ever-so kind of you to let me wait here while my motorcar is being repaired. I hope you don't mind, but I was just going through your medicine dispensary and putting a few things in order."

I glanced at the bottles of colourful liquids. "I trust you *know* about dispensing medicines?"

"A little, yes. I'm studying for my apothecary's examination. You see, I prefer chemicals to nursing."

"Really? Not very keen on blood. eh?"

"Oh, I don't mind blood. But I enjoy working alone, and it's fascinating to discover the effects that these chemicals have on one's body."

I realised that the bottle in her hand was sporting a skull and crossbones motif. "And I assume that this one would have a very final effect on one's body!"

She smiled kindly. "You're right, your ladyship. But you see, it's the dosage not the chemical that's dangerous. For example, cyanide can be found naturally in apples and almonds, which are perfectly safe. But if the cyanide is distilled and given in a higher dosage, then it will be fatal."

"Yes, I see. And what's this you're doing here?"

"Oh, this is a sleeping draught that I've prepared for some of the men. The nurse mentioned that a few of them are having dreadful nightmares."

Charlie spoke severely. "Poor chaps have been through hell."

The young woman winced. "So I believe, sir. And I'm sure this will help. But I will warn the nurses to

212

be careful. It's far too easy to take too much of this drug. You only need a quarter of a teaspoon for it to be effective – and just a few grains can be too many. Then it's all over."

A realisation trickled into my brain. "Wait a minute, you said it's a sleeping draught?"

"Yes, it's called barbitone. I do wish doctors would stop prescribing it to the general population. You see, the trouble is, it takes about an hour to work, so often people will take more when they think it's not working. Then they've taken too much and… they've had it."

My thoughts shuffled into place. Becky Hengleberg had said that her uncle sometimes took a sleeping draught. And Neville Baron was showing clear signs of substance abuse…

"Is it addictive?" I asked.

"Oh yes – highly."

I took Charlie to one side. "Listen, I know I'm clutching at straws here, but I wonder if Herr Hengleberg's sleeping draught has something to do with Neville Baron? What if Neville was unable to get his usual supply of dope, and he knew Hengleberg had some in his flat, so he thought he'd invent the air raid and steal it?"

"It's a bit of a reach, Lady Joanie."

"Yes, but…"

I realised the dispenser was watching us carefully. "Everything all right, your ladyship?" she asked with concern.

I smiled reassuringly. I was reluctant to distress this nice young woman with the details of a grisly murder. "Everything's quite well. So, um… where did you gain your exemplary knowledge of drugs?"

She spoke proudly. "In Torquay – at the war hospital. I met some thoroughly decent chaps there. Some of the Belgian refugees were particularly mysterious. Clever too."

"Oh? Mr Anderson and I have both been to Belgium. I was… I *am* an auxiliary nurse."

"We *are* there," Charlie muttered.

The young woman fiddled with her potions. "Actually, pharmaceuticals aren't my real interest… I'm a writer of novels."

"A writer? Or novels? But how wonderful!"

"Well, I'm calling myself a writer, But, alas, my novel was rejected."

"Oh I am sorry. But I'm sure you're terribly clever."

"You're very kind, your ladyship. And I ought not to be worrying about my own trivialities when there's a war on."

"Oh but you must! Now more than ever we need to escape into fiction, or music, or a new dance craze. It's what life's all about – what makes us *feel* alive. I wish you the best of luck. Tell me your name, so I can say I've met you when you're famous!"

Her eyes twinkled. "I'm Mrs Christie, your ladyship. Agatha Christie… Oh I say, your ladyship, you've got very pale. Are you quite all right?"

Charlie drew me into his arms. "She's all right, Mrs Christie… Come along, Lady Joanie, let's leave Mrs Christie to her poisons… And… Mrs Christie, as her ladyship said, don't give up on your novel. I have a feeling it's going to be a terrific success!"

Chapter Ten

Charlie supported me by the arm as I staggered back out into the October sunshine. I was trembling all over… *I'd just met one of my literary heroes!* How marvellous!

Charlie was excited too. "Hey, we should ask Agatha Christie to help us solve the murder!"

I pulled my arm away from his strong, commanding grip… *swoon*… "We can't ask Agatha Christie to help us solve the murder, Charlie. Uncle Frog said we mustn't change anything. We're not even supposed to be here."

"Lady Joanie, Agatha Christie is *the* Queen of Crime! What harm could it possibly do?"

"Well, for starters, she doesn't yet *know* she's the Queen of Crime… what if she enjoys solving our murder so much that she decides to join the police, or something? I'm not being held responsible for depriving the world of *The Murder of Roger Ackroyd*! It's one of the cleverest plot twists in the history of literature. Come on, let's put the murder on the backburner for now and try and think of a plan to get the golden lion off Lord Vilnius when we get back to London."

"Without *him* stealing the silver rose from us…"

"Precisely."

We strolled across the lawn in silent contemplation. Charlie halted. "There is one thing that would definitely work."

I stopped too. "Oh yes?"

"Yeah." He raised a sly eyebrow. "We hit him where it hurts…"

"Er… you're not actually talking metaphorically, are you?"

"Nope."

I considered this. Could something *that* base ever work against one of the most powerful sorcerers in all of Marvelton? Well, everyone had their weak spot, didn't they? "It's actually quite a good plan, Charlie. But we'll need to lure him to us – take him unawares. Hey, perhaps we can set a trap. Use the silver rose as bait!"

"I like your thinking, Lady Joanie. Right, how about this? When we're about to leap back home, we'll entice him to us, then *you* pretend to hand over the silver rose. At that moment, I'll knee him in the whatsits, you shove him to the floor, and we'll both grab the golden lion and time controls – then we'll leave straight away for 1926. Agreed?"

"Agreed!" We shook on it. His vibrant energy tingled up my arm like a fizzing tonic of pure loveliness.

Charlie turned to inspect the outside of the manor house, with all its beautiful surroundings. I was pleased he liked it here. He gestured towards a barn that stood on the woodland-side of Locksleigh Manor. "What's in there?"

I felt like a tour guide. "That's the Long Barn, darling. It's a working barn, and full of nothing very interesting. Just farming machinery, sacks of animal feed, and bales of straw – boring."

He grinned, "Boring… unless you like rolling around in the hay."

I shrugged. "Been there, tried it… found it too prickly…"

He laughed, then turned to the barn on the other side of the lawn. "And that one?"

"That barn's currently being used as a canteen for the officers here. Mrs Evans supervised the conversion, and she's created a lovely space for the men to relax and enjoy decent, home-cooked food."

Charlie gazed pensively down the long winding driveway. "You know what, Lady Joanie? That officer's barn would make a great location for a tearoom after the war. The villagers could walk up the driveway there, enjoy a refreshing cuppa in the café, then stroll around the grounds. You said you needed to make money in 1926 to support your various houses. What do you think?"

"Can you really imagine *me* serving tea and cake to the public, Charlie?"

"Yes, actually I can! You'd be very entertaining. But, of course, not any old cakes. They'd be Magic Cakes!"

I allowed his enthusiasm to buoy me up. Perhaps when we got back, Charlie and I might run it together… No. *I* was going to become a senior witch and serve the magical community in that way. Someone else would have to do Charlie's Magic Cakes Café idea. One of my relatives, perhaps…

"What's around the back of the house?" he asked.

"I'll show you."

With little Wispu trotting beside us, we made our way to the back of the Tudor wing, where Uncle Frog had recently planted a baby magnolia tree. It was fragile and tiny, with its golden leaves falling all around. I hoped one day, in decades from now, it might be as tall as the house…

We turned away from the magnolia tree at the sound of men laughing.

"Oh look," I said. "Some of the fitter chaps are putting on a play. What fun."

We sat on the grass to watch. Wispu flopped down on my lap and I stroked her soft fur.

"What play is it?" Charlie asked.

"*Romeo and Juliet*," I said. "I love this play. I was there at the opening night of the very first production."

"What! It's Shakespeare, isn't it?"

"Yes, darling. He was never sure about the… what?"

"How old *are* you, Lady Joanie?"

"Old enough to know never to answer questions like that."

"My apologies. But you must've known so many different people. Don't you ever get… lonely?"

"I must admit I'd never understood all that *star-crossed lovers* nonsense before…" I trailed off, gazing into Charlie's lovely eyes, and feeling the fizzle of fireworks in my heart.

"But something's changed?" he asked sincerely.

"Let's watch the play. Juliet's about to kill herself. Such jolly good larks."

I tried to ignore him as he inspected the side of my face. He spoke in a low voice. "I like being here with you, in the sunshine. It's better than my life in 1926 with Inspector Parry. And it's certainly better than where I currently am in 1916."

"Don't think of it, Charlie. You survived."

"It's strange wearing an army uniform again."

I glanced at my own oversized uniform. "Well, *I* have plenty of clothes here to change into, and I know Uncle Frog has a suit or two you can try."

"Hold on, is Uncle Frog here? The Uncle Frog of this time, I mean?"

"No. He spent most of the war in Marvelton. It was around the time of the evil princess debacle. She's probably kissing him into a frog-headed wizard as we speak."

Charlie leaned a little closer. "I wonder what *I'd* turn into if *you* kissed me. Nothing bad, I'm sure. Perhaps you could turn me into a handsome prince."

I turned to face him. "Well you're already jolly handsome – as I'm sure you know. And *I've* always believed that status is a state of mind. Do you *feel* regal?"

"I do when I'm with you, Lady Joanie."

"Well then, there's no need for me to kiss you. You're already a handsome prince."

I turned back to watch the play, wishing Charlie didn't have such a hold on my heart. But I quickly relaxed as two butch soldiers jovially acted out the final scene of *Romeo and Juliet*. Both actors were sporting impressive, bushy moustaches – even the one pretending to be a teenage fair maiden. It was all very silly and jolly good fun.

Romeo theatrically drank the poison and then Juliet awoke to find her beloved dead, so she melodramatically stabbed herself with his dagger, staggering around and taking ages to die. None of the soldiers could stop laughing – even the ones on stage.

Then, after a round of bows, curtsies, and manly backslapping, the soldiers bustled off for tea and biscuits.

"If only Juliet had waited a few minutes more…" I mused.

"I don't really understand what just happened," Charlie said. "It's like a foreign language to me."

"Oh, well you see, Romeo and Juliet wanted to be together against the wishes of their rival families. So they devised a cunning plan. Juliet sent Romeo a message saying she would pretend to be dead and await Romeo in her family crypt, then they'd run off together. But Romeo didn't get the message, so when he found her and *thought* she was dead, he glugged down an entire bottle of poison and died. Juliet then woke up, found *him* dead, and killed herself."

Charlie stroked Wispu, who'd fallen asleep. "That must be how George and Becky feel. You know, because of Neville Baron not approving of their relationship. And Rolf Hengleberg not wanting her to grow up and leave him."

"Yes… I wonder how Sergeant Parry's getting on with his murder enquiry."

"Haven't *you* got any ideas, your ladyship? You worked out the last one in 1906."

I thought about the case. "The trouble is, it could've easily been an intruder off the street, couldn't it? The anti-German brigade."

"But it *could've* been Neville Baron. He's possibly been using dope, and perhaps he *did* want to steal the sleeping draught from Herr Hengleberg's flat – as you suggested."

"It's possible, isn't it? And whatever this thing was that he needed *back* from Hengleberg, well… it might've been damning proof of his drug habit. Neville said he was going through Hengleberg's coat pockets, so maybe a letter, or something?"

"But," Charlie said. "If Neville was in the Palace of Westminster at the time of the murder – as he claims he was – then he'll have alibis coming out of his ears."

"True. I'm sure Sergeant Parry will be checking those very closely."

"He certainly will. So… then there's George. He had the perfect opportunity to stab Hengleberg while we were down in the cellar with Becky. We saw him leave."

"And George's motive was to set Becky free from her uncle?"

"Hmm… there must be something we're missing. It might be nice to go back to the bakery and have a proper look around. We haven't been able to do that yet."

"Yes," I said. "We might discover something the police have overlooked."

Charlie nodded. "And also, it'll be good to know more about the nature of the victim. It might give us a clue. I read that in one of Mrs Christie's stories."

My heart squeezed with affection – I'd met Agatha Christie! And now we needed to think like her little Belgian detective… "Charlie, there's something that did strike me as strange at the bakery. You'll say it's nothing, but it's on my mind. Why were there thirteen cups but fourteen saucers? It feels… wrong."

"If I may say, that sounds rather superstitious, Lady Joanie." He gazed tenderly at me. "But we probably shouldn't dismiss *your* instincts."

"Quite right! And if Becky and George are due to die tomorrow – as Uncle Frog said – then we should try to prevent it if we can."

"Or at least discover who did it, so they can face justice."

"Yes. And we ought to return the plane to Hyde Park. Uncle Frog told us not to change anything – and stealing a plane is quite a big something."

He grinned playfully. "I suppose I'm on the wing on the flight back, am I?"

I laughed. "You could catch the train if you'd prefer?"

"I don't want to let you out of my sight. What if Lord Vilnius pops up again?"

"You're sweet, but I think I can probably keep him at bay with my magic."

"Exactly – why do you think I want to stick with you!"

Chapter Eleven

It was late afternoon by the time we got back indoors, so Charlie and I split up to bathe, rest, and change. I dug out a pair of tweed culottes and a simple blouse, and Charlie dressed himself in a quality suit of Uncle Frog's.

We intended to get going straight away, but the smell of dinner persuaded us to stay, so we ate at the long table in the lavish dining room, sharing stories, laughing like loons, and opening up to each other.

I wasn't known for my sentimentality, but sitting there opposite Charlie, eating good food and drinking fine wine… we could've easily been husband and wife – this could've been *our* home.

But, like Romeo and Juliet, we were too different. Actually… we weren't very different. In fact, we had a lot in common. But we were from different backgrounds. And apparently that mattered a lot to society, even in our time of 1926.

But perhaps society was wrong?

As the sun rose over England the next morning, I flew us back to London, and we left the plane on the dew-soaked grass of Hyde Park – scarpering before anyone caught us. Then we hurried to Maida Vale, hoping to have a snoop around Hengleberg's flat above the bakery – where we might find a clue to his murder.

When we arrived at the bakery building, the police were nowhere to be seen. Good – we didn't want them interfering! The local streets were gently waking up to this new day, but the bakery was silent and lifeless. Becky was staying with her friend, so a good snoop was in order.

To save my magic, Charlie set about picking the lock. "This shouldn't take long…"

I hugged myself to keep warm. My breath came out as mist. "Did you break into many places before the war?"

"I never said I was a nice person, Lady Joanie."

"Oh but you *are*. That's how I know you must've had a reason."

"I was taught by bad people. I've told you that already." The lock clicked and he held the door open for me. "I never burgled a home when I was a thief. I broke into one shed and one shop. I knew it wasn't right for me. That boat I stowed away on saved me from a life of crime."

"I'm glad."

We shared a smile.

It was strange being back inside the bakery. It felt empty and… dead. But we didn't dare turn on the electric lights or even light a candle, in case the police rumbled us.

I sat down at one of the tables and pressed my Amulet of Seeing. "Let me just check in with Uncle Frog…"

His image whooshed up on my wrist. "Joanie, I'm having difficulty locating the exact spell to get you home. I'm not exactly sure what went wrong when you left 1906, and I'd like to find out before you try time travel again. Have you got the golden lion?"

"Not yet, Uncle – Lord Vilnius has it! We had an encounter with him, but thankfully escaped. And I still have the silver rose."

Charlie grinned. "Lady Joanie and I have come up with an elaborate plan to get both the golden lion *and* the time controls from him, which involves kneeing him in the whatsits."

Frog frowned. "In the what?"

"The whatsits," I said. "You know… his… *whatsits*…"

Frog croaked. "Oh there! Well… jolly good."

"But, Uncle, I wanted to check, are Becky and George still alive? You said they were due to die today."

"They're due to die this evening, so they ought to be fine for the moment. Oh, and by the way, I've also discovered that in the original history, Rolf Hengleberg's coroner found signs of liver damage during the post-mortem."

"Liver damage?" I said, confused. "Can you *get* that from being stabbed in the neck?"

"Perhaps it was caused by the sleeping draught?" Charlie said. "Becky implied that Rolf took it regularly for his sleeplessness. And Mrs Christie said barbitone causes all sorts of problems."

A thought buzzed in my brain. "I wonder… did one person try to poison him, then someone else stabbed him? Two killers; one victim?"

"Don't know, Joanforth," Uncle Frog said. "Whoever killed him was never caught. But if you can solve it, it might give you that extra boost for your journey home."

"We're trying to solve it," Charlie said. "And we'd better get on with it."

"Quite right, that man! Be in touch soon. Frog out!"

We went upstairs to the flat. I'd been up here yesterday after the murder, to change into Becky's 1916 clothes, but I hadn't discovered anything useful. Hopefully now that we were alone, Charlie and I could have a proper rummage.

The flat was rather old and creaky, with quite basic furnishings and scuffed whitewashed walls. Inside the main door, we were presented with a short landing and two bedroom doors. "You take Herr Hangleberg's room," I said. "I'll search Becky's."

Most of Becky's room was taken up by a single bed, an old wardrobe, and a writing desk. The carpet was threadbare, and she didn't have many clothes or possessions – but then again, she had packed a suitcase yesterday to take to her friend's house.

There was a large washbasin in one corner of the room and, as I stood in front of it, I noticed a smudge on the mirror. Oh... something had been *written* on the glass... written with someone's finger...

I turned on the hot tap, gasped in surprise, then called across the landing. "Come and look at this, Charlie!"

He stood behind me. "What is it?"

"Look, it's steaming up. Oh it's astounding!"

Charlie stared at me in the reflection. "It certainly is, Lady Joanie."

"Stop flirting with me, young man, and look at the writing It says *Exeunt*."

"What does that mean?"

226

"It means 'exit'."

"Why would Becky write that on her mirror?"

"No idea. I imagine she stood here gazing at her own reflection and… wrote it."

"But what was she exiting? Was she predicting the murder?"

"I don't think she's inherited her uncle's psychic powers."

Charlie stepped away from me and sat on Becky's bed, which boinged beneath him. "I don't mean to be rude to the deceased," he said. "But if Hengleberg was psychic, why didn't he see his death coming?"

"I think his temporal nodes were out of sync. That's why he predicted that I'd meet you after we'd already met."

"So what now?"

I stepped over to the bed and stood in front of Charlie. "Find anything in his room?"

"Nope. Not even a helpful bottle of barbitone."

"Hmm… I wonder if a fortune demon might assist."

His face remained deadpan. "A what?"

I rested my foot on the bed at his side, then pulled up my long skirt, revealing my magic wand tucked into my garter. Charlie's eyes bulged – possibly at my stocking-clad thigh. But perhaps also at my impressive wand.

As I held it in my hand, it tingled with magical potency.

He hadn't taken his eyes off it. "I saw this before, when I searched you at the nightclub. You said it was…"

"My magic wand."

"Blimey – s'cuse my language. What does it do?"

"It channels magic. As long as I have it about my person, I can cast spells. But soon, when I'm a senior witch, I won't need it anymore."

He gazed up at me from the bed. "How do you become a senior witch?"

"Hard work and lots of exams. I've recently passed my telekinesis exams with flying colours, which means I can now move objects with the power of my mind – providing there's enough magic available, of course."

"That's… incredible."

"Thank you, darling. And I jolly well hope magical time travel counts towards my final exams too!" I waved my wand through the air for effect. "Now, let's try summoning this fortune demon, yes?"

We both stood in front of the washbasin again, and I directed my wand towards the plughole, secretly hoping to impress my hunky partner in time travel… And for my next trick…

I closed my eyes and pretended to go into a trance. It wasn't necessary for the spell, but I felt sensual, tilting back my head and pouting seductively. I spoke in a low rumble. "*O fortune demon, foul and mighty, I command you come to Blighty, where I will ask for advice, then cast you back in just a trice!*"

As I opened my eyes, the plughole started to steam like a smouldering swamp in a haunted forest. The edges of the room faded and the air hissed like sand

228

falling through an hourglass. Charlie gasped as the head of the fortune demon slowly materialised upwards through the solid porcelain sink.

The demon certainly looked frightening, with his red reptilian skin, sharp fangs, and goat horns. But... weirdly, he was dressed in a satin opera cloak, with a top hat perched on his scaly head. And in his clawed hand he was clutching a silver-topped cane. Um... I hadn't been expecting him to be dressed like *this*...

"Woah..." Charlie whispered.

I spoke quietly to Charlie. "I'm allowed to ask him one question. And he's obliged to answer."

The demon fixed his beady eyes on me. His voice should've been booming and commanding, but actually he spoke in a reedy cockney accent. "Oh blinking heck, why now? You've just pulled me out of the opera. *La Witcha*. It's one of me faves."

"We'll put you back in a moment, demon. Now then..."

"Could we hurry this up, lady? I'm about to sing my aria."

"*You're* in the cast?"

"What's an aria?" Charlie asked.

"An operatic solo, darling."

The demon scowled. "Oh not *you*. Joanforth Eldritch, ain't it?"

"*Lady* Joanforth Eldritch. Have we met?"

"Is that your question? I'm only obliged to answer one, and so far you've asked me two."

"Don't get pedantic with me, O Foul and Mighty One. I have no recollection of ever meeting an opera-singing, cockney-speaking fortune demon before."

He waved a clawed hand. "Listen, missus, I operate on a multi-phase, quantum-dimensional, many-layered reality. I remember *everyone* I've met, will meet, and might meet in the grand scheme of time – be they human, witch, or... who's this?"

Charlie tipped his hat. "Detective Constable Charles Anderson."

The demon snorted suggestively. "Oh yeah, detective, is it? *I* see."

"What does that mean?" I asked. "What do you see?"

"If I had a shilling for every witch who becomes romantically entangled with an 'andsome copper, I'd be the richest demon in the underworld."

"Does it happen often?" Charlie asked.

"Witches and 'andsome coppers? More than you could ever imagine, me old mucker. Now can we get on? I've been training for my aria for seven millennia..."

"Yes. My question is... seven millennia? Opera wasn't even *invented* then..."

"I did just explain about multi-dimensional, time-dilating, quantum –"

"Yes, yes – enough of that. Right, my question is: how can we prevent the deaths of Becky Hengleberg and George Baron?"

The fortune demon's eyes snapped shut as he started to hum *Land of Hope and Glory*.

"What's it doing?" Charlie whispered.

The demon opened a red eye. "Oh '*it*', is it? How very charming. Demons are people too, you know."

"I thought you were keen to get back to your aria, Mister Demon," I said pointedly.

He scowled at me, then closed his eyes and started humming again.

I spoke quietly to Charlie. "I think he's having a rummage around in his quantum suitcase. Or something like that. Something to do with cats, anyway…"

The demon's eyes flew open. "Right. All I can tell you about Rebecca Hengleberg is that her mother was a magician's assistant back in Germany."

"Just like *you*, Charlie," I said playfully.

"And…" the demon said, "There's an engagement ring in her future. And an hotel. And then… death… Can I go now?"

"But… what does *that* mean?" Charlie asked. "I thought he was going to tell us how to prevent her from being killed. How to solve her uncle's murder."

The demon leered at Charlie. "Tch, so ungrateful. I am merely a conduit of information, matey – *you've* gotta work it out in your brain. Honestly, the treatment I get… I'm thinking about starting a union…"

I ignored the demon's gripes. "Is there anything you can tell us about The Right Honourable Neville Baron?"

"Oi! I'm only obliged to answer one question."

"Oh please help us, do!"

"Right, right, keep yer hair on… let's see… Oh, you might wanna check your Shakespeare, Lady Joanie…"

"Shakespeare? Why, is that something to do with Becky? Is *that* why she wrote *Exeunt* on her mirror? Becky and George are like *Romeo and Juliet*, is that it?"

The demon grinned knowingly. "Romeo and Romeo more like, hur hur."

"What does that mean?" Charlie asked.

My mind was suddenly filled with an image of the soldiers at Locksleigh acting out their moustached version of *Romeo and Juliet*. "Oh... I think I see what you're getting at."

"Right, good. Now, can you banish me please? If I hurry, I might get to perform the last forty-five minutes…"

I clicked my fingers. "Yes, be off with you."

The demon started to sing in Italian, as he was sucked back down the plughole.

Charlie stared at the white porcelain long and hard. "Did that really just happen?"

"I'm afraid so!"

We headed back down to the bakery. "Right, Charlie, let's have a think about what the demon just told us. A hotel is in Becky's future… Did you notice how quickly she packed her bag? She *said* it was because she was frightened of the anti-German brigade. But what if she was actually *planning* on leaving in a hurry?"

"You mean, to stay in a hotel? But where?"

"That's precisely what I intend to ask her."

Charlie followed me into the main space of the bakery. "How can we find her?"

"I could cast the Locator spell. But the trouble is, after summoning the fortune demon, I'm running out of magic."

"Is there no way for you to get more magic? In an emergency?"

"There are three ways I can replenish my magic – but it'll still be jolly weak."

"Oh yes?" He stood in front of me, wrapping me in his blue and brown gaze.

I was about to elaborate, but... the universe shifted, and *I* was under *his* spell. How infuriating! He was standing so close to me now that we were almost touching, and his intense gaze was drilling into me – making me feel scrutinised and squashed. I was *never* like this. *I* usually took whatever I wanted and had fun whilst I was about it. But this one mortal man made me feel... incredible...

I could see his very soul in those gorgeous eyes, and they reflected my own pure essence back at me.

The tension crackled in the air all around us. He stepped a little closer. "Lady Joanie? You were saying? About replenishing your magic?"

"Er yes. I can replenish my magic with either blood, sugar, or... se-haa*ha*..."

"Pardon?"

Oh drat! I'd never felt so helpless and yet so powerful in all my life. Quite frankly, I was desperate to kiss Charlie – to inform him that the other way for me to replenish my magic was with sex. Ha! That would shock him, wouldn't it – Mr Old Fashioned!

But I knew if I kissed him now, there'd be no going back. My heart and soul would forever belong to him. And that was… frightening.

He smiled tenderly. Oh, those luscious lips… I could easily stand on my tiptoes right now and claim him – just once to find out what it was like. But *that* would be like licking honey off a bumblebee. Sweet, fuzzy… then… spiky. Ouch!

Charlie took my hand in his. "Lady Joanie, you're trembling…"

"Yes… because… because my magic needs replenishing." I forced a cocky smile. "Luckily, we're in a bakery, so there's bound to be meat and cake galore!"

I strode off to the kitchen. Charlie followed. "But… what were you going to say?"

I rummaged through the pantry. "Hm? Say what? Oh look… I wonder what these big white beans are… Let's see, the label says 'butterbeans'. What the devil are those!"

"Lady Joanie? The other thing?"

"What other thing, darling?"

"You said there were three ways to replenish your magic. Blood, sugar, and…?"

I spoke through a mouthful of apple pie. "Er… I forget. But never mind. Look, I'll just eat all these cakes, and then I'll cast the Locator spell and we can find Becky – for a few more questions."

And then hopefully Charlie and I could return to our separate lives in 1926 – for my own sanity!

Chapter Twelve

It didn't take me long to scoff all the sausages, pies, and cakes – which topped up my weak magic a tad. Then, determined to speak to Becky, we rushed out to the street, closing the bakery door tight behind us.

"Where now?" Charlie asked.

"I'll quickly cast the Locator spell and then we can… *Oh look at this*!"

I stopped in my tracks, as I realised there was a chemist situated right next door to the bakery. It was a small, old Tudor building with tiny windows and a low, crooked door. But I'd just had a brainwave… "Let's pop inside."

The small shop was dominated by a wooden counter, which held a hefty cash register, and out the back was a cavernous room, crammed with shelves of pills and potions.

Standing behind the counter was a smart young woman wearing a crisp white coat. "Good morning, madam… sir…"

I spoke to Charlie out the corner of my mouth. "Take her out the back and distract her."

Charlie looked offended. "I beg your pardon!"

"Don't be so prudish – I don't mean seduce her. Just… take a sudden interest in chemistry."

"What are you going to do?"

"Snoop…"

Charlie folded his arms across his chest. "We could just try asking her."

I narrowed my eyes suspiciously. "What?"

"Allow me to demonstrate…" Charlie tipped his hat to the young woman, who was watching with interest. "Good day, miss… er…?"

"Miss Hawkins, sir."

"Miss Hawkins. I'm Detective Constable Anderson and this is Lady Joanforth Eldritch. I'm investigating a murder…"

"Oh good heavens, how dreadful, sir."

"It is. But her ladyship would like to ask you something." He gestured for me to step forward. "Your ladyship…"

I was briefly annoyed about having my exciting plan scuppered, but it probably *was* easier this way. "Miss Hawkins, thank you for agreeing to help. I was wondering if you could tell us anything about a prescription of barbitone you might've fulfilled for a Mr Rolf Hengleberg?"

She bent to open a filing cabinet under the counter. "Hmm… the name rings a bell, but… ah yes, here we are. Not for Mr Rolf though. It's for Miss Rebecca Hengleberg. See… the doctor prescribed it for her last week. She hasn't paid yet, but we're happy for patients to pay on tick, weekly, like."

"*Becky* was prescribed the sleeping draught?" I said. "Not… not her uncle? Charlie, I wonder if Becky asked the doctor for the barbitone on her uncle's behalf? She obviously knew he was having trouble sleeping. But perhaps he was too proud to ask for help himself, so she asked *for* him?"

"Oh no, madam," Miss Hawkins said. "The doctor wouldn't prescribe a strong drug like that without seeing the actual patient. Miss Hengleberg must've needed it for herself. Been having trouble sleeping, I expect. It's a worrying time for us all."

"Yes… trouble sleeping…" And slowly, another piece of the jigsaw slotted into place. "Thank you, Miss Hawkins."

I ushered Charlie back out into the street.

"What, Lady Joanie?" Charlie asked. "You've worked something out?"

"Why did Becky tell us that her *uncle* was having trouble sleeping if it was *her* who was under the doctor?"

"Well, as you said, perhaps she wanted it for her uncle. I mean, sleeplessness is easy to fake, isn't it? You probably just need to yawn a lot and play-act all drowsy like. Tell the doctor you're tossing and turning all night. That sort of thing."

"She faked her symptoms?"

Charlie shrugged. "Perhaps. But we do know that Herr Hengleberg showed signs of liver damage in his post-mortem. Your Uncle Frog said *that's* what the coroner said. So perhaps he did take the barbitone himself."

"Could Herr Hengleberg have *died* from the barbitone? Did he mean to take his *own* life?"

Charlie frowned. "He was alive when I was making the tea. And that stab wound to the neck – well, he would've died from that, undoubtedly."

"Yes. But, Charlie, I'm thinking about something Mrs Christie said…"

I was unable to finish my train of thought because Charlie had suddenly caught the attention of two women. Probably nothing unusual there. But these two were adorned with the purple, green, and white sashes of the Suffragettes… and they were carrying large white goose feathers.

Charlie tensed angrily as they halted in front of us.

The older of the pair proffered a white feather to Charlie. "For you, sir."

He scowled. "Don't be ridiculous."

"You're not in uniform," said the younger Suffragette.

"I am in uniform… somewhere…"

The older Suffragette frowned. "What on earth does that mean?"

I stepped forward. "It means, I should leave him alone if I were you."

But Charlie apparently wasn't going to leave them alone. "I don't understand you lot. I'm on *your* side. As a working-class man in 1916, *I* still don't have the vote neither. *I* support universal suffrage for women. But by going around humiliating men who ain't in uniform… you're doing the government's dirty work for them!"

The older Suffragette sneered. "How can you lecture us, when you ought to be in France, fighting for King and Country!"

"That's right," the younger Suffragette said. "If you're not in uniform, you get a white feather."

The older Suffragette snorted. "*Or* if you are in uniform but you disgrace it!"

"What does *that* mean?" I asked.

She searched for an example. "Well, such as yesterday… there was this young chap wearing his clean new uniform, and I sees him with me own eyes

238

coming out of an *anti-war* meeting down at the Town Hall."

The younger Suffragette tried to stuff a feather into Charlie's coat pocket as she spoke. "Yes, that was a real to-do – young soldier attending an anti-war meeting in *uniform* – I ask you!"

"Would you stop that!" Charlie said, moving away from her feather.

She ignored Charlie and continued with the story. "So I shoves a feather in his uniform pocket quick as I could, like. Naturally, the fella starts shouting at me, but then some German bloke starts defending me! Had a right old barney they did – in the street. So undignified. Un-British…"

"Yes, it was an odd business," the older Suffragette said. "The German fella was telling the young soldier that he oughta be proud to serve his King and Country. The world's turned on its head."

That sounded like George and Herr Hengleberg…

I gazed at the younger Suffragette's bundle of white feathers, suddenly realising that the long shafts were roughly the thickness of my little finger. *Ah-ha!* So it wasn't a piece of *bone*, after all.

I was about to ask them if they'd caught the names of the German man and the soldier but, as I glanced at the bakery door, I realised it was ajar. And I knew Charlie and I had shut it properly when we'd left.

It probably wasn't the police in there – because they didn't tend to sneak about in the dim light. In fact, judging by the smashed lock, it looked exactly like someone had broken into the bakery whilst we'd been in the chemist.

And I wanted to know who it was.

Chapter Thirteen

Charlie slipped his knuckleduster onto one hand and held his baton aloft with the other, then he led the way through the bakery door.

In the dim October light, we saw a man sitting with his back to us – bolt upright… very still… deep in thought.

He glanced at us as the door swung shut.

Charlie raised his baton higher. "Well, if it isn't the Right Honourable Neville Baron. What, may I ask, are *you* doing here?"

I resisted saying, *Returning to the scene of the crime…*

Neville Baron's face was deathly pale, emphasising the dark circles under his eyes. His voice was gruff. "I might ask *you* the same thing."

Charlie spoke smugly. "Well, I asked first. And *I'm* armed with a baton and knuckleduster."

"I… I came to say goodbye to my old friend."

Charlie tutted. "You *came* to find whatever it was you lied about the air raid for."

"No, I told you, I found that already. Yesterday morning – when I found the train ticket."

Charlie and I moved around to stand in front of Neville. "And what *was* the thing you wanted so badly from Herr Hengleberg?" Charlie asked. "Evidence of your hypocrisy and drug-taking junkie… ness?"

Oh dear. *I'd* worked this out earlier from the fortune demon's info. But the penny obviously hadn't yet dropped for Charlie.

"Er, Charlie...?" I said.

Neville Baron had shot to his feet. "How dare you, sir! I'm against drugs with every fibre of my being!"

"Oh yeah? So how do you explain the burn marks on your fingers? Because to *me* that's clear evidence of smoking a crack pipe."

Neville was aghast. "Crack pipe, indeed! You'd better explain yourself, young man!"

"I will," Charlie said. "When we saw you yesterday, you had black marks on your fingers. And don't try saying they were from smoking an ordinary tobacco pipe."

"I won't."

"Good."

"They were ink marks from my fountain pen. I've washed them off now, as you can see." Neville held up his hand. His very *steady* hand. Oh dear…

"And what about dark circles under your eyes?" Charlie asked. "And the being out of breath from walking? Clear signs of drug abuse!"

Neville spoke flatly. "I have asthma."

"Asthma?" Charlie asked quietly.

"Yes. And as for the dark circles under my eyes, well, I barely slept a wink the night before last because – as you know – I was ransacking Rolf's flat."

"And the shaking? You were shaking when we confronted you outside the Palace of Westminster."

"You'd just told me that my dear friend had been killed. It was a shock. And also... I was worried..."

"Worried we were *on* to you," Charlie said. "Because we were about to expose you as a murderer!"

Neville Baron's voice was suddenly flat and lifeless. "No…"

I spoke up. "You were worried that people might discover how you really felt about Rolf Hengleberg. *That* was what you were looking for in his flat, wasn't it? Evidence of how much you cared for him?"

Neville Baron glared at the table so hard I feared it might catch alight.

Charlie was baffled by this revelation. "*What*?"

"Think about it, Charlie – Rolf and Neville were two confirmed bachelors who were once very close but had a falling out. Do you understand what I'm suggesting?"

"Yes, Lady Joanie. But I'm shocked to hear such a suggestion coming from *your* lips."

"Nonsense. I know more than anyone how it feels to be different."

Charlie spoke primly. "Nevertheless, what you're suggesting is illegal, whether we like it or not."

I sat down with Neville, who was still angrily glaring. But he hadn't denied it.

"Mr Baron," I said in my kindest voice. "If I've hit the nail on the head here, please be assured that whatever you say will go no further than this bakery. I just want to know the truth. You've known Rolf for twenty years… that's what *he* said. You… fell in love with him?"

The air was thick with tension. Charlie was right – my suggestion was illegal. And if it got out, not only would Mr Baron's career as an MP be over, but he could also face imprisonment.

Mr Baron swallowed. Then he raised his eyes to meet mine. He nodded imperceptibly.

"You don't have to say it," I assured him. "But my guess is that you fell in love with Rolf when you were youngsters? Did he feel the same?"

Neville's voice was full of sadness. "No… he felt nothing like it. So I took myself out of the equation – engineered an argument over something trivial – I can't even remember what now. But I just needed to be shot of him. It was too awkward. Impossible…"

"But you found him again by accident?"

"Yes. I was given this constituency by my party just over a year ago – it's a safe seat which they knew I'd win. They have high hopes for me, you see. Well, you can imagine my surprise when I walked in here for a coffee and saw him…" Neville chuckled tenderly. "Alas, my feelings were just as strong as ever. I was drunk one night last week and I–"

"Drunk?" Charlie said. "I thought you were anti-drugs and alcohol."

Neville held his head high. "I'm against the working classes having access to gin. It's ruining them – making them idle and workshy."

Charlie opened his mouth to argue. I held up my hand. Charlie relented.

"You were saying, Mr Baron? You were drunk and…?"

He sighed heavily. "I stupidly wrote to Rolf, saying far too much. We'd been getting along well, you see. He'd made me feel so welcome here, and we were becoming good friends again. I... I know he didn't feel the same, but... well, the deadly drink makes one behave recklessly."

"Did he threaten you with the note?" I asked. "Threaten to tell the authorities?"

"When I asked him for the note back, he said he wanted to keep it, because it might come in handy if he ever needed a friend in high places. I told him not to be stupid and that I'd always help him. *He* reminded *me* that I'd voted for the internment of aliens and that he didn't trust me."

"So you decided to pretend there was an air raid to get him and Becky down in the cellar – giving yourself access to all areas to find the letter?"

"Yes. I didn't expect George to be here. Or you two. Anyway, I found my letter in Rolf's coat pocket the next morning and burnt it straight away, so it's gone forever."

"Alas, so has Herr Hengleberg," Charlie said quietly.

"I would *never* hurt him." Neville paused for a moment, then he smiled affectionately. "He was a good man who took life in its stride. The truth is, I was jolly surprised when I found that train ticket in his pocket, because he wasn't the sort of chap to break the rules. He always adapted to life's problems, you see? That's one of the things I lov... admired him for. He always stopped to smell the roses. There was always time for a second cup of tea. Or coffee in his case."

"I'm not surprised he needed two cups of coffee," I said. "Poor man was having trouble sleeping *and* he had to be up at the crack of dawn to… wait a minute… The second coffee cup! Romeo and Juliet! Oh my word… that's it!"

"What's it, Lady Joanie?" Charlie asked eagerly.

I sprang to my feet. "The train ticket! Rolf Hengleberg wasn't planning on leaving – it belonged to *Becky*! Think about it – why would a young couple elope to Carlisle?"

Neville slapped the table. "Gretna Green! The legal age for marriage in Scotland is only fourteen, and they don't need their parents' consent. Gretna Green is the first village on the border *after* Carlisle!"

And like the clouds parting on a summer's day, everything became clear in my mind. "Rolf must've caught Becky trying to leave in the middle of the night – suitcase packed, train ticket in hand. She still needed to collect George from the cellar of course… whereas previously they'd *planned* to meet at Euston Station. But you'd scuppered their plan with the air raid hoax, Mr Baron."

"You said you heard raised voices during the night, Lady Joanie," Charlie said. "It must've been Rolf and Becky arguing."

"Yes. He would've seen the danger of the plan, because you're not allowed to run away from the army, are you? They get awfully funny about that sort of thing and end up shooting people at dawn."

"That's why they were having such a serious conversation when I took their coffee over," Charlie said. "They were still discussing it."

"Yes. And the reason she packed her suitcase so quickly was because it was already packed!"

Neville frowned. "But what's this got to do with a second cup of coffee?"

"I'll explain everything. But first, I suggest we get to Euston Station, before it's too late!"

I stepped towards the door but Neville grabbed my arm. "Wait!"

Charlie grabbed Neville. "Unhand her!"

"My apologies, Lady Joanie. But... now, just hold on a moment, please. Are you suggesting my *nephew* killed Rolf? Because if you are, then let me tell you, it's impossible!"

"It's absolutely possible, Mr Baron. You see, George and Rolf had a massive falling out earlier that day."

I quickly turned and fished inside my camisole, pulling out the small piece of bone. "This is the remains of a feather. A *white* feather."

I stepped over to the fireplace. "George was burning it when we walked in. You remember when we first arrived, Charlie, Herr Hengleberg was taking off his overcoat and hanging it up in the kitchen? *That* was because he and George had just got back. I believe Rolf had seen George leaving the anti-war meeting and encouraged those two Suffragettes to embarrass him for being a conscientious objector."

Charlie frowned. "Why did he burn it though?"

"Well, it's rather humiliating isn't it? Being accosted in the street like that. I'd imagine he was furious and threw it on the fire the moment he arrived here with Herr Hengleberg."

"Yeah, that makes sense. The tension was thick between them when we arrived."

"That's all very well," Neville said. "But I can assure you, George wouldn't kill anyone. He's far too… namby-pamby."

"I think the word is 'sensitive', Mr Baron. And none of us can help how we're made." I raised a poignant eyebrow at him.

"Well, anyway. He's always been 'sensitive'. I repeatedly took him on hunting trips when he was a boy, and he bally-well blubbed the whole time. Wouldn't even kill a bird. Didn't even like *fishing*. And not only because he didn't like killing the fish – but he cried when I showed him how to hook a worm!"

"George is a pacifist?" Charlie said.

Neville scoffed. "That's one word for it."

"But..." Charlie said pensively. "Would George have killed Herr Hengleberg to prevent *himself* from being shipped off to kill countless other men? Or to… I don't know… to be with the woman he loves?"

Neville Baron was resolute. "No, absolutely not."

I pulled open the door. "Well, if that's the case, then it's even worse than I feared! We must go to Euston Station. Becky and George are still due to die today!" I waved my arm frantically at a passing car. "I say, *taxi*!"

Chapter Fourteen

Euston Station was one of the oldest railway terminals in England, boasting beautiful Victorian architecture and history galore. But this was no time for sightseeing. We had a train to intercept!

Neville, Charlie, and I rushed from the taxicab, running together under the station's magnificent marble archway, then across the large concourse – which was busy and bustling, as always.

Charlie grabbed a porter by the shirt in one strong fist. "The Carlisle train?"

The small man spluttered. "Er… um?"

"Quick, man, which platform!"

"Platform Two, squire!"

"Thank you, sir. Now, fetch the police. Sergeant Parry from Scotland Yard!"

We dashed across the Great Hall, with our footsteps echoing off the hard stone floor. Why was Platform Two so far away!

Neville Baron's asthma was playing him up. He wheezed as we ran. "The second coffee cup, Lady Joanforth – I must know!"

We split apart to dodge a refreshment trolley laden with cakes, then he was at my side again. "Becky drugged her uncle with the barbitone," I said. "She must've disposed of the cup – *that's* why one cup's missing. But where did she hide it?"

"*Becky drugged Rolf?*" Neville asked in disbelief.

The long platform came into view, but… oh no! A ticket collector was blocking our entry, and beyond him, a metal barrier stood firm. "Tickets please, tickets please!"

"Can you jump it, Lady Joanie?" Charlie asked.

"Jump it? What am I – a racehorse!"

Charlie bulldozed the ticket collector out the way – but not too forcefully. All the strong young men were away at war, which left either children or the elderly running the country. Oh… and women, of course.

"Stop, help!" the ticket collector yelled, as I scrabbled over the metal barrier.

"It's all right, I'm a copper," Charlie said, leaping over the barrier too.

Becky and George were sitting on a bench further down. They noticed our frantic approach and clambered to their feet.

Neville gasped and wheezed as he spoke to George. "What's all this about, my boy?"

"We're leaving," George said. "Running away."

"Oh no you're not."

"Oh yes we are. The train's due in ten minutes. We're getting on it and you can't stop us."

"The police are on their way," Charlie said.

George bunched his fist at Charlie. He was braver than I'd realised. "You traitor! You've told the police I'm deserting?"

Charlie stayed calm. "Not yet. It's not too late."

"And *that's* not why the police are coming," I said.

"Why are the police coming?" Becky asked innocently.

"Allow me…" I wrenched Becky's suitcase from her hand and flicked open the clasps.

"Hey!" Becky said, trying to wrestle it back.

Ignoring her, I rifled through her clothes. "Of course, if she was clever, she would've smashed the missing cup into a million pieces or thrown it in the river. But... here it is!" I held it aloft like the Holy Grail. "It's been rinsed, but the police might find traces of barbitone. Ah, and here's the bottle of barbitone itself. You couldn't risk leaving any evidence behind, could you, Becky?"

"Lady Joanforth," Neville said. "It's not getting any clearer."

"*This* is the second cup, Mr Baron. Or, more accurately, it's the *first* cup. You see, Herr Hengleberg had a cup of coffee in the very early hours of yesterday morning. Before any of us were even awake."

"And that's when she poisoned Rolf?" Neville asked. "But... who stabbed him?"

I gazed at Becky. "Would you care to answer that, young lady?"

Becky held eye contact with me for a strained, tense moment. Then, realising she was beaten, she sprang to life and fled towards the barriers.

Charlie ran and grabbed her, clapping on the handcuffs. "I'm arresting you in the name of the law!"

Hmm... handcuffs? I didn't know he had those!

Sergeant Parry and a uniformed officer ran to join us. "All right, let's be havin' you... what's going on here then?"

"Well, Sergeant," I said coolly. "Allow me to explain precisely what happened to Herr Hengleberg. And how his niece *Becky* killed him!"

Chapter Fifteen

Sergeant Parry eyeballed me. "Let me get this straight… you're saying this young lady killed her own uncle?"

"That's precisely what I'm saying, Sergeant."

"I'm all ears, your ladyship. In plain English please."

I cleared my throat. "Plain English, of course. Here we go… George and Becky fell in love. George got conscripted into the army. He didn't want to go. Becky came up with a plan: Let's elope in the middle of the night – we'll meet at Euston Station and marry at Gretna Green! She bought the train tickets and packed a suitcase. But on that very same night, Neville Baron turned up at the bakery with his story about an air raid."

Sergeant Parry narrowed his eyes at Neville. "Yes, sir, what was that in aid of?"

"It was just a mistake," I said quickly. "Anyway, back to the murder. In the very early hours, Herr Hengleberg caught Becky red-handed, leaving with a packed suitcase and a train ticket to Carlisle – which would ultimately take her and George to Gretna Green to marry. Herr Hengleberg confiscated the train ticket – putting it in the pocket of his coat, which was hanging in the kitchen."

"Where is this train ticket?" Sergeant Parry asked. "I don't know anything about this."

"It's here," I said, handing it over. "*I* found it in Herr Hengleberg's coat and forgot to give it to you."

Sergeant Parry treated me to a long silent glare. Then he waved for me to continue.

"My guess is that Herr Hengleberg threatened to tell the War Office about George's plan to desert. Becky and her uncle argued for ages while we were all still asleep in the cellar, but then Becky came up with a new plan. She said to her uncle, 'Let's sit down and talk about this.' She ensured he was sitting in the chair with his back to the room and made him some coffee – adding a large dose of barbitone."

"Barbitone?" Sergeant Parry asked.

"Sleeping draught," Charlie said.

"Yes," I said. "But Mrs Christie told us that barbitone takes an hour to work its magic. So uncle and niece sat down at the table, discussing Becky's future, as Herr Hengleberg slowly nodded off… into a very deep sleep."

Charlie scrunched up his handsome face. "So Herr Hengleberg was *already* drugged when I was making your tea – making *their* coffee?"

"Yes, it's the only thing that makes sense – that he was *already* unconscious at that point. Charlie, you said their heads were bent together. Herr Hengleberg had his back to you. You never actually saw him up close…"

"But he moved…"

"He moved when *Becky* patted him on the arm – making him move! But she knew he was deeply sedated. You're lucky he didn't start snoring, young lady."

Becky threw me an evil glare.

Charlie frowned. "So, Becky *pretended* to be chatting with her uncle when I was there, but he was already out cold?"

"Precisely. You gave *Becky* the coffees, didn't you? You had no direct contact with Herr Hengleberg. And then you brought down my tea, and Becky followed shortly afterwards, giving plenty of time for an 'intruder' to come in and stab her uncle."

"What intruder?" Sergeant Parry asked.

I shrugged. "There wasn't an intruder, Sergeant. *Becky* stabbed her uncle."

"But how *could* she have stabbed him?" Charlie asked. "We were there the whole time."

"It was a matter of sleight of hand with the ice pick," I explained. "Her mother was a magician's assistant, and presumably Becky must've learnt a trick or two. And *that's* how she managed to–"

I raised my voice as the Carlisle train rumbled noisily into the station. Great puffs of smelly steam spewed out of the twenty-ton iron beast, filling the platform with a black cloud of sticky vapour. It was impossible to be heard as the train squealed to a halt and stood there tooting to let off steam. The guard blew his whistle and shouted, "All aboard!"

Blocking out the hubbub of the passengers embarking, I re-created the murder in my mind... Yes, that was precisely how she'd done it... After we'd finished our breakfast, Becky had gone over to her heavily drugged uncle, and acted like she was merely catching him napping. She'd shaken him – pretending she wanted to wake him. But as she'd shaken him she'd eased him forward, so he'd woozily slumped into her. *That's* when she'd quickly stabbed him in the throat with the ice pick – which she'd been gripping in her hand all along. She'd pushed him backwards and skilfully distracted us with a scream… Charlie and I had never seen a thing…

I said this out loud to my small audience, as the train chugged away, trailing billows of steam behind it – fogging up the platform like thick mist.

"You see," I continued. "After he'd fallen to the floor, Becky was the only one who'd touched Hengleberg. *She'd* checked his wrist and said he had no pulse. But he *would've* still had a faint pulse at that point because he was actually in the process of dying. But he was so drugged that he didn't thrash about or even move at all. *Becky* said he was cold to the touch, but again, it wasn't true. Charlie didn't check the body because he rushed off to the police station, and I didn't, because I set about comforting Becky."

Charlie spoke pensively. "The ice pick remained in the wound, stemming the blood, so we had no idea that the blood we *did* see was extremely fresh."

"Precisely. Becky made it look as if someone had stabbed Hengleberg when *we* were down in the cellar with her. And then she 'discovered' him dead using *us* as her alibis. And of *course* she seemed upset. She was shaking because it takes guts to blatantly stab someone in front of witnesses. She was probably terrified about what she'd just done."

Neville frowned. "Lady Joanforth, you said that George and Becky were due to die today. What was that all about?"

"Ah yes. Sergeant Parry, if you send some officers along to the banks of the Thames, they'll find a pile

256

of George and Becky's bloodstained clothes – presumably stained with animal blood, or at least I hope so!"

"They faked their deaths?" Charlie said, laughing at the cleverness of it all.

"They did – *that* was their plan all along. It was the only way to get George out of the army. And then they could've married with new identities, sat out the war, and started their lives together in Scotland – or wherever they decided to go."

Neville sighed wearily. "George, what you've done is tantamount to treason. Faking your own death to evade fighting for your King – how could you!"

George trembled with emotion. "It was all Becky's idea!"

Becky gasped at his betrayal. "George!"

"Well, you've killed someone! How ghastly!"

"I did it for us! For you!"

"I never asked you to. It's wrong. Killing's wrong!"

Inspector Parry spoke firmly. "Right, missy, you're about to spend a very short time in prison…"

"Short time?" Neville asked, confused.

Parry hauled the handcuffed Becky to her feet. "With a very *final* full stop at the end of her sentence."

Becky struggled in Parry's arms. "I love you, George! I'm sorry!"

George bit his lip to stop his tears of emotion. Neville rolled his eyes at his nephew's blubbing. But

I knew Neville was pleased really. Better to have a pacifist as a nephew than a cold-blooded killer.

Becky's voice rang around the platform. "I don't see why *I* should be judged for killing one German, when George is being sent off to kill as many as he can!"

"Because it's murder," Sergeant Parry said. "Now come on…"

Sergeant Parry told George not to leave London, then he led Becky away.

After they'd gone, George pulled himself together. "I'm not going to war."

"You'll be sent to prison, you stupid fool," Neville said. "You're in enough trouble as it is."

"I don't care. I'm going to stand up for my beliefs."

Leaving George and Neville to argue, Charlie and I strolled to the other end of the platform, where the plumes of steam from the recently departed train were still thickly swirling. Perhaps we could use them as cover to summon up Uncle Frog…

"George will be lucky if he only gets prison," Charlie said. "A lot of deserters are getting hard labour. And that's not to mention the ones that are shot outright."

"What a ghastly time we're in, Charlie. I think it's time to get back to the fun, carefree 1920s, what do you say?"

"I say, get Uncle Frog beamed up here, right this instant!"

I smiled and lifted my arm to engage my Amulet of Seeing. But… hullo… what was this? A shape was approaching through the lingering clouds of steamy

258

vapour. The atmosphere sizzled with tension. I held my breath…

Out of the steam strolled a very tall, *very* muscular man, dressed in a leather jacket and fedora hat. Oh drat… why did he keep popping up just when we needed him least?

Lord Vilnius halted in front of us. The anticipation buzzed off the metal train tracks. He wanted the silver rose, but I was adamant he wasn't getting it. *I* wanted the golden lion…

Perhaps it was time for Charlie and I to enact our cunning plan. I needed to stall for time…

"You cast the Locator spell?" I asked.

His voice was cool as ice. "I hated to waste my magic on you, but yes I had no choice. When my master, the Empower, lost track of you, I–"

"The Empower's tracking us?" I asked with dread.

"But he couldn't locate you. So *I* was forced to use the Locator spell."

My wand tingled in my garter. "I know your magic is weak in this time, Vincent. You won't have much left, so don't try anything."

"But perhaps I have more magic than you, Joanforth, if you've been casting spells. I hear there was a fortune demon summoned recently?"

Oh drat! That's how the Empower had tracked us. Fortune demons famously left traces in space and time, didn't they?

But there was nothing we could do about that now. Our immediate problem was the Empower's extremely skilled – and to be honest, jolly attractive – student.

Lord Vilnius presented himself to the world as a cool cat, but I knew below the surface bubbled a mad, rabid wolfhound, coiled like a spring, eager to rip out your throat. Rage boiled from every pore.

I raised my chin determinedly. "We seem to have reached an impasse."

Lord Vilnius chuckled sinisterly. "I don't think so. You know what I want."

"There's two of us," Charlie said. "And *we* want the golden lion."

Lord Vilnius glared at Charlie so hard that even my brave copper seemed to flinch.

Right… how were we going to get out of this one? In the pounding silence, the distant rumbling of a train drifted into my ears. I realised that further down the platform, new passengers were arriving. *Another train must be approaching.* Perhaps Charlie and I could carry out our plan to knee Lord V in the whatsits, grab what we needed from him, then jump aboard to escape? But how could I prevent Lord Vilnius from boarding too?

He grinned nastily. "Come along, Joanie, don't draw this out – I do hate awkward farewells. Give me the silver rose, and I'll be on my way."

"No. You give me the golden lion."

"Oh dear. I really didn't want it to come to this… a magical battle on Platform Two of Euston Station."

"Don't! The humans will see."

"Yes. And *that* leaves them susceptible to the Beings of Evil. So I win twice."

"You're not a Being of Evil, Vincent. Not yet. Give me the golden lion."

"Do as she says," Charlie commanded.

Lord Vilnius hadn't taken his deep brown eyes off me. "Allow me to demonstrate exactly the lengths I'll go to, Joanforth!"

He raised his hand to shoulder height. Then, after discharging a sinister crackle of metal-tasting magic, he squeezed his fingers in mid-air.

Charlie's hands flew to his throat as he started to choke. *Oh no*, He was telekinetically throttling Charlie!

"Leave him alone!" I shouted.

Lord Vilnius laughed, squeezing harder.

I steeled myself and rolled up my sleeves. Righty-ho, if it was a telekinetic battle he wanted, then he'd just picked a fight with the Marvelton Magical Academy's Telekinesis Best in Class!

Even though my heart was thumping desperately at the sound of Charlie's choked groans, the only thing that would help him now was for me to focus hard. I closed my eyes and dug deep inside, gathering every last drop of magical juice from the air, from my veins.

My wand buzzed in my garter, tingling against my thigh… I shouted the spell at the top of my lungs. *"With the strength of London's Tower, I'll move this object with my mind's power*!"

My eyes flew open as telekinetic animation crackled through my fingers. Yes! I thrust my arm towards Lord Vilnius, and strained against the air, hitting him with every iota of my magical might. The truth was he was extremely powerful – easily able to choke Charlie with one hand and deter my magic with the other. It was like arm-wrestling a solid mountain.

But of the two of us, *I* was more determined. Lord Vilnius might have no qualms about killing Charlie. But he didn't *want* to kill him as much as I wanted to save him. I *had* to save him. *I* had to win.

Lord Vilnius's growling voice rang in my ears. "Give me the silver rose, or I will kill him, Joanforth. You can't beat me!"

Tiredness crept into my arms. Oh no, what if he was right! My magic was depleting fast. Lord Vilnius was strong, and my own strength was ebbing into a black hole of panic.

But I was Lady Joanforth Eldritch. I did not lose to the likes of him!

As the rumbling train continued its approach, the engine's thunderous roar smothered poor Charlie's chokes. The squealing brakes on the metal tracks set my teeth on edge.

I tried to think. *Must stop him!* I scrunched up my toes and dug even deeper – deep down to my very core, to the place where I wasn't even me anymore – there I found the purest essence of all Beings of Magic – of *every* living being; the golden spark that existed in all life. And with one giant heave, and with one guttural groan, I finally forced Lord V's fingers apart, releasing Charlie from his deadly grip.

Wasting no time to catch his breath, Charlie rushed at Lord Vilnius and grabbed him by the throat with both hands – suddenly becoming as unstoppable as the fast-approaching steam train. "This ends this now – with me killing you!"

Lord Vilnius struggled against Charlie's firm grip. His voice gurgled. "You can't kill me – you're a policeman!"

"In that case, consider yourself nicked, sunshine!"

Charlie punched Lord Vilnius hard in the face – forcing him to stumble backwards to the platform's edge. Lord Vilnius flailed his arms around, grabbing onto the nearest solid object, which happened to be the arm of Detective Constable Charlie Anderson. But Lord Vilnius had already passed the point of no return, and thrashed like a hooked fish against his own crumbling balance.

One step back, and they were both going over…

"We're *both* going over!" Charlie shouted, flinging his arms around Lord Vilnius.

"What are you doing? Get off me, you stupid boy!"

"Get ready with the time controls!"

"There's a bloody great train coming!"

"I *did* warn you I was going to kill you!"

"You'll kill yourself too, you idiot."

"I *said*, get ready with the time controls!"

And then it happened... Charlie threw himself forward and gravity dragged both men down to the white-hot metallic trainlines. Charlie landed on top of Lord Vilnius, who immediately started to kick and punch.

The heavy train ploughed on, inches from them now. My insides melted with terror. "*Charlie!*"

Gripping his prisoner tight, Charlie fumbled for the time control cube hanging from Lord V's belt, jabbing it with his fingers.

I held my breath as the inches slid away. The train was too close. They'd never escape. The roaring locomotive's squeals filled the air, mixing with my own shrill screams. It was going to hit them! And then–

And *then* reality shifted as Charlie jabbed the button. Time surged; space warped. Electric blue flashes zinged off the hot metal tracks and crackled over the two men, as the steam engine bulldozed over them… over exactly where they'd just *vanished*.

The train drew to a halt, but my eyes were fixed on the after-image of Charlie and Lord Vilnius wrapped in each other's arms — floating like the ghostly outline of a lightning flash.

Where had they gone? Back to 1926? How on earth was Charlie going to defend himself against Lord Vilnius alone? Lord V's magic would undoubtedly be weakened after our magical showdown, but still… if he was back in the correct timeline, his powers might return with full strength.

Wherever they were – whenever they were – I needed to find Charlie.

Behind me, I realised the entire platform was now deathly silent.

Someone coughed. "Er… are they okay?"

My tension snapped. "Of course they're not okay – they've just been squashed by a bloody great steam train!"

The gathered passengers muttered to each other about this terrible tragedy, but they needed to believe

264

it. Otherwise, say what? "Actually, both men are fine because they magically time travelled just at the last second. And in fact one of them is an evil sorcerer and I'm a witch…"

Besides, I needed to get out of here! My heart lurched as I ran to the other end of the platform, stepping behind a convenient guard's hut, and summoning up Uncle Frog on my Amulet of Seeing.

His image zoomed up on my wrist. "Joanforth, good to see you. Have you saved George and Becky?"

"Sort of. In the original history they ran away and faked their own deaths – it was Romeo and Juliet gone right."

"Cunning. And what about Lord Vilnius?"

"He still has the golden lion."

"Dashed villain, that man."

"Quite. And… he and Charlie have gone somewhere. Charlie arrested him. Then they time travelled together."

Uncle Frog looked impressed. "Charlie *arrested* him?"

I chuckled wearily. "I know. He's like that."

"Bear with me a moment, Joanie."

Uncle Frog grabbed a large crystal and slotted it into a panel on the front of his time machine. Then he chanted an incantation in a magical language I wasn't familiar with.

I watched agog as four clockwork dials on the machine spun into position. "One, nine, two, and three? What does that mean, Uncle?"

"They're in 1923, Joanforth."

"Oh no, poor Charlie."

My uncle blinked his froggy eyes. "Can *you* rescue him?"

I shrugged. "Delighted. Tell me the spell and I'll be on my way."

"Good woman, that witch." Uncle Frog told me the magic words, wished me luck, then signed off.

Even though I wasn't with Charlie, I said the words out loud, for luck. "*Now I leave nineteen sixteen, I'll never forget what I have seen. But before back home I hop, first to '23 I'll stop.*"

And so I left the first big shake up of our modern times – the Great War of 1914 to 1918. Unquestionably, it'd been dreadful. A bloody awful business. But in four short years the restrictive roles that had been fixed for centuries were finally eroded just a little.

In the muddy trenches of France, ordinary men had lived side by side with high-born officers. At home, women had driven buses, shovelled coal, or worked the land – in trousers! The Great War had absolutely been the darkest of dark times, but often from darkness comes light and hope, and this dismal few years had ushered in a brand-new era with wonderful new freedoms – new *rights*. Votes for women; rights for workers.

And whether they'd known it or not, *these* were the freedoms that those beautiful souls had fought and died for. And we must never forget them. Because they gave us our lives. Without a doubt, their bravery made us who we are today.

Chapter Sixteen

As always, I landed with a thud. But, alas, not on top of Charlie this time.

Wherever he was, I prayed he was all right…

Lying on my back, I opened my eyes and blinked up at the bright blue sky. I touched the ground below me… Ah, I'd landed on a hard stone surface. But the pain in my shoulders could've told me that…

I was just about to sit up and explore when, to my astonishment, the face of a Roman soldier suddenly heaved into view. Now this was a turn-up! The hunky soldier was wearing a feathered brass helmet and a gleaming breastplate. But the odd thing was, he looked exactly like Charlie – right down to the sculpted cheekbones, differently-coloured eyes, and bare bulging biceps. Gosh, I'd ever seen such muscles!

Don't ask to see his spear, Joanie!

"Am I in ancient Italy?" I asked blearily.

The Roman soldier smiled amiably. Ah yes, he probably couldn't speak English. It was a common affliction amongst foreigners. I searched my memory banks for my best schoolgirl Latin, then spoke loud and slow. "Ciao, bella… is this old Italiano? Er… arrivederci? Um… Romanes eunt domanes? Hail Caesar?"

The Roman grinned. "It's *me* Lady Joanie. Charlie. And we're in the 1920s. We're home!"

As he helped me to sit up, I glanced down and realised he was wearing a thigh-length leather skirt with knee-high lace-up boots… *Gah*! His quadriceps bulged even more than his biceps. I wondered what else on him might bulge and, when I had a sneaky peek, *my eyes* bulged like bursting balloons.

"It's very hot, isn't it?" I whispered. "Um, Charlie, why are you dressed as a Roman centurion?"

"This is a film studio, your ladyship. Look…"

Oh *yes*.... We were in the backyard of a cream Georgian mansion, with the River Thames flowing along the bottom of the large sparse lot. There were several caravans dotted around, and a couple of women with clipboards chatting nearby. Thankfully, they were too engrossed to have seen me beam in.

But I was delighted to be back in the 1920s! The women were wearing skirts to the knee, with high heels and scarfed blouses. One of the women sported a stylish cloche hat over her short hair, with a solitary kiss curl on the side of her face. Ah… never again would I need to wear a corset… Was that good news? *Corset* was!

Charlie offered his hand to help me stand. I leaned against him as I tried to get my bearings, treating myself to a surreptitious squeeze of his gleaming muscles…

A couple of ancient Egyptians wandered past. "Charlie, what happened to Lord Vilnius? Are you all right?"

"I am now *you're* here. And I must admit it's good to be back in the correct decade again."

"And Lord Vilnius?"

Charlie's face clouded with thunder. "Lord Vilnius scarpered the moment we landed – coward that he is. I gather he ran out of magic during your showdown and couldn't face me man-to-man."

Not many could, with you dressed like that, darling...

Charlie brightened up. "I'd just started to wonder what to do next, when a young lady with a clipboard asked if I was a supporting artist. I thought to me-self, what would Lady Joanforth do? So... I said yes."

"Glad to hear you're embracing your inner-Joanie, darling! Now, let's see... what does this sign over here say?" I gasped with realisation. "Oh, good heavens, this is the back lot of Golden Magic Flicks. If this is 1923, then they're currently filming *The Egyptian Queen*. Charlie, I've been here before... and the last time I was here, there was a murder!"

Will our heroes locate Lord Vilnius and knee him in the whatsits before he finds the next magical gem? And what of this murder Lady Joanie spoke of? And how many more times will she squeeze Charlie's muscles while he's dressed as Roman? Probably at least 1923 times!

Turn the page to follow their adventures!

A Witch in Time 1923

Chapter One

"A murder?" Charlie asked.

And… *cut*!

Ah hello, darlings! Lady Joanforth Eldritch here – solver of murders, soon-to-be senior witch, and lover of fun!

And *what* fun I've been having, travelling around the twentieth century with my dishy sidekick, Detective Constable Charlie Anderson. It was strange to think we'd only known each other a short while. It felt like we went back years…

We were slowly edging home to 1926, but I'd stopped off in 1923 to rescue Charlie – who'd arrived here before me, after bravely tackling the evil Lord Vilnius in 1916.

I'd just materialised in the backlot of Golden Magic Flicks, and discovered that while Charlie had been waiting for me, he'd been recruited as a supporting artist by the film company, hence why he was currently dressed as a Roman soldier…

He looked delightfully hunky in his brass breastplate and leather skirt, and I shall give you a moment to drool… and now, on with the story!

Action!

"Charlie," I said. "I've been here before. And last time, there was a murder!"

"A murder?" Charlie asked… again…

Before I could explain further, a woman dressed in a 1920s knee-length skirt and frilled blouse approached. She was brandishing a clipboard. "All supporting artists come with me *now*!"

She grabbed Charlie's upper-arm – probably enjoying a feel of the ol' biceps. Then she dragged him towards the Georgian mansion, which was the headquarters of Golden Magic Flicks.

I followed, feeling frumpy in my long 1916 skirt, cotton blouse, and prim little hat – all of which made me look dowdier than an Edwardian dowager – especially in the 1920s.

But I shouldn't be worrying about my clothes – what about this impending murder? And where had Lord Vilnius run off to? I tried to fix my mind on those questions, but as I stepped into the film studio, my thoughts were smashed sideways. The only way to describe the chaos was like… it was like entering a builder's warehouse, located in a giant ants' nest.

People wearing the latest fashions scurried hither and thither, and every free bit of floorspace was covered with clutter. Planks of wood, tins of paint, and reams of cloth had been pushed up against the walls – with hand tools scattered all around. Towering plywood boards had been painted on both sides with extravagant scenes – the canals of Venice, a Wild West town, an enchanted forest.

Still following the clipboard lady, Charlie and I suddenly found ourselves in the middle of ancient Egypt. A River Nile made of blue silk was framed by a backdrop of pyramids and palm trees. Oh yes, of course, they were filming *The Egyptian Queen*!

I halted to gawp at a couple of topless gladiators sparring with wooden swords. Charlie yanked me away so hastily that we almost crashed straight into a young woman in a negligee, who was theatrically miming "No, no, no!" as a man in a toga tied her to his Roman column.

The column wobbled as she wriggled.

We finally reached the epicentre of the chaos, where a semi-circle of men wearing knee-length trousers and large flat caps were positioned around Cleopatra's boudoir. The heavy, static camera was pointing at the starlet… the beautiful Gillian Everett.

Filming was yet to begin, so Gillian was reclining in a director's chair in the middle of the set, filing her nails and looking bored. Make-up ladies buzzed around her like drones around the queen bee. One brave woman was trying to puff white powder onto Gillian's already pale face, but Gillian coughed and waved her away. Another lady bent to add more black eyeliner to Gillian's already panda-like eyes.

A wardrobe lady approached…

"Your headdress, Miss Everett," she said reverentially.

Gillian sat up tall as the heavy jewelled headdress was carefully affixed, before a couple of women helped her to her feet, like tugboats to Gillian's luxury liner. Gosh… what a transformation. An attractive Englishwoman was now the notorious Queen of the Nile. No one could deny how glamorous she looked, how beautiful. In 1923 the 'sex icon' was a thoroughly modern phenomenon, and Gillian Everett oozed appeal.

"Are we finally ready?" a haggard-looking man asked.

I assumed this was the director. He was standing in the middle of the semi-circle, wearing the biggest 'plus-four' trousers and most-ridiculous flat cap I'd ever seen. Next to him, a younger man sat in front of the film camera, preparing to turn the handle.

"Title card?" the director shouted. "Where's the bloody title card boy!"

A portly young chap plodded over, clutching a stack of placards. He held one up to the camera, which said: *Later at the Palace of Cleopatra…*

Gillian Everett rummaged around in her floaty white dress and pulled out a cigarette case.

The director grabbed a megaphone. "Do NOT smoke in here!"

The megaphone was unnecessary – he was only a few feet away.

Gillian Everett froze, glaring at him with icy blue eyes.

A pianist – who'd been playing an upbeat tune all this time – paused with his fingers over the keys, waiting for the inevitable explosion.

Gillian stamped her foot. "Stop shouting at me!"

The director's tone became saccharine. "Miss Everett, I apologise. You're wonderful."

"Quite right." Gillian flopped into her chair. "And where's my bloody drink!"

"Here, Miss Everett." A young lady wearing a plainer costume – perhaps that of a handmaiden – stepped over with a pink cocktail. Gillian took a swig, then handed the glass back to the handmaiden without saying thank you or even looking at her.

Time ticked on; the director spoke quietly to the cameraman. Gillian adjusted her heavy headdress and… wait a minute, *hullo*! Did I detect the next magical gem nestled amongst all those fake jewels? I needed to get nearer to be sure… *if* I could plough through the clouds of tension wafting around Gillian Everett…

But then the gloomy clouds dissipated as the leading male, handsome hunk Rhett Mantel, swaggered over, dressed as Mark Anthony. Gosh he was scrummy, so much like the real Mark Anthony… if the real Mark Anthony had worn dark lipstick, face powder, and more eyeliner than Cleopatra herself.

The director shouted, "Action!" and the cameraman turned the handle. The piano player launched into a jaunty jangle, as Gillian and Rhett began their melodramatic choreographed kiss. After some hammy overacting from the pair of them, Mark Anthony bade her farewell and strutted off. Cleopatra swooned around for a moment, then danced over to a wicker basket and pulled out a rubber snake. She wrestled with it for much longer than necessary, then performed a dramatic death of a thousand facial expressions.

"Cut!" the director shouted. "Everyone take five!"

As if a switch had been flicked, the spell of the silver screen was smashed and everyone went back to normal. Well, normal for *this* place. Gillian Everett swished off towards a corridor, which presumably led to her dressing room – and everyone else dispersed too, going off for a quick cuppa or cigarette.

I turned to Charlie. He was clearly impressed about being here, but *I* had something even more impressive for him… and I wasn't talking about my gorgeous little bot…

"Charlie, did you notice Cleopatra's sapphire? I think it's the next jewel!"

Charlie raised his voice above the hubbub. "You mean that blue stone in her head-thing?"

"Yes and, actually, it's a rather famous jewel – the Blue Stuart Sapphire. It was historically part of the English Crown Jewels, but King James the Second smuggled it out of the country when he left in 1688. This is obviously where it's ended up. But these people clearly think it's just a piece of costume jewellery!"

"*We'd* better get it before Lord Vilnius comes back."

"Agreed."

Charlie glanced around the bustling space. "Did you know that this building is a nightclub in 1926?"

"Of course, darling, The White Russian, it's one of my favourites." I raised a flirty eyebrow. "Do you come here often, Charlie?"

"Only as a policeman. I carried out a raid here a few weeks ago, well, in 1926." He inspected me with his blue and brown eyes, making me swoon a little inside. "You said there was a murder last time you were here? But what were you doing here? Are you interested in the flicks?"

"I'm interested in handsome actors. I snuck in to get Rhett Mantel's autograph!"

"Rhett Mantel?"

"The chap playing Mark Anthony."

"Ah. And did you get his autograph?"

"That's not all I got, darling."

Charlie rolled his eyes. "That's all we need – *you* turning up and ruining everything."

"Don't be like that. Oh but look, here I am now…"

I watched my 1923 self striding into the film studio, dressed in the latest to-the-knee skirt, sailor blouse, and barred high heels. Our lovely sheepdog/poodle cross, Wispu, was walking beside me, looking adorable – with her black-and-white coat all woolly. My heart soared with affection. I'd missed that lovely pup since I'd been travelling in time.

As my 1923 self scanned the scene for Rhett, Wispu sniffed the air and turned to look directly at *us*. Her cute face seemed to smile with recognition. But, *uh-oh*, was she about to give the game away? My 1923 self noticed Wispu looking over and followed her gaze…

I pushed Charlie behind a pillar. "Oh drat, Wispu's seen us!"

"Well, I'm sure she won't say anything!" He fell serious. "She can't talk, can she?"

"Not exactly, but… I know what I'm like – if I find out I'm here, I won't be able to resist interfering with myself."

Charlie deciphered this. "That *does* sound like an accident waiting to happen. Let's make sure we stay out of her way."

"Agreed."

As he gazed down at me, I realised we were standing jolly close behind this pillar… if I stood on my tiptoes, we'd be kissing…

"So, what happened with this murder then?" he asked.

"Oh yes… right." The memories of that day drifted back. "I was standing over there, talking to Rhett…"

"Like you are now?"

"Exactly like that, yes."

"And then?"

"And then… the director shouted something. What was it…?"

The director's voice shouted, "Places everyone!"

"*That* was it! And… then, a bell rang."

Charlie pointed in the air. "Like that one?"

"Yes. And Rhett said he had to go..."

We peeked around the pillar and saw Rhett and my 1923 self still happily chatting.

"But you continued to flirt with him..."

"How did you guess?"

"Because I'm watching you do it. And then what happened?"

"We-ell, I was about to ask Rhett to dinner, but there was this blood-curdling scream..."

"The *murder*! Hey, perhaps we can stop it!"

The sound of a blood-curdling scream pierced our eardrums.

"Or perhaps not," Charlie said blankly. "Then what happened?"

"And then everyone ran to that corridor over there. *That's* where the scream had come from. Shall we?"

278

I stepped out from behind the pillar, but Charlie pulled me back.

"Wait, your Uncle Frog said we can't interact with our alternate selves, otherwise the universe will implode like a flan in the hot oven of space/time… or something."

I remained calm. "It's all right, darling. Look, as you can see, I've slipped outside. I didn't want to get involved. Come on, let's try to swipe the gem while everyone else is distracted!

Chapter Two

If it was true what fictional detectives said about the attitude of the victim leading to clues about the murder, then the gold star on the dressing room door spoke volumes.

Charlie and I squeezed inside, joining the crowd of crew, cast, and staff who were captivated by the beautiful leading lady lying on her velvet chaise-longue. Under usual circumstances, she probably would've enjoyed the attention. But these were *not* usual circumstances… it was unlikely she'd be enjoying much ever again…

Gillian Everett's dressing room was extravagant – just like the starlet herself. A mahogany dressing table down one end held a box of glistening jewels, pots of make-up, and bottles of perfume. And every surface was laden with gift boxes, greeting cards, and flowers from adoring fans.

But the eye was drawn to the woman herself, lying there motionless…

Her heavy headdress had slipped to the floor. *Ah-ha!* Perhaps now might be a good time to swipe the sapphire!

I elbowed my way to the front of the crowd, then bent to check her pulse. "I'm sorry to say… she's dead."

"That's terrible!" The director gasped. "Now how are we going to finish this picture?"

He suddenly realised how callous this had sounded and started to backtrack. But he was interrupted by the wardrobe lady, who shouted. "Good heavens, is that a snake!"

The crowd gasped and gawped as if they thought they were watching Miss Everett's latest picture.

Her co-star – the snake – slithered warily from under the chaise-longue, flicking its tongue to sniff the air. It was a biggun – four-foot long with brown scales and beady eyes.

"Look at the fang marks on her wrist!" Someone shouted. "It must've bitten her!"

As everyone craned to look, the snake coiled into a spring and hissed defensively.

Charlie faced the crowd, arms out wide. "Everyone, stay back."

"On whose authority?" The director asked.

Charlie glanced at his outfit. "Er… in the name of Caesar."

While Charlie took care of crowd management, I tried to piece together what had happened. Well, it wasn't too hard to guess… A wicker basket was lying on the floor, with its lid strewn open, so Gillian must've thought the basket contained a gift, put her hand inside, and then… got a wristful of snake fang.

Which meant someone had *purposely* left her a poisonous snake.

I turned to inspect the faces of the people here. Most of them looked shocked. But one man stood out, and not only because he was strong, rugged, and dressed in a battered leather jacket and grubby fedora hat. But also, he looked worried.

The director spotted him too. "One of *your* snakes, Mr Lambourne? You're always bragging about how you're a snake expert as well as an archaeologist."

Mr Lambourne spoke in a growling American accent. "Even if it was my snake, Mr Bunter, I can assure you, this little guy ain't venomous." As Mr Lambourne took his hands out of his pockets to gesture to the snake, he dislodged a business card, which fell to the floor.

I was about to alert him to the card, but Mr Bunter interjected. "We all know *you* wanted the leading role in this picture, Lambourne, but Miss Everett insisted on Rhett."

Mr Lambourne squared up to the director. "Listen, Bunter, I flew all the way from California to star in your movie – and *you* allowed *that* woman to demote me from leading man to Egypt consultant. If I was gonna set a snake on anyone, believe me, it would be *you*!"

"So it is your snake?" Mr Bunter said. "You admit it?"

Mr Lambourne's face flashed with guilt. "Lemme check…"

Charlie intervened. "The police will want to inspect the snake, sir. We'd better leave everything as it is."

Mr Bunter turned to the crowd. "Yes, someone call the police! And find me another leading lady!"

Cleopatra's handmaiden stepped forward. "*I* could play Cleopatra, Mr Bunter."

"You? A chorus girl?"

"I know all the movements, sir. I've watched Gillian closely."

Hmm… *how* closely? Had this young lady decided to kill off the competition?

"I'll think about it," Mr Bunter said. "I need to speak to my sponsor. Somebody get my sponsor!"

As Bunter's people jumped to it, I suddenly realised that Wispu had snuck into the room and was sitting near Mr Lambourne's dropped business card. That was the great thing about sheepdogs – they were cunning, clever, and stealthy. Wispu winked at me in a *watch this!* way, then she snuffled her nose to the floor and picked up the card in her sharp teeth.

Oh, good girl!

Wispu padded over and gazed at me with her puppy-dog eyes. I took the card, giving her ears a ruffle – then she trotted off. Bless her, she was adorable.

But, hmm... this was the business card of a Doctor Scott at the London Hospital of Tropical Medicine. Poor Edgar Lambourne must've contracted an exotic illness on his travels in Egypt. But was his illness connected to Gillian Everett's murder?

I glanced at the beautiful Blue Stuart Sapphire in Gillian's headdress. Was *that* a motive for murder? But surely the killer would've taken it with them, wouldn't they? And no one around here seemed to know its true worth.

Nevertheless, I needed that magical sapphire – and I needed it before Lord Vilnius turned up. Alas, the police were on their way, and if I was caught stealing jewellery from a murder victim, I might end up as a suspect myself!

Chapter Three

The crowd dispersed, leaving the snake and the corpse in the dressing room, with the door firmly shut. Right… first thing's first. I needed to change.

I snuck into the room next door and was delighted to discover an overspill of Gillian Everett's sumptuous wardrobe, so I quickly pulled on an expensive skirt, chiffon blouse, and lovely cloche hat. Well, Miss Everett didn't need them anymore, did she?

I met Charlie in the corridor. He'd swapped his centurion costume for some outrageous 1920s menswear. But he was so handsome that he actually looked gorgeous in the knee-length 'plus-four' trousers, complete with colourful sleeveless jumper, shirt, tie, and oversized cap. He exuded even more star appeal than the lovely Rhett Mantel.

Obviously, I couldn't tell *him* that though. "Are you wearing those clothes for a bet, Charlie?"

He smirked. "I stole them off your boyfriend."

"Rhett Mantel is not my boyfriend. Come on, let's get out of here and contact Uncle Frog – see if he can confirm my theory about the sapphire being magical."

We were about to slip out the backdoor, but our path was blocked by two huge policemen.

They were followed by a familiar grumpy face. "Lady Joanforth Eldritch, strike a light – it *is* you!"

"Detective Sergeant Parry… how have you been in the last decade?"

He tipped his hat. "It's *inspector* now, Lady Joanforth. And I've been –" His eyes bulged at Charlie's fashionable outfit. "*Good lord*, Constable Anderson, get back into uniform this instant!"

Charlie smirked like a naughty schoolboy. "Yes, sir…"

He stepped out to the backlot, trying not to laugh.

Inspector Parry looked me up and down. "'Ere, didn't I see you outside a moment ago dressed differently?"

I shrugged. "I don't know. *Were* you outside a moment ago dressed differently?"

"*I* wasn't! But I could've sworn…" He frowned. "What have you got in your hand?"

I was still holding the business card, so I quickly cast the Duplicator spell and slipped the copy up my sleeve. "It's a business card, Inspector. I found it on the floor of Gillian Everett's dressing room. It fell out of Edgar Lambourne's pocket. Here, you should take it."

"I will. And I'll be coming to find *you* later for questions."

"There's nothing I wish to ask you, Inspector."

"*I'll* be asking them. Starting with, why were *you* removing evidence from a crime scene?"

"Well, I –"

"Stay out of this, I really mean it!" He swept off.

I spoke to his retreating back. "Do come and find me any time… preferably *after* I've left for the day…"

Huh… *I* won…

Outside in the spring sunshine, Charlie was stealthily watching the film director, Mr Bunter, as he argued with – presumably – his sponsor.

The sponsor was more like a London gangster than a glamorous film financer. He was wearing a camel hair coat with leather boots, and his cockney accent was laced with gravel and rust. He wouldn't have been out of place selling fruit and veg from a Billingsgate barrow.

His eyes were pinned to Mr Bunter. "Y*ou're* ultimately responsible for this mess – you're the owner of Golden Magic Flicks. It won't be my name dragged through the dirt, but the name of Bertie Bunter. And it won't be *my* face dragged through the broken bottle factory if I lose my investment, but the face of Bertie Bunter!"

Mr Bunter held up his hands. "Please, Mr Lange, I implore you. We need more time."

Mr Lange puffed on his cigar. "Listen, Bunter, this picture has been over-budget and over-time since it *started*. I don't give a monkeys if there's been a murder. The show must go on!"

I spoke quietly to Charlie. "That gives me an idea…"

He sounded worried. "What, Lady Joanie?"

I stepped forward. "Excuse me, Mr Bunter. Might I have a word?"

Mr Bunter tutted. "Look, who *are* you? I don't believe we've met."

"I'm Lady Joanforth Eldritch. And I was wondering, do you intend to continue filming *The Egyptian Queen*?"

"We do!" Mr Lange growled. "I've invested a lot of dosh in this, and I want it finished *yesterday*!"

Bertie Bunter wilted under his sponsor's glare. "Steady on, old chap. I couldn't have planned for *this*, could I?"

"But who will replace Gillian Everett?" I asked innocently.

Bertie Bunter shrugged. "The handmaiden volunteered."

"*I* could do it," I said.

"What!" Charlie asked.

"You?" Bertie Bunter said.

"Yes. I look more like Gillian Everett than the handmaiden. And once all the heavy make-up is in place, then…" *Then I'll have access to the sapphire!*

"I'm not sure," Bertie Bunter said. "We don't know you. The *public* don't know you."

I smiled amiably at the sponsor. "I'll do it for free."

Mr Lange slapped Bertie on the back. "We'll take her. Now get back to work."

"But… the police?" Bertie Bunter said.

"We could set the filming up at the other end of the studio?" Charlie suggested. "Then we'd be out of their way."

Mr Bunter scrutinised Charlie. "And *you* are, sir?"

"This is my… agent," I said. "Charles Anderson."

"You were dressed as a Roman a minute ago," Bertie Bunter said.

"Yes," Charlie said. "I'm a supporting artist."

"She just said you were her agent."

"I support artists in *all sorts* of capacities."

288

Mr Bunter waved his hand. "Very well, Lady Joanforth, you're our new Cleopatra."

He told us to hang around for the wardrobe lady to do a fitting, so we stepped back towards the Georgian mansion.

Charlie shook his head in awe. "You've got guts, Lady Joanie, I'll give you that."

"Thank you, darling. Now tell me, do you think Mr Bunter or his sponsor might've killed Miss Everett?"

"Why would they?"

"Perhaps to pay a replacement less money? Gillian Everett was probably jolly expensive. Not to mention demanding. She had all those fresh flowers in her dressing room and a big bowl of... what's wrong, Charlie?"

Something over my shoulder was making his face a picture of panic. He glanced at me briefly, then suddenly grabbed my upper-arms and pushed me against the wall, before kissing me passionately.

Gosh!

I instinctively clenched my fist to punch him round the chops. But... actually... I relaxed and melted into the most wonderful kiss I'd ever experienced.

And I'd experienced plenty, thank you very much!

Charlie pulled away slightly and gazed deep into my eyes. His voice was a whisper. "Sorry about that."

I straightened my hat and cleared my throat. "Well... I know I'm irresistible. But really, Charlie, you must try to control yourself."

"Um, yes. And..."

I turned to see my 1923 self breezing past, with Wispu trotting beside her… Oh, he'd only kissed me to hide me from her. But… ah yes, *that's* right, *she* was returning to finish chatting up Rhett Mantel.

Oh dear, my heart sunk as Bertie Bunter accosted her. "Ah, there you are, Lady Joanforth. If you'll come this way? The wardrobe lady will get you ready."

Wispu barked and growled, as if she was trying to intervene in this terrible case of mistaken identity.

My 1923 self reached down to soothe her. "Shh, girl, it's all right." She frowned at Mr Bunter. "Did you say, wardrobe lady?"

"Yes, your ladyship. If you're going to be our new Cleopatra, you'll need to get changed. See you on set – we'll take it from the kiss scene with Mark Anthony."

My 1923 self grinned. "Oh… I suppose we'd better rehearse *thoroughly* then."

She followed Mr Bunter back inside, clearly delighted by this turn of events.

Charlie was flabbergasted. "I can't believe she just went along with that! You're… I mean, *she's* now playing the role of Cleopatra!"

"So typical of me!" I said proudly. "I never question anything – just go along with the fun!"

"How are we supposed to get the sapphire now? With you… *her*… interloping?"

I glanced up at the bright blue sky, feeling hopeful. That kiss had stirred my not-particularly-latent passions. "Let's contact Uncle Frog. Perhaps he can think of something."

"All right."

"And, Charlie?"

"Yes, Lady Joanie?"

I linked my arm through his. "That was quick thinking with the kiss. Well done."

Chapter Four

We strolled to the bottom of the backlot, where the River Thames meandered peacefully on this lovely spring day. The lush green riverbank stretched for miles in one direction but, up ahead, beyond a scrub of trees, a stone path led to a large brick building.

"Hopefully we can be alone in there, Charlie… to contact Uncle Frog, I mean."

"Of course, Lady Joanie."

I chatted nineteen-to-the-dozen – feeling unhinged after our kiss. "We'll talk to Uncle Frog and then try to get the sapphire. And then… and then… we might even have time to solve the murder – won't that be jolly good fun! But Lord V will still be lurking – you can mark my words. So we'll need to watch out for him!"

Charlie threw me a funny look. "Yeah... So how are we going to get the golden lion and time controls off your boyfriend then?"

"Lord Vilnius isn't my boyfriend, Charlie! As I told you, we were once betrothed, but I ended it a long time ago."

He smiled playfully. "My apologies. But… what do you think? Should we stick with our plan to knee him in the whatsits and basically mug him?"

"Perhaps. But before *that,* we need to let him know where to find us." I sighed. "If only there was some sort of communication device we could carry around with us all the time."

Charlie sounded incredulous. "What, like a telephone in your pocket?"

"Why not?"

"Impossible."

"It might be possible one day."

Charlie looked pensive. "I can't see it taking off – you'd need a very long cord, and they'd keep getting tangled up… But anyway, doesn't Lord Vilnius have an Amulet of Seeing, like you and your Uncle Frog?"

"He does. But after I broke with him, he changed his contact spell and blocked me."

He shrugged. "Then all we can do is wait for him to find us. And be ready this time."

We reached the brick building and peered through the large open door. "It looks like a motorcar garage," Charlie said.

The cavernous garage had a stone floor, electric lighting, and tool-cluttered shelves, but it was the cars that seized my attention. Proudly parked, like soldiers on parade, stood several stylish Rolls-Royces, as well as a few American cars.

I knew the sporty little Dodge belonged to Rhett Mantel – I'd ridden in it myself. The other cars presumably belonged to the film crew as well as the people who occupied the flats and offices on the upper floors of the Georgian mansion. But whoever owned them, they were all stunning. How I loved 1920s cars – always so elegant in the Art Deco style. And so much fun to drive!

I inspected a lovely Rolls-Royce Silver Ghost, which was an open-topped blue beast, with four leather seats and big white wheels.

"Come on, Charlie, let's sit in this one."

"Be careful, Lady Joanie." Charlie grasped my arm, preventing me from kicking over a bucket of soapy water.

"Thanks, darling. We've had enough people kicking the bucket for one day."

Charlie chuckled. "I like your sense of humour. Do you…er… do you want to hear something else funny?"

"All right."

He grinned. "I think I'm in love."

"S… sorry? What?"

"Yeah. The object of my affection is so beautiful. Almost flawless!"

"Flawless? Really? Gosh…"

"Yeah." Charlie gazed at the Rolls-Royce and affected a posh English accent. "The leather upholstery is to-die-for!"

"Oh, you're in love with this car, are you?"

His blue and brown eyes sparkled. "What else would I be talking about, your ladyship?"

"Hmm… You know, Charlie, *I've* always preferred physical humour."

A smile skirted across his lips. "Physical? Really? Like, when I kissed you just now?"

"No…" I picked up the bucket of soapy water. "Like slapstick. For example, this bucket of water over *your* head."

Charlie held out his hands. "Hey no, come on, Lady Joanie, I was just joking."

"It's rather warm in here, isn't it? Would you like to be cooled down?"

Stifling his laughter, Charlie edged away. "Lady Joanie, put the bucket down!"

I propped the heavy bucket on top of the windowless door, enjoying our flirty game. I was about to relent and leave him dry, but my hand slipped and knocked the bucket sideways – spilling the dirty water all over the cream leather backseats. Ohhh... drat...

In the tense silence, Charlie said, "Whoops..."

I gazed at the damp seats. "Whoops, indeed. Hopefully it'll dry out before the owner returns. Or at least before they catch us! Come on, let's sit in the front and contact my uncle."

Charlie opened the car door for me, so I got comfy in the driver's seat.

As he climbed into the passenger seat, I pressed my Amulet of Seeing to connect with my frog-headed uncle.

His image whooshed up on my wrist. "Joanforth, delighted to see you!"

The 1926 Wispu barked a hello. Her pink tongue flopped cutely.

Uncle Frog played with her woolly ears. "Joanforth, how's 1923? Have you found young Charlie?"

"I'm twenty-eight," Charlie said sternly. "I'm not young."

I took my Amulet off my wrist and placed it on the dashboard, so my uncle could see us both. "Charlie," I said. "Uncle Frog's older than *me*, and I've met Shakespeare... And yes, Uncle, we're in 1923, safe and sound. Lord Vilnius apparently fled as soon as he got here, but I think I've found the next gem! Is it a sapphire?"

"It is, Joanforth, jolly good work! Can you get it?"

"Unfortunately, it's part of a murder scene in a film studio. But I've volunteered to be the new leading lady, so I plan to swipe it."

"Good plan."

"Yes… and no. My 1923 self has turned up and the director thought she was me. So now *she's* getting ready to kiss Rhett Mantel."

"Just do what you can, Joanforth."

"Is there anything you can tell us, sir?" Charlie asked. "Anything we should watch out for? Apart from the dastardly Lord Vilnius."

Uncle Frog grabbed his runes. "Can you give me a little background on the situation?"

I explained about Golden Magic Flicks, *The Egyptian Queen*, and the death of Gillian Everett.

Uncle Frog threw the small white runes to the carpet, then frowned. "Hmm… right… oh… yes, I see…"

"Well?" I asked.

He cleared his throat. "Um, Joanforth, there's a slight snag."

"Oh dear. Is it *really* a slight snag? Or is this an example of British understatement in the face of disaster?"

"Yes," Uncle Frog said ambiguously. He cleared his throat again.

"Have you got a frog in your thr…" Charlie began. "Sorry…"

"The thing is," Uncle Frog said. "In the original timeline, another cast member called Edith Parker also died shortly after Miss Everett."

"Edith Parker must be that handmaiden!" I said. "*She* would've been given the role if I hadn't volunteered."

Hmm… I was starting to see where this slight snag was leading…

"Yes, Joanie," Uncle Frog said. "You've saved her life. But now, the trouble is, *you* die instead – the day after tomorrow!"

"So we need to save her," Charlie said. "Save *you*. But we can't interact with our alternate selves – or the world will end?"

"Precisely, young man. Would you like my advice?"

"Catch the killer before anyone else dies?" I suggested.

"Good suggestion, that witch. Stay in touch and I'll see if there's anything else I can do. Frog out!"

Charlie and I exchanged a weary look. His lovely face morphed into a gentle smile. "Don't worry. We'll figure this out. I won't let you – or your 1923 self – come to any harm."

"You're sweet."

Our tender moment was interrupted by the sound of two men approaching. We jolted to attention.

"Hopefully this isn't one of *their* cars," I whispered.

We strained to listen. One of the voices belonged to Rhett Mantel. "Someone's stolen my favourite trousers and hat!"

Charlie adjusted his flat cap. "Wonder who *that* was…"

The other voice was Bertie Bunter's. "Now that I've finished with the police, I'm off to take the motor for a spin."

"Are you still driving that cheeky little Silver Ghost?"

I hissed at Charlie. "Oh no, this is *his* car!"

"I jolly well am," Bertie said to Rhett. "See you later at the pool party. All cast and crew are invited. Royal Grand Hotel in Westminster. I know we ought to call it off after what's just happened, but they won't return my deposit, so we may as well go."

"Right-o. Enjoy the spin in your motor!"

I grabbed Charlie's shoulder. *Gosh, he was muscly!* "We've ruined his upholstery! Go and stall him!"

Charlie scrambled out the car and grabbed a spanner from a nearby shelf.

I sat stock-still, listening.

Charlie swaggered outside and spoke in a rough accent. "Nah, sorry geezer, no entry."

"Get out the way. My car's in there."

"I said no!"

"Listen, matey, who the devil do you think you are?"

"I'm… the mechanic."

"That was a rhetorical question, you imbecile. You've already told me you're Lady Joanforth's agent. *And* apparently a supporting artist. Now, if you'll excuse me."

"I'm afraid there's something seriously wrong with your car, sir."

"Oh yes?"

"It's complicated."

"Just tell me. I do know a thing or two about cars, thank you very much."

"Okay. Well, the floating piston in the brake junction is intermittently leaking through the contact switch. And also, the… er… flux capacitor is… fluxing."

Bertie pretended to understand. "Is it? Oh dear, that's not good. *Is* it?"

As Charlie continued to stall Bertie, I realised I'd better get out of here. I glanced around and saw an open window further along the wall – so that would have to do. I grabbed my Amulet of Seeing and, as I fumbled to put it back on, I dropped it. Drat.

It'd rolled under the seat, so I felt around and, *hullo…* what was this? I pulled out an envelope the size of a hardback book.

I checked Charlie was still distracting Bertie, and tipped the contents into my palm. Oh blimey… it was a stack of twenty photographs – *explicit* photographs – of Edith Parker the handmaiden!

What were *these* doing in Bertie Bunter's car? No time to dwell on that, I needed to get out of here!

Taking the photos with me, I scrabbled out the window and plopped to the ground. Judging by Bertie's raised voice, he was getting pretty hacked off with Charlie.

"Dashed it all, man, would you *move*!"

"Wouldn't you rather walk? It's a nice sunny day."

"I don't want to walk!"

"How about the bus?"

"Why don't *you* get the bus?"

"I don't want to go anywhere."

"Well, I'm sure Lady Joanforth needs you somewhere. Where is she anyway?"

"She's gone to learn her script," Charlie said. "I don't expect we'll see her again for a long time."

I strolled around the corner, approaching behind Charlie.

Bertie frowned at me. "Won't see her again for a long time, eh?"

"Not for ages I don't expect," Charlie said.

"Hullo, chaps," I said jovially. "Ah, Mr Bunter, police finished with you, have they?"

"What's it to you?"

"I expect they asked you all sorts of questions, did they? Where were you at the time of the murder? How well did you know the victim? Was she a huge pain in the neck and costing you a fortune? That sort of thing."

Bertie Bunter eyeballed me. "Lady Joanforth, the murder weapon was a venomous snake. First thing I knew about it was when Miss Everett screamed, and we all went running. It's obvious who the culprit is. Our resident Egyptologist and snake expert, Edgar Lambourne."

"What makes you say that, sir?" Charlie asked.

"Gillian Everett was a tough cookie, but I got the feeling she was frightened of Edgar Lambourne. He was always trying to scare her with outlandish tales of Egyptian curses – claiming that the real Cleopatra would haunt her for her dreadful acting."

"You heard him threatening her?" Charlie asked.

"Lots of people did – just ask anyone. And not only that but, yesterday afternoon, I actually overheard Edgar Lambourne and our handmaiden Edith Parker plotting to *do away* with Miss Everett!"

"They were plotting to kill her together?" Charlie asked. "I assume you've told the police this?"

"Of course I have. Now, if you'll excuse me."

"How well do you *know* Edith Parker?" I blurted out. "For example, have you seen any interesting photographs of her?"

Bertie threw his hand to his hip. "And what exactly do you mean by that?"

I was reluctant to whip out the risqué photos of Edith here. What if it put her in danger again? I decided I'd better speak to the woman herself.

"Never mind," I said.

"Right. Now, Lady Joanforth, if you want the starring role in this film, I suggest you go and learn your part!" He swept into the garage.

I gazed at Charlie. "One, two, three, four, fi—"

Bertie's anger echoed off the walls. "What the bloody hell's happened to my car!"

We scarpered – hurrying along the banks of the river, before halting under an ancient weeping willow.

Charlie was a little out of breath. "I don't think he believed I was really a mechanic, your ladyship."

"Don't worry, darling, you were superb." I held up the envelope in my hand. "But look what *I* found hidden under the seat of Mr Bunter's car. You might want to brace yourself, Charlie. I know how terribly old-fashioned you are."

Although… after that kiss, who knew what passions might be lurking…

I showed Charlie the first of the photographs, and his eyes almost popped out of his head. He blushed bright crimson, then stepped away and fiddled with his tie, clearing his throat. "Lady Joanforth, I'm shocked that you'd show me such pictures – and *you* certainly shouldn't be looking at them…"

I chuckled. "But didn't you see who the lady in the photograph was?"

"I did not and I care not neither!"

I slid the photographs back in their envelope. "They're of Edith Parker."

Charlie turned slowly. "Why does Bertie Bunter have *erotic* photographs of Miss Parker?"

"No idea. But if they're both somehow involved in the death of Gillian Everett, it might be interesting to find out."

"Well I'm certainly not asking her. Or him."

"No, all right. But we'll take ourselves along to the Royal Grand Hotel tonight for the party they're having. I'll take Miss Parker to one side, woman-to-witch."

Worry skirted across his face. "Will they let *us* into their party?"

"Why not? Bertie Bunter said it was for all cast members. And I'm the leading lady!"

Chapter Five

One thing I loved about the 1920s – as well as the liberation, fashion, cars, and music – was the avid interest in ancient Egypt, which was known as Egyptomania. This craze had actually begun in the Victorian era – well, hadn't everything! But it was Howard Carter's discovery of the tomb of Tutankhamun that had sent Egyptomania into overdrive – influencing the beautiful Art Deco styles that defined the decade.

In my few hundred years on this planet, I'd always loved dressing up, and the 1920s had given me the confidence to do so with a vengeance. Back home in 1926, I loved emphasising my eyes with dark sweeping eye-liner, akin to King Tut's lavish gold funerary mask. And, until I'd adopted my waved blonde crop, my hairstyle had been a poker-straight black bob – a fashion also inspired by ancient Egypt.

Charlie and I strolled back into the film studio, hoping to get closer to the sapphire. But I was dismayed to see that my 1923 self was now wearing it – and *totally* embracing the Egyptian style that we *both* loved! Just like Gillian Everett before her, 1923 Joanie strode regally onto the set, looking glorious in Cleopatra's jewelled headdress, floaty white robe, and leather-sandalled feet.

Charlie gasped. "Woah…"

I was tempted to reach up and close his jaw. Well, here was a strange sensation. I was envious of myself! "Come along, Charlie."

I grabbed his arm and ushered him away, worried that if she spotted this handsome young man, she might steal him off me…

Charlie grinned. "You look beautiful, Lady Joanie – a real Egyptian queen."

I patted my cloche hat, feeling frumpy again. "Thank you, Charlie."

We hid behind a billboard that was painted to look like the inside of a tomb. Charlie chewed his lip. "But… what if I bump into her, thinking she's you? How will I tell you two apart?"

"Don't be silly, darling, *she* won't know who *you* are. Although, if she sees you, she'll undoubtedly try to seduce you."

He brightened up. "Will she?"

"But you're far too young for her. Innocent and naïve. She'll worry she'll corrupt you."

He looked annoyed. "Innocent and naïve, really? Well, she's far too hoity-toity for me."

I glanced at my fingernails. "That's true. And also, you're human and she's a witch. It'll never work."

"Fine."

"Fine."

We turned to each other suddenly. Charlie lowered his face to mine. *Oh golly!*

"Charlie?" I whispered.

"Yes, Lady Joanie?"

"You're standing on my toe…"

"Oh, I do apologise." He shifted his weight – bringing his face even closer to mine.

My heart fluttered with longing… But, thank goodness, Detective Inspector Parry was heading this

306

way, so I stepped away from my lovely hunk to observe the policeman from our hiding place.

DI Parry was deep in conversation with a serious-looking, bespectacled man wearing a brown overcoat. They halted at the other end of the tomb, so Charlie and I crept along to eavesdrop.

"But you're *certain* the snake isn't venomous?" DI Parry asked.

The man wrung his cap in his hands. "I'm positive, squire. You're welcome to get another opinion, of course."

"No, no. If I can't trust London Zoo's very own snake expert, then I can't trust anyone. It's just the coroner's saying Miss Everett died from a lethal dose of highly toxic snake venom. And she has those fang marks on her wrist, so…"

The snake expert shrugged. "Well, inspector, *I* handled the animal and suffered no ill consequence. But then again, I was bitten so many times out in Africa, I'm practically a walking/talking antivenom!" He laughed nervously.

DI Parry spoke severely. "The coroner said the victim would've died almost instantaneously with a strong venom like that. Agree, do you?"

"Oh yes, sir. A lethal dose of highly toxic venom would've caused immediate heart failure. Some snakes contain enough poison to kill two-hundred men!"

"Why, what've they got against 'em?"

"Oh no, you see, Inspector, snakes need extremely potent venom because mice have a tendency to run away once bitten – so snakes bite first and ask questions later. Unfortunately, when the lady delved her hand into the basket, the snake would've struck straight away." He pushed his glasses up his nose. "Why *did* she put her hand in the basket, do you think?"

DI Parry sighed. "There was a handwritten card on the lid, which said *To Darling Gillian, From Kevin Smithers*. But I've traced it, and it looks like the card was moved by the killer from a wholly innocent bunch of flowers."

A uniformed constable joined the two men. "Sir, a witness has just informed me that Miss Gillian Everett seemed frightened of the American man, sir."

"Edgar Lambourne?"

"That's right, sir. Snake expert and Egyptologist."

"Why was she frightened of him?" DI Parry asked. "And who was this witness?"

"One of the catering blokes, sir. Overheard Miss Everett and Mr Lambourne arguing the day before yesterday." The constable read from his notebook. "*Miss Everett sounded frightened, which was odd as usually she was a stuck-up piece of goods.* Witness's own words, sir."

"All right, good work." DI Parry waved them both away.

I turned to talk to Charlie, but my 1923 self was now heading this way!

DI Parry stopped her. "Right, Lady Joanforth, it's time for me to ask you some questions." He frowned. "It's strange, you know, you don't look a day older than when I saw you ten years ago."

She patted her jewelled headdress. "Oh… thank you. We've met then, have we? Sorry, what did you say your name was?"

"Don't get funny with me, Lady Joanforth. You know who I am. Detective Inspector Parry."

"Hmm… I usually never forget a face. Although in your case I can see why I made an exception."

From our hiding place, I guffawed at my own wonderful wit.

"Shh!" Charlie said, laughing too.

DI Parry folded his arms across his chest. "Yes, very drole. Listen, I need your assurance that you won't go poking your nose into my business this time."

"I promise you, Inspector, I will not poke anything of mine into *anything* of yours."

"Good. Right. Where were you at the time of the murder?"

"Oh, has there been a murder?"

They walked off together, with DI Parry grumbling about how strange she was acting.

I turned to Charlie. "Interesting about the snake situation."

He nodded. "Yeah… why did that London Zoo man say the snake wasn't venomous when – oh blimey – excuse my language – there's Edith Parker… Oh, your ladyship, I can't look at her!"

I grinned. "Stop being such a prude. What do you think *I* wear under *my* clothes?"

He flushed. "I would *not* care to speculate!"

I linked my arm through his. "Come on, let's talk to her…"

We caught up with Edith at the refreshments table. I helped myself to a plate of sandwiches. Edith was making herself some tea.

"Excuse me, Miss Parker," I said. "Might we have a word?"

She looked surprised. "Lady Joanforth, you've changed back into your civvies? We're about to re-shoot the kiss scene."

"Um, yes… I… never mind that now. But I was wondering, have you lost any photographs recently?"

Miss Parker's wrist went limp with shock, and she yelped as the tea burnt her. She blushed crimson – but quickly pulled herself together. "Photos? Lost? Me? No…"

I held up the white envelope. "So you wouldn't mind if I showed *these* to your mother?"

"Or the police," Charlie added grimly. "Obscene Publications Act, 1887."

"Don't be silly, Charlie – sometimes the law is *wrong*."

Edith tried to grab the envelope. "Please!"

I held it out of her reach. "It's all right, my dear, you can have them back… but first I must know, why were they in Bertie Bunter's car?"

"Mr Bunter's car?" She looked genuinely surprised. "I've no idea. All I know is that they were stolen from my bag a few days ago."

"Who by?"

"I don't know. *Please*!"

"All right, here…"

She grabbed the envelope and held it tight with relief.

"Just one more thing," I said. "Mr Bunter said he overheard you and Edgar Lambourne plotting to do away with Miss Everett. And it was *his* snake that bit her… Is this true?"

Edith sighed. "Yes, but we weren't planning to *kill* her. We just… we wanted her off the set… off the film."

"And so…? You planted a basket containing a deadly snake in her dressing room?"

"Edgar did. We hoped to scare her. But honestly, Edgar promised me the snake wasn't venomous. You should speak to him – he'll back me up."

"Have you told the police all this?" Charlie asked.

"Of course not – they'll think *we* killed her. But… what are *you* going to do?"

I stood tall. "We're going to talk to Edgar Lambourne. All the evidence seems to be pointing his way!"

Chapter Six

I relished the feel of the April sunshine on my face as Charlie and I traversed the front lawn of the Georgian mansion that served as the headquarters of Golden Magic Flicks.

This lovely green space would ordinarily be a tranquil haven but, at the moment, Edgar Lambourne was chatting loudly to journalists and posing for photographs. There was a hefty crowd around him, so Charlie and I slipped into the huddle.

A reporter near the front shouted a question. "Mr Lambourne, did you *really* just say that Miss Everett's murder is due to the curse of Cleopatra?"

Edgar Lambourne's gravelly American accent was laced with joy. "Well, as I say in my new book – which I have here – we really don't know what sort of magic those ancients were capable of."

"So it *was* the curse that killed her?"

"I'm just saying we don't know…"

He smiled for a photograph, then another reporter asked, "Can you tell us more about your travels in Africa?"

I spoke quietly to Charlie. "Nothing like a juicy murder to sell a few copies of his new book…"

"My thoughts exactly, Lady Joanie."

I opened my mouth to ask a question of my own, but realised I'd caught the attention of someone I'd met in 1916. "Ah… I should've guessed *you'd* be here, Mr Volfson."

The journalist's yellow werewolf eyes inspected me. "Lady Joanforth Eldritch, we meet again."

"Shh!" another journalist hissed.

"Getting all the news, are you?" I asked. "Sniffing about?"

"Something like that."

"Shh!"

Mr Volfson eyed-up Charlie. "Why hasn't this human aged in the last ten years?"

My mind raced for a bluff. "This is… his… younger brother."

"He looks identical."

"Shh!"

"Yes. They're… twins."

"Twins… born ten years apart? Now there's a scoop."

"It's as believable as everything else you write in your newspaper."

"Shh!"

He laughed humourlessly. "And what's this one's name?"

"Er… Charlie."

"Is that a fact? And the other guy was also called Charlie?"

"Yes. His parents were avid fans of King Charles the First. And… King Charles… the, um, Second."

"Shh!"

The werewolf's fangs extended slightly. "Lady Joanforth, tell me the truth, have you invented magical time travel?"

I snorted. "Don't be daft."

"Shh!"

"And I will *not* shh!" I waved and shouted. "Coo-ee, Mr Lambourne, I write for the *Daily Witch*. Please be honest, did *you* kill Miss Everett by leaving her a gift-wrapped deadly snake to play with?"

Mr Lambourne gawped at me, but slickly recovered. "Me? Of course not! Is it not written that anyone who dares to portray the Queen of Egypt will be cursed to face a similar fate?"

"*Is* it written?" I asked. "Apart from in the book *you're* currently hawking?"

Mr Lambourne raised his hands. "No more questions…"

The journalists reluctantly dispersed, leaving Charlie and I to face the Egyptologist.

"Who *are* you?" he asked irritably. "A lady journalist? Our replacement Cleopatra? Or…" He glanced at Charlie. "An undercover cop?"

"What makes you say that?" I asked. "Hiding something from the police?"

Charlie loomed. "*I* have a question. Earlier you said that *you'd* originally been cast as Mark Anthony – but Miss Everett insisted that Mr Mantel be the leading man instead. That must've annoyed you?"

His confident act deflated. "The truth is, I didn't like her – I *did* want to get rid of her. You see, it was her who got in touch with me originally to star in this picture – she said she'd heard all about me. So I flew all the way from California three weeks ago. But then at the last minute she insisted on Rhett Mantel as Mark Anthony, and *I* was cast aside – demoted to Egypt Consultant, which is a joke! There's nothing authentically Egyptian about this movie – *or* about Miss Everett. She was as fickle as she was beautiful."

"So you set your snake on her?" I asked. "For revenge?"

Mr Lambourne sighed. "I admit I did do that, yeah."

"You admit it was *your* snake that killed her?" Charlie asked optimistically.

"No! Listen, my snake is *not* poisonous. I brought him in a pet shop in Croydon a few days ago – the police are already verifying my purchase."

I narrowed my eyes suspiciously. "Don't the police think it's rather strange that an American tourist would buy a snake on holiday in England?"

"No, because I'm a snake expert. I've always loved snakes. And I'm not on vacation, I was here for a job – which was taken from me."

"Perhaps you should tell us the truth?" Charlie suggested.

Mr Lambourne stared at him for a moment, then shook his head. "Okay… here's what happened: A couple-a evenings ago, after yet another day of Miss Everett upsetting poor Miss Parker and me, I was in my hotel room… alone, relaxing with my snake."

I laughed unintentionally. "Sorry. It's just it sounded like a… um, carry on."

"Well, I was struck with this cool plan… which I shared with Edith Parker yesterday."

"The plan being?" Charlie asked.

"We decided that I'd leave my snake in Miss Everett's dressing room, in the hope that – along with all the curse stuff – we might scare her away forever."

"So the snake was just part of your 'curse of Cleopatra' ploy?" I asked. "Trying to give Miss Everett enough of the willies to walk?"

"It sure was."

Charlie clicked his fingers. "*You* moved the gift card in her dressing room?"

He glared at the grass. "Yes. But I just wanted her to *leave* – not die. I assure you, Sedrick is not venomous!"

"Sedrick?" I said, smiling.

Charlie raised an eyebrow. "Mr Lambourne, I must ask, are you and Edith Parker – *ahem* – involved?"

"Of course not! I like Edith, she's a good kid. I wanted her to have the starring role." Mr Lambourne glared at me. "But now *you've* got it instead."

"You're not accusing *me* of murder?"

"I guess only the killer knows who he or she really is." Mr Lambourne took off his hat and wiped his brow. "Now, much as I've enjoyed our little chat, I'm busy."

Charlie and I watched him march back towards the mansion.

"I'm sure he did it," Charlie said. "Him and Edith Parker are in this together. All that 'just trying to scare Miss Everett off the film' nonsense is a smokescreen."

"You might be right, Charlie. But *whoever* the killer is, and however they managed to get Sedrick to kill Miss Everett, one thing's for sure: *I* might be next!"

Chapter Seven

After an afternoon of filming, Charlie and I saw my 1923 self leave for her date with Rhett Mantel – meaning she should remain safely alive tonight. Admittedly, it was possible that Rhett was a suspect, but we'd tried all day to come up with a motive for him – and failed. So we felt fairly confident that she/I should be fine. It would hopefully just be a repeat of what happened last time… and there was no way I was depriving myself *or* her of that deliciousness!

"And now, Charlie, let's dine out…"

I knew he'd probably feel uncomfortable in my favourite restaurant, the Ritz, so we chose a nice little pub in Camden. I tucked into a big plate of sausage and mash, washed down with a glass of ale. The truth was, I could feel comfortable anywhere. Especially with Charlie.

And next stop, the pool party! We'd need some decent evening togs to be let in, so I took Charlie shopping to my favourite boutiques. I paid on my 1923 self's account – she wouldn't mind. I also bought a large carpet bag for our day clothes, which we could store in the cloakroom at the hotel while we were at the party.

Gosh it was fantastic to feel glamorous again! I cast my mind back to my various time-travel outfits. I'd first arrived wearing my 1926 dress, of course, but then there was the Edwardian tea gown with copious undies and that dreaded corset. And my frumpy, but freer, 1916 clothes.

But *this* outfit was much more me: a green knee-length dress, decorated with sparkly diamantes. The tassels at the hem tickled the tops of my shins, leaving nothing to the imagination. And with the peacock feather stuck in my matching headband, I looked a sensation.

And of course, Charlie looked delightful in his tuxedo and black bow tie – very modern for 1923! I was proud to arrive at The Royal Grand Hotel with him on my arm.

We stepped into the glittering ballroom, and I gasped. If rainbows could dream, then *this* is what they'd dream of – fabulous, frolicking fun.

How wonderful to see the hundred-or-so guests dressed in their expensive fashionable clothes, chatting, drinking, and schmoozing. And they were apparently insatiable! The waiters carrying trays of colourful cocktails couldn't move fast enough to satisfy these hedonistic, pleasure-loving bright young things.

But the best part of this den of delight was the five-piece jazz band making merry music on the stage. My body swayed of its own accord. I eyed-up Charlie, hoping we might dance.

A waiter proffered a tray. "Cocktail, Charlie?" I purred.

"Don't mind if I do!"

We clinked glasses, then inched through the throng, wondering what fun we might find. But, like a puddle of gloom in the middle of paradise, I spotted Edith Parker arguing fiercely with Bertie Bunter.

I spoke above the music. "Do you think he's wondering where her risqué photos have disappeared to?"

"Perhaps – if he was planning to blackmail her with them."

"He looks rather cross. I think we should intervene."

Charlie pulled me back by the upper arm. *How forceful he was!* "Wait, Lady Joanie. Edith Parker clearly wanted to play Cleopatra. I know you think she's a sweet young woman, but what if *she's* the killer – and now plans to kill the new leading lady?"

"But Uncle Frog said *she* was due to die until I showed up."

"Yes, but we know from before *that* doesn't mean she's innocent!"

"You're right. But it would be nice to know what they're arguing about…"

Bertie Bunter suddenly shouted at Edith to leave him alone, so she strode off into the crowd – getting swallowed up by the glamorous, air-kissing partygoers.

"Let's follow her," I said.

We caught up with her as she strode through a wide ornate door, which led to… Oh good heavens – an indoor swimming pool!

I grabbed Charlie's shirt in excitement. "How marvellous! Let's join the fun."

It was the most lavish indoor pool I'd ever seen, and the sparkling water was jolly inviting. Most people were simply dangling their feet in the water, but a few were swimming in 1920s bathing costumes, which only a decade ago would've been classed as underwear.

Speaking of underwear… "Look, Charlie, there she is – sitting on that sun lounger."

We sidled up behind her. "Miss Parker?"

She turned, Champagne glass in hand. "Oh… it's you."

"May we join you?" I asked.

She gestured to a nearby lounger, so we sat.

"We saw you arguing with Bertie Bunter just now," Charlie said. "Was he attempting to blackmail you over the photographs?"

Edith gulped her Champagne. "Look, the truth is, I don't know how my photos ended up in his car, so I just decided to ask him straight out if he planned to blackmail me. He got angry and said he didn't know anything about any photos – and if I ever accused him of anything like that again, he'd remove me from the film. And I do so want this job."

"Someone else put the photographs in his car?" Charlie said.

"Do you know who that *was*, Miss Parker?" I asked kindly.

Edith gulped her drink again. "It might've been… Well, it was *Gillian* who had them last."

"Gillian Everett?" I asked. "*She* was threatening you with them?"

Edith's eyes welled with tears. "The photographs were taken over a year ago, but I always keep them in my bag for safekeeping. Well, Gillian Everett found them. Waved them under my nose, saying she'd make sure I never got above my station again. *Bitch*."

"That's enough of *that* talk, thank you," Charlie said. "But... Let's get this straight: Miss Everett was blackmailing you, so... you killed her?"

"No! Look, I do realise that this looks bad on me, because I did want to get rid of her – off the film. I *did* plot with Edgar to plant the snake in her dressing room. But she was a bully. A nasty person. I'm not sorry she's dead. But I didn't kill her."

"So who did?" I asked.

Edith shrugged her shoulders. "I don't know."

Charlie frowned. "What I don't understand is, why did Miss Everett put your photographs in Mr Bunter's car?"

"Again, I don't know. Perhaps it was simply a good hiding place where she knew I wouldn't look. Or maybe she wanted Mr Bunter to find them and sack me."

An idea occurred. "Do you think Edgar Lambourne might've acquired *another* snake? A venomous one? And Sedrick is a red herring?"

Charlie spoke pensively. "A *second* snake as a red herring? Interesting theory..."

"It's just an idea but, as a snake expert, Mr Lambourne would know how to handle even a highly lethal snake."

Edith scoffed. "And where does one *hide* a deadly snake? Stuff it down his trousers, did he?"

I opened my mouth to make a suggestive joke, but Edith stood up. "I've told you everything. I'll see you tomorrow."

I watched her walk away. Charlie gazed at me. "Now what?"

"Fancy a dip?"

He laughed. "I'm not donning a bathing suit, Lady Joanie. Not even for you."

"So you'd prefer to just jump in naked? Oh Charlie, don't look at me like that, I'm joking! Come on, how about a dance?"

He stood up and held out his hand. "That sounds more like it. Shall we?"

I linked my arm through his as we made our way to the main space. The dance floor was empty, because most people were drinking cocktails, chatting, and schmoozing.

"Looks like it's just we two," Charlie said.

I was hoping for the Charleston, but it hadn't arrived from America yet. As Charlie and I stood opposite each other, the musicians struck up a sultry blues number.

I gazed into Charlie's gorgeous brown and blue eyes, and just for a moment, nerves gripped me. But that wouldn't do. I lifted my chin and threw him a cocky smile.

He raised a flirty eyebrow, stepped away, and started to circle me like a confident alley cat. Had he learnt to dance in the lusty bordellos of Argentina or something! Not to be outdone, I stepped in time with him, and we strutted around each other, held together by tension, music, and smouldering eye contact.

As the tempo increased, Charlie wrapped his arm around my waist, effortlessly pulling me towards him. He linked the fingers of his other hand through mine at shoulder height. "Let's dance," he said.

"Delighted…"

He drew me close then stepped between my legs, leaning into me, and gently forcing me backwards. Our bodies were suddenly pressed together so tightly that I could feel his heart beating against mine. And like that, we glided gracefully around the dancefloor, losing ourselves in the music – and in each other's eyes.

This delicious dance was so different to my experience with Captain Sebastian Loveday back in 1926. Dancing with Charlie made me feel alive… like a raindrop in the sunshine. Glee surged through me and I grinned.

I wanted to kiss him…

Like a mind reader, Charlie lowered his face to mine. I braced myself. He smelt of honeysuckle and masculinity. My heart thumped hard. Our lips were close now… just one hair's breadth and we'd be–

The unwelcome sound of brass whistles frantically tooting sprung us apart. My heart pounded harder, but this time with fear. "What's happening!"

Charlie grabbed my hand. "It's the old bill – a raid, let's go!"

We squeezed through the crowd. "Charlie, why? We haven't done anything wrong!"

He spoke as we ran. "They're probably here for the owner – London nightclubs are always getting done for breaking so-called morality laws. And it might be something *actually* illegal, like dope or guns." We dodged a group of scattering people. "But worst of all, *I* currently work for Scotland Yard – my 1923 self, I mean. And my fellow coppers might start wondering why I'm here at this posh hotel with a member of the aristocracy!"

"Good point," I said. "Quick, let's go through here!"

I pushed open a heavy wooden door, which led to a calm back hall of the hotel, where only staff and servants were supposed to come. We ran all the way up a flight of wooden stairs, then through another door – from which we burst into an extravagant hotel corridor.

We caught our breath and walked slowly down the hallway. *I* was more familiar with this sort of opulence than Charlie, but even to me this corridor was spectacular. It was like stepping back two hundred years to the sort of décor Marie Antoinette would've been accustomed to. Gold leaf dominated the lofty ceiling, the walls were decorated with embossed panels, and the carpet was fluffy enough to sleep on.

"Even the doors are posh," Charlie said in awe.

"Yes…" An idea floated into my mind. "Charlie, we don't have anywhere to stay tonight. How about we employ our lockpicking skills and sleep in a nice comfy bed?"

He stifled a smile. "We'll need *two* rooms, Lady Joanie. But… what if we get caught sneaking around?"

"Oh we won't be sneaking around, darling. I'll have a word with the manager – and charge the bills to myself!"

Chapter Eight

I slept like a queen in the snuggly hotel bed – alone, alas. But I was delighted when Charlie woke me from my snoozy slumber the next morning with a tray of eggs, bacon, and tea. He was still wearing his tux, minus the bowtie.

"Breakfast! Thank you, Charlie. How did you manage that?"

"Disguised meself as a waiter." He helped himself to a slice of toast. "You just have to act like you ought to be somewhere and people believe you."

"Cunning, darling. I like your style."

"Thank you, Lady Joanie. I'm quite keen on your style too."

I sipped my tea and grinned. "Come on, we'd better eat up and try to get that sapphire. Lord Vilnius has been rather quiet, and *that* worries me immensely."

"Yeah, all right. We also need to make sure your 1923 self remains unmurdered."

We dressed in our day clothes, then headed back to the film studio. My plan was to sneak into Cleopatra's new dressing room and swipe the sapphire, so we headed in that direction. But we halted as we saw Bertie Bunter standing in a little glass booth at the end of the corridor, messing about with a gramophone.

We walked into the booth to the sound of sweet bird song. How lovely and soothing.

Bertie Bunter took the needle off the record. "Oh, I thought you were getting changed, Lady Joanforth. As I said, I've arranged for some promotional photographs to be taken before we all need to stop for the big event."

"What big event?" I asked – genuinely clueless.

"Very funny. Anyway, what can I do for you?"

"Oh… I wanted to ask you something…"

"Well?"

Oh drat, we actually had no reason to be in here! "Er, um… Charlie, what was it we wanted to ask Mr Bunter?"

"Yes, thank you, Lady Joanie," Charlie said through gritted teeth. "It was… are you interested in music, sir?"

Bertie Bunter glanced at the record in his hand. "Oh, I'm always on the listen-out for new sound effects. My dream is to use this little booth to create plays on the wireless. I've had a tip-off that the newly formed British Broadcasting Corporation will be needing content, and I'm hoping they'll let me broadcast some serious drama from here. Get some proper actors in. For when the bottom falls out the flicks, you know?"

"You don't have faith in the cinema, Mr Bunter?" I asked.

"Not sure. I hear over in the United States, there's something called 'soundie films' on the way. But I'm not certain how popular *that* would be."

"Sound in films?" Charlie asked. "Would it really be possible?"

Bertie shrugged. "Probably not here in England. But I'm sure a clever chap in America will sort it all out."

I glanced around the booth. "Well, we've already got the wireless. I suppose it can't be long until we get sound in film."

"Yes. The dynamic loudspeaker already exists in theatres and for radio broadcasting – so they just need to find a way to attach the sound to the film."

Bertie started riffling through his records, but further down the corridor, I heard my own voice, talking loudly. "Yes, thank you, Doris, I appreciate all your help... yes, the headdress *is* very heavy, darling, but I have exquisite shoulders, as you can see!"

I pulled Charlie around a convenient corner. My 1923 self halted at the sound booth door. "Well, Mr Bunter, I'm ready when you are."

He almost dropped the record in his hand. "How... how did you get changed so quickly?"

She straightened her headdress. "Quickly? It's taken me ages to get all this Egyptian garb on. You wanted some promotional photos, yes? But can we hurry this up please? I've got a wedding to attend in an hour..."

"We'd better get out of here," I whispered to Charlie. "We can't grab the sapphire while she's wearing it. Come on, let's go somewhere away from *her* and think of a plan..."

We strolled through the streets of London for the next hour or so, chatting about the case, the film industry, and the first thing we planned to do when we got back to 1926.

"I'm going to give Uncle Frog and Wispu a big hug," I said. "And then suggest that he dismantle his time machine!"

"And I'll report back to Inspector Parry," Charlie said. "And ask for a pay rise after helping to solve all these murders!"

We ended up strolling along a fashionable, tree-lined thoroughfare known as The Mall – a lovely wide street connecting Trafalgar Square to Buckingham Palace. This area of Central London was relatively clean, and on this sunny April day a brass band was playing all the crowd-pleasers, creating an uplifting, festival vibe.

Actually… there must be something happening today. The streets were lined with thousands of people – many of whom were waving Union Jack flags. Whatever the occasion, it was wonderful to see all walks of life represented: middle class gents in bowler hats, factory workers in their Sunday best, military men in uniform… and of course, the ubiquitous London bobbies, who were patrolling in their tall police helmets, looking for pickpockets and hawkers.

My eye caught a banner fluttering above the street: *Westminster wishes all happiness to the Bride and Groom.*

"Oh, Charlie, it's April the 26th 1923! *That's* the wedding my 1923 self was referring to earlier – the big event that Bertie Bunter mentioned. It's the royal wedding between Prince Albert, Duke of York and Lady Elizabeth Bowes Lyon. How lovely."

330

"Watch out, Lady Joanie – here they come…"

We stepped out the way as four white horses trotted along the street, followed by the royal carriage. The bride and groom – just married – waved at their adoring public. I caught a thrilling glimpse of Lady Elizabeth in her ivory chiffon dress. And the Duke was proudly wearing his RAF officer's uniform. They made a splendid couple.

The carriage was like something out of a romantic fairy-tale – dreadfully old-fashioned in modern 1923. But the truth was, the English couldn't resist all this pageantry, pomp, and ceremony. It was excessive archaic folderol, but it was *ours*.

Charlie waved as the carriage sped by. "She's very queenly, isn't she? Almost as if she was born for a queen."

"Her new husband is only second in line to the throne, Charlie. But you never know…"

"Know what?"

"Well, you've surely heard the rumours about the love-life of the Duke's older brother, the Prince of Wales?"

Charlie tightened up. "Lady Joanie, I've pledged allegiance to serve my King and country *twice* – once as a soldier, then as a policeman. I do not listen to royal gossip. And neither should you. It's… treason."

I smiled kindly, surprised to hear him 'knowing his place'. But class mattered tremendously in England. We were taught that a posh accent and a well-stuffed bank balance somehow made you a better person than a poor worker who dropped their aitches. What a strange country we lived in…

But on this lovely April day the atmosphere was fun and light, no matter what social status you belonged to. And my mood spiralled further, as I spied a young policeman over yonder, standing to attention in a sunbeam.

"Oh look, Charlie, there you are – doing your patriotic duty. Gosh, you look even more dashing in your uniform than I should ever have imagined!"

He chuckled. "I *did* police the royal wedding, it's true. Are you around here somewhere too, Lady Joanie?"

"I'm actually inside Westminster Abbey, so no chance of us bumping into me."

His expression froze. "You didn't go dressed as Cleopatra, did you?"

"Not originally, because I wasn't involved in the film the first time around. But I wouldn't put it past me this time! Actually, here's an idea, once I get my hands on that magical sapphire, I could send it to the Royal Couple as a wedding gift for safekeeping. I only got them a toaster before."

Charlie sounded impressed. "A toaster? Very modern."

"Oh look, something's happening…"

Keeping up with the bustling crowd, we followed the royal carriage to the end of the Mall – where the King's lavish residence, Buckingham Palace, stood majestically in pride of place. As the Bride and Groom appeared on the balcony, their loyal subjects erupted into stirring chants of *Long Live the King!*

You couldn't help but feel proud and jubilant. But, while half of London was here, now might be a good time for Charlie and I to try to swipe the sapphire. *If* my 1923 self hadn't gone to the wedding wearing it, of course!

Chapter Nine

The film studio was quiet when we got back, because practically everyone in London was out cheering the royal couple. But, sitting peacefully at his desk as always, the young title card boy was hard at work.

"I wonder if he can tell us anything about Gillian Everett," Charlie said. "He spends a lot of time around the set, but blends into the action – just like the title cards he designs."

"Let's talk to him," I said. "He might've seen or heard something that we haven't yet discovered. I'd especially like to know who might be plotting my 1923 self's murder!"

Charlie and I stepped over to chat. He was a fresh-faced, stocky young chap with slicked-back hair and a trimmed moustache. He seemed rather serious and stern for one so young, as if he might've been more comfortable back in Edwardian times.

"Excuse me, young man," I said.

He stood up quickly, knocking over the card he was working on.

Charlie picked it up for him. The swirly writing said: *Later That Da…*

"Sorry to interrupt your work," I said. "But we were wondering if you'd seen anything important regarding the murder that happened yesterday?"

He spoke in a pompous voice. "As I told the police, I saw nothing – I *heard* nothing. I'm far too busy creating my cards. I don't have time for thinking about cruel and unusual ways of killing off beautiful young blondes."

"You really can't tell us anything?" Charlie asked.

"Look, all I know is, if I don't finish this card, Hollywood will have invented sound – and *I'll* be out of a job."

Bertie Bunter strode over. "Alfred, how are those cards coming along?"

"Oh, fi—"

"Good. I've instructed everyone to get back here by three so we can continue filming. And if they aren't back, they won't get paid. Simple as…"

Bertie walked off, calling over his shoulder. "Chop, chop, Mr Hitchcock, no time for chatting."

Gripping his pencil in his fist, Young Alfred Hitchcock glanced at his retreating boss, then slashed the implement up and down like a knife.

Charlie and I took a step back – just in case he was some sort of… psycho.

Alfred shrugged his shoulders. "They do say the pen is mightier than the sword…"

Leaving him to it, Charlie and I crept towards the corridor for the dressing rooms. Time to get that sapphire!

"Charlie, you wait here and keep watch. Don't let *anyone* pass."

"Right you are, Lady Joanie."

Gillian Everett's dressing room had been roped off by the police since the murder, so I assumed my 1923 self must be using a dressing room further along. After rattling a few doorknobs and glancing in a few rooms, I soon found the right one. I recognised a 1923 handbag of mine, as well as Cleopatra's headdress – complete with glistening, magical sapphire! *Yes!*

I quietly closed the door. My fingers prickled with anticipation. Right…

Knowing myself to be a practical witch, I grabbed the handbag and rummaged around for my Swiss army knife. There was no need to waste magic, when you could simply use a small blade, a corkscrew, a mini tin opener, a tiny pair of scissors, and… whatever this last one was for…

I easily prised the sapphire out of the headdress and clasped it tight in my trembling fist. It tingled with magic. *I* tingled with excitement!

Had we really just outsmarted Lord Vilnius?

I still had the silver rose brooch from 1906 pinned to my camisole, so now we just needed the golden lion and the time controls, and we'd be home and dry!

I rushed to the door, eager to tell Charlie, but it was flung open from the corridor, hitting me squarely in the face. "Ouch!"

My 1923 self lowered the newspaper she'd been reading, "Oh, I do beg your pardon, I didn't realise there was anyone in here!"

Luckily, I was now covering my face with my hands – due to the bonk I'd received on the nose. I staggered backwards, grabbed a bushy moustache from a props box, and held it to my upper lip. Then in my best macho voice, I said, "I was just repairing your… um…"

"My *um*?" She sounded like she was enjoying this.

Wispu barked a tender woof at me, wagging her tail. *She* was enjoying this too!

I ran to the open door. "All fixed now. Goodbye…" I stepped into the corridor, calling over my shoulder. "Be careful, won't you? Just in case someone tries to kill you!"

My 1923 self would undoubtedly think *that* prospect was just jolly good larks.

Leaving her there, I rushed back down the corridor, cursing Charlie for not keeping an eye out. But I was secretly proud of my 1923 self – she'd presumably put the charms on Charlie and convinced him to let her through. Well, I could be very persu— *oh no!*

As I careered around the corner, Charlie was standing nose-to-nose with Lord Vilnius.

My triumphant mood plunged to terror. My heart thrashed in my chest. *Don't you dare hurt him!*

Lord Vilnius grabbed Charlie's throat. "I *said*, where is she!"

"And *I* said –"

"Leave him alone, Vincent!" I shouted.

Lord Vilnius dropped Charlie – turning his ire on me. "Joanforth, how – wait a *minute*, are those magical vibes I detect? What's that in your hand?"

I thrust the sapphire behind my back. "Nothing."

"Give it to me."

"No…"

He grabbed my wrist and squeezed hard, making me yelp and drop the sapphire into his palm.

Charlie leapt on his back, but Lord V's magic was now fully replenished. He swiftly cast the Strength spell and, with a mere jerk of his shoulder, sent Charlie crashing into a stack of fake urns.

I raised my hands to hurl a fireball, but Lord Vilnius moved as fast as lightning –shoving me to the floor and storming off with the magical sapphire.

Charlie helped me to my feet. "Stay here."

"Charlie, wait!"

He waited, but agitatedly so. "He took the sapphire!"

"I know. But, Charlie, I've got an idea… *You* stay here."

"Where are *you* going?"

I gazed into his earnest eyes. "Listen, there *is* one thing that Lord Vilnius wants. Something *I* can give him."

"The silver rose?".

I glanced at the floor. "No…"

"Not *yourself*, Lady Joanie – no, surely not!"

"Please, Charlie. Just wait here. Let me talk to him."

Before Charlie could stop me, I ran to the secluded backlot and found Lord Vilnius striking a match on a wall for his cigarillo.

He blew out the smoke and spoke in a growl. "I'm not giving you the sapphire – you can forget that."

"I know. But… I think we should talk."

He snorted. "*Talk*? About what?"

"About… all this."

"Why should I talk to someone who a couple of days ago wanted to throw me under a moving steam train?"

"You were choking Constable Anderson – I had no choice. Look, I don't want to argue with you. I want to talk. Sensibly. Like adults."

"All right. Let's talk sensibly about how you're going to give me the silver rose."

"Not now – I can't talk now. But please, let's meet at – I don't know – Trafalgar Square. Seven o'clock tonight."

"Why Trafalgar Square?"

"It's out in the open. Plenty of witnesses."

"You don't trust me?"

"Of course not."

He smirked, cat-like. "Sensible. The feeling's mutual." He smothered me with his deep brown eyes. "Don't bring that human."

"No. Just us."

He threw his cigarillo to the ground and strode off. Litter bug…

I wandered back inside with my thoughts full of what I might say to him.

Charlie was leaning against the wall. He watched me carefully.

"Did you get all that?" I asked curtly.

"You're making a big mistake, your ladyship. Meeting him. Alone."

"Not alone. We'll be in a public place."

"You know what I mean. Without… me."

I wanted to say, 'I've managed perfectly well without you for the last few hundred years, thank you very much.' But that would be spiteful. "Charlie, you two keep fighting whenever you see each other. I'd like to try something different."

"What about our plan to knee him in the whatsits?"

"Please, I know I sound naive, but what if I can convince him to come back to the good side? Perhaps I can persuade him to betray the Empower. I sense there's still good in him."

Charlie squeezed my hand. "I know you have a soft spot for him, but *I* have no sympathy for the devil."

"I'm not planning to seduce him, if that's what you're thinking."

Charlie scoffed. "That's none of my business."

"Quite right. But I'm not."

"What did you ever see in him?"

"He was nice… once."

Charlie scrutinised me, then suddenly gasped. "Lady Joanie, your eye's all black and puffy! Did that villain lay his hands on you? Just wait until I get *my* hands on him!"

"Calm yourself, Charlie. It wasn't Lord V who hit me in the face."

"Then who?"

As if on cue, my 1923 self's voice drifted over. "Yes, yes, I am coming Mr Bunter. But I was just reading this article by a Mr Volson, which says that the leading lady of your last film died too! Should I be worried about *my* life? A mysterious stranger just warned me to watch out. Is it the curse of Cleopatra, do you think?"

Mr Bunter was walking beside her. "No, no, dear lady of course not! My last film was set in the court of King Arthur, so the ghost of Cleopatra would hardly haunt there, would she! It's just a dreadful coincidence. Now if we could get some filming done today? My sponsor's breathing down my neck…"

Mr Bunter snatched the newspaper from her hands and, without looking at us, shoved it into Charlie's chest.

Charlie unscrunched Mr Volfson's article.

"Look at that headline," I said. "*Fear-Amid the Pyramid!* Is that what passes for grammar these days?"

Charlie read the article out loud. "*Golden Magic Flicks owner, Albert Bunter, in Golden TRAGIC flicks scandal! Leading lady, Gillian Everett, took her role as Cleopatra a little too far yesterday, when she was bitten to death by a venomous snake! FANGS a lot, Sedrick! Observant readers of this newspaper will agree that Bunter's dying queens sure are ADDER-ING UP! Remember the tragic accident last year of Queen Guinevere? When that leading lady slipped over in the armoury, it wasn't just the film that got axed! Ladies, if Mr Bunter offers you a regal role in his next flick, give him a de-NILE, and run screaming for your MUMMY!*" Charlie closed the newspaper. "Hmm… perhaps we'd better have a word with Mr Volson."

"To recommend a nice writing course, sort of thing?"

"To *ask* him if he knows anything about the murder."

"Oh… yes. Well, perhaps we'll see him later. But more pressingly, *I* need to prepare for my date with the dark side!"

Chapter Ten

The humid London drizzle reflected my own tense mood this evening. Uncle Frog would probably call me half-insane for arranging to meet up with Lord Vilnius. But I had to try – otherwise I'd regret it forever.

The trouble was, I was a glass half full sorta witch, and I was thinking if I could persuade Lord V to come back to the good side, then perhaps he'd abandon his quest to collect the magical gems, and we could all live happily ever after.

It did sometimes happen that way, didn't it? In fairy tales…

The rain hung in the air, soaking my hat and coat with a fine layer of London dampness. I wiped my face with my gloved hand and steeled myself. I could do this. I was Lady Joanforth Eldritch for goodness sake – soon-to-be senior witch and all-round jolly good egg!

Anyway, it was impossible to be too distressed amid the hustle and bustle of London's fashionable Trafalgar Square. This world-famous plaza was vibrant, fun, and slap-bang in the centre of London. In fact, it was *the* centre of London, for it was the place where all distances from London were measured.

The centre of Trafalgar Square (the *centre* of the centre of London!) was dominated by the 150-foot-tall Nelson's Column, as well as four monumental bronze lions, and several large water fountains –

which had actually been built to prevent protesters from gathering! Welcome to England, where you have the *right* to protest, but not the space!

Thankfully, no one was in a protesting mood at the moment. 1923 was the year of hedonism, liberation, and letting the good times roll! Tonight, men and women were gathered in abundance, dressed in the latest fashions, as they headed off to dine, dance, and definitely consume copious cocktails!

I knew I'd easily find Lord Vilnius – just follow the negative vibes.

Charlie had insisted on walking me here, but now that we were on the outskirts of the square, it was time for us to part. "I'll be all right, Charlie. Don't look at me like that."

He spoke firmly. "I'll be here if you need me. Just holler."

"Thank you. My magic feels all right at the moment, so I should be able to defend myself. I've got one spell in me, I think."

"And if all else fails, we'll go back to our original plan…" Charlie smirked at the prospect of kicking our nemesis in the whatsits.

"And I can always hit him over the head with this…" I held up the Champagne bottle I'd bought at dinner just now. I'd also swiped a couple of glasses…

"Is that your weapon of choice?" Charlie asked. "Getting him blotto?"

"Something like that." I smiled into his eyes. "I'll be fine. I'd better go."

He leaned tantalisingly close. "Shout if you need me – I really mean it."

I swallowed my clashing nerves. "You just stay out of sight. He'll know I've betrayed him if he sees you."

"All right. But I'll be lurking…"

I nodded gratefully, then held my head high and strode across the square, disturbing a flock of resident pigeons – who flapped frantically away. Lord V's dark vibes called to me like a Geiger counter seeking out radioactive material. I halted in front of Nelson's Column, and… ah yes…

My once-betrothed – now evil sorcerer – stepped out from behind a brass lion. He looked devilishly dashing as always. But my witchy senses detected a nuclear furnace of pent-up anger inside him, desperate to explode. He'd always been blessed with an authoritative air that I found appealing. If only I could persuade him to use it for good.

"Joanforth. Delighted."

"You came…"

"Naturally. I want the silver rose."

"No rush. Look, I've got Champagne."

He snorted. "Surely you didn't think you could get me *drunk*, Joanforth? This isn't a Gilbert and Sullivan operetta."

Blast, he'd seen straight through my plan! "Of course not."

I popped the cork, which banged. A few people looked over.

I poured us both a glass of bubbly, then clinked his glass. "Cheers… oh, you know where the tradition of clinking glasses comes from, don't you, Vinnie?"

He sighed. "It was traditionally done so the liquid from the glasses spilled and mixed – just in case one of them was poisoned."

"Well then, our liquid has spilled and mixed, so… *up yours*...."

"I beg your pardon!"

"I mean, bottom's up. Cheers."

"Cheers." He swigged his drink. "Now, what do you want to *talk* about?"

I tried not to wilt from his intense stare. But he was scrutinising me like a man in command of the universe. *That* was probably what the Empower was offering – *Stick with me, kid, and I'll make you a star.* And we all knew how powerful and destructive stars could be.

And how full of gas…

I refused to let his arrogant air get under my skin. "I know there's still good in you, Vincent. Otherwise, why am I still alive?"

"Because I haven't decided to kill you yet."

Good answer… "Nevertheless, you were once a decent Being of Magic with good intentions. I know the war affected you. It affected all of us. But we didn't all go rushing off to hook up with the evil Empower. And it's not too late for you to stop this."

He was apparently finding this amusing. "You're wrong. The Empower is my teacher and master. And one day the student will become the master. And I shall be lord of all Marvelton – and *all* the magical realms."

"Vincent, what do you know about ruling Marvelton – or anywhere?"

346

He gestured grandly. "Well, if you insist, I'll gladly impart my expertise."

"Oh really? Does that mean you're going to remain *silent*?"

"Very amusing, Joanforth. Anyway, I *will* be the ruler of Marvelton. You cannot change my mind – or my destiny."

"Then why did you agree to meet me?"

He glanced at his fingernails. "The Empower is interested in you."

"*You're* trying to recruit *me*!" Oh dear…

"My master has foreseen that your children will be powerful. He is keen for you and I to… rekindle our alliance."

Oh blimey, how romantic… "Children?"

"That is what the Empower has foreseen. Your descendants pose a threat to him – to all Beings of Evil. But if you align yourself with me again, I will protect you – *and* our offspring. It's up to you now, Joanforth. Are you with me or are you against me?"

"This is ridiculous. Come with me, Vinnie. Back to 1926. You can be good. It's not too late."

"You don't understand the power of the darkness, Joanie. If you're not with me, then we will forever be enemies. We will fight. To the death."

Well, that was clear! "You would kill me?"

"I would have no choice."

"Then we – the Beings of Magic – the good beings, we'll stop you *and* your master."

"You cannot."

An idea surged in my brain. "Yes! We'll create a Beings of Magic Committee – a strong alliance to keep you out. And this committee, it can protect all the magical *and* human realms with powerful incantations. And… a representative from each type of magical being can serve. And we'll be united against our common enemy – you and the Empower!"

Lord Vilnius swallowed me up in his big brown eyes. "Thank you for revealing your plans."

Oh drat! Now we'd forever need to disguise our committee as an incompetent bunch of local rag-tags, whose main aim was to discuss biscuits, bus shelters, and bandstands. Yep, *that* would fool the evil ones!

Lord Vilnius held out his hand. "Join me, Joanforth."

"No, *you* join me!"

"Never."

I was about to appeal to him again, but a movement over his shoulder caught my eye.

Charlie!

He gestured with a frantic circle of the wrist – keep him talking!

I focused on our nemesis. "Very well, Vincent. If you've made up your mind, then I only have one thing to say to you."

"Oh yes?"

"This conversation is *over*."

"In that case…" Lord Vilnius raised his hands to cast magic but, in one swoop, Charlie bonked him hard with his heavy wooden baton. Lord Vilnius collapsed to the ground, smashing his glass with a crash.

"What a waste of Champagne," Charlie said.

Lord Vilnius groaned, tried to stand, but fell again. The message took a second to get to his brain, but thankfully *now* he was out cold.

Charlie drew back his foot to kick him in the whatsits, but paused. His enemy was incapacitated, and Charlie had no need to be cruel. Charlie was probably as surprised as *I* was that in the end it'd been that easy to incapacitate someone who claimed to be so powerful! But we all had our weak spots, even Lord Vilnius.

Charlie cupped his hand to his ear. "Did I hear you holler, Lady Joanie?"

"You did not – I was coping perfectly, thank you! But excellent work, darling. Now, let's get what we need!"

It was still very busy in Trafalgar Square, so Charlie dragged Lord Vilnius behind a brass lion, just in case anyone thought we were mugging him – and tried to stop us.

"Let's mug him," Charlie said. "Before anyone tries to stop us."

"Right-o!"

I crouched to swipe the time control cube from Lord V's belt, while Charlie's nimble fingers searched his aviator jacket for the golden lion and sapphire.

"Got them!" Charlie pocketed both gems.

"Fantastic! Now we just need the magic spell from Uncle Frog, and we can send this villain back while he's still out cold. We'll keep the time control cube, then once we've prevented my 1923 self from being killed, *we* can use it to get home!"

Checking no members of the public were nearby, I pressed the button on my Amulet of Seeing. Uncle Frog whooshed up on my wrist. "Joanie, how goes it?"

"All right, Uncle. Bit of a hurry, we've got Lord Vilnius, all the gems, *and* the time controls. If we send him back to 1926, where will he end up?"

My uncle blinked his frog eyes. "Possibly right here in my workshop. But you *must* do it. We can't leave him flapping about in time."

"All right. Do you have the magic words, Uncle?"

"I've just finished working on them and was about to contact you myself!"

Uncle Frog told me the magic words, reminded me to change the 'sender' to Lord Vilnius – then congratulated us for being so clever and brave. "See you both back here for tea and crumpets. Frog out!"

How I adored my Uncle…

On the dirty ground of Trafalgar Square, Lord Vilnius started to stir.

"Better hurry, Lady Joanie!" Charlie said.

"Yes, here goes." I took a deep breath… *Now I send Lord Vilnius home, no longer throughout time he'll roam. To celebrate him going back, I'll now consume a tasty snack."*

Lord Vilnius leapt to his feet and swung woozily at Charlie, but blue crackles shot through the air, zapping his seven-foot bulk with an electrical jolt of magic. He writhed and roared in fury, screaming vengeance like a rabid animal. Then, as reality lurched sideways, I grabbed Charlie and held my breath – watching time tear itself in two like a frantically thundering freight train. And finally, with a magical POP, Lord Vilnius vanished... leaving the damp stones of Trafalgar Square crackling with swirls of spell-heavy lightning.

I stared at the empty space – terrified that the dastardly villain would have a last hurrah. But... nothing... I exhaled... My heart pounded like a hammer in my chest. Did I dare smile? Was it true? Had he gone?

"I think we've *won*, Charlie," I whispered.

Charlie squeezed my shoulder. "Did you ever doubt it, your ladyship?"

Perhaps... a little...

But now... a glorious banner of joy unfurled inside me. I unfroze, cheered triumphantly, and threw my arms around Charlie for a hug. He picked me up and twirled me around – both of us laughing with glee.

He placed me back down. "Tasty snack?" he asked, bemused.

"Yes, I know – any excuse for dessert! Hey, I wonder if Herr Hengleberg's is still a bakery?"

"Only one way to find out." Charlie offered his arm. "Shall we? After all that excitement, I think we deserve a cup of tea and a slice of cake!"

Chapter Eleven

With the sizzle of triumph swirling around us, Charlie and I crossed the road and stood in front of another famous London landmark – St-Martin-in-the-Fields. It was an old Norman church that had started out as a Roman burial ground, hence the Roman columns at the front, with the beautiful cathedral-like spire behind.

Charlie and I started to decide which direction to head in, but the weather gods of England always loved a laugh. This evening they seemed to be messing about with water-filled cosmic paper bags. As they popped them, they sent rumbles of thunder banging across the sky, and floods of icy rain pouring down my collar, gah!

I grabbed Charlie's hand. "Let's go inside!"

"Inside the church?"

"Yes, but around the back – it's all right!"

Splashing through the puddles, we ran to a spiral stone staircase that led to the darkness below. I shouted above the hissing deluge. "Be careful on the slippery steps!"

Charlie peered to the bottom. "What is it?"

"The St-Martin-in-the-Fields Crypt."

"Crypt!"

"Come on, it's all right. There won't be anyone down there. No one alive anyway."

"*That's* what I'm worried about!" He grumbled as we jogged down the steps. "I mean, since meeting you… do *zombies* exist? And vampires? I know witches do!"

I ignored his questions and pushed open the heavy, creaking door. "In here…"

Charlie gasped. "Woah…"

This huge underground crypt was indeed impressive, with its brick vaulted ceilings and tombstone-covered floor. It was cold and echoey, dark and damp – but perfect for sheltering from the rain.

We stood opposite each other, out of breath and soaking wet. Charlie burst into laughter from the exhilaration, then he pinned me with his gorgeous gaze. "You're a bad influence on me, Lady Joanie."

"I fairly doubt that, Charlie."

My heart fluttered with affection. Then it thumped with desire. We had two options. We could either kiss passionately or…

"Let's think about the murder case," I said, stepping away. "Might as well try to catch the killer whilst keeping my 1923 self alive."

"All right," Charlie said, pacing. "*I* think the killer can only be Edgar Lambourne. All the evidence is pointing his way."

I paced too. "Yes, it's probably him. He's hungry for publicity, and Gillian Everett promised him Mark Anthony, but she stitched him up and gave it to Rhett."

"And Bertie overheard him plotting with Edith to 'get rid of' her."

"And Edgar *admits* putting the snake-filled basket in her dressing room. He *claims* he only wanted to scare her. But he would say that, wouldn't he?"

"He can't deny that it was *his* snake that bit her," Charlie said.

"Yes. He vows Sedrick isn't harmful, but… what if he *is* venomous after all?"

"The snake expert said he wasn't," Charlie said.

"But the coroner said she'd died from a lethal dose of snake venom, so…?"

We both halted and sighed. Then we tightened our resolve and paced again…

"Right then," I said. "How about Miss Edith Parker? Gillian was blackmailing Edith over those risqué photographs, and Edith not only wanted the pics back, but she also wanted the starring role. *And* she was a fellow-plotter with Edgar, hoping to 'get rid of' Gillian."

"But she was very upset at the pool party, though, wasn't she?"

"Yes, but don't forget, Charlie, she's an actress."

"A *film* actress – which means she's good at doing this…" He raised his hands and waved them about, gasping like a guppy.

I laughed. "That's true… Come on, let's pace again – it helps me think…"

Our footsteps echoed around the cavernous crypt.

"How about the director, Bertie Bunter?" Charlie asked. "Why would *he* want to kill his Cleopatra?"

"Well, her death is certainly bringing his film a lot of publicity. The film is over-budget and over-time, so perhaps the interest from the press is helping to keep his sponsor sweet."

"But don't forget, your ladyship, after his Queen Guinevere died last year, *that* film was doomed to be cancelled. So surely he'd just expect a repeat of the same?"

"You're right. But… *because* this film is so over-budget, had he decided to permanently remove the costly diva, and install a lesser-known actress, such as Edith Parker?"

"Edith Parker whose indecent photos *you* found in Bertie Bunter's car? Perhaps he was forcing her to do the film for *nothing*?"

"So he *did* know about the photos after all?"

"Maybe. They *were* arguing at the pool party."

We stopped pacing and faced each other. "Well, that's that."

"There is one thing that might help," Charlie said pensively.

"Oh yes?"

"We could search Miss Everett's dressing room. It's been shut off by the police since the murder. But perhaps if we go to the studio now, we might have a stealthy late-night snoop."

"I like your thinking, Charlie."

"Good! I'm keen to leave this creepy tomb before the residents start requesting our assistance with *their* murders!"

Chapter Twelve

The film studio was dark and secluded as we let ourselves in with Charlie's lock-picking skills. I fumbled around with a stage light near the door but, rather than illuminating the place, it just created eerie shadows on the walls and floor. The vast space was cluttered with so much Egyptian paraphernalia that I felt like *I* was in a silent film, creeping through an ancient tomb.

Of course, I *had* just been creeping through the actual tomb of St Martin's, but I knew where I stood with real dead people. It was the illusion of the movies that made this place seem… dead yet still alive. Spooky.

Hoping to leave as quickly as possible, I led Charlie towards the corridor for the dressing rooms, trying to reassure myself that nothing could harm me here.

Charlie grabbed my arm. "Watch out, Lady Joanie!"

I jumped at his frantic command. But… it was just a wooden crate blocking my path. I exhaled, stepped around it, and headed towards the dressing rooms again.

Just beyond the scope of my vision, the shadows flickered, playing creepy tricks on my mind. But I forced myself to get a grip. There was nothing to be frightened of but fear itself… *and whatever that was!*

A gigantic man loomed by the wall. I leapt into Charlie's arms. "Wah!"

Charlie held me tight but laughed gently in my ear. "It's just a piece of painted cardboard, Lady Joanie. Look…"

I stood up straight and pulled myself together. The magic of the movies was doing strange things to me. I wasn't usually the 'leaping into a man's arms' type. Although it had been jolly nice.

I straightened my hat. "I'm just feeling a bit… jangly."

Charlie smiled. "Everything's fine. We've beaten Lord Vilnius and… oh bloody hell – excuse my language – but what's *that*?"

Turning slowly, I realised with dread that a corpse was sprawled on the floor. But surely it was just another lifeless prop… wasn't it?

Alas, no. We edged closer, and I saw it was definitely alive… or *had* been.

Now it was very dead.

Charlie crouched to inspect him. "Edgar Lambourne… looks like he was bashed on the head with that…"

I picked up a golden statuette in my gloved hand. It was a one-foot-high golden knight, holding a sword downwards. The knight was standing on a reel of film… How strange…

Charlie searched Edgar's pockets – presumably for evidence and not valuables. "Oh look at this!"

He passed me a handwritten note: *Meet me at film studio at six, come alone. We need to discuss…*

"Why would anyone kill Edgar?" I asked. "Something he saw or heard?"

Charlie stood up. "Presumably whoever wrote *this* lured him here to silence him."

A memory drifted into my mind… something *else* Edgar had kept in his pocket… The business card that had fallen out just after the murder! I took it out of my own pocket and looked at it again. It belonged to a Doctor Scott at the London Hospital of Tropical Medicine.

Tropical medicine… ohhh… wait a minute… was *that* the answer to this puzzle? Could it be?

"Why are you staring at that card, Lady Joanie?"

"Charlie, I'd assumed Edgar had this because he was suffering from a nasty disease that he'd picked up in foreign parts. But what if he'd picked up something *else*?"

"Like what?"

"Like… yes, that would make sense. Edgar spoke to Edith about scaring Miss Everett with his snake, didn't he? But what if…hmm…"

"Lady Joanie?"

"I'm not entirely sure. I thought I had something, but…" I gazed at the late Edgar Lambourne. "What do we do with him now, Detective Constable?"

"We should contact DI Parry."

"All right. But we might as well snoop in Miss Everett's dressing room anyway. That's what we came here for."

"Agreed. You do that, I'll go and – *now* what!"

Several male voices were shouting in the backlot. We ran to investigate.

Outside by the banks of the river, Charlie and I lurked in the shadows, watching as Bertie Bunter argued with two burly blokes.

"I know those two thugs," Charlie whispered. "They work for a local gangster –known to the police as Mr Big. Those two men are his heavies. You see the huge bloke with watermelons for biceps?"

"The one resembling an outhouse? Yes?"

"That's Mr Vega. And the other one – the skinny one who looks like a rake – he's a knife-wielding maniac called Mr Jackson."

"What do they want with Bertie Bunter?"

As if to answer my question, the giant thug, Mr Vega, growled. "I'm telling you, the boss has had a change of heart…"

Bertie stood tall. "Pity he wasn't able to have a change of *face*."

Mr Vega thumped Bertie, sending him flying. "*I* can gladly rearrange *your* face!"

Bertie cowered on the ground. "What does he want!"

"He wants his money back," Mr Vega said.

Mr Jackson sneered. "Yeah."

"*And* the deeds to this place."

"Yeah."

"And he wants… everything you got!"

"Yeah!"

"And if he doesn't get it tonight, you're gonna die. Or *worse*! Bring the money, the deeds, and everything to the Grand Theatre in Shaftesbury Avenue in one hour. Or else."

Bertie held up his hands pleadingly. "Oh come on, chaps, surely we can discuss this as adults?"

Mr Vega loomed. "*We* can discuss it like people who'll smash your face in if you don't do what the boss says!"

"All right, all right. I promise to give Mr Lange everything I've got. I'll be at the theatre in an hour."

Mr Vega punched Bertie once more, then the thugs walked off, leaving him concussed on the dirty ground. Charlie and I ran to assist.

Bertie gazed at me through bleary eyes. "Oh goodie, my leading lady… I've got leading ladies coming out my earholes."

Charlie squinted at Bertie's ear. "He's delirious."

"Where do you live, Mr Bunter?" I asked. "We'll take you home."

He pointed blearily at the Georgian mansion. "Live there…"

"In there?" Charlie said. "What, in one of the dressing rooms, or something?"

"Perhaps in one of the *other* rooms of the mansion?" I suggested. "On the upper floor?"

Bertie nodded. "Upstairs."

Charlie and I supported one side of him each, and carried him to the first-floor corridor.

Whilst I'd grown accustomed to the film studio being in a hectic mess, I now saw that this entire building was in disrepair. The corridor was grubby and the carpet was threadbare – a shadow of its former Georgian opulence.

Bertie wasn't coherent enough to give us directions to his room, but his feet knew the way. They led us to the end of a grotty hallway, where a padlock hung on a large, peeling door.

"I suppose we'll find the key about his person?" I said to Charlie.

Charlie glanced at the wobbly man between us. "Hold him tight. I'll get this open…"

He made quick work of the padlock. Once inside, I flicked on the electric light. There was no lampshade over the single lightbulb.

Poor Bertie. My heart surged for him. This room was the epitome of squalor – and Bertie's confident film director act was clearly that… an act. His bed was an old mattress on the floor, under a curtain-less window.

"Home sweet home," Bertie whispered.

"I assume the motorcar's just for show, Mr Bunter?" I said. "How long have you been in such dire financial straits?"

Bertie spoke woozily. "House in family for years. But now money sink…"

I nodded sympathetically. "Charlie, remember what I said about all the big English houses struggling after the war? I suppose Bertie must be in the same situation."

Charlie lowered Bertie to the mattress. "But what about the people renting the offices on this floor? Don't they pay you rent, Mr Bunter?"

"Barely cover heating… taxes… maintenance – place crumbling. Roof leaking."

"So you borrowed money from *gangsters* to make your film?" I asked. "In the hope of making some much-needed cash?"

Bertie nodded. "High-interest loan from Mr Lange. Can't pay back."

"Mr Lange is the film's sponsor," I said. "We met him yesterday just after the murder..." A gloomy shadow crept over me. "Oh Charlie, have we completely missed a suspect? Did *Lange* kill Gillian Everett? Or his thugs?"

We turned to Bertie for confirmation, but he snored loudly on the bed.

"Why would the film's sponsor kill the leading lady?" Charlie whispered. "It makes no sense."

"We'll need to think about it a bit more. But let me just check Mr Bunter's vitals. After being punched like that."

"Don't come any closer, Lady Joanie! This mattress contains more life than a 1920s nightclub. More vermin too, I shouldn't wonder."

"Don't be silly, Charlie. I saw worse than this as an auxiliary nurse."

I checked the sleeping Mr Bunter's pulse, breathing rate, and temperature. "It's just concussion. I dealt with this a lot in Flanders. He'll be all right in a bit."

Charlie plumped Bertie's pillow. "Your medical skills are very impressive, Lady Joanie."

"Not really. They're just a souvenir from that dreadful war."

Charlie pulled his hand out from under the pillow, gripping a revolver. "So's this…"

"Gosh. Well, I suppose he might need it if he's in trouble with gangsters."

I glanced around the dirty room, hoping to find some new information about the case, but there wasn't much to see… instead of a kitchen, there was a portable gas stove, and instead of a bathroom, there was a cracked washbasin. In the far corner, a fitted wardrobe stood glumly with one door hanging low on its hinges.

"Shall we see if he has any skeletons in his closet?" I asked.

Charlie and I crept over to the wardrobe and eased the door open. It creaked. Bertie Bunter snuffled in his sleep.

We slipped into the large wardrobe, closing the door behind us… and then we were alone together in a small, dark space.

"I can't see anything," Charlie whispered.

I secretly hoped to impress him. "Let me see if *I* can shed some light on the matter." I closed my eyes and focused hard on the spell. "*If it's dark where I am going, then like a star, I shall start glowing!*"

As I held out my arms star-like, my body flushed with a golden glow, illuminating the wardrobe. My heart shone with ruby red rays, and I grinned – shimmering all over.

Charlie's eyes reflected the light, making them sparkle. "Wow, Lady Joanie… you look… twinkly…"

I chuckled. "Let's be quick. The spell won't last long – my magic is weak."

My glow slowly faded as we searched the wardrobe. Luckily, Bertie didn't own much – just a few clothes, books, and… "A shoebox containing *a lot* of cash…"

Charlie took it from my hands. "Blimey, that *is* a lot. And what's that down there?"

I unfolded the old yellow document. "The deeds to this mansion."

I stepped to the back of the wardrobe, where my fading glow shone over a pile of official-looking envelopes. With trembling hands, Charlie and I tore them open.

"It's legal speak," Charlie said. "I can't make head nor tail."

"These are court summonses, Charlie. Mr Bunter is being sued by the financier of the last film he was involved in – the other one where the leading actress died."

"Why's he being sued?"

I carefully translated the jargon. "Because… because he still owes *that* financier money for the film, even though it was cancelled."

"He *kept* the money from his last film? Even though it never got made?"

"So it would appear."

"But isn't that… well, it's sort of… stealing?"

"I think the technical term is embezzlement."

Charlie and I realised it at the same time. Charlie spoke slowly. "And now that Gillian Everett's dead, Mr Bunter's going to embezzle the money for *this* film? What an idiot! Stealing from a London gangster is tantamount to suicide."

An idea struck me. "Charlie, you said that this building is a nightclub in 1926. I'm wondering, did the gangsters seize this place? Those thugs said their boss wanted the deeds *and* the money."

"It *is* owned by a racketeer in 1926. It's a right dive – a haven for dodgy deals."

"Such as?"

"You name it… money laundering, cocaine… all sorts of nasty stuff."

"What nasty stuff?"

"Anything you want. Inspector Parry was poised to nick Mr Vega last month – in 1926 – for selling opium. But the big boss is powerful, and he weaselled Mr Vega out of it."

"Have you met the big boss?"

"I haven't had the pleasure. I don't even know his name."

"You do now."

"Mr Lange?"

"Precisely… Oh dear… Charlie, I've just had a dreadful realisation…"

"Oh yeah?"

I was about to elaborate but the room door slammed. *Bertie!*

We rushed out the wardrobe. "He's gone…"

"And he's taken the gun with him!" Charlie frowned. "But… he promised those thugs to give their boss *everything*. So why's he left the money and deeds here?"

"Well, if he's taken the gun with him, perhaps he was talking *metaphorically*."

Charlie sighed. "We'd better follow him. He's going to get himself killed."

"Yes, but, Charlie… just now you said those gangsters can get their hands on anything. Well, I was wondering, what if the bite marks on Miss Everett's wrist weren't from a snake at all? If it's true that Sedrick isn't venomous, then what if the gangsters armed themselves with lethal snake venom and injected *that* into her?"

Charlie's jaw dropped open. "Could be. But *why*?"

"Let's get to the Grand Theatre in Shaftesbury Avenue and find out!"

Chapter Thirteen

The Grand Theatre in Shaftesbury Avenue was an old Victorian building, which had once been a music hall venue. It was currently in disrepair and closed to the public – the perfect hideout for London gangsters to concoct their dodgy deals.

Charlie and I strolled into the empty foyer and made our way to the auditorium. Even without Uncle Frog's time machine, it was like going back years – a proper old-style theatre with a large wooden stage, an old-fashioned proscenium arch, and red velvet curtains.

The ramshackle chandelier looked like it might come crashing down at any moment – but hopefully *not* because someone planned to drop it on us.

Charlie and I halted halfway up the aisle, between the rows of flip-down seats.

"There's no one here," I whispered.

"Or at least, we can't see anyone…"

"I wish you hadn't said that, Charlie."

My wand tingled in my garter, and I regretted wasting all that magic with the Glow spell. Why did I always need to show off?

Well, he *was* terribly handsome…

Charlie's instincts were also twitching. He slipped his knuckleduster over his fingers, then raised his baton to shoulder height.

The silence pounded in my ears. "Film is nothing like the excitement of theatre."

"Yeah, I've always said the flicks would never take off."

Just when I thought I might burst from the stifling tension, the scene sprung into life. From somewhere backstage, a man shouted, "*No, no!*"

"Who was that?" Charlie asked frantically.

"I couldn't tell where it came from – let alone who it was!"

Charlie scanned the stage. "It could've come from left, right, centre… or perhaps from that loudspeaker."

A bell of clarity clanged in my brain. "Oh good heavens – I've worked it out! Charlie, go and call the police."

I fled towards the stage, but Charlie grabbed me. "It's too dangerous!"

"It's all right, darling, I'll cast the Shielding spell!"

"But you've just cast that glowing spell! Lady Jo—"

"Don't argue with me, Charlie. Call the police, please!"

I ran off, hoping he'd do it. Then, hitching up my knee-length skirt, I clambered onto the dimly lit stage. Caution trickled down my spine. *Beware!*

I tried to calm myself, but even just the *set* made me feel uneasy. This large performance space had been abandoned mid-run, and it now resembled an Edwardian drawing room – with the decorators in. It was adorned with the usual old-fashioned furniture and props – but also, a tall step ladder, paintbrushes, and buckets of whitewash.

A movement in the darkness! "Who's there?"

Silence…

Dash it all, why did I always try to be so brave? Ah well, I'd come here to catch a killer, so I'd better get on with it…

I crept into the wings, holding my hands high, ready to cast magic – or throw a nifty judo chop. It was dark back here, so I paused to get my bearings, resting my gorgeous little bot on a handy ledge. But, *argh*! A frenzied clanging pierced my eardrums. *What!* Ohhh, I'd accidentally pushed a lever on a self-playing piano.

The swirly, fairground music did nothing to calm my nerves. But I couldn't see how to switch it off – and there was no one back here anyway. So I left the music tinkling as I crept onstage, stealthily scanning the shadows for assailants.

"Mr Bunter?" I called.

No answer.

Perhaps he was over the other side? I headed to the opposite wing, but halted with dread as Mr Jackson and Mr Vega barred my exit like a terrifying Laurel and Hardy.

Mr Vega raised a fist. "What do we have 'ere then?"

Mr Jackson brandished a dagger. "Looks like a girl."

Well, really. A girl, indeed!

Smiling sinisterly, the thugs approached, like icebergs converging on a ship.

Mr Jackson spoke in a patronising tone. "Now listen, darlin', I don't want to hurt a woman."

"Oh good." I kicked him in the shin, then shoved him backwards.

I frantically tried to cast a spell, but my magic wouldn't catch, *drat*!

The bearlike Mr Vega stepped forward. "Come 'ere…"

I pointed hysterically over his shoulder. "What's that!"

Amazingly, he fell for it. As he spun to look, I leapt on his back and pulled his hat over his eyes, making him stumble blindly.

"Gerroff me!" We bucked together like a wild horse and novice rider.

I fell to the stage in a heap. "Oof!"

The jaunty music pricked my ears, reminiscent of a vaudeville skit. Hmm… all right, what would Charlie Chaplin do?

The two men ran at me again, so I rushed to the middle of the stage, and unwound a rope dangling from the rigging. It was attached to a sandbag and, as I yanked the rope, I flew into the air. The men crashed into each other – falling on their backs like upturned turtles.

They leapt to their feet as I landed back on the stage.

With the thugs hot on my heels, I ran up the step ladder, realised I had nowhere to go, clambered over, then climbed back down the other side – grabbing a nearby bucket of whitewash. For want of a better weapon, I threw the paint all over Mr Jackson's jacket, then the bucket at Mr Vega. It clanged off his head and rolled away.

"Come 'ere!" Mr Vega growled.

"Yeah," Mr Jackson said.

"We're gonna getcha this time."

"Yeah!"

I raised my hands as they closed in on me, desperately trying to cast a spell. Mr Vega pulled back his fist to punch me, but I ducked and punched Mr Jackson instead. Mr Jackson's fighting instincts took over and he automatically punched his colleague back. As they launched into a slapstick scuffle, Bertie Bunter ran onstage.

He raised his gun. "Stop or I'll shoot you!"

"Yeah," I said.

"I meant *you*, your ladyship…"

"Ah…"

Despite the make-believe setting, the gun looked very real. I coiled my muscles to leap out the way but, for the second time tonight, Charlie appeared over my assailant's shoulder – this time in the wings.

Charlie glanced up, then unravelled a rope at the side of him. Another sandbag, perhaps?

I looked up, and *ah-ha!* The chandelier rattled on its rope and crashed down over Bertie Bunter, trapping him inside – and saving my life.

I waved at Charlie. "Thanks, darling."

"Look behind you!" Charlie shouted.

I kicked backwards like a frenzied mule, sending Mr Vega flying across the stage.

Mr Jackson tried his luck, but Charlie ran onstage and caught him in a headlock – losing his hat as he threw the thug over his shoulder. "Honestly, I leave you alone for two minutes, your ladyship!" he shouted playfully.

With the thugs in a heap, and Mr Bunter trapped in the chandelier, I called into the darkness. "Mr Lange, are you there?"

A gravelly voice came from the wings. "Good guess, your ladyship…"

Mr Lange swaggered onstage. Sticky silence stifled us like a thick velvet curtain.

The seconds ticked cruelly by. Someone had forgotten their lines!

But Bertie Bunter took the cue. He swiftly struggled out of the chandelier, then raised the gun again. "I'll kill you, Lange. Make peace with your maker!"

I grabbed Charlie. "Let's take a bow!"

We bowed deeply as the bullet flew over us and struck Mr Lange deep in the shoulder. A climax worthy of a standing ovation!

But then came the curtain call. Blowing their brass whistles and brandishing their batons, five uniformed police officers burst into the auditorium and leapt on the stage. They wrestled the gun from Bertie and arrested him – as well as arresting Lange and his heavies.

I grinned at Charlie. "That's all, folks!"

"Let's go?" he said.

Charlie grabbed his hat and we strode victoriously up the aisle towards the exit. Our work here was done; we could go home.

But, alas, we bumped into Inspector Parry in the foyer. "Lady Joanforth, Constable Anderson – you'd better explain yourselves!"

I pulled Doctor Scott's card out of my pocket. "Inspector Parry. I know where the snake venom came from that killed Gillian Everett. You need to telephone *this* chap – then I'd be delighted to explain everything."

Chapter Fourteen

Despite being defunct, the theatre foyer was lavish – with a red carpet, gilded rails, and marble columns. There were several velvet sofas near the box office, so Charlie and I sat with Inspector Parry, while Bertie Bunter and Mr Lange stood in handcuffs.

A uniformed officer joined us. "Sir, I've confirmed with Doctor Scott of the London Hospital of Tropical Medicine that he did indeed expect to receive a phial of lethal African snake venom from Edgar Lambourne whilst he was here in London. But Doctor Scott never received the venom, sir."

DI Parry eyeballed Charlie. "Perhaps Constable Anderson would like to explain how *he* came to be involved in this? And not in uniform again, Constable?"

For a Detective Inspector, it was surprising that DI Parry still didn't realise he'd met Charlie back in 1916 with me. But human minds did tend to block out anything that might upset them. And the thought of magical time travel would *definitely* upset a logical man like DI Parry.

"I'm off duty, sir," Charlie explained. "I was helping her ladyship."

DI Parry looked like he was about to quiz Charlie further, so I leapt in. "Would you like to hear about this murder, Inspector Parry?"

He grunted. "Let me guess, it was the gangster all along? The film sponsor here?"

"No… it was Bertie Bunter."

DI Parry glared at me. "What?"

"How ridiculous," Bertie Bunter said weakly. But he knew I was onto him…

I shrugged. "Yes, Inspector. Bertie Bunter killed his leading lady, because he *wanted* the film to be cancelled – just like the last film he'd worked on."

"Embezzlement," Charlie said.

"You'd better explain your theory, Lady Joanforth," DI Parry said. "I'm particularly interested in how Mr Bunter convinced a non-venomous snake to bite and kill Miss Everett?"

"Well, he didn't… He made it *look* like Gillian Everett had opened the basket and put her hand in – *seemingly* resulting in the snake biting her. But really, when everyone went for a break, Bertie followed Gillian into her dressing room, and made up an excuse to hold her wrist – perhaps saying something like 'What's that mark on your arm?' type thing. Then he injected her with a syringe of lethal snake poison, straight into her bloodstream."

"Injected?" DI Parry asked.

"Yes, with a medical syringe."

"I never found a medical syringe," DI Parry said.

"No. Mr Bunter went for a spin in his motorcar after the murder – which is when he presumably disposed of the needle and venom phial."

"He *was* rather keen to get to his car, sir," Charlie said.

"You see, Inspector," I continued. "Gillian Everett died almost immediately after Bertie injected her. We know from the London Zoo chap that such lethal venom is almost instant. So once she was dead, Bertie quickly upended the basket containing Edgar's

378

snake, to make it *look* like the snake was the killer. And of course, snakes have two fangs, so Bertie poked the syringe needle back into her wrist an inch away from the first prick, to make it look like fang bites."

Charlie spoke pensively. "But, Lady Joanie, everyone ran to the dressing room *straight after* we heard the scream. How did Mr Bunter have enough time to arrange the scene?"

"Ah yes," I said. "That's because Gillian Everett *didn't* scream. She died far too quickly for anything so dramatic."

The men around me frowned. Apart from Bertie, who wilted.

I nodded. "Yes, that was the clever part. After he'd arranged the scene, Bertie slipped out of the dressing room and set up one of his sound effects records – the sound effect of a woman screaming – which could be heard via the dynamic loudspeaker in his sound booth."

"The scream was a sound recording?" DI Parry asked.

"Yes. And he even left a gap of silence at the beginning of the recording, so he could get back on set and give himself an alibi of sorts. Of course, sound amplification is still very rudimentary, but the scream was amplified enough to make everyone run. And Bertie simply joined the crowd, making him seem wholly unconnected to the murder."

Charlie shook his head in awe. "He used *sound* to alter the time of the murder – well, to alter what time *we thought* the murder happened."

I winked at Charlie. Of course, another of our murderers had used a similar technique on our travels but, now in this modern era with its wonderful technology, *this* scream had been even more cunning and diverting.

DI Parry had questions. "Ere, hold on, what about this snake that belonged to Edgar Lambourne? Bit of luck that he just happened to put *his* snake in the dressing room on the same day Mr Bunter decided to kill Miss Everett with deadly venom, wasn't it?"

"Not a coincidence at all, Inspector," I said. "In fact, it was Edgar Lambourne who gave Mr Bunter the idea. Remember? It was *Mr Bunter* who told us that he'd overheard Edgar and Edith plotting to put the snake in Miss Everett's dressing room, in the hope of scaring her off the film. So Mr Bunter simply took their plan one step further – then left them to get the blame!"

Bertie snorted. "This is rubbish. How would *I* know how to get black mamba venom?"

Charlie raised an eyebrow. "Who said anything about black mamba venom, Mr Bunter?"

"Oh…er… I was guessing."

The uniformed constable nodded curtly. "Very *good* guess, sir. That's exactly what Doctor Scott said the venom was."

"And I'm glad you asked, Mr Bunter," I said. "Because obviously you broke into Mr Lambourne's hotel room and stole it."

"But how did I know it was even *in* Mr Lambourne's hotel room?"

"Well, I can't know for sure, because I wasn't there. But I know how angry Edgar and Edith were when they were plotting against Miss Everett. I'd imagine Edgar must've said something like, 'We could even kill her if we wanted. I've got some black mamba venom in my hotel room.' Something like that."

DI Parry sighed wearily. "Why did Edgar Lambourne not mention this to *me* when questioned?"

The uniformed officer spoke up again. "Sir, Doctor Scott was reluctant to talk to the police, coz it was all happening under the counter, like. So I assume Mr Lambourne was equally reluctant. But I do believe Mr Lambourne's intentions were honourable. He was keen to help the Doctor create an antivenom for a deadly snake – and save a few lives."

DI Parry tutted. "Dealing in black market snake venom, dear me."

"Black *mamba* snake venom, Inspector," I corrected.

DI Parry treated me to a glare. "Nevertheless, I shall be having strong words with Mr Lambourne."

"You'll be having them via a medium, sir," Charlie said.

DI Parry groaned. "Oh marvellous. Killed him too, did you, Bunter?"

"I'm not saying anything without a solicitor."

"Very wise." DI Parry turned back to me. "Lady Joanforth will, I'm sure, fill in the gaps?"

"Yes, poor Mr Lambourne. The murder weapon *was* his venom, but of course he knew he was innocent. So when the police told him that *Mr Bunter* had overheard his conversation with Edith, he must've figured out what had happened. He confronted Mr Bunter – who then lured him to the film studio and bonked him over the head with a statuette."

DI Parry stood up. "Bertie Bunter, you're under arrest."

Bertie muttered glumly. "I'm already under arrest."

"That was for waving a gun about. This is for murder! But… if you'd care to grass on your old chum Mr Lange here – and all his dodgy dealings – then we might convince the jury to spare you from the gallows."

Mr Lange spoke severely. "Bunter, if you squeal, you'll be *begging* for the gallows!"

And with that, DI Parry marched off, leaving his officers to deal with the prisoners.

Charlie and I stepped out into the busy London thoroughfare.

"Another one solved," I said. "And now I think it's time to go home."

We found a quiet alleyway. This time we didn't need the magic words from Uncle Frog because we already had the time control cube.

"Hold hands?" Charlie asked. "One last time."

"Absolutely…"

I gripped the time controls and – with our fingers linked – we pressed the button together…

And so we left the era of silent movies… and all that jazz. That thrill-fuelled golden age when women wanted to look like boys, and men wanted to look like they'd just stepped off the golf links.

When cropped hair, to-the-knee skirts, and ladies with jobs were still shocking, but finally accepted. A time of cocktails, gay dancing, and bright, young liberation. This fabulous decade was the first truly modern era. And its influence stretches onwards – because every fashion, film, and frivolity since has been built on the foundations of the wonderful, glorious, roaring 1920s!

Chapter Fifteen

But of course, the 1920s was *our* decade. 1926 was home.

To my delight we didn't drop to the floor and land in a heap but, instead, we materialised inside the cavity of the spinning, sparking time machine – beaming back with dignity. Through the flashing lights, I scanned Uncle Frog's workshop, feeling glad to be home, but uplifted by my travels.

I threw Charlie an excited grin, and we stepped into 1926.

With the time machine whirring behind us, we stood opposite each other. Charlie's brown and blue eyes twinkled with joy. I wanted to embrace him, but my nerves suddenly crushed me like a debutant at her first ball. So silly…

Besides… this was goodbye.

I swallowed my emotion. "I'll… I'll lend you that Agatha Christie novel I promised."

His voice was smooth and tender. "Please do. Now that I've *met* her!"

"Yes. And we'll perhaps go to the cinema and watch a Chaplin flick. See if he's incorporated the banana-peel gag!"

"I'd like that… Um…"

"Yes?"

"Lady Joanie… I didn't say it at the time, but…"

"Yes?"

"When we were in Mr Chaplin's dressing room in 1906… and we shared that banana?"

"Ye-es?"

"I… well… I wanted to ask if *you* thought that *I* – like that banana – had a peel… Um… Appeal…"

I burst into laughter. "It's a good job Mr Chaplin didn't incorporate *that* joke into his act, or we might've killed off his career before it'd got going!"

Charlie laughed too. "Shall I take that as a yes, your ladyship?"

I gazed into his eyes. My heart pounded hard. The time machine whirred gently behind us. I opened my mouth to speak, but then… but then I realised what was missing from Uncle Frog's workshop. "Charlie… where's Uncle Frog?"

He stepped away. "Er…?"

"And Wispu!"

I glanced frantically around. How had I not noticed before? The study was a mess – Frog's books had been thrown off the shelves and his ornaments scattered and smashed. Granted, it *had* been like that when we'd left, but Uncle Frog would've tidied up.

So why…?

And then I saw it lying on the carpet. *Uncle Frog's Amulet of Seeing*. I grabbed it with trembling fingers, but dropped it again in surprise. A silent recording whooshed up from the device, revealing the flickering images of Lord Vilnius fighting with Frog in this very room… Uncle Frog was struggling valiantly but Lord Vilnius was forcing him and Wispu into the time machine… *Oh no!*

My voice was a whisper. "Uncle Frog must've dropped it on the carpet for me."

Charlie sounded worried. "Look, Lady Joanie, the dials are set to 1936!"

386

"Oh Charlie, I bet Lord Vilnius materialised back here and kidnapped Frog – forcing him to find the next gem!"

Charlie punched his palm. "I knew we couldn't trust that bast… dastardly villain!"

I gazed at the spinning time machine. "I'd better rescue him. *And* stop Lord Vilnius from taking over the world. Again."

"But, Lady Joanie…. 1936 is in the future!"

"Yes, I've always wanted to see it, haven't you? What do you say, Charlie – will you join me on my next adventure? Or you can stay here for cocoa and an early bath?"

His eyes twinkled. "Cocoa and an early bath do sound appealing. But how could I refuse another adventure with Lady Joanforth Eldritch?"

"Splendid! Right, let me just cast a strong protection spell around the silver rose, golden lion, and Blue Stuart Sapphire, so they'll be safe while we're away."

"All right…. Got the time controls then, Lady Joanie?"

"I certainly have, Charlie. Ready?"

"As I'll ever be!"

We held hands and leapt into the spinning time machine once more…

I tried to stay calm, but my stomach looped and my mind warped, as space/time hurtled us into the unknown. Into the *future*…

With little regard for this giant leap for witchkind, space/time unceremoniously spat us out again. I stumbled and staggered, trying to stand straight.

But… hold on… why was the world still shaking and rumbling!

As I was thrown forward into Charlie's arms, my cloche hat fell in front of my eyes. "Is it an earthquake!" I shouted.

He sounded confused. "We're on a train, Lady Joanie."

"Oh…" I pushed up my hat. Hmm… this was no ordinary train. We'd landed in the empty restaurant car of a very opulent carriage. I grabbed a menu from a walnut table.

"We're on the Orient Express! The most luxurious train in the world. I *like* the future!"

Charlie smiled. "There's definitely worse places to land."

"Quite right. And we're perfectly safe here. I mean, who's ever heard of anything bad happening on *this* train?"

He chuckled. "Yeah, it's not like there's ever been a *murder* on the Orient Express!"

I was about to suggest we find a porter and grab some tea, when I was interrupted by the heart-wrenching sound of a scream…

"Ah… first time for everything!"

Can our heroes rescue Uncle Frog, defeat Lord Vilnius, and get a nice cup of tea on the Orient Express? Join them in 1936, as they solve the murder, save the day, and flirt their way through history. Funnier, flirtier, and murder*ier* than ever, the next instalment of *A Witch in Time Solves Nine* is coming soon! In the meantime, stay in touch and get a FREE

fun download when you join my newsletter at
https://www.subscribepage.com/joanie

If you're new to my books, you can discover the adventures of Joanie's granddaughter Evelyn Eldritch in the **English Village Witch Cozy Series**, starting with Book One – *Murder at Magic Cakes Café*. Scan the QR Code to see the entire series  Or   visit **amazon.com/author/rosiereed**

Printed in Great Britain
by Amazon